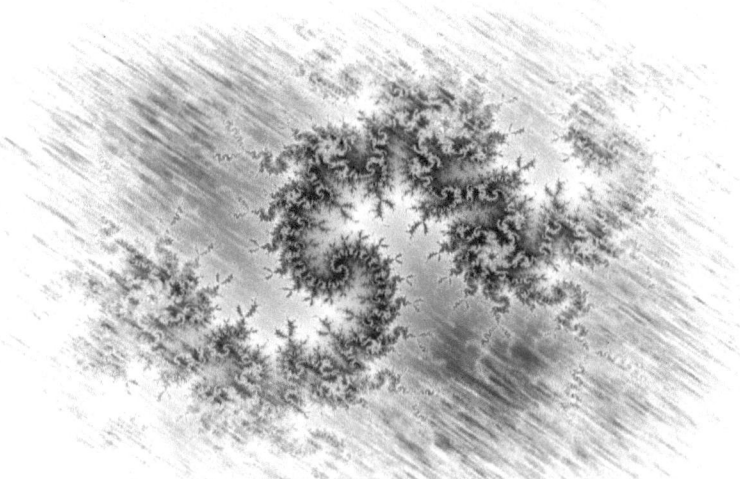

BRAIN CHILD

BY

ALAN K. GARRETT

For my wife, who said I *should*
For my mother, who insisted I *could*
And for the friends who read it
And told me I *did*

Contents

Part One

Home

I

How it Started (sort of)

I

January 2007.
From an on-line chat room entitled,
"I'M OKAY, YOU'RE OKAY."

<u>MyAlterEgo</u>: I wasn't sure if anyone would be in here this
  early.
<u>bArElYtHeRe</u>: i try to get up with the chickens.
<u>WottaNut</u>: i get up with the lemurs
<u>MyAlterEgo</u>: I'm not going to ask
<u>OneBrikShy</u>: *has entered the room.*
<u>MyAlterEgo</u>: I'm glad you're all here. I'm looking for moral
  support.
<u>OneBrikShy</u>: not sure my support will be very moral ego.
<u>bArElYtHeRe</u>: just try not to make it profane brik
<u>OneBrikShy</u>: you know me bare. if i can't think of something
  nice to say i ...
<u>OneBrikShy</u>: ...

OneBrikShy: ...

bArElYtHeRe: LOL

OneBrikShy: what's up this morning?

MyAlterEgo: I'm going to a meeting with my kid's school principal. He's been a royal pain.

WottaNut: the kid or the principal?

MyAlterEgo: (laughs weakly) I might not feel like chatting later. I think the kid may have really stepped in it this time.

bArElYtHeRe: go easy on him. her. whoever. or not. just don't get in trubble

WottaNut: just remember: pressure gets to be too much, fake a seizure. can you drool convincingly? bite your tongue?

OneBrikShy: take it easy ego.

bArElYtHeRe: HUGS

II

Sheila sat with me in the school office. I was nervous, but not too nervous. I'd seen this coming. Sheila should have seen it, too, but it wouldn't be the first thing to escape her notice.

In describing her mood, the word "adjivated" came to mind. She could blow up at me, cry, or blow up at someone else. Blowing up wasn't like her, but anyone can learn it, given reason.

No clicking typewriters or ringing phones in the oven-warm office. We were quiet, too. No communication, other than my attempts at telepathy.

Watching Sheila's emotional struggle was exhausting.

Drowsy-ing, at least. I yawned. The way she looked at me, you would think I'd leapt onto a chair and broken wind. I lowered my eyes and kept my lips zipped. I was getting good at that.

Before I got antsy enough to pace the floor — something else that would grate on Sheila's nerves — Mrs. Bowman came out of her office. She frowned for a moment, then sat and addressed Sheila.

"I don't know if there's anything else we can do, Mrs. Bledsoe. There's no improvement. Scott is still disrupting class. He's very bright, but that just doesn't cut it." She took a deep breath. "The school board policy calls for extended discipline."

"What does that mean?" I asked.

Mrs. Bowman folded her hands. "Expulsion. At the very least, suspension pending a stringent reform agenda."

"Excuse me?" asked Sheila. I knew what the principal meant but I kept my big mouth shut. Sheila had enough to deal with.

Mrs. Bowman handed Sheila a form. "A psychological review. School board's rules. No regular classes until your child has been deemed fit to return."

"I see."

Silence again. My ideas weren't wanted so I twiddled my thumbs. I considered yawning again to break the tension, but I just rolled my eyes.

"You need to take this seriously, Mr. Bledsoe." Mrs. Bowman pinned me with a look. "Being expelled from school means long months of trouble. It's not a vacation." She turned back to Sheila. After a moment, she softened.

"There is an alternative. If you'd like to hear it, that is."

I had expected to see tears, but Sheila's cheeks were dry as she nodded.

"You could home school Scott."

Sheila gave her a blank look. Mine probably matched hers.

"I could?" Sheila asked.

"Yes. Scott's records say you and your husband are college graduates." Sheila winced but Mrs. Bowman didn't see. "I'm not sure of your work schedules, or what you would do in the event Scott has to be left at home, but I'm sure that — what is it?" Mrs. Bowman stopped when she saw Sheila shaking her head.

"My husband died before Scott was born."

Mrs. Bowman deflated a little. "I'm ... sorry."

Sheila ignored her. "Tell me about home schooling."

Her manner subdued, Mrs. Bowman told of a regimen that sounded like something I might have invented: requisite number of hours in study, standardized tests provided and graded by a third-party institution. It sounded like the way to please everyone.

Sheila appeared to agree. "That really does sound ideal." She lowered her head, as if she couldn't look at me. "Do you think you can handle that, Scott?"

"Sure." I kept my voice calm, but my legs kicked back and forth. Easy since my feet didn't touch the floor. I stopped when Mrs. Bowman saw me. She might think I had planned the whole thing.

And she'd have been right.

2

Revelation

I

"Just put that on the table, please," Sheila said, putting her own grocery bag down. "Hang up your coat, please." Two "pleases" in as many sentences. She was feeling the single parent role. I felt bad for upsetting and embarrassing her but thought she needed to stew a little longer. Was I practicing psychology now? Was it a medical analogy, like pricking a boil already about to burst?

Sheila didn't want to stew.

"What do I do, Scott?" She played with the zipper pull on her jacket and didn't look at me. She could have been asking how to operate the thing. "Six times. *Six times* I've had to leave work." She folded the coat over her arm and didn't look at me. "My boss doesn't think you're cute."

I nodded. She didn't see me, but it didn't matter. She wasn't finished.

"I don't get it. This ... behavior." She pushed past me, a rudeness she deplored in other people, and hung her coat on

7

the rack, above the spot reserved for mine. She straightened it, then tugged on it so hard I feared she might pull the peg out of the rack. "Where did it come from, Scott?"

I shrugged and, not for the first time, considered my mother's mental and emotional health. It was almost time to tell her. She was ready, and boy did she need a break.

My shrug didn't impress her. Sheila put her hands on her hips and gave me a look that could wilt silk flowers. She looked like an ad model. *Disappointment* by Calvin Klein.

I turned from her withering gaze. If I had to look at it any longer, I might blurt something out. This required planning and I headed to my room to do some.

"Supper will be early tonight," she said to my back. "I have to catch up on some of the work I missed today, so bedtime's at seven. I want you in your jammies when you come to the table."

Without answering, I went to my room and closed the door. I got out my pajamas and unfolded them. How would Sheila react when I unfolded my secret?

II

The silence at supper rivaled our alone time in Mrs. Bowman's office. When I was sure she was finished, I picked up Sheila's plate and my own. She watched skeptically, wary of the brown nosing as I loaded the dishwasher.

But when I returned to the table I took her hand in both of mine.

"We need to talk."

She said nothing. Right then, I thought she knew. It didn't matter. I had to say it out loud.

I took a deep breath and tried to exhale some butterflies. "I'm not normal. I think you know that."

She still said nothing, but her hand squeezed mine.

"You wouldn't believe how long I've worried about how to tell you."

Sheila still said nothing. I hadn't expected this to be so one-sided.

"Do you understand?" I asked. "I'm afraid of what might happen if people find out. It's why I act out at school. I ... " My eyes fell away. "I didn't want to be a bad kid, but that place was driving me insane." I raised my eyes to her face and saw no change. "I couldn't tell anyone. Now, I *have* to."

"What do you mean, Scott?" Her words were almost too flat to be considered a question.

"I have to tell you," I said. "I have to start with you, I mean. Other people will come later." Despite twenty minutes of preparation, I was in danger of rambling. "Do you understand?"

She shook her head. "You're scaring me a little, Scott." She didn't look scared, though. Relieved, maybe.

"We need to find help, first," I said. "Like a lawyer. It'd be expensive, but we need someone who knows the law and can keep our secret."

She squeezed my hand, much harder than before. *"What secret, Scott?"*

There was the question I'd been waiting for, and I was almost too chicken to answer.

"I know ... things."

She waited, mouth open.

"Things I couldn't know. Things I really *shouldn't* know."

My voice shook and I swallowed a lump. "But I really do know them. Known them my whole life, and that's too long to pass off as just weird."

She squeezed my hand again, and now she did look scared. "You don't want to go back to school, do you?"

"No," I said. "I'm sure I creep the other kids out, anyway."

III

A precursor to expulsion ...

It hasn't been a good morning. Lessons so tedious I want to explode with impatience. Four hours doing arithmetic, reading comprehension, phonics, and a laughable little science experiment with magnets. Almost time for lunch.

Peanut butter and jelly. I can barely contain the thrill. At least it won't be *this*.

Mrs. Miller is the teacher. She bothers me, too. Keeps opening a desk drawer to look at something, maybe a dying animal she keeps checking for signs of life. For all I know, it really could be. Poor thing, if it is. This year has witnessed the passing of three gerbils and a tankful of goldfish. I'd bet money Mrs. Miller has a house full of brown things in pots. She might believe in Winston Churchill's admonition to never, never, never, never give up, but I'll bet every pet she ever owned opted for early retirement.

It's not an animal. A telltale reflection in her eyes tells me that Mrs. Miller is hiding a small television. Whatever she's watching, it has more of her attention than the twenty-four first graders in the same room.

No fair, I think. If I have to sit through this tedium, why doesn't she?

I take a paper — doesn't matter which one, just a reason to get up — and approach her desk. She is turned in her chair to view her program. I get within a yard of her before letting her have it.

"Missus Miller? I need h— wow! What's that?"

Slapstick isn't my favorite comic medium, but the scene is perfect: her hand slams the drawer shut, with her thumb inside. But before she makes a sound, her face stirs one of my unexplained memories.

She looks just like Lee Harvey Oswald when he was perforated by Jack Ruby.

She looks like Harpo Marx doing the old piano-lid-on-the-fingers shtick.

Mrs. Miller stifles an agonized curse. For a few moments I'm sorry I've done it. Then I get over it.

Mrs. Miller gets up, tells us kids to stay put while she steps out for a moment of respite.

First aid from the first grade. I feel a similar sentiment.

When she's gone, I circle the desk to see what she's been viewing.

A mark of my particular mental oddity is finding novelty in many modern conveniences more commonplace now than televisions were in the 1950's. I'm amazed to see American Idol playing on the tiny screen of an iPod. How could she enjoy a music program with the volume turned all the way down?

"I'm gonna tell!"

I look up from the drawer. A boy in the front row smiles

at me. What's his name? Cody? Coby? One of those trendy names filling the school roster.

"You aren't supposed to touch Miss Miller's desk," he says. "I'm gonna tell."

I close the desk drawer and our eyes lock. In a few seconds the smile fades from his face. Suddenly, he looks as though he might need to go potty. I move to his desk and look down at him. I don't even speak, just let him have it with the old hairy eyeball.

When I'm a jerk, I don't usually discriminate, but Cody/Coby is a mean tattletale. I lean toward him, widening my eyes and showing my teeth. When my nostrils flare, he tries to melt through the back of his chair, never taking his eyes off me. I walk away. My work is finished here.

One girl — named Barbara, I think — has been watching me. Now, as I leave Cody in my dust, she wears a grin. It seems I have a fan.

At my desk, I stare at the clock, waiting for lunch.

"You don't have to be so mean," Lizzy, a girl to my left hisses at me. "You don't 'posed to touch the teacher's desk. And I *know* you don't 'posed to open it up!"

I turn to her. How best to discourage the attentions of a little girl? In a moment of inspiration, I root in my right nostril and collect a magnificent specimen, green and sparkly.

I hold it between us like a glowing hot brand. Her eyelids peel back and disappear. I reach to wipe it on her and she squeals and squeals until a teacher comes to investigate.

It's the only fun I have at school all day. It won't get me expelled, but it'll help.

3

Anonymity

A week or so earlier, despite my behavior at school, Sheila had given me an early birthday present. A child-sized computer keyboard. I asked and she delivered, bless her.

I think she was just happy I hadn't asked for a chemistry set.

I tried a few on-line learning programs. Piece of cake. Before, I had never done much more than play solitaire. After graduating from card games, the speed of my progress was a little disturbing.

When it came to computers, I felt an affinity I didn't understand. The same way I liked baseball, even though the closest I came to it was a classmate wearing a Cal Ripkin Jr. tee shirt. I was a natural at computers, but it wasn't *natural*.

I was drawn to the news service websites right away. I watched some television news, but I was limited to early morning and early evening broadcasts because we couldn't afford cable. Now, I pulled up Reuters anytime I wanted, or as soon as the dial-up connection allowed.

News was nice, but before long I yearned for something interactive. Dozens of pop-up ads about dating services were interesting. And cruel. Except for my mother, I didn't have any friends, much less a girlfriend. How would my personal ad read? *SINGLE WHITE MALE, NONSMOKER, NONDRINKER, NO DRIVER'S LICENSE ... LIVES WITH MOTHER.*

It was a bad idea to go one-on-one with anyone I met online. Chat rooms, on the other hand, were group forums. Visiting a chat room was like going to a party in a completely dark room where everyone's voice was the same. Safe as long as one remained anonymous.

I chose a nickname both anonymous and appropriate, "MyAlterEgo," and I tried a couple of "social rooms." The category suggested *someone* might talk to me. No one did, but according to the roster on the right side of the screen, nearly two hundred people were signed on. Too many people to notice one more little guy.

All the chat rooms had titles, but the more general the name, the larger the population. I changed my search parameters and looked for a room that had nothing to do with sexual orientation, sports, geographic patriotism, politics, etc. I wound up with a list of nearly a dozen rooms, all of which had fewer than ten guests.

One caught my eye immediately: *"I'm Okay, You're Okay."*

bArElYtHeRe: ooooooo look! we got new meat
WottaNut: (struggles to curb his enthusiasm.)
OneBrikShy: Welcome, MyAlterEgo! Please tell us your age, sex and location.

MyAlterEgo: Excuse me?

bArElYtHeRe: don't worry. its an old bot. turn that off brik??? eh?

MyAlterEgo: I was about to go elsewhere. I thought the whole point was anonymity.

OneBrikShy: i keep it on to discourage kids.

MyAlterEgo: I guess that's a good idea. You didn't advertise as an adult site though.

bArElYtHeRe: anonymity's out ego. yer giving yerself away :P

MyAlterEgo: How did I do that?

OneBrikShy: use of punctuation

WottaNut: mature syntax

bArElYtHeRe: kinda stuffy

OneBrikShy: this is informal ego. lay off the caps and punctuation all you want

MyAlterEgo: I think I'd have to cut off my pinkies to keep from hitting the shift keys.

WottaNut: 2 down (winks at *bArElYtHeRe*)

OneBrikShy: just 2?

MyAlterEgo: Yes, I only have two pinkies.

OneBrikShy: no man. 2 out of the 3. a/s/l

MyAlterEgo: I'm still trying to catch onto the abbreviations.

bArElYtHeRe: Age/Sex/Location silly

WottaNut: i bet i got you on 2 out of 3

MyAlterEgo: Impressive. Which ones do you think you've uncovered?

OneBrikShy: over 21, prolly WAY over, and male

MyAlterEgo: Why do you think so?

WottaNut: caps are hard to put down for people who

learned how to type before emails and ims

bArElYtHeRe: cutting off fingers is gross, ergo MALE

MyAlterEgo: Impressive, but I'm not confirming anything. Out of curiosity, though, why did you think they might have had all three, um, Brik?

OneBrikShy: nut figures he can place people by word choice :D

MyAlterEgo: That would be really impressive. After all, it isn't spelled "Bah Habbah."

OneBrikShy: convenient but too easy. he goes by little things

MyAlterEgo: such as? (look, lowercase!)

WottaNut: in some places people say "my wife bought a dress up to the mall"

MyAlterEgo: Lots of places, I think

WottaNut: yeah but "Bah Habbah" puts you in the usa. north america at least. who else makes jokes about that?

MyAlterEgo: oops.

WottaNut: from the south?

MyAlterEgo: Better and better.

WottaNut: we'll stop there. no sense in driving you off by invading your privacy.

MyAlterEgo: I appreciate it.

WottaNut: we'll invade your sanity >:)

OneBrikShy: I'm from chicago if it helps you relax.

WottaNut: and I'm from boston. not quite bah habbah

OneBrikShy: bare won't tell us where she's from.

bArElYtHeRe: I'm from Venus.

MyAlterEgo: but you know she's a she?

WottaNut: we HOPE she's a she. there's been a lot of flirting

OneBrikShy: I keep wondering if bare is a guy who looks like newman on seinfeld

bArElYtHeRe: hello jerry ROFLMAO

MyAlterEgo: That's funny.

2hot2handle has arrived

OneBrikShy: Welcome *2hot2handle* ! Please tell us your age, sex and location.

2hot2handle: this bites

2hot2handle *has left the room*

MyAlterEgo: that was interesting

bArElYtHeRe: brb afk

MyAlterEgo: I need a list of all these abbreviations.

OneBrikShy: they start to come natural after while

MyAlterEgo: I've got a couple. Be Right Back and Away From Keyboard.

WottaNut: there you go with the shift key again

MyAlterEgo: sorry

WottaNut: wait til you discover smileys

MyAlterEgo: and who's Rolf Mao?

OneBrikShy: LOL

WottaNut: BOL

It was *so* much more fun than first grade.

4

Honesty

If Sheila had known I liked coffee — or had been willing to let me drink it — we might have put away three pots. Instead, we sat at the table in our pajamas and put away leftover Christmas cookies and a half gallon of milk. I told her the whole story and she pretended not to freak out.

What I told her:

I was Scott Bledsoe, age 5 years 11 months and 16 days. Or at least I thought I was. There were a number of hitches in that theory.

I spent the first six months of my life trying to talk to my mother. I couldn't, though. My vocal cords were brand new.

I wanted to ask her, or anyone, what in the world was going on.

I needed to know because on January 4, 2001, I was born at Memorial Hospital in Roanoke, Virginia. I didn't know why I was aware of it, but I was definitely being born. I'd seen it on enough TV shows and movies to recognize the event.

Or had I?

If I was just coming into the world, I thought, how could I have known about childbirth, or about TV and movies? Understand the doctor's words when he said, "It's a boy?" Recognize his Virginia accent?

I tried to talk but it didn't work. All I got was a squeak. I tried again and heard only small mewling sound. I tried screaming. *That* worked. The doctor told my mother I had a great set of lungs.

Now, I munched on milk-sodden shortbread and remembered for Sheila.

"At least I knew you were my mother," I said. "Everyone kept calling you that."

She smiled at that but her eyes were a little glassy. I might have trusted her reaction better if she had fainted or cried or something. She just sat and took it. Like bad news.

After three hours' worth of troubling anecdotes, Sheila had a couple of questions.

"What do you want to do, Scott?"

I already had the answer. "I want to find out what I can do with my life."

She looked down at the beige crumbs collected in the bottom of her milk glass. "How could this have happened?"

That one wasn't directed at me.

We were both silent for a few moments. I soaked cookies and munched. Sheila breathed with an odd rhythm.

She reached for my hand. "Sweetie? How long ... ?"

" ... has this been going on?" I blew a jet of breath through my bangs and then I blushed. "Well, my earliest memory is from before I ... came out."

She had held out long enough and it was time for a cry. The tears flowed, though I think they were for me, not her. I didn't begrudge her the weeping. I felt like crying myself, but some deep part of me shied away from the release, as if it could hurt me. Same reason I didn't try shaving.

"I knew there was something," she said through tears. I was a good boy and handed her a Kleenex. "I just knew you would be one of those kids. Learning how to do calculus by age 10 and graduating college before you can vote." She sniffed and turned her eyes on me, smiling. "Do I need to start saving for dorm room furniture?"

I shook my head. "It's not like that." I twisted in my chair so I wouldn't see her tears. "I'm not just smart. Maybe not *even* smart. I just ... know things."

Sheila wiped her eyes again. "Other than how to talk like an adult?"

"Come here." I took her hand and led her to the computer desk. I got my extra booster chair from under the desk. At the computer, on my special, cartoony keyboard, I typed.

"January 10, 2007. This morning I decided to tell Sheila the truth. She already knew things aren't all hunky dory. She is going to have her hands full with me, now even more. I let the cat out of the bag. I hope that she can forgive me someday."

"I ease along at about seventy-five words a minute," I said. "I'm pretty sure I can go faster, though." As I mentioned, I got the keyboard the week before. I didn't state the obvious, that I didn't learn to type seventy-five words a minute in a week. Or shouldn't have.

Sheila leaned close, read and reread. She squeezed my arms a little too tightly but I let it slide. She released my shoulders and leaned down to kiss my cheek. "There's nothing to forgive, Scotty. Whatever is going on can't be *your* fault." Then she slumped so hard I felt the wind. "That means that something I ... " Her hands covered her mouth and her eyes bulged.

I pulled her hands down. "Come on," I said. "This isn't because you didn't take enough prenatal vitamins. You didn't smoke or drink, did you? Take LSD?"

She shook her head and held in a gasp.

"Attend any occult rituals involving livestock?"

She released her held breath in one syllable that was more laugh than sob.

I held out my hands. "There you go."

"But what do we do?"

"We have to find someone who can help us," I said. "I can't do any more myself. It's making me crazy."

"But who?" she asked.

"Try looking at work," I said. "Maybe someone you work with could help. We can't afford a lawyer but someone there might help us out." She wasn't looking at me. "You okay?" I asked.

She put a hand to her cheek and looked at the screen again. "Do you really think of me as Sheila instead of Mom?"

5

Recruitment

A couple of days later, Sheila came home with a name.

"His name is Charlie Bailey," she told me as she prepared the salad for supper. "Bonnie Lockhart says he's *extremely* well-read."

"Is that a nice way of saying he's a student?" I was hoping for someone on staff.

"Oh, no," she said. "He got his degree. Doing grad work now."

"Degree in what?" I asked.

"Art." Sheila brought the knife down, decapitated several carrots in one blow.

"Oh, well *that's* useful."

Sheila shook her head and kept slicing. "Bonnie said he's very, very smart. Doesn't give up until he's found his answers."

"How many years did the degree take him?"

She sighed. "I didn't ask."

"Charlie Bailey," I said. "What is this, a Frank Capra movie?"

Sheila stopped slicing. "You already got me to take you out of school. You don't have to act like that anymore."

There it was. I wasn't a normal kid, but my mother was still in charge. Chastened, I exhibited unfeigned interest.

"Did you tell him?"

She started in on the veggies again. "No, I didn't tell him, Scotty."

I snorted. "Would you mind not calling me that? I have enough on my mind without feeling like I'm named after a dog breed."

She didn't reply, but I knew I'd hit bone.

I felt bad but I couldn't let it be. "What, am I supposed to spring it on him? 'Introducing Scott, the Middle-Aged Grade-schooler?'"

She dropped what she was doing and turned to look at me. "Middle-*what?*"

"Never mind," I said. It was too much to explain. "We're just inviting him to the freak show?"

She kept slicing, but her breath got hitchy. Despite momentary self-loathing, I almost stirred things up again. I didn't know why.

Then I relented. "I'm sorry. Let's give it a shot."

"You want to see him?"

"Yeah," I said. "Info I've got. It's know-how I lack. And guidance."

Sheila smiled but it was relief, not happiness. That made me feel like a real jerk. She shouldn't have to feel that way.

II

Before meeting the Talented Mr. Bailey, I wanted to see what we were getting. Sheila arranged for him to meet me for a *téte-a-téte* in an online chat room. I was comfortable with that format now, mostly because I didn't have to measure myself next to a yardstick in order to ride.

MyAlterEgo: Thank you for coming.

CareerStudent: First things first ... you're not the person I spoke to before, are you?

MyAlterEgo: No, but that person can be contacted for verification.

CareerStudent: OK. Next ... I don't want to get involved in anything illegal

MyAlterEgo: Nothing illegal on this end. Should I be worried about you?

CareerStudent: No, but cybercrimes abound, and I don't want to get caught in one. Or a pyramid scheme.

MyAlterEgo: I appreciate your caution. Don't worry, there's nothing illegal, immoral, or unethical about what we're doing.

CareerStudent: What are we doing?

MyAlterEgo: Now? Testing the waters. Getting a feel for each other.

CareerStudent: Without meeting? A roommate of mine chatted online with a "woman" for weeks before finding out the truth. I don't want any romantic entanglements.

CareerStudent: Are you still there?

MyAlterEgo: Sorry, I had a laughing fit. Please don't worry

about romance.

CareerStudent: I don't even know what you want from me. Why contact me if you're going to be so secretive?

MyAlterEgo: This format is for my protection. I wish to remain anonymous for now. What I want from you: I need an observer, or tutor. With academic credentials.

CareerStudent: I'm not sure you read my dossier correctly, 007. I'm still a student.

MyAlterEgo: Got a degree in art, right? Doing grad work?

CareerStudent: Yes. Grad studies and a full-time job. I might not have time for this. Plus, I tend not to be popular as a tutor.

MyAlterEgo: Why is that?

CareerStudent: Because I LOOK like an art grad student.

MyAlterEgo: Personal appearance doesn't mean much to me. I don't actually need a teacher or a tutor, but this has to remain secret. There's no non-disclosure contract, but you must not go to anyone else with what you see or learn without express permission from me.

CareerStudent: I understand that, but there's that specter of questionable legality.

MyAlterEgo: I assure you, I will not involve you in anything illegal. But my situation is delicate.

CareerStudent: How so?

MyAlterEgo: You'll find out if we meet, and only if.

CareerStudent: Are you going tell me how to prepare?

MyAlterEgo: The phrase that best sums up my predicament is "identity crisis." You can prepare accordingly.

CareerStudent: Maybe you just need a shrink.

<u>MyAlterEgo:</u> The thought has occurred. It may still be an option, but not my first choice.

Charlie seemed like a sharp guy. Is that high praise coming from a six-year-old? With stuff like "the specter of questionable legality," I wanted to meet him just for the conversation.

6

Alliance

Sheila went to answer the doorbell. I stayed at the kitchen table. The front door opened and someone stepped inside. There was a change in the house. Nothing unnatural about that, I supposed. We didn't have many guests.

I sort of sensed Sheila leading the way, heard her approaching voice but not her footsteps. They drew closer but I knew Sheila was in front. She'd had second thoughts the night before, but when she finally realized that I would never, ever enjoy a normal childhood — or normal life — without help, she put her worries on the back burner.

Sheila led our guest into the kitchen. "Mr. Bailey," she said, "this is my son, Scott. He's the one you're here to see." Then she disappeared.

"Hi, Scott," he said. "I'm Charles Bailey. Most people call me Charlie."

This didn't feel right. Maybe it *was* his appearance,

despite what I had said. He was right about looking like an art student. Art *grad* student, even. Cleaner hair and a finer cut of flannel. That wasn't it, though. I didn't have all my faculties figured out yet, but something nibbled at my worry.

He wasn't as surprised as he should have been. Since he had been chosen on the basis of open-mindedness, it should have done him credit. But he was too cool. Too soon.

"Nice to meet you, Charlie, but I think we've wasted enough of your time."

"How so?" He sat down and got some things out of an ancient canvas backpack.

"I think you've already made up your mind about me."

Charlie put thin books and notepads in a neat stack and got a pencil from his bag. Not a pen. *That's an artist for you,* I thought.

"And what have I decided?"

Since Sheila had left the room, I climbed onto the table and sat cross-legged. "Sheila didn't tell you how young I was. Now, you think I'm just a really smart kid and you want to do tests to find out exactly *how* smart."

"I did bring along an I.Q. test, but you gave me the idea, when you mentioned psych tests. That was before I even knew your age, or even what this was about."

"An I.Q. test isn't going to help," I said. "This isn't about intelligence but knowledge. Stuff that can't be deduced or figured."

"Like?"

"I only started typing last month, something like forty words a minute from the get-go."

Charlie frowned. "You were a lot faster than that in our little on-line interview."

I nodded. "I'm closer to a hundred, now. All it took was a keyboard better suited to my hand size. Sheila bought me the Spongebob Squarepants model."

Charlie's frown deepened. I thought something was happening inside his head, but babies frown when they're filling their diapers, too. "An I.Q. test might not register correctly, but would you take it to humor me?"

I folded my arms. "If you start asking the right kind of questions."

"You in a big hurry? Got some kind of deadline?"

"I just don't want to waste time. I'm already way behind." I didn't tell him I thought I might go crazy if I didn't get answers soon.

"What kind of questions should I be asking?"

"Don't ask me," I said. "I'm the test subject. That's your job."

"Who was the first President of the United States?"

"George Washington. Got one other six-year-olds couldn't answer?"

"And the president now?"

"George W. Bush," I said. "You're not scoring any points."

"Is this his first or second term?"

"Second." That one took me a moment.

My hesitation was enough for Charlie. "And who was Richard Nixon's veep?"

"Spiro Agnew," I answered, then added without thinking, "then Ford."

Charlie flipped open a notebook and scribbled something.

"Now how about Nine-Eleven?"

"What about it?"

"What do you know?

I shrugged. "I know it happened right around the time I was learning to stand up."

"Then that's where we'll begin. Good a place as any, I guess."

"What do you mean?"

"We now know of a way to track your knowledge. Not much, but something. Something to catalog. Straight data with no math involved, unless it's just subtraction." Turned away as he was, I couldn't tell if he was answering me or talking to himself. His gravity was almost amusing.

"What?" I said. "What are we cataloging?"

"Maybe some kind of event calendar," he said, still not facing me. "Pictures, newspapers, music —

What are you talking about?" I yelled.

"Aren't you the test subject." He could have smiled to let me know he was joking. He didn't.

"I just wanted to get your creative juices flowing," I said.

He looked at me over the tops of his glasses. "You came to me, remember?"

"Geez, I'm sorry." I sounded like a petulant child giving a forced apology. Help was here and I was being a brat. "Really, I'm sorry. Please don't let the voice fool you."

He looked at me for a long moment, then smiled. "I'm going to have to ignore your voice. Spiro Agnew sounds creepy in the mouth of a child."

"Don't I know it."

I realized then what an independent observer might have

noticed right away: Charlie didn't condescend to me. Didn't set himself up in the lead adult role of *The Kid That Knew Stuff.* Didn't treat me like a credulous child or a dumb animal.

However ...

"Speaking of watching your mouth," Charlie said.

I had been about to climb down and behave. "Yes?"

"I'll bet your mother is at a loss for what to do with her 'special boy,' but I'd like you to think about something."

I retained my perch on the table. I might have to smack the guy. "What's that, Charlie?"

"It's mostly just that. She's at a loss. You're an amazing kid but she has no idea what to do with you. Coming to me was a desperate act."

"Wait a second," I said. "You misunderstood. This was my plan, not hers. You just come cheaper than a lawyer or a doctor."

If Charlie was insulted, he didn't show it. Instead, he looked embarrassed. "It's going to take awhile for me to quit assuming your mother makes all the decisions around here."

"She makes most of them," I said. "No matter what kind of weirdo I am, she's still the boss."

"Well, yeah," he said. "She's your mom."

"I just said that."

He squinted at me and exhaled a long breath. "I know you're an exception, but kids who speak rudely to adults — like you spoke to me earlier — usually learn by practicing on their parents." He gave me a meaningful look and pursed his lips. "You see what I'm talking about?"

"I don't talk to *her* that way," I said. "With you, I was

conducting a negotiation."

"Yes, but I see something you probably don't. I don't know if it was specific to my visit, but your mother is walking on eggshells. I can't imagine what it must be like for her, but I want *you* to try."

"Excuse me?" I wanted help, not guilt.

"You might be comfortable with your condition, or at least used to it. Your mother is not. She still thinks of you as the little boy she needs to protect and nurture and all those things that mean she's being a good mother. Do you understand what I'm getting at?"

"Yes," I said. "You want me to be nice to my mother."

He shook his head. "I don't know if you see. When she led me into the kitchen, it was like she was trying to avoid setting off a bomb."

"Maybe you don't see," I said. "My mother just divulged a closely-held family secret to someone she just met. I'm sure she feels antsy about that. If someone committed a desperate act," I tapped my chest, "it was me. Not her."

"Maybe," he said. "And maybe both of you are desperate."

7

Experiment

I spent the next few weeks going through a battery of tests Charlie devised himself. The tests impressed and really challenged me, maybe for the first time in my life. I had come to believe I had something like a world-class search engine between my ears. That somehow I had access to major data stores and could retrieve it with the right keyword.

Considering the intensity of the tests, it was more like assault and battery. Day after day, hour after hour, quart after quart of Sugar-Free Kool-Aid, I answered questions, performed tasks and responded to stimuli. I took tests until I thought Charlie might just name a whole new branch of science after me. *Scottology,* of which he would be the founding father.

"Do I get to ride the space shuttle?" I asked one day. "This feels like astronaut training."

Charlie smiled. "I know it's tough, but look at all the

useful information we've got." He pointed to a steno pad full of his scribbling.

"Useful" was a relative term, and logically speaking, all information is useful for *something*. I almost said so, but then Charlie would ask how I knew about logic, how much I knew about it and why I felt that way. I was too weary for a new line of questioning.

"And what have we learned?" I asked. I rubbed my eyes, stretched and tried not to sink back into the deep chair.

Charlie flipped open a manila envelope and grabbed a fresh, sharp pencil. "First, the IQ test tells us that on paper you're a very bright kid."

"I sense a 'but' coming on."

Charlie smiled. "But that test told me something else."

I waited.

"I'm not just talking about the results," said Charlie. "I watched you while you filled out the paper to see how you answered. Questions that should have required a modicum of calculation, you just answered in passing. What I call 'pencil-whipping.'"

"Did I get those right?"

"Almost all of them."

"So I scored pretty high?"

"Yes," Charlie said, "but you told me at the start that you're not worried about your intelligence." He looked at the page. "You did okay on some of the math-based questions, but you excelled at spatial reasoning. However, those questions were the ones you spent the least time on. Almost no thought."

"So I'm smart at that type of questions?"

Charlie frowned and shook his head. "More like you knew the answers already." Then he smiled. "Like you'd cheated, memorized the test beforehand."

"Weird."

"Yes, but your age and seclusion rule that out." He opened another folder. "Now, the tests that have nothing to do with cognitive ability." He whipped a sheet of paper out of the folder and laid it before me. "I gave you standardized spelling tests all the way up to high school level. Then I added some words from the hardest section of the National Spelling Bee study book."

"How'd I do?"

"Out of six tests at two hundred words apiece, you missed nine words, all of them from the spelling bee list. Even on the ones you misspelled, you came really close. Like educated guesses."

I frowned. "But educated guesses have a lot to do with cognitive ability."

Charlie squirmed in his seat and rubbed his hands. "This is great! Not only do you have all this unlearned information, you intuit partial solutions. It's another mystery!"

"Why are you so excited?" I asked. "I don't want more mysteries! I'm looking for answers, not more problems! Why do I prefer RC to Coke or Pepsi? Have you ever known Sheila to let me have soda? Why do I prefer Dodge trucks but Honda sedans? I've never driven!"

I got up and tapped my knuckles on the table. "I can quote from The Godfather. I can do Hamlet's soliloquy." I picked up Charlie's car keys from the table. "I could open the hood of your car and tell you the name of everything in there!"

"Really?" Charlie asked. He flipped his notebook open again to jot down this latest information.

"Stop it!" I took a few steps back and climbed onto my chair. I gripped the chair rungs and glared at Charlie. "I can't know this much stuff. For God's sake, I'm six years old and I feel like I'm drowning in whole lifetimes of experience!"

The door opened and Sheila stuck her head in. "Sweetie, are you okay?"

I held the back of the chair, half ready to try throwing it, but I didn't say anything.

Charlie took that as an invitation to explain. "I think my irrepressible optimism is getting on Scott's nerves."

I stood on my chair and glared at him, saying nothing.

Sheila came in and put a hand on my back. "You've been at this for days. Maybe it's time to stop for a while." I wasn't too upset to appreciate the way she said "for a while" instead of "for today." She left the decision up to me.

Charlie looked at me and then Sheila. He sniffed and stuffed his bag full, one piece at a time. He still had that devious twinkle in his eye, but he had the good sense not to smile.

"It'll work out, Scott," he said. "We'll figure it out."

"Not today." My voice hurt. "Goodbye, Charlie."

He left without saying another word. I remained on my chair and seethed. My frustration with Charlie didn't depart when he did.

Another mystery, he had said. Joy.

Sheila's hand squeezed my shoulder. "Are you okay, Scott?"

I nodded without turning.

"I don't think I've seen you cry since you bumped your head climbing out of the playpen when you were two."

I turned and saw her through tears I hadn't noticed.

"Are you really okay?" she asked once more.

"No," I moaned. I fell into her waiting arms and buried my face in her neck and cried and cried and cried.

I thought I had a good excuse.

8

Theories

MyAlterEgo: you guys ever play sports?

WottaNut: fantasy football. the cop that wrote me a ticket last month suggested nascar

OneBrikShy: basketball. i lettered 4 years in hs. a little in college too. bare?

bArElYtHeRe: a long time ago i was a cheerleader. less sweat, nicer duds

WottaNut: nothing more violent? like lacrosse or field hockey? I think of you as the violent type

bArElYtHeRe: (*drop kicks WottaNut's head through the goalposts*)

MyAlterEgo: it may be cheerleader I'm thinking of. Or maybe a coach, but more Lamaze than basketball.

WottaNut: you in a family way ego?

MyAlterEgo: (chuckles) no, but there's this ... colleague who's not as helpful as he thinks. but he's so excited he drives me up the wall

OneBrikShy: does he pat you on the back? lots of new age

38

office lingo? game plan? think outside the box? does
he pronounce it para-dijum?

MyAlterEgo: no, thank goodness. but his priorities are little
off

bArElYtHeRe: can you fire him?

MyAlterEgo: maybe, but i'd rather not

OneBrikShy: is he a friend?

MyAlterEgo: we haven't known each other very long

WottaNut: we aren't exactly your lifelong buddies, ego

MyAlterEgo: yes, but when I get advice from you, you never
know if I follow it.

II

Of course, I let Charlie come back. Sheila made me.

One day, in between torture sessions, Charlie sat on the
couch and drummed on his head with both fists. At first I
thought he was doing an old Spike Jones percussion riff. But
he was really going to town. Not drumming but hammering.

"What are you doing?" I asked over the knocking sound.

He stopped, eyes still closed. "I had a thought. A new
one." He clenched his teeth. "It slipped away."

"You're just tired," I plopped down in a chair. "So am I."

"But it was new!" he said. "Really!"

"Then why beat yourself up?"

He gave a long, tuneful sigh. "If I distract myself with
discomfort, sometimes I can recall things that have just
slipped my mind."

"That's stupid," I said. "You'll hurt yourself."

He opened his eyes, took off his glasses. "No more stupid
than smoking. People use cigarettes to help them think

straight all the time."

"Sure," I said. "Nicotine has a calming effect. It also temporarily improves synaptic response."

"Where'd you learn that?"

I just looked at him.

"Well, even if it might do the trick, no cigarettes for you."

"Do you really think it might work?"

"No," Charlie said. "Plus, Sheila'd kill me."

"I wasn't serious."

"Good," he said. "Anyway, I'd rather have bruises on my scalp than tar in my lungs."

Sheila picked that moment to enter and gave both of us odd looks. "What're you two talking about?"

"Scott and I were discussing the pros and cons of using chemicals to improve — or rather alter - brain performance and—"

"You're not thinking of getting Scott drunk, are you?"

Charlie and I shared a look that said "Why not?"

I grinned at Sheila. "Come on, I skipped my birthday party. How about a kegger?"

"Not on your life," said Sheila.

"Killjoy," Charlie chuckled.

"No cigarettes, either?" I giggled and Charlie let out another sound of glee. Weights were being removed from the stack on my shoulders.

Then Sheila gave me the hardest look I'd ever seen on her face. No, the hardest look ever directed at *me.* The kind reserved for adults.

"Promise me you won't," she said.

Sheila said she was okay with my calling her by her first

name. This wasn't a time to try it out.

"Mom, we were just kidding around."

Sheila relaxed everything but her face. "I know," she said, and slumped into her chair. "But I've seen you. You've got a nervous habit. A fidget. For the life of me I don't know where you picked it up."

"Drumming my fingers on the table?" I asked. "Inappropriate scratching?"

Sheila shook her head, folded her arms and crossed her legs. Defensive posture, the weird brain said. I told it to mind its own beeswax.

"Patting his pockets, right?" asked Charlie. Sheila looked up and nodded, but Charlie's eyes were still closed. He had stopped beating his head and now pinched the bridge of his nose. Maybe he had actually given himself a headache.

"What do you mean?" I asked.

Charlie got up and demonstrated a sort of hand jive: right hand on right breast pocket, ditto the left. Right hand on right back pants pocket, ditto the left. "Like you're looking for something you know you don't have on you," he said. "Glasses, maybe."

I was a little disturbed. Now that it had been brought to my attention, I remembered doing it. Lots of times.

"Like Detective Columbo on TV." I thought of the way Peter Falk looked like he had misplaced something or accidentally walked into the ladies' restroom.

Sheila shivered when I mentioned Columbo. She still wasn't used to me talking about things I shouldn't know about. It helped make up for the times I didn't know things I should, like how to relax and sit through first grade.

"Not glasses," Sheila said. "It's the way my dad used to pat his pockets looking for his Lucky Strikes." She tightened her folded arms. "Spooky."

I nodded, sure it must be.

"And you were talking about alcohol and then cigarettes, and then acting like you were considering it … . " She stopped and looked down at her arms again, winding them even tighter.

"What," I said, "do you think I'm channeling my grandfather's spirit?"

"Scott!" said Charlie. He gave me the speech about being careful of Sheila's feelings again, in a single glance.

"I'm not being flippant," I said. "We never considered anything like that like that before. Or I haven't."

"I don't believe in ghosts or spirit channeling," said Charlie. "That's one reason."

"Me neither," I said, "so far. I'm just saying we hadn't considered it." I looked at Sheila. She had withdrawn a little and seemed close to tears.

"Sheila," Charlie said. "What's wrong?"

She looked up, but not at him. At me. "My dad died of lung cancer," she said, and I saw where her thoughts were taking her.

"I'm sorry." I'd never heard him use that tone before. "You aren't still worried about Scott smoking, are you? I mean, we weren't serious."

"I don't think that's it," I said.

"What, then?" he asked. "I don't mean to pry, but it sounds important to you."

She sighed. "Jamie died of lung cancer, too."

"Who?" asked Charlie.

"*My* father," I said.

"Oh," said Charlie, and was then silent.

"I just hoped I could believe it was something else. With a genetic tendency from both sides of the family, I mean. What do poker players call it? When they give things away with body language?"

"Tells," Charlie and I said together.

Sheila nodded. "Right. Tells. I kept hoping it was glasses you were patting for, but you don't do anything else that people with glasses do. Pushing a finger up the bridge of your nose, like Christopher Reeve in the Superman movies. One of my coworkers had the laser surgery and he still does that, so I thought maybe if you —"

Charlie shot to his feet. "That's it!" He grinned like a lottery winner. "That's the idea I lost!"

"I guess distraction worked," I said. "What was the idea?"

He shook his head. "Come on," he said. "*Superman!*" He waited for me to guess. I waited for him to remember that I wasn't clairvoyant.

"Okay," he said. "You didn't have — don't have — a normal childhood ... "

"Must you keep bringing it up?"

" ... and so you've missed out on some of the things kids do." He acted as if I hadn't spoken.

"I filled my share of diapers."

Charlie grinned at Sheila.

"Yes," she said. "But you also expressed interest in going to the toilet before you could walk."

"Really?" asked Charlie.

"It was so cute," said Sheila. "I'd go to change his diaper and it would be dry and clean. Then he'd give me this look, crawl to the bathroom and pat on the door."

"Wow," said Charlie.

I rolled my eyes.

"I guess he just didn't have the fine motor skills or he would have been using sign language." She looked at me and got misty again. "About a month later — he couldn't have been more than eight months old — he started talking."

"What was his first word?" asked Charlie, having the tact not to bring out his pencil and notepad.

She nodded. "'Newspaper. Well, 'paper,' anyway." She looked at me again. "Recently, he told me it had been a request."

Charlie shook his head. "Amazing."

"After Scott finally confided in me," Sheila said, "He said he'd been trying to find out what was happening in the world. To see if it matched what was in his head. He had to settle for a newspaper. When I couldn't tell six o'clock news from celebrity gossip, I just quit watching."

I cleared my throat as if I were trying to cough up a newspaper. They looked at me. "Either of you two adult people familiar with the word 'tangent?'" I asked.

They gave each other knowing looks and smiled.

"What I meant," said Charlie, "is that you missed out on entertainment kids your age are into."

"I've filled my share of coloring books, too, thank you." Boy, had I.

Charlie shook his head but that infuriating, knowing smile was still there. "Not coloring books, Scott. *Comic* books."

I made a vague gesture. "I still don't get it."

"Superheroes!" he shouted, as if he were cheering for a team. "I thought of it earlier but it slipped my mind. When Sheila mentioned Clark Kent, I remembered."

"Yes," said Sheila, "we were all here for that. What about it?"

Charlie sat down but still looked like he was dancing. "It means we have some direction. Specific possibilities to explore."

"Superheroes?" I said. "Like Superman and Batman?"

"Superman," he said, "yes. Batman, no. Spiderman, yes. Iron Man, no. See the pattern?"

"Names starting with 'S?'" I sounded obtuse, but he sounded ludicrous. I still didn't get it, though, so I gave him a blank look.

He frowned. "Maybe your knowledge doesn't extend to that field."

"Superman," I said, ticking off points on my fingers. "Created by Jerry Siegel and Joe Schuster. First appeared in Action Comics #1, 1938."

That must have unnerved him a little. He waited a moment before continuing. "I don't mean vital statistics. I'm talking backgrounds."

He had my attention but I was still in the dark and said so.

Then Sheila's eyes widened and her cheeks rounded in a smile. I could tell she'd had a "eureka" moment. I felt more than a little left out.

Sheila put a hand on mine. "Do you want us to tell you," she asked, "or do you want to figure it out?"

I sank into my chair. "I've reached my figuring limit for the day."

"Let me try one more time," said Charlie. "You'll feel better if you make the connection yourself."

I shrugged and nodded.

He smiled and took off his glasses, his own little Clark Kent impression. "How did Superman get his powers?"

I spoke up right away. "Earth's yellow sun."

"And Spiderman?"

Realization came just before I answered. Superman and Spiderman, yet neither Batman nor Iron Man. These but not those.

I grinned. "It's a nice idea, Charles, but I think my mother would remember pulling me out of an impact crater or treating me for radioactive bug bites."

Charlie frowned and shook his head. "I doubt we can pin down anything specific this afternoon, but we've really narrowed our focus. Until now, all we've done is stand back, say 'wow,' and record data. That amounts to a nice chunk, but we haven't spent any time with how and why."

"Maybe *you* haven't," I said. "It's practically all I think about."

Sheila patted my hand. "I think Charlie's saying that since you now have a real approach vector, you can begin asking specific, educated questions."

I looked at Sheila with surprise. *"Approach vector?"*

She shrugged. "I went to college, too."

"She's right," said Charlie. "I think my subconscious has been trying to tell me, but I've been too driven to stop and smell the roses."

"The theory is nice and all," I said, "but how do we test it?"

Charlie shrugged. "No idea, but Sheila's right about the approach vector. While we can theorize on how this came about, what happened to cause it and why it affects you this way, we won't be totally lost. We now have a guiding theory."

"And you think the theory that my unusual scope of knowledge has superhero-like origins is sound?" I meant to sound cynical. My hopes were rising and I wanted to stop them before they go so high any fall would dash them. "That there's a far-fetched, even miraculous, plausible reason for all this?"

"Yes," said Charlie.

"But you don't believe in ghosts?"

9

More Theories

What now?" Sheila asked. "I keep a pretty good day-planner, but I can't tell you every little thing that might have caused ... " She made a vague gesture. I thought she meant the situation instead of me, and it was sweet. Wrong, but sweet.

"Any ideas, Charlie?" I asked, "or is one your daily limit?"

Charlie gave me a dirty look and Sheila followed with one of her own. Charlie's was a smile, though. Sheila didn't get it, probably because she was a woman, but maybe because I'd been closer to Charlie for the last few weeks. We had a rhythm going, a guy thing.

"Oh, I've got plenty, squirt," he said.

"Do I need to step out?" asked Sheila. "I feel like I'm in the middle of a contest I'm not equipped for." Maybe she did get it.

"You picked up on Charlie's cockamamie idea before I did, and I've got enough stuff in my head to fill some pretty big notebooks."

Charlie grinned again. "That's more true if you replace the word 'stuff' with the word 'sh—"

"Charlie!" Sheila hissed.

"Shinola," Charlie said. "That's what I was going to say."

To be honest, I was a little jealous of Charlie. He worked with knowledge he'd gotten from years of study. Practice at understanding. My knowledge was undefined. I had no idea what I might come up with.

Even that wasn't the whole reason. I could hold up my end of conversation while talking to him, but Charlie had an ability I didn't. He could swear.

I didn't know why — some kind of mental block, maybe — but I couldn't utter profanity. Nor could I write or type it. I once tried singing it, but to no avail. I could think it, and often did, to my discredit. Verbally, though, I was limited. It really chapped my patootie.

II

Charlie had brought it up, so it was his baby. It was an awesome idea. Romantic, even. But comparing my mysterious mental state to super powers felt like a waste of time.

So why did I find the idea so fascinating?

If I were normal — a description I feared would forever elude me — I would be thrilled to have someone compare me to a superhero. But the idea didn't just euphemize my personal problem. He used it as a clue to the origins of the dilemma. Maybe to its cure.

"Maybe it didn't happen in the conventional way," said

Charlie. He stood up and looked at the floor.

"What conventional way?" I asked and sat back in my chair. I wanted my feet out of the way if he decided to pace. "In a theory based on fictitious events, the word 'conventional' doesn't even come into it."

"You know what I mean."

"Don't hold me to it."

He paced. I pulled my feet up and sat on them.

"You're not from outer space," he said. "You weren't bitten by anything radioactive."

"Oh, that," I said. He couldn't see my eye-roll so I did it for Sheila. But she had her eyes on something else, out of sight.

"What other ways did superheroes get their abilities?" Charlie asked. "Come on, Scott. Put that search engine to use."

I almost retorted, but active thinking cheered me up. "Okay, let's see." I held up fingers as I named some popular superheroes and brief descriptions of the events that brought them fame. "Bruce Banner became The Hulk after being subjected to massive amounts of gamma radiation."

"I thought you'd mention The Leader," Charlie said. "Samuel Stearns got a super gamma dose, too."

"But he wasn't a hero."

"True," he said, "but I can't imagine morality has an effect on it. We ought to keep him in mind." He paced some more.

"There's the whole X-Men mutant gene theory," I said, "but I think that's a bust."

"Why?" asked Charlie.

"You think mutation could put unlearned knowledge in my head?" I asked. "Typing skills? Automotive knowledge? Vocabulary?" I shook my head.

"What if you read someone's mind?" He said it in mid-turn, completed another lap.

"Awfully selective mind-reading," I said. "No personal info, just general knowledge?"

Charlie stopped pacing. "And personal preferences," he said. "Don't forget those. Bias with no corresponding experience." He started moving again.

I nodded to myself. I had forgotten and told myself it was easy to do so. I never drank any of the soft drinks I professed to prefer. Nor the beer. Nor the wine. Never drove my favorite car makes and models. Never voted Republican, Democrat or Other, though I *did* have a soft spot for Ralph Nader.

I kept thinking but dismissed several possibilities before I could speak them aloud. For the first time since I met Charlie, I had trouble keeping up with him. He looked at me after each circuit around the coffee table. I didn't answer his look, just kept searching my memory for superhero origins.

When Sheila spoke I realized she was still in the room.

"Are there any superheroes that got their powers from ... " she swallowed, "lightning?"

I could think of a couple right away, but Charlie answered first.

"The Flash," he said. "Barry Allen was a scientist in a lab. Bolt of lightning came in through the window and zapped him, *through* a rack of chemicals in beakers and flasks. Next thing he knew, *POW!* Breaking sound barriers all day long."

Sheila did not appear to be listening. She had folded her arms and put a hand over her mouth. Her expression was more resigned than worried. Well, resigned and nauseated.

Charlie noticed. "Don't tell me Scott was struck by lightning." He smiled at me. "Or, I don't know, *do* tell me. It would explain a lot."

I got out of my chair and stood in front of her. "What made you think of lightning?"

"I can't believe I didn't think of it before." Her face blank, she probed her memory. "It happened so fast. It was over so quick. I just didn't think of it until now."

Charlie squatted beside me and looked up at Sheila. "You're serious?" he said. "Scott got struck by *lightning?*"

She shook her head. "Not him."

"*You?*" We both looked at her as if she were still glowing from the strike. "When you were pregnant?"

Sheila shook her head. "I wasn't struck, but lightning was involved." She looked at me. "I was in the last minutes of labor. There was a thunderstorm and a power surge."

"That isn't uncommon," Charlie said. "That's why hospitals have emergency generators."

Sheila shook her head again. "The generator didn't even come on. The power came back on a few seconds later. But there was something wrong." She looked at me. "The thing that recorded the baby's — your heartbeat and my contractions ... "

"Cardiotocograph," I said. Charlie didn't say anything but he grinned.

Sheila nodded. "It was a lot quieter because when that thing was going, it sounded like a recording of the inside of a dishwasher. I got worried and asked if you were okay because I didn't hear the sound anymore. My coach held my hand and calmed me down while they looked for the problem. Turned out the power surge had fried the machine."

"You'd think hospitals would have circuit breakers galore on things like that," I said.

Sheila nodded. "The doctor said that but didn't bother about it. Just brought in another machine and changed out the sensors on my belly like changing earphones on a stereo."

We sat in silence for few moments.

"And you just thought of this now?" Charlie asked. "Scott winds up like he does and it didn't occur to you?"

Sheila huffed. "I *was* in labor. The doctor didn't worry, so I didn't, either."

Was it significant? It *could* pass for a superhero origin. Could we ignore a possible coincidence like POWER SURGE plus ELECTRONIC SENSORY DEVICE equals AMAZING MENTAL ABILITIES?

Like a supposedly new Honda with a sudden output of five hundred horsepower and a suspicious odometer.

Charlie was in a pensive, insightful mood so I left him alone and turned back to Sheila. "Was it really such a nonevent like you said? I want answers, but I'd like to rule this one out."

Sheila shaded her eyes. "Hon, I only remember they had to change machines. It seemed like forever at the time, but it wasn't more than fifteen seconds. Lights went out, lights went on. All that was missing was that sound from the heartbeat monitor. They brought in a new one, and you were born fifteen minutes later."

III

While we spent the morning exhausting our brains on theories and memories, the weather turned stormy. Charlie suggested we break for the day and have an early supper. He volunteered to go out and get the food and promised Sheila it wouldn't be Buffalo Wings and beer.

He returned later with a couple of pizzas, a two-liter RC Cola, and a small DVD player. He also carried a plastic shopping bag from a video rental store. Sheila evaluated Charlie and his cargo for a few moments before letting him in.

The pizza smell filled the house. The bottle of RC looked at me with a mix of familiarity and adventure. Sheila left me to ruminate while she got out glasses, plates and silverware.

"What's the occasion?" I asked. "Sorry. I meant to say, 'thanks very much for the unsolicited free meal.'"

Charlie smiled. "I just like to have pizza when I watch a movie."

"What's the occasion for the movie?" Sheila asked.

Charlie spun the lid off the soda bottle. "We spent the whole day working the hides off our brains. Isn't that enough?"

Sheila had managed to get her hands on the movie store bag and looked at the cover of the box. I saw no pictures but I could make out the title: *The Matrix*.

Sheila read it, too. "Doesn't this have something to do with —?"

Charlie yanked the case out her hands. "Don't spoil it for Scott! It's a great flick, and I'm not talking about acting at all."

"What are you talking about?" I asked. I poured myself some RC, feeling wicked doing it in front of Sheila. She didn't like me to have any caffeine. "A subtle way of avoiding work for a while?"

Charlie shrugged. "I think you'll like it. Kids loved this movie, too."

"How well you know me, Charles."

He was on our good side by now. The RC for me and vegetarian pizza for Sheila got him off to a good start. If only the movie was as good as he claimed.

Sheila's comments began before Charlie started the DVD. "You say kids liked it, too? It's rated R. What for, pray tell?"

Charlie counted on his fingers. "Violence, violence and violence. A couple of minor potty mouths, too." He took a bite of pizza just as the studio logo came up on the screen. "Oh, yeah," he said around peppers, onions, olives and cheese, "a little bit of violence, too. But it's essential to the story." He winked at me. "Sorry, Scott. No sex."

I snorted.

IV

The pizza went fast. Two Thousand Seven was a very good year for RC Cola and I'd had about a pint and a half. The movie wasn't bad, either, for action/sci-fi. And Charlie was right. The violence in the first ten minutes exceeded anything — change that to *everything* — I had seen in my whole life.

Around the time the plot was really getting somewhere, I saw why Charlie had decided to take this particular break from brainstorming. Our Hero had just heard the this-is-why-you're-the-main-character speech and had an electronic plug inserted in his brain. The thing that made Charlie think of screening the movie occurred to me, too: electronic data was being transferred directly from computer chips to human brain. Our Hero — or his friends — could download skills and knowledge, almost instantly, and integrate them as if they had been learned.

Did Charlie think this kind of thing was possible? If so, could I come to believe it?

She had a quiet sort of *Aha!* moment a few seconds after I did. I was glad I got it first. After that, though, I expected her to say she got the gist, she'd had enough movie violence for one evening, and goodnight, Charlie.

But she didn't. She watched, oohed and aahed and gasped with the rest of us. I thought maybe she hadn't done anything this close to pure leisure since her husband — my father — died. We didn't have many family nights.

We ought to make this a regular thing, I thought later. *But next time, a comedy. Genuine goofing off is just what we need.*

"Whaddaya think?" asked Charlie after the movie was over.

"One thing kept occurring to me," Sheila said. She looked into space and tapped her chin.

Uh-oh, I thought. *Playtime's over.* But I was wrong.

"If the bad guys could dodge bullets ... " she began.

" ... why could they be hit with punches and kicks?" I finished.

We all laughed.

"And speaking of the suspension of disbelief," I said, "why is it that in martial arts movies, no person flying though the air ever follows a parabolic path before hitting the ground?"

When no one laughed, I shrugged.

We didn't talk business the rest of the night.

The Aura of Good Feeling stayed with Sheila through the next few days. I thought it sad that it took so little to achieve. Then I was envious. Such a small thing improved her mood for days. It didn't last that long for me.

I wished I didn't have such a high standard for happiness.

10

Containment

I often wondered what might happen if my secret slipped out. Maybe someone would notice that my home school papers were graded by the same hand that completed them. An observant bank employee might notice that, starting near the end of January, Sheila's utility payment checks were written in a different hand.

I was getting really tired of living like a spy in foreign lands. The temptation to confide in someone was always there. Even someone at random.

Psst! Hey, garbage man, want to hear a secret? I'm a really weird kid. You might think you've seen weird, but I've got them all beat. You see, it's like I had organ transplants from several different people, only instead of liver, kidneys, or a heart, I know how to type business correspondence, rebuild a transmission and quote Shakespeare.

Keeping it to myself was safest, but next was telling someone who would never believe me, like another kid. But that was awkward, too. If a kid didn't get the transplant analogy, I'd have to explain what organ transplants were. Then he'd either say "gross!" and gag, or he would say "gross!" and grin.

And a kid probably wouldn't focus on the right details. Kids never did. Tell them the story of The Three Bears and they'd want to know if Goldilocks had a Playstation.

Charlie had a thing about details, too. Often, during normal conversations, he would ask me to repeat something I'd said that wasn't consistent with my age. My answers weren't helpful. Were Charlie's questions having an undesirable effect, e.g. that they might fog my memory?

After my discovery of the events surrounding my birth — and after I had begun to label the toys in my attic — I visited the chat room again. I thought it would be a great way to unwind. Instead it turned out to be a great temptation.

MyAlterEgo: Seriously, guys, I have an unexplained problem. I have no idea who I am. I have ideas and knowledge that I didn't acquire the normal way.

I don't know how many times I typed that, but I had reconsidered enough times to wear away the lettering on the "delete" key.

One day my resolve was put to the test. The topic was compulsory education. I had a few opinions that had been in the crockpot too long and had to come out.

MyAlterEgo: yes, most kids need to go to school, but there are some who are wasting their time there.

OneBrikShy: better explain what you mean ego

MyAlterEgo: I just mean that some kids don't need to be in school. Especially with teachers who are next door to incompetent.

OneBrikShy: i had a chem teacher like that. couldn't pronounce anything. didn't really know anything. caused a fire and got canned because she didn't know how to put it out

MyAlterEgo: yeah, but not just that. What if the child is a genuine case of unnecessary schooling??

WottaNut: thats state sponsored day care. who else gonna take yer younguns on tax money alone?

OneBrikShy: kids need school, ego

MyAlterEgo: Most kids need the rudiments, yes. But the smarter kids who have to sit through hour after hour of 4+4=8 and read entire books whose sole purpose is to describe sentence structure?

bArElYtHeRe: give the man a soapbox

OneBrikShy: ego, why dont you pipe up like this when we discuss politics?

MyAlterEgo: Because I won't be old enough to vote for almost twelve ye—

Delete, delete, delete ...

The delete key had been almost totally worn away.

In school, I had acted out, but in protest. Attention was a side effect. From my stunts and my demeanor, I guessed I'd be regarded as gifted or psychotic, and maybe both. But when I got to that point, after years of keeping this secret, I wasn't concerned with everyone else's opinion of me. It wasn't all that rational, but what do you expect from a little kid?

After I stirred the cesspool, the discussion continued with very little input from me. I was just thinking about logging off to do something less stimulating when a new window popped up.

bArElYtHeRe has invited you to a Private Chat

There were two buttons, one for accept, one for decline. It was like something from the school system I had just finished raking over the coals. DO YOU LIKE ME? CHECK THIS BOX.

I clicked the "accept" button.

A blank window popped up.

MyAlterEgo: What can I do for you?

bArElYtHeRe: you have some real issues with the public school system

MyAlterEgo: I've seen my fair share of ugly little secrets swept under the rug

bArElYtHeRe: same here. your kid dissing teachers at school? that why you had that conference?

MyAlterEgo: Yes and no. His teachers were competent but otherwise oblivious. He aced schoolwork and made constructive comments, but just couldn't get through to them.

bArElYtHeRe: so he caused trouble. got himself noticed?

MyAlterEgo: Big time. Nothing violent, but he got noticed.

bArElYtHeRe: how so?

MyAlterEgo: acting out. he took it out on a couple of mean kids and a teacher.

bArElYtHeRe: not too bad then. i hope i'm not being too forward

MyAlterEgo: Not at all. I've already brought it up plenty of times.

bArElYtHeRe: i mean i wanted to ask you something.

MyAlterEgo: (grin) you already have my take on the benighted school system.

bArElYtHeRe: (smiling) wanna call me and talk about it?

MyAlterEgo: On the phone?

bArElYtHeRe: duh yeah the phone. i'm sure you got one. your connection pauses like a dialup whenever youre in the room

MyAlterEgo: Doesn't this defeat the purpose? Anonymous people meeting in cyberspace to chat?

bArElYtHeRe: just a talk on the phone. its not a dinner date

MyAlterEgo: I'm not ready to try that right now.

bArElYtHeRe: just an idea

MyAlterEgo: It's okay. I'm just a little shy.

bArElYtHeRe: don't worry about it

I suppose it could have been worse. She might not have taken no for an answer. Real hackers comprised a scary percentage of the Internet's users. Bare might be able to discover that the person who used this URL belonged to a young, single mother who lived alone with her six-year-old son. Bare didn't seem like the type. Then again, if Nut's instincts could be trusted, she might just be a fat, beady-eyed television actor.

The way she accepted my polite refusal simultaneously relieved and enhanced my anxiety. I was happy she took it well, but what if she asked again? I just wouldn't bring it up. I would leave it up to her. Him. Whomever.

I made the painful decision to stay away from the chat room for the time being. I *did not* want to think Bare was a stalker. Until I found out otherwise, though, I was in danger of blabbing everything to her.

II

"It'll have to be you," I said to Sheila. Charlie nodded his agreement.

Sheila looked at each of us in turn, then looked at her plate and pushed it away.

Charlie had fixed dinner. It was pretty good, an Asian noodle dish with beef and veggies. We were surprised he didn't order pizza. Living his extended college life, Charlie still depended on pizza delivery three or more times a week.

"Why me?" Sheila asked.

Charlie shrugged. "Because we can't."

"I can't get the voice right," I said. I had tried, but I still sounded like a kid calling school to excuse his own absence.

Scotty won't be at school today. He's sick.

Okay, and who is speaking?

This is my mother.

"Charlie can't do it because he can't keep up the act," I said. Charlie frowned but I made no apologies. I had waited long enough in the tunnel and now I could see a flicker of light.

"You think I can do better?" she asked. "I've never been

good at acting."

"Scott's pretty good at acting," Charlie said. "He fools everyone. Cute and innocent and all that."

I ignored him and returned my attention to Sheila. She looked at her plate as if she couldn't believe she had eaten Charlie's cooking. "Come on," I said. "A phone call can't hurt anything. We just have to prepare. How to answer certain questions, how to ask for the specific information. That kind of thing."

Sheila flicked at the end of a noodle hanging over the edge of the plate. It swung back and forth like the wattle on a turkey's neck. "How do you even practice for something like this?"

She had stopped arguing. She was going to do it.

III

Sheila sat at the kitchen table, the phone held to her ear, and followed her checklist with a ballpoint pen.

Charlie and I could stay in the room if we kept silent. So we listened from the adjoining room.

" ... and what did *they* say?" I heard her ask. I couldn't tell how well it was going, but Sheila had done a first rate job. Maybe she had missed her calling. She ought to try Hollywood.

I hoped this didn't constitute insurance fraud.

"I bet *he'll* be getting a phone call soon," Sheila said. Then she chuckled. "Poor guy. Oh well. Anyhoo, thanks for your help, Charlene. Have a good time this weekend."

Charlie looked at me and mouthed, *"anyhoo?"*

Sheila hung up the phone, entered the living room, and

collapsed on the sofa with a forearm across her brow. She wore a huge grin. "Am I good or what?"

She uncovered her face, jumped back up and left the room. Charlie and I gave chase. In the kitchen, Sheila munched another mouthful of Charlie's cooking and twirled a fork in the noodles. She looked triumphant. For Sheila, a second helping was the equivalent of popping a brewski.

She flicked her gaze back and forth between Charlie and me as she tried to smile and chew at the same time. She swallowed and grinned again. "You ready to hear what I found out?"

"Yes!" we chorused.

"Charlene seems like a great person," Sheila said. She abandoned her plate and flipped open the legal pad. Most of a page was covered with her loopy script, but I couldn't read it upside down. "I'll have to figure out a way to accidentally 'meet' her one of these days."

"What did she have to say about the date?" I asked, careful not to seem impatient.

Her smile seemed to charge up, as if someone wound a key in her back and the spring tension showed in her cheeks. "There was indeed something going on that day." She sat down and leaned over the table at us.

Twenty minutes ago she would have denied the possibility, but Sheila was proud of herself. There was going to be a story. I got out the vanilla wafers.

"I was sure that she was going to have to get a supervisor or something." Sheila waves her hands when she talks excitedly. It really draws attention. "But she is so friendly. Asks what she could help me with.

"So I say I'm new at the company and stuck with the grunt work. I'm double-checking claims about to reach the seven-year resolution mark. She says she knows all about that, and she's *so* sympathetic!"

Charlie grinned and looked at me. I grinned, too. Much more politic than jumping to my feet and demanding that she spit it out.

"And so to the date in question. I say, 'I have one claim, January of '01, for a machine on the maternity ward,' and she says, 'yes, that's the Hewlett-Packard Cardiotocograph. An electrical storm fried it when the GFCI outlet failed.' We already knew that, but I say 'yikes! That's got to be a big worry during a storm. What does the machine do?'"

I just processed cookies, didn't really taste them. Charlie cadged a few, and I had handed them over without even looking at him. On with the show, already.

"So she explains it to me and says it's funny that I should call right then because the hospital was reviewing the same date."

I stopped chewing. Charlie tried to inhale a cookie and began coughing.

"Someone at the hospital?" I asked while Charlie hacked. "About the same date?"

Sheila nodded. "So I tell her, 'That *is* interesting,' but suggest that one of the other rookies in my office might be checking on the same policy and claim, but she says no. 'It was another claim,' she says. 'There was this guy doing something in the lab attached to the maternity ward, and the same master circuit fried his computers, too.'

"'The same circuit as the cardio-whatsis?' I ask her and

she says yep. 'He had these two computers set up and all these test subjects sitting outside. The story was he was doing some kind of psych experiment with questionnaires and whatnot and when the power surge hit, his computers went kablooey.'

"I try to sound like a ruthless insurance person and say, 'I'll bet acts of God weren't covered in his case, if they were his own computers,' and she says, 'you got that right.'

"So I think we're done when she says something else. She says, 'and you know who this guy was?' 'Who?' I say. 'A famous writer!' she says. Her boyfriend was a big fan of his books, but she forgot his name. It was right there on the incident report, though." She turned the legal pad around and pushed it across the table at us. Near the center of the page, circled, was a name.

George McCullough

"Oh, wow," said Charlie.

I felt the same way.

"You know who this guy is?" Sheila asked.

"Well ... yeah!" Charlie said. I was nodding in agreement.

Sheila held out her hands. "Well?"

"Like the lady on the phone said," I answered. "He's a writer."

"Okay, help me out here. Journalist? Self-help? Novelist?"

"Novelist," Charlie said. "Epic science fiction and space opera stuff. Totally awesome."

I nodded, amused at Charlie's word choice.

"Is this a lucky break?" Sheila asked. "Does knowing who he is help us at all?"

"Yeah," Charlie said. "It means we won't be knocking on

Mitch Albom's door."

"The sports writer?" I asked.

"He's written a few books, too. They're a bit mushy. Cute motivational stories."

"*Tuesdays with Morrie* was a good book," Sheila said. She crossed her arms and gave Charlie a challenging look and a grin just a little too feminine for comfort.

I took the legal pad from Sheila's hand and looked at the name. "Let's stay on Mr. McCullough, shall we?"

"Sure," Charlie said. "Sorry for dissing your favorite author, Sheila."

"He's not my favorite," she said, "but I'm sure you'll take shots at the rest, too."

"Guys!" I wanted them to get along, but this was too close to flirting. After that, who knew what would happen? "For the moment, George McCullough is *my* favorite author, whether or not I've read anything he wrote."

"Have you?" Charlie asked. "I mean ... you know?" He tapped his head.

I thought about it. "No," I decided. "I kind of see his name on lists, next to Piers Anthony or Dan Simmons. Maybe Harlan Ellison. In big letters on book covers. But I haven't read any of them."

"I have," Charlie said. "He's got deep pockets."

Sheila blinked. "You mean he's rich?"

Charlie shook his head. "No, I mean he's got fantastic ideas. He reaches in and pulls out the most amazing stuff."

Sheila tightened her crossed arms. "He's not an occultist, is he?" She looked like she might burst out laughing, although I didn't see anything that might be hilarious.

"No, no," he said. "He's just got a great imagination."

"I just get the willies when someone with 'a great imagination' fiddles around with electrical stuff at a hospital where children are coming into the world." She unfolded her arms and rubbed her neck, still rigid, looking like she was bracing against a shiver.

I did shiver. Sheila had the willies, and they were contagious.

II

Contact

to: gmccullough@spg.com
from: smbledsoe@uva.edu
Re: Roanoke Memorial Hospital 1/4/2001

Dear Mr. McCullough,
I was a patient at Roanoke Memorial Hospital in 2001, around the same time you reportedly conducted some kind of procedure. The thunderstorm that caused damage to your computers also damaged equipment in my hospital room ...

"More shocking," I said. "It's gotta grab his attention."

Sheila threw her hands up. "I'm not a writer. I don't know how to do that. Plus, I'm leery of writing anything that sounds like a threat or grab for money."

"Good thinking," Charlie said. "We shouldn't send anything hostile to a person who makes money for other people: movie stars, pop singers or famous authors. They have people to protect their investments."

Sheila and I just looked at him.

"You know what I mean," he said. "George McCullough may not be the best seller, but he's certainly up there." He ticked off points. "Hardbacks and paperbacks mean money, sure. Plus there are the audio books, film rights and all that." He grimaced. "Even if this is is just his fan mail address, if we make him nervous, someone on his end could drop us in legal trouble. We'd never get close enough to him to ask the real questions."

"Do we have to contact him by e-mail?" I asked. "Maybe it would help to send him an old-fashioned paper-in-envelope fan letter. I could put a bunch of stickers on it or something." I rubbed my head, tried to avoid tears. Since Charlie's first visit, I had felt the urge to cry more than in the whole rest of my life.

In fairness to Charlie, though, it wasn't his fault. He could be a pill, but we'd never have made any progress without his help. Or his cockamamie ideas.

"Check his website for a list of public appearances," suggested Charlie. "Shoot, he may be on a writing workshop or book-signing tour." He smiled at me. "In a case like that, your being a kid might work to our advantage."

I frowned. "How, exactly?"

Charlie grinned. "Imagine: Scott Bledsoe, age six, in line at a book-signing, holding a copy of the latest fifteen-hundred-page book." He raised his voice an octave but failed to sound anything like me. "'I really enjoyed the book, Mr. McCullough, but are you ever going to write anything about the experiment in Roanoke?'"

I blinked. It sounded feasible. "How do we know he hasn't, though?" I asked.

Charlie shrugged. "I've read all his books. The plot doesn't ring a bell."

"Maybe it was just a vague reference," I suggested, watching George McCullough's web page fill the screen at a crawling rate.

"No," said Charlie. "That kind of experiment, there's probably a whole book involved. I wouldn't be surprised if — man, this thing is slow! Why don't you guys get a cable modem?"

Sheila raised her upturned palm, not taking her eyes from the display. "You gonna pay for it, itchy britches?"

God bless her, my mother is so Southern it's sometimes embarrassing, ranging from Southern Belle to barefoot hick. It sounds good on her, though. A twangy drawl sounds so clever. It's why people like Tommy Lee Jones sound so credible.

Charlie paced around the coffee table. "Next time," he said, "we'll do this at my place." If this was a veiled attempt at hitting on Sheila, she ignored it and kept her eyes on the screen.

Then her face fell. After I looked at the screen, I'm sure mine did, too. Charlie noticed our expressions and left off pacing to come look over our shoulders.

"New Zealand?" he said.

The caption that finally emerged told us that after a book-signing tour, George McCullough would be staying in Wellington, New Zealand to work on a new book.

Sheila lowered her face into her hands. "Oh, Scott," she

said. "I can't afford that kind of trip."

"Shoot," said Charlie. "I'll bet it costs as much as a year's tuition."

I looked at him and sighed. We already knew it was out of our reach. Did he have to count off the strikes against us?

Charlie looked really upset. If anyone's hopes and dreams had dashed, mine had. But both Sheila and Charlie looked more put off than I felt. Had they wanted to meet McCullough that badly?

Then one more thing materialized on the web page, filling the last empty spots on the screen.

IF YOU OR YOUR ORGANIZATION WOULD LIKE GEORGE MCCULLOUGH TO APPEAR AT YOUR CONVENTION OR OTHER EVENT, PLEASE CONTACT NANCY BARTHOLOMEW AT:
STEINMETZ LITERARY AGENCY
PHILADELPHIA, PA

We had McCullough's fan club e-mail address.

This message offered a phone number.

"Take a look," I said, tapping the screen with a fingernail.

They both looked at the screen and were silent for a few moments.

"You think it would be that easy?" Sheila asked.

We looked at Charlie who shrugged.

"How hard would it be for 'Sheila' from Leverage Insurance Co. to become 'Sheila' from the University of Virginia at Roanoke's Sci-Fi Book Club?"

"I don't think it would be hard at all," I said, taking hold of Sheila's hand and smiling encouragement.

Sheila did not share my enthusiasm. "I don't know," she said. "I could do the other call because I speak office lingo. I don't know the first thing about Sci-Fi."

"That's not important," Charlie said. "The main thing is that famous novelists usually get paid for appearances like this."

Sheila's eyes went wide and her brow creased. "How much money?"

"That's not really important, either," he said. "This is just to get in touch with him."

Sheila frowned at Charlie. She gave me a kinder look, then got up and paced. All twenty-eight of her knuckles popped while she did a dozen laps. To Charlie, she must have looked nervous and evasive.

But I thought I recognized the behavior. She was psyching herself up. Charlie remonstrated with her about the details, but it wasn't necessary. She was going to fly solo.

She was doing it for her boy.

II

When it was over, I realized Sheila hadn't even given her name.

When the other party picked up, Sheila said "Nancy Bartholomew, please." Her tone said she didn't say "please" very often. A moment later, she launched into, "Nancy! Hi! ... " and delivered the most eloquent malarkey I've ever heard. Her accent was a little heavier, just shy of over-the-top. Her voice was loud as a car horn and her recitation without pause.

After almost a whole minute of nonstop chatter, Sheila paused to take a stifled breath. Then she said, "Sure do appreciate it, hon. Bye!" She finished jotting down a number as she hung up the phone.

"Wow," said Charlie, and joined me in a round of applause.

Sheila handed me the scrap of paper with the magic phone number and clapped a hand over her eyes. "She must not like George McCullough very much. I think she wished me on him like a plague. You boys are gonna have to do without me for a bit." She staggered past the knee-barking furniture. "I feel like I've been channeling Dixie Carter. I need to lie down."

III

Sheila took a short nap and — no joke — brushed her teeth. Later, we sat around the phone and watched it as if Mr. McCullough might call us. Weirder things had happened. I was one of them.

Sheila reached for the phone, then withdrew her hand.

Charlie looked at the phone as if trying to dial it by telekinesis. It didn't work.

Sheila got up and went to the counter. She looked at the stove and a couple of pans. Then she came back.

I picked up the phone. When it rang in my hand, I almost wet my pants. The cordless receiver dropped and bounced on the kitchen table while I backed away. All sorts of foreboding thoughts rushed through my head. It sounded like a giant toilet flushing.

Sheila picked up the phone. A moment later she spoke in

a more violent version of the voice she had used to call McCullough's publisher. "My number is on the National Do-Not-Call list, and you are in violation, ma'am. If you would like to get your company slapped with a $10,000 fine, by all means, stay on the line." A moment later, "I thought so." She put the phone down.

I was still in shock from the phone's ringing in my hand, but Charlie gave Sheila a high five. "I need to make a recording of you to play for the folks at Sallie Mae," he said. "They hassle me whether my payments are up to date or not."

A deep breath steadied my nerves. "Do you need another nap?" I asked.

She smiled for me. "No, I'm feeling pretty up now."

"Me too," I said. All my anxiety melted away and was replaced by a feeling of confidence. I couldn't tell if it was Sheila's inspiring performance or my years-old readiness for answers.

Instead of handing Sheila the phone, I dialed the number she had written on the pad and put the phone to my ear. While it rang, I realized it was probably the first actual phone call I had ever made. The line rang three times before it was answered. Other than disappointment, I didn't know what to expect.

"*Hello,*" a voice said with no upward inflection. The word was not a question to this person.

I expected to have trouble speaking, but my voice went on its own. "Have I reached Mr. McCullough's office?"

There was a pause.

"*Okay, whoever you are, the only people who are supposed to have this number don't call me that."*

I nearly fell off my chair. It was the man himself.

"I got your number from Nancy Bartholomew," I said. I didn't want him to hang up. "Want me to call you 'George?'"

"What I want is to know why I'm navigating Pittsburgh traffic and talking to someone who shouldn't have my personal number." A car horn blared and George McCullough responded with an obscenity Charlie and Sheila could probably make out. *"You've got about two seconds to identify yourself and explain why you're calling me at this extremely inconvenient —"*

"The experiment at the hospital," I blurted. "Roanoke, Virginia, January 2001."

"What?" Another blast from a car horn. *"Say that again!"*

"Mr. McCullough," I said, "I was in the hospital when you did your experiment." I hated to yell, but I was competing with traffic noise and intermittent cell phone signal.

"Are you serious?" he asked.

"Totally serious! I need to ask you some —"

I jerked the phone away from my ear as a loud pop came from the receiver, nearly knocking me down. Through my ringing ear I heard car horns, screeching tires and a few yells. I held the phone back up to my ear, horrified.

I listened and listened. I still heard traffic, but McCullough did not respond when I yelled his name. "I think I killed him," I said. I kept the phone to my ear.

A couple of minutes later, someone came on the line.

"Hello!" the voice said. *"Anyone there?"*

I sighed in relief. "Yes! Is everything okay?"

"No, everything is not okay! You had better be for real or you owe me a new Porsche!"

12

George Cometh

The doorbell rang. It may have been the first time since Charlie first came around. We were a lonely bunch of people.

Lonely as we were, none of us moved to answer the door right away. Sheila slid to the edge of her chair but stayed there. Charlie sat still, but it wasn't his door to open. I sat on the glider rocker and kicked my legs. My feet just brushed the rug.

Sheila got up but moved like someone trying not to aggravate a hernia. I knew how she felt. It was as if we were avoiding bad news, like a doctor telling us something was inoperable.

A sharp rapping came from the storm door glass. We all got to our feet but stopped halfway to the door. I reached to answer the rapping but Charlie stepped in front of me. Sheila pulled me around and behind her as if trying to stow me in her pocket. I was too excited to take offense.

"I know you're in there!" I recognized the voice as the one from the phone call. "Come on, folks. You invited me, remember?"

We waited another moment.

"I don't think your neighbors like me very much," he called through the door. His voice got more intense but quieter. He was facing away, aiming away from the house. "Get lost, lady!"

"Oh, for heaven's sake," Sheila said. She flung the door open and emerged onto the porch. "Mister McCullough! There is no need for —"

Charlie and I went to the door to see why she stopped talking. Sheila stood at the edge of the porch and looked out at the empty neighborhood. McCullough's target had not been frail Mrs. Peters from next door but Sheila's limits of discretion.

"It's about time," McCullough said. He slipped past Sheila to Charlie and me. "I thought I was gonna have to create a whole cast of characters. You know, elderly neighbor lady, married to her binoculars. Middle-aged widower who lives to mow his lawn." He looked at Sheila. "Attractive single mom, her bright but misanthropic son and her geeky, college student boy toy." Charlie actually preened at "geeky," but Sheila blushed at "boy toy."

"Sorry," McCullough said at Sheila's red face. "I meant to say 'gentleman friend.' Look, I don't mind having this meeting on the porch, but can we, like, get this thing underway?" I couldn't tell what he expected. Maybe he was just used to running things.

Sheila held the door. "Please, Mr. McCullough. Won't you

come inside?"

"With pleasure," McCullough said, and he dashed inside. Charlie and I were intrigued but Sheila was mortified. She checked the streets again for witnesses.

Inside, Charlie and I were like sleepy animals watching a large fly while McCullough rounded the room, looking at books and knicknacks. Sheila joined us, as self-conscious as a young bride on her mother-in-law's first visit.

"Can I get you something to drink?" she asked him.

At the sound of her voice, McCullough spun around so fast his hair flopped. The move reminded me of someone, but he himself looked different with every change of posture. Right then, he was halfway between Howie Mandel and John Denver.

"No, no, thank you," he said. His voice was fast, but the rest of him was calming down, as if he were solar powered and coming inside slowed his motor. The alteration slide settled on John Denver. *Perfect,* I thought. *We finally got him here and he's gonna tell me the secret is all about sunshine on my shoulders.*

He looked at the shelves and ran his fingers along the book spines. It sounded like a kid with a stick rattling a picket fence. We had several books, but he wasn't reading titles.

"What, none of mine?" His smile didn't slacken and it started to look a little loony.

"I've got most of them, Mr. McCullough," said Charlie.

"Did you like them?" McCullough asked.

Charlie smiled. "I kept buying them, didn't I?"

McCullough grinned. "Good answer. And you, Mrs.

Bledsoe?"

"I haven't had the pleasure."

"Your loss," he said with the same grin.

McCullough didn't know why he was there, I thought. Maybe he was trying to figure it out. Or maybe he thought to pry it out by small-talking us to death.

Something else, too. McCullough had a real knack for reading people and situations. There was indeed a nosy octogenarian with a pair of Minolta binoculars next door. A widower a few years her junior lived across the street and kept a perfectly planar fescue lawn.

He'd pegged us pretty well, too, except for the Charlie/ Sheila thing. I knew Charlie liked Sheila. Sheila knew it, too, but we had other things to talk about.

George McCullough was the guest of honor, but I was the conversation piece.

"Please sit down, Mr. McCullough," said Sheila, the good hostess.

"You bet," he said and checked out the couch. He moved to the far left, the spot none of us used. But he didn't sit.

We stood that way for a few moments, seventy-five percent of us bursting with impatience, both astounded and relieved that the other twenty-five percent was really there. McCullough looked as excited as a kid waiting for birthday cake, or better yet, presents. Something was a little off about his look, though. His smile wasn't fake, but neither was it real.

God bless Charlie. He jumped right in and broke the ice.

"Mr. McCullough, I'm Charles Bailey and I'd like to thank you for coming."

McCullough's smile tilted without the rest of his head and his eyebrows went up. "Think nothing of it," he muttered, making me think of a beginner ventriloquist.

"Let me start by saying I've enjoyed most of your books."

"Really?" asked McCullough. "Which ones left you wanting more?" It was hard to tell if his question was innocent or derisive.

"Sorry," said Charlie. "I meant to say I enjoy your work."

"That's very nice, Mr. Bailey. How am I supposed to feel about that?" The smile strained his cheeks.

Charlie looked hurt. "Sorry, I just meant I liked your books. I'm not looking for an autograph."

"Oh, you weren't, were you?" McCullough eyed Charlie and his expression looked more real. The smile had faded.

"No." Charlie was suffering. I didn't think I'd ever seen him embarrassed before.

McCullough wasn't through yet.

"I mean, am I supposed to be so overcome with flattery that I won't notice what you're doing?"

Sheila stepped close to McCullough. I could feel the energy in the air. Just a hiss coming through the amp, but the knob was turned up to eleven.

"Mister McCullough," Sheila said, "you came here by your own means and on your own schedule and so far you have done nothing but cause us discomfort. Now you accuse a guest in my house of having an ulterior motive for choices you made by yourself. What do you think we want from you?"

McCullough looked as if he were trying to come up with a retort. Then his shoulders slumped and his face fell. He dropped his head forward. "I knew this was a mistake." He turned to Sheila. "Apologies, ma'am. I got my undies in a twist and tried to do the aggressive thing. Wanted to do this on my own."

He shoved his hands in his pockets and turned away. "I didn't tell Nancy I was coming. She would have insisted I bring a lawyer. *Two* lawyers. Or send two lawyers while I sit in my den with Valium and Vaughan Williams."

Sheila swallowed. "Why would you bring a lawyer?"

Our guest looked at her, then at Charlie. He still gave me no more than a passing glance. "You aren't suing me?" he asked.

Charlie shook his head. "No."

"You're not a lawyer?" asked McCullough. He squinted at Charlie through circular, rimless lenses.

Charlie looked offended but didn't lose his smile. "No. This isn't a lawsuit, Mr. McCullough. Nor are we obsessed fans. But we *do* need to ask you some serious questions. So, won't you please sit?"

"You got my attention with the mention of Roanoke and the date." He started to sit, but then straightened. "I'm telling you that right away because I usually don't travel four hundred miles to visit someone who shocks me into wrecking my car."

McCullough told Sheila he hardly had any wine with dinner, so that wasn't the cause of the wreck. The Breathalyzer backed him up. He said it all without even looking at me. Sheila had his complete attention.

Not because she had mesmerized him with her good looks, either. I think Sheila is highly attractive — or a knockout, or a babe — depending on which part of my weird mind is doing the assessment. No, he talked to her because he thought she was the caller who caused him to bang up his ride.

Of course he thought that. I hadn't even gotten around to telling him my name before he wanted to know where we could meet. After he confirmed that I lived in Roanoke, he just asked for the address and told me when he would arrive.

Sheila was steadfast against McCullough's ramblings for a few moments. She didn't bat an eye but gave him stern looks. Dixie Carter was still in her holster, if Sheila wanted to engage her. I hoped she wouldn't have to. It might leave McCullough in tears.

For another full minute, nothing meaningful came out our guest's mouth and he *still* remained on his feet.

Sheila cleared her throat. "Mr. McCullough," she said, "won't you please have a seat? We've been so anxious to meet you."

McCullough eyed the two taller people in the room and still ignored me. "Does money enter this in any way?"

Sheila and Charlie looked at each other, then shook their heads. "No," Sheila said.

McCullough shrugged. "I don't know what to tell you, then. I could have gotten new computers, but my input hardware was completely sizzled. One of a kind item, too." He shook his head and *tsked.* "I didn't follow insurance guidelines, got in dutch with my sponsor and lost interest in the experiment real fast."

"We have a problem of our own." Charlie said. "We believe your experiment may have had a side effect. If so, you may be the only person who can help us."

"Why couldn't the hospital?" McCullough asked.

"I don't think they have a department for this kind of thing." My mouth offered my two cents on its own.

I was used to patronizing looks from adults. George McCullough gave me one now. "Is this of special interest to you, young man?"

I was so wound up I wanted to knock his block off, but I'd settle for his socks. I bugged my eyes out at Charlie and Sheila. They didn't get it, so I gestured to McCullough. Let them fill him in.

"Mr. McCullough," she said, "this is my son, Scott. I didn't speak to you on the phone. He did."

That got him to sit down.

II

A few minutes later, emergency glass of water in hand, George McCullough was still staring at me.

"Funny," I murmured to Charlie. "You didn't have this reaction when you met me."

Charlie grinned. "Not outwardly, anyway. Of course, I never had the impression someone thought I was responsible. He must feel a little like ... " He stopped and looked embarrassed.

"Like what?" I pressed.

Charlie looked at me with a pained, apologetic smile. "Like Dr. Frankenstein." I could have been angry, but I had thought worse things about myself and my creator, be He God or be he man. I had invited Charlie on this mind trip and

I couldn't expect him to keep everything to himself.

Without looking, McCullough uncapped a prescription bottle, popped a pill, and dry-swallowed it.

Sheila's eyebrows shot up. "You're not taking anything illegal, are you Mr. McCullough?"

McCullough's eyes went wide. "Nothing like that," he said. He stuffed the bottle in his breast pocket and covered it with his hand. "A mild tranquilizer is all. If there were no children present, I might have asked you for a glass of Scotch. And please, call me George." For all his clarity of speech, he still looked like the lone survivor of a recent plane crash.

George looked back and forth between us with an uncertain smile. "Didn't you have some questions for me?"

"The last one still stands," I said. "What was the experiment at the hospital?"

"What makes you want to know?" he asked. He didn't even sound defensive. Maybe the pill was already working.

"Stop evading the question!" I barked.

"Scott!" Sheila gave me a very maternal look.

I ignored her. "When Sheila told you it was me on the phone, you fell on your butt."

"So? That was obviously why she did it." George put his water glass to his lips, maybe to plug his mouth.

I pulled the glass away before he could take a sip. "Why are you so anxious about me? *What was the experiment?*"

George's slight shoulders slumped even more. "I will answer your questions," he said. "But may I ask you one first? Just one?"

I frowned. I looked at Charlie, who shrugged. Then I

looked at Sheila, who looked at George. I looked at him, too. "Fine. I guess I'll get the answer someday."

George pondered for a moment before speaking. "Where would I get a water pump for a 1971 Volkswagen Beetle?"

Talk about left field. I blinked at him, then cocked an eyebrow at Charlie. It reminded me of when Charlie had first come. All those random questions. This was far from random.

"None of the old Beetles came with a water pump," I whispered. "The engines were air-cooled." I got to my feet. "How did you know I'd know that?

"I'm getting to that," McCullough said. "One more question." He jotted something down on a pad he took from his breast pocket. He handed me the pad. "Can you read this?"

I looked at the pad for a moment. Charlie looked over my shoulder. "What is it? Sanskrit or something?"

"It's Gregg Shorthand," I said.

"But what does it say?" pressed George.

"'Last question. I promise.' I doubt that, though." I looked at George. "I'll bet you've got a million of them."

"But you answered the only ones that matter right now," George said. He tossed the notebook aside and wiped his eyes with his fingertips. "You poor kid."

13

George Explaineth

Sheila made coffee. Decaf, so I got a cup, too. We sat around the kitchen table, drank coffee, and ate anything that went with it. Among us, we emptied a box of doughnuts and a tin of snickerdoodles. Sheila always shielded me from caffeine but gave me sugar as if tooth decay were mythical.

"First off," George began, "the experiment was never completed. The fried equipment saw to that."

I wasn't in the mood for a recap so I hurried him along with my eyebrows.

He patted my hand. "I'm getting to it, but it needs context. It'll work better if you know a little bit of the reason for the experiment."

I pulled my hand away and nodded for him to continue.

"I've published books for years," he said. "The genre never mattered to me. Whatever made the readers happy.

"But once — and it only takes once — the definitive review of my book, *The Abstract Scribe,* wasn't just critical commentary but a personal insult."

"That can't be uncommon." I made a mental note to try one of his books. Charlie liked them. Then again, Charlie was odd.

"Yeah," George said, smiling. "Of course, there's an unspoken rumor that publishers bribe critics to harp on sore points, so the publisher can harp on the writer."

Sheila frowned. "I hate to say it, but that doesn't surprise me even a little."

"Yes, well," said George, "the critique in question wasn't really like that. It actually named my own pet peeve about my work."

"And that was?" I asked. I kept prodding and hoped to poke the right button.

He smiled and got out his wallet, a blue nylon tri-fold, fastened with Velcro. Big surprise. With the ripping sound that signified a nerd showing his credentials — and George McCullough *was* a nerd — he opened the wallet and pulled out a flimsy plastic card. It was a magazine clipping with sections highlighted in green, laminated to last while riding around on George's butt.

He handed it to Sheila who read, " *... and though McCullough has real talent, his readers have the right to expect more. His ability, combined with real effort, could produce magnificent work. Instead, he has limited his scope to fanciful stories, full of imagination but lacking in substance and, therefore, quality.*

"*Also, the urgency with which McCullough ends a tale shouts of impatience, as if he cannot focus and give the piece resolution. With such open laziness, I wonder that publishers continue to print his work. Perhaps they believe in the power of positive reinforcement. A pity, then, that the work will fall into obscurity, and each will pay the price for the other's shortcomings."*

Sheila finished reading and returned the card to McCullough.

"That was pretty harsh," Charlie said. "One of the publishing periodicals?"

"Boston Globe, actually," George said and stowed the clipping again.

Charlie grimaced. "Oh, nice."

"A mainstream newspaper?" asked Sheila. "Where anyone could read it?"

George nodded. "Anyone."

Sheila shrugged. "Still, he's just a critic. Maybe the old saying about 'those who can't' could include 'criticize.'"

"But that would be wrong," George said. He got the card out and forced another look at it, like penance.

"It sounded like criticism to me," I said.

George shook his head. "No, I meant the saying." He waggled the clipping in front of me. "The man that wrote this can write circles around anybody."

"Who?" Charlie and I asked together.

"Gabe Hamilton."

I sighed. "Oh." Charlie sat back as if he had lost a chess match. Only Sheila looked lost.

"Who?" she asked.

"Major cult writer." Charlie answered.

George nodded. "Best of the best. Hollywood's always after the movie rights to his books and he keeps telling them 'no way.'"

"Why have I never heard of him?"

Charlie smiled at her. "You're not a nerd."

I scratched my chin. "Is it odd for a critic to be so, I don't know, *parental* in his criticism?"

"No," George replied, "but I might have guessed you'd notice that." He waited for me to beam with pride. When I didn't, he said, "Gabe had a vested interest."

"Was he perhaps one of those bribed to badmouth you?"

George sputtered before answering. "Good Lord, no! He was my *mentor*." He raised a cookie to his mouth, almost took a bite, then lowered it. "Any idea what it's like to get raked over the coals by someone you worked most of your professional life to impress?" He crammed a snickerdoodle into his mouth and chased it with a swig of coffee. "Feel like you really made it and have your hero tell you you're not trying?'"

"I can't imagine," said Sheila. "So, what was your pet peeve?"

"Gabe called it laziness," he said, "but it wasn't. It was lack of focus."

Charlie sat forward. "It's a lot of work to write a book. If I wrote day and night for ten years, I doubt I could catch up to you. All that editing and rewriting. Where's the focus problem?"

George gritted his teeth and scratched his head. "That's more embarrassing ... and potentially harmful. I ask that it not leave this room."

I snorted. "I just told you something that would get me Oprah, Larry King and every major news service in the same day. I'm good at keeping secrets."

George didn't bat an eye. "Telling you also breaks a contractual obligation. I've just decided it's the least of several evils."

I raised my hand. "I promise no one will learn anything about you from me. I haven't even read any of your books." Sheila and Charlie took similar oaths.

"Okay," he said. "Here's the dope: I don't edit my own work at all."

We all just looked at him.

"What I mean to say is that an *incredible* amount of editing went into them. I supplied the pieces and the editors put them together." We still didn't say anything. "I have a terrific agent," he added, as if that explained it all.

I covered my face with my hands. "Please tell me you're not just an ideas man."

"I'm not even a scientist," he said. "What you see is what you get."

Charlie cleared his throat. "About Scott's questions?"

"That's what I'm telling you," George said. "I'm not a scientist. You'll probably learn more from the history of the experiment than I did by conducting it."

"You know *something*," Sheila said. "The moment Scott started talking, you pushed exactly the right buttons to confirm whatever prompted you to come here!"

"And no more nonsense about not being a scientist," said Charlie. "You weren't at that hospital to sell bedpans."

George popped open his bottle and dry-swallowed another pill. He didn't pocket the bottle but set it on the table. I could just read the label. *Ativan.* A benzodiazepine. If he took another, he'd never make it out the door.

"This is where my history becomes integral to the explanation," he said. "I used to turn in complete stories. Agonized over, rewritten and edited to death. I could never quit fiddling with them before they fell apart. Like a stone sculptor who can't stop chiseling and winds up with marble gravel."

Sheila picked up the bottle. "You take benzos and your editing habits sound harmfully obsessive. Do you have OCD?"

George shrugged. "I don't know. Maybe. I never actually went to the doctor." He smirked. "Nancy thought real treatment might impair my effectiveness. She found a doctor that would just calm me down."

Sheila slid the bottle toward George and took a deep breath. "You avoided treatment of a potentially crippling anxiety condition ... on the advice of your literary agent?"

George waved it away. "It doesn't matter."

I rapped my knuckles on the table. "Good enough. Now, about the experiment?"

He shrugged. "I was mapping mental and physical reactions to certain stimuli."

"What kind of stimuli?" asked Charlie. "Like the questions you asked Scott?"

"In a way." George slipped a small notepad from his inside jacket pocket. "Johns Hopkins University gave me a small grant to fund the experiment. I would do the research and put my name on the findings, but hardcopies of the data would be the property of the University."

"I guess I've seen too many movies," Sheila said, "but I have to ask. Was the government involved?"

We all looked at her, surprised. Charlie was impressed. She'd thought of it first.

"Not that I know of," said George. "Just the legalities 'adherent to operating foreign equipment in a hospital environment,' or something like that. More liability and such than anything else."

"Why's that?" I asked.

"The test subjects were actual patients of the hospital, but this was not, strictly speaking, medical treatment. They were invited to take part in the test. I chose them for their occupations."

"What kind of occupations?" Sheila asked. "Anything to do with why you asked Scott about Volkswagens?"

"*Everything* to do with it," George said. He pulled some file folders out of his attaché case and opened one. In the upper left corner was a headshot of a bald, stocky man in his sixties. "Test subject number two was Jarvis Tracy, car mechanic for forty years."

"And the shorthand?" I asked, but I already had a guess.

"Subject number four," said George. "Marie Huntsacker, former personal secretary turned office manager at Dominion Resources, a Fortune 500 company based in Richmond."

"How many subjects were there?" Charlie asked.

"An even ten," said George. "But only four were tested."

"Why only four?" I asked. I thought knew the answer, but I didn't want to get ahead of myself.

George smiled. "You already know the answer to that one. *Zap!*"

"Fortune 500 office manager?" Charlie asked. "That's

pretty swanky. Not the kind of person I'd expect to answer an ad reading 'Test Subjects Needed.'"

"They didn't answer an ad," George said. "They responded to an invitation. But yes, there *was* pretty serious money involved, and it didn't all go into the electronics."

"The power surge," said Sheila. She looked overwhelmed but I didn't see why. We had figured out the first part. Maybe George had — pardon the pun — brought it home.

"You just recorded brain waves from your test subjects?" I asked.

"Much more than just brainwaves," George said. "Loads more."

"Like what?" I asked.

"We recorded all kinds of body functions," he said. "Elizabeth Croyden, an electrical engineer I know — she works for Sprint now — designed this helmet that recorded electrical activity. Looks like a salon hair dryer, works like an EEG but it records vibrations – both audible and outside the range of human hearing – and galvanic skin response. Plus, it tested for blood oxygen saturation, and changes in perspiration chemistry that might signify hormone production."

"It recorded their voices?" Sheila asked. "Why not just use a microphone?"

"No," said George. "Not their voices. It listened to the body's systems. Heart rhythm, arterial pulse, involuntary muscle contractions. Even intestinal peristalsis."

Sheila frowned. "Why?"

George smiled. "A friend of mine called it a 'glorified polygraph.' That's not far off, but it was much more. And it was cheaper to build than to rent an MRI for an extended period."

"Can you tell me about the test subjects?" I asked. That was what I really cared about.

He pulled a folded sheet of paper from another file. "Here's the list of the questions for Kevin Adams. He was a computer programmer for an industrial machinery manufacturer. I thought him of as the quintessential nerd."

Look who's talking, I thought and unfolded the paper George handed me. There was a small snapshot of a hilariously goofy guy photocopied onto the paper with his vital statistics. The photocopy didn't help his appearance.

Charlie chortled. "He looks like Napoleon Dynamite." When I looked blank, he said, "A movie character. I'll rent it sometime. You'll love it."

I turned my attention back to George. "It measured their bodily reactions to a list of questions?"

"Yes," George said. He frowned at Charlie, who was still getting a kick out of Kevin Adams's Xeroxed image. "There was no speaking involved. The subjects were instructed to read the questions one at a time, then think the answers."

I looked at Charlie and Sheila before returning to George.

"Pardon me for saying so," I said, "but that sounds hokey." Charlie nodded in agreement.

"I knew you'd think that, but that's how it worked. It's why I brought the documentation. I wasn't sure why I was invited here, but I had to have something to show."

Sheila shook her head. "Still sounds like science fiction to me."

George pulled a cell phone a little larger than a Zippo

lighter from a pouch on his belt. "Just ten years ago, this would have blown the engineers' minds." He opened it and pressed a few buttons. "And it can hold eight *gigabytes* of information. In this case, MP3 files of around *two thousand songs.*" Though I would've expected "Thank God I'm a Country Boy," it played a tinny version of "Woodchopper's Ball" before he snapped it shut. "It's only science fiction as long as we quit trying to accomplish it."

I sighed. "We've already been through our own list of unorthodox theories. I guess this is no cornier than any *our* hypotheses, but it's still a humdinger." I sighed again. "But I guess it sounds feasible. Or it does *now.* It sure didn't take you long to make the intuitive leap and start asking pertinent questions."

He held out his hands and shrugged. "It's what I do for a living."

Sheila cleared her throat. "What good is it, though?"

George folded his hands and sat forward. "If you have a computer, you've thought of it. Imagine you have a stroke, lose parts of your memory, mental abilities, etc. We know through modern medical research that the brain is an incredibly adaptive organic computer. If it's damaged, it can reroute certain paths in order to maintain functions. Those who have lost the power of speech often regain it by accessing hitherto unused parts of their brains."

"I've heard of that," said Sheila.

"Now imagine," said George, "that you could make a monthly, weekly, even *daily* backup of your brain."

Charlie smiled. "You could treat a stroke like a hard-drive crash."

I shook my head. "That's not a new idea. In fact, dozens of sci-fi writers have exhausted the subject."

George smiled. "Yes, but how many of them had ideas that got them university grants from one of the top medical schools in the U.S.?"

The three of us sat in awe of the brilliant man before us.

"So how did the data get passed on to Scott?" asked Charlie.

The brilliant man shrugged. "Beats me."

14

George Explaineth Further

I

"All this is very interesting," I said, "but I just want to know how to reverse it."

George blinked. "Reverse it?"

"That's what I said."

George took off his glasses and pulled at his face. "I'm not sure how this happened in the first place. I'm sorry, but I think you're stuck. I don't have the first idea how to undo it."

"Stuck?" I wadded a napkin in my fist. "Try again."

"You want rid of the mental stuff?" he asked. "The first, easiest thing that comes to mind is getting quadruple amnesia. Ever hear of anyone who benefitted from a blow to the head?"

Charlie cleared his throat. "Actually, I —"

"Shut up!" I was speaking to Charlie, but Sheila jumped.

I ignored her. "Come on, George! Scientists have been at

this kind of thing for years. Hypnosis, electro-shock therapy ... lobotomies!"

Charlie swore under his breath. Sheila made a noise I tried to ignore.

"Yes!" said George. "All of those have been around for decades. But what would you do with hypnosis? Try to forget your knowledge of the wider world? Your zillion-word vocabulary?"

I gave a violent shrug and scowled.

"Lobotomy," he continued, "would be like cutting off your hand to prevent hangnails. And, to my knowledge, electro-shock therapy has had exactly one beneficial use: treating clinical depression."

I slapped the table. "I *am* depressed!"

"You know better than that," he said. "In the annals of human medicine, transferral of mental abilities or memories has never been documented."

"Any non-human cases?"

George nodded. "Several."

"Monkeys?"

He shook his head. "Moth larvae. And flatworms. The first generation learned to navigate a maze. Then the second generation could navigate the same maze on the first attempt. But this is nothing like their methods."

"How do you know?" I asked.

George frowned. "Because they puréed the first generation and fed them to the second."

Sheila made an urping noise.

"You're experiencing something brand new," said George. "No one ever succeeded at this, so there are no books on how to *un*-succeed." He reached toward me. "All this stuff in your head was stored in a computer. Somehow it was transferred to you. Maybe through the electrical system. I just don't know." He shook his head. "But it sure is remarkable."

"Why does everyone keep saying that?" A lump had formed in my throat. "It's not remarkable, it's terrible! Before, I just knew stuff. Now I'm full of other people! They didn't come out of a blender, but they're in me Without them and that knowledge, I don't know who I am!"

"Scott," said Charlie, "this *is* you. The search for identity is a defining characteristic *of* your identity."

I threw my wadded up napkin across the kitchen. "I don't want my identity to be based on trying to find out what it is!"

Charlie threw up his hands. "But *everyone's* is!"

"You know what I mean!" I put my hand to my face and felt my wet cheeks. "I'm tired," I whispered. "I don't want to talk anymore."

"Will you tell me something?" asked George. "It's not a test. No parameters to gauge, nothing like that." He came and put a hand on my shoulder. I still couldn't get people to quit treating me like a little kid. At least he wasn't patting me on my little head. "For just a moment, forget methods. What do you want, Scott? End result, I mean."

I closed my eyes. I wished I had foregone the parting comments and just split. But I considered the question. Tried for a real answer.

"I want to be a regular kid." I ran my fingers through my hair. My scalp ached. After seeing Jarvis Tracy's photo, I remembered a quiet fear of baldness. "I know enough about innocence to know I never had it." I looked at George. "Did you know I can remember what it felt like in the womb?"

George shook his head. Sheila gasped for the umpteenth time.

"I think the only thing that kept me sane was my extremely short attention span. I heard babies are like that, physiologically. They don't have much short-term memory. I remembered other things, though." I looked at Sheila. "The day I was born, I wanted to ask you to turn off the CD of Pachelbel's Canon because I hated it. Because I had *always* hated it." Sheila smiled but it looked strange in the dim light. I realized she was crying.

"Your father couldn't stand it either," she said.

To ignore Sheila's tears, I had to return my attention to George. "All I had to learn was toilet training, and that was more like physical therapy. Instead of relearning to walk, I was relearning to hold my water."

I fell silent.

"So that's it?" asked George. "You want a happy childhood?"

"I want *any* childhood! Don't I deserve it? Doesn't everyone? A time when I don't have to feel responsible?"

No one answered me.

"Sheila's my mom," I said. "I'd love to call her 'Mom.' Think 'Mom,' instead of 'Sheila.' I don't because I don't feel young enough to be her child." I swallowed and looked at her again. She wasn't smiling through her tears now. "I want my dad. I know I can't turn back time, but I want a dad! I want someone to *be* my dad! To teach me and raise me and be with my mother, to tell me everything will be okay, even when it won't!" I stopped and sighed. "Even if I don't believe it."

I looked all the tall people in the room.

"I want to know what it's like not to be a ... " I stopped.

"A what?" asked Charlie.

I mumbled at the floor. "A freak."

Sheila left the table and then I heard her sobs in the hallway. I threw my head back and cried at the ceiling. The tears ran into my ears.

Charlie was at my side in a second and took hold of my elbow. "Go after her."

"Not now," I said. I wiped my face with my sleeve and sat on the couch.

"Why not now?" he asked.

"Because I'm still mad."

I didn't hear him move, but a second later Charlie stood before me. "Scott, if you don't go apologize to her, I'm through with you. You're not the only one suffering. Your mother had a baby, the most precious thing to her in all the world, more so since her husband died. But he's not a normal baby, so she can't feel like a normal mother."

He was right. Sheila had lost her husband, and then begun to lose her child. Not to illness, but to something far more difficult to understand.

I stood and made for the hallway. I looked back, but Charlie's eyes prodded me through the door.

I searched the house for Sheila, not desperate enough to call to her until anger had finished turning to grief. Then I found her, in the back seat of the car, crying into a tee shirt I wore as an infant. I opened the car door and crawled in, put my arms around her and let myself be pulled into her lap.

There we both cried, for each other.

II

Later, Sheila and I entered the house together. George sat with Charlie at the kitchen table. I didn't think they had even talked.

"Should I go?" George asked. "I feel I have a duty here, but I don't know how I can help."

Sheila took George's hand. "Please stay for supper, Mr. McCullough. We might still accomplish something."

Despite his need for tranquilizers, George was an honored guest. We didn't treat him — as he once feared we might — as a negligent mad scientist. Instead, we asked more about the long-lost experiment that yielded no primary data but one gollywhopper of a side-effect.

George asked more questions, but I didn't mind so much now because we finally had answers.

The questions, derived from the questionnaires, covered some general knowledge but were mostly specific to the test subject. On those, I knew more than Sheila, Charlie and George put together.

George set his empty stew bowl aside. "This one's not exactly a question, Scott." He smiled at Charlie and Sheila. "Sherlock Holmes and Watson are investigating a burglary. They camp out on the grounds to catch the villain unawares.

"Holmes stares up at the sky. 'Are you awake, Watson?' he asks.

"'Yes, Holmes,' Watson replies.

"'Look up at the sky,' Holmes says, 'and tell me what you see.'

"'I see the sky,' Watson says. 'Thousands of stars and unimaginable distances. Makes one feel small and insignificant.'"

"'And do you know what I see, Watson?'

"'What, Holmes?'

"'The thief has struck again!' Holmes says.

"'How the devil do you know that, Holmes?'

George winked at Charlie and Sheila and then looked at me. "Do you know his answer?"

"'Elementary, my dear Watson.'" I wiped my mouth and laid down the napkin. "'He stole our bloody tent!'"

Charlie grinned, but Sheila chirped, choked, then tried not to spray us with another helping of stew. I was glad I knew the Heimlich maneuver if the need arose.

"So, these four people," Charlie said after Sheila had recovered. "Each one contributed mental content, and Scott downloaded it?"

George shook his head. "Before today, I would have scoffed at it. I'm still not sure it all fits."

"Then why does he know all these things?" Sheila asked.

"Sorry," George said. "I didn't say it right. Other people usually edit my explanations of things. What I mean is they didn't contribute part of their minds, exactly. Not real memories but the preferred ways of doing things."

"Like the RC-Pepsi-Coke thing," I said.

George nodded. "Right."

"Charlie," Sheila said, "thank you *so* much for being Scott's caffeine enabler."

"Don't mention it." He offered another slug from the two-liter bottle and I accepted with a grin.

"But Mr. McCullough," Sheila said.

"George, please."

"George, then. How did Scott get all these memories? All this information?"

George sat back and gave it some thought. I thought he'd have the answer on the tip of his tongue. I knew I had a good enough idea. "We tested brain and involuntary body reactions as each subject followed his or her own individually tailored questionnaire. Jarvis Tracy had questions about automotive engineering and little else. For Mrs. Huntsacker it was management and efficiency. For Kevin Adams, it would have been computer stuff. For Mark Norton, investing."

Sheila looked at me, then frowned at George. "But Scott knows things that don't fall anywhere in those fields."

"Did you actually record the test subjects as they recalled the answers?" I asked.

George nodded. "That's right."

"Then that makes sense," I said.

"It does?" Sheila asked.

"Sure," I said. "When you think about something, especially when you're remembering, your mind is never completely on one thing and nothing else."

"Aha!" George cried, and Sheila almost jumped out of her chair. "Sorry," he told her.

Sheila ignored George and looked at me. "Like when you think 'I have to go to the supermarket,' and really quick, you think about everything involved? Getting your keys, getting in the car, starting the car, driving the car ... all that stuff?"

"Yeah," I said. "For mechanics, so much is tangential anyway. Each of Mr. Tracy's questions would connect to more and more bits of info, splitting into maybe hundreds or thousands of branches. What if all that data made it through the funnel?"

"Reminds me of fractals," said Charlie.

"Fraggles?" Sheila asked.

Charlie laughed out loud. "Not Fraggles. *Fractals.* Interconnected pieces, all the same shape but different sizes ..." He shook his head. "No, that's not right. Help me out, George."

George looked blank. "I'm not sure I see the connection. Math's never been my strong suit."

I thought I understood. "Like those drawings by M. C. Escher. Patterns of animals or shapes. Row upon row, they get smaller and smaller, still the same shape, but eventually they're so small you can't really tell what they are."

"Those are fractals?" she asked.

"I think so," I said. "I *hope* so. How could I tell if the person I got it from was wrong?"

George sat forward on his chair. "Maybe it's not them, Scott. I don't know much about fractals, but I think I recognize them when I see them. The comparison, though. Maybe it's just the six-year-old part of your mind making a connection an informed person would not."

Charlie pouted. "*I'm* the one who brought it up."

"I meant whether Escher's artwork represented fractals."

"Oh."

"Anyway," George continued, "Scott's — for lack of a

better word — Scott's *adopted* knowledge isn't facts but entire thought processes. If we ask Scott about car engines in general, can he just give information without someone having to elicit it?"

"How do you mean?" Charlie asked.

George pursed his lips. "I know Scott can read shorthand, but could he write it?"

"We've got that ground covered," Sheila said. "Scott types faster than I do."

"You type?" George asked. "Well, I guess you could have gotten that from any of them. Everybody seems to type nowadays." He grunted. "Except me. I still do everything longhand."

III

Later, I showed George my *Spongebob* keyboard and a few pages of my journal. I thought about introducing him to my on-line chat group but decided against it. Anonymous or not, it was an exclusive club. I knew *I* would resent an unannounced, unknown observer. Keeping a public forum secret might seem silly, but I had gotten almost as close to those pseudonymous guys as I had to Charlie.

At first, I had been uncomfortable with the idea of keeping the journal. It meant committing to posterity a record of my ... self. Until now, it all might have been a bad dream. Despite everything I had experienced, I had trouble believing I was the person everyone else saw.

Solipsism doesn't mesh with PB and J.

Then came George and his *deus ex machina*. It was like getting a telegram — or an e-mail — saying I had passed some kind of test and could now enter a new realm of awareness. To top off the cliché, my messenger was also my maker.

As with other celestial harbingers, though, there were complications.

"I know this won't come as a shock," George said, "but you start saying 'look what I can do,' it's going to attract a lot of attention. Most of it unwanted."

We all nodded.

"I considered it," I told him. "Even before contacting you. You *do* make your living telling things to people."

He smiled. "At this point in my career, if I mentioned this to someone I knew, they'd tell me to shut up and send them a plot synopsis, outline, and the first five chapters."

"I don't think we've ever talked about that before," Sheila said. "We spent too much time on what Scott could do, how it happened and all that." She poured coffee for Charlie and patted his arm. "Charlie has been a real godsend, but I'm sure he's a rare breed." Charlie smiled and raised his cup to her.

George smiled. "Well, you lucked out when you got hold of me."

"It was Sheila's assertive phone presence," Charlie said and winked at her. "Not luck."

"I don't think that's what he meant," I said.

George nodded. "Scott's right. I mean you hooked the right fish. I will not — except under torture — reveal what you've told me today without your approval." He looked deep into his cup before taking a sip. "In that respect, I am in the minority."

"'Under the spreading chestnut tree   ... '" Charlie murmured, sipping his coffee.

"What?" Sheila asked.

"It's from a book," George said, frowning. "I don't remember which, right off the top of my head."

"*Nineteen Eighty-Four*," I said. Only George stared at me that time. "It's an ironic retooling of a Longfellow poem, depicting betrayal as a dutiful way of life." I recited, "'Under the spreading chestnut tree, I sold you and you sold me ... '" I sipped at the short java ration Sheila had given me. "A business world theme song if I ever heard one."

Charlie grinned at George's expression. "Anyone in Scott's head an English scholar?"

George grunted. "Obviously."

Sheila had read between the lines, though. "George, knowing these people like you do, what would you recommend?"

George rubbed his eyes under his glasses. "I'm probably not the best person to ask, if my own contract negotiations are any sign."

"Do you mean we should get an agent?" Sheila asked. "Or stay away from them?"

George was appalled. "I mean you should get a lawyer!"

Sheila almost smiled, then gave up. "I might have known it would be something beyond our means."

"Don't worry," George said. "My guy will do for you. Later, who knows?" He looked at me. "Maybe you'll need an agent."

"Your guy?" Sheila asked. "You mean *your* lawyer?"

"You got it," George said. He put both palms on the table

and looked at all of us. "Not to denigrate Charlie's valued help, but let's get some professionals working on this." He looked at me. "If I can't help, let's find someone who can."

15

Sharing the Joy

MyAlterEgo: you guys remember when I told you about my identity crisis?

WottaNut: which time? it was ALL you talked about for a while.

MyAlterEgo: is that supposed to be moral support?

WottaNut: i like you man but you don't comment on other stuff. no problems. no inadequacy at work. no marital problems. no erectile dysfunction.

OneBrikShy: i don't think that last one qualifies as a psychological problem

bArElYtHeRe: but it may be why we never hear him complain about marital problems :D

MyAlterEgo: all non-issues, those, but there's a new development

OneBrikShy: have an epiphany?

MyAlterEgo: more of an outside influence. I discovered a whole new realm of possibilities.

bArElYtHeRe: sounds like a credit card commercial
WottaNut: what did you find out?
MyAlterEgo: any of you ever met someone famous?
OneBrikShy: for all we know, we could any of us be famous
WottaNut: i still think bare is wayne knight
MyAlterEgo: who?
bArElYtHeRe: newman on seinfeld. ROFL
OneBrikShy: you met someone famous, ego?
MyAlterEgo: moderately so, yes.
OneBrikShy: what did you learn that has you all bubbly?
MyAlterEgo: in one way, you could say we're related.
bArElYtHeRe: we cant help unless you give us a little more
    to go on ego baby
WottaNut: yeah, was it a celebrity or a politician?
MyAlterEgo: yes
WottaNut: and you might be related to him/her? trying to
    scam some cash?
OneBrikShy: i don't know why we let you in here nut
WottaNut: coz nobody plays bad cop like i do >:)
MyAlterEgo: no scams, nut. I just got a handle on who I
    might be, now or someday
bArElYtHeRe: far out man. like looking in a mirror and
    seeing yourself years later?
MyAlterEgo: no, just see myself a lot clearer, what i can do
    about it, if it matters ... stuff like that.
OneBrikShy: yep, thats an epiphany. come here to gloat?
bArElYtHeRe: awww, thats mean brik
OneBrikShy: i was kidding before, you know that, right ego?
MyAlterEgo: your barbs never go deep, my friend
bArElYtHeRe: your what? oh never mind

OneBrikShy: how can we help you ego?

MyAlterEgo: you guys know anything about brains?

WottaNut: good with eggs

bArElYtHeRe: oh barf

OneBrikShy: you mean brain medicine and stuff?

MyAlterEgo: yeah.

OneBrikShy: I couldnt write a paper on it but i know the conventional stuff i guess

OneBrikShy: (looks at nut) with or without eggs.

WottaNut: (cackles insanely)

MyAlterEgo: there may a be a logical reason i can't figure out who i am

WottaNut: check your wallet

bArElYtHeRe: (slaps nut upside his nut)what reason, ego?

MyAlterEgo: something happened when I was a baby, and no, nut, I wasn't dropped on my head

OneBrikShy: what kind of something? illness? alien abduction?

WottaNut: or regular abduction? (look he's being serious)

MyAlterEgo: the gist? I had no idea who I'm cut out to be. along comes the famous person and tells me why. first time in my life, i get real help.

WottaNut: (still serious) Deepak Chopra?

OneBrikShy: as i said (no snotty tone this time) sounds like youre making progress. how could we help?

MyAlterEgo: i guess i just need to talk to someone who doesn't see the problem every day and get bored with it

bArElYtHeRe: we'll let you know when we get bored, hon. don't worry

Once again, I avoided harmful disclosure. I had talked to them regularly for weeks and months. But, as Nut said, one of us could still be Wayne Knight.

And Brik was right. I did go there to gloat. Or to pat myself on the back.

I couldn't help but feel conceited. Partly, I wanted to encourage them. If I could gain ground in my struggles, then Nut might conquer his fear of not being the funniest guy around. Brik might not feel the need to take charge all the time. Bare could affirm that she wasn't a Seinfeld co-star.

My new relationship with George McCullough made me feel adventurous. After our meeting, I realized the number of people in the know had increased by a third. Telling George had been so cathartic, I had to be careful not to spill the beans online ... to everyone.

16

Plans are Made

I

Leo Radcliffe, George's lawyer, flew down from New York. We had a business lunch at the Hilton. I was so eager to try out the hotel restaurant's cuisine I almost forgot my fear of exposure. Once our mouths were full, however, no one paid us any attention.

"Leo," George said, "Let me start by saying, no, this isn't a custody dispute or child support case."

Leo, who probably looked like a lawyer in his pajamas, gave me the first in a series of long looks. Searching for genetic similarities between George and me, perhaps. He turned to George. "Looking to adopt?"

George chuckled. "No sense in corrupting someone else's upbringing. No, I want to retain you to represent Scott here."

Leo looked at me again. "What did you do, kid?"

I choked on a laugh and almost sprayed him with half-chewed baked scrod. "I didn't do anything," I said after I had calmed down and swallowed. "If anything, I'm a victim."

Leo raised an eyebrow at George. "There's no jet lag between New York and here, but I seem to be missing something."

"Okay," George put down his knife and fork. "Remember the thing I did at the local hospital a few years ago?"

"The scanner thing? For Johns Hopkins?"

"Yeah, more or less. They funded it and had access to my research, such as it was."

Leo huffed. "What research? Didn't you lose everything with the burnt-out computers?"

George nodded. "Including my mind, for a while. Power surge zilched all my research data but the experiment might have been saved, but I hadn't started on 'the pill' yet." He smiled, but it looked sad. "I scrapped the whole project and wallowed in self pity for month or two."

"And that's why Johns Hopkins contacted me griping that you hadn't provided them with any research."

George shrugged. "What can I say? I was messed up." He looked at me. "Anyway, let me set the stage. You ever see an out-of-date movie? A big hit you just didn't make it to see when it was hot?"

"Uh, sure." Leo gave me another quick glance. I just stared at George, fish forgotten.

George continued. "So, when you see this years-old movie, you're like, 'hey, that's a good movie.' Then a week later, they announce a sequel to that same movie. Hollywood was just waiting for your approval and *BANG!* There's your sequel."

Leo joined me in staring at his client.

George was unfazed by our blank looks. "The computer crash doesn't fit the analogy very well," he said, "and the sponsors are probably still ticked at me. But the sequel, Leo. The *sequel!*"

Leo checked me out again.

I shrugged. "I guess I'm the sequel."

George told Leo everything we had told him, in less detail but with far more verve. He was probably more used to talking than listening, but he paid attention. He held the gaping to a minimum.

"Just so I have this straight, George," Leo said, "These people got your private phone number, found out about your failed experiment and called you to say what, that you'd left a little something behind?"

I shook my head. Leo was a lawyer all right. For someone who relied so heavily on editors, George had told a cogent story. Leo just dug for worms. And the guy was supposed to be on our side.

George threw his hands up. "Weren't you *listening?* I went there *expecting* a scam. But Scott was born fifteen minutes after my gear got wasted!"

"Have you seen the birth certificate?"

I shook my head again. "Mr. Radcliffe, George tried to make you understand how this *could not be* a hoax. I can confirm everything he told you. Without my mother or anyone else coaching me."

Few adults could maintain a straight face at expostulation from a small child. Still, Leo sipped his iced tea to show how unimpressed he was. "I'm sure you have a demonstration to prove your claims." He smirked, ready to find the flaw in our program.

I turned to George. "I don't think I want someone who cross-examines his own clients."

George turned to his lawyer. "What will it take to convince you, Leo?"

"We don't need to," I said. "He's supposed to protect your interests, not question them. He wants a performance to critique."

George pounded his thigh. "But you *can* show him!"

"It wouldn't convince him," I said. "No matter how good the story, lawyers are human hole-punches. He could claim I simply memorized a bunch of facts, which proves nothing more than a good memory. It wouldn't convince him."

George pulled at his face. "So what do you want to do?"

I gave Leo Radcliffe a dead look. "Finish your coffee, George. I'm ready to go."

George gaped at Leo, perhaps realizing that "lawyer" was not a synonym for "pal." I laid my napkin on the table and stood.

"Wait," Leo said. "You got my attention." He sat up now, but still wore his lawyer smile. "That speech was pretty good, kid. Got anything else?"

I tipped my chair back on two legs. "Like what? Want me to name the state capitals? List the presidents? I don't know if I can. Not even sure I should. I'm not here to show off or be quizzed."

Leo shook his head. "Sure you are. Gotta show something original or else you're just a freakishly well-spoken kid."

My face grew hot. He'd used the "F" word to my face! It didn't help that he was right. He was the last guy I wanted to hear it from.

George looked at me and squirmed. "How about *you* ask him a question, Leo?"

Leo sat back and tapped his bottom lip. "George tells me you have the skills and experiences of four people packed inside your head."

"That's what he tells me, too." My chair was still tipped back and I looked elsewhere. Sheila wasn't there, so George pulled my chair out and set all four legs on the floor. Leo grinned. I ignored it.

"In no particular order," Leo continued, "they were a successful young banker, a mechanic, a high-level office manager and a computer programmer."

"Is that a question?" I asked.

"No," he said. "Remember, I'm a lawyer. I'm just laying groundwork." He stood and walked around the table, hands behind his back. "Sorry. I'm used to being on my feet when asking questions." He stopped with his hands on the back of George's chair. "Young man, do you know the capital of Nevada?"

I looked at George and sighed. "Carson City."

He paced another leg. "Texas?"

"Austin." I had thought him shallow, but now I could tell he was building up to something. I wanted to be ready. Curve balls might hurt me or help me, but if he tricked me into an answer, I might be more surprised than Leo at the answer.

"Sri Lanka?"

"Colombo." I remembered my reference to the Peter Falk series and smiled.

"Myanmar?"

I blinked. "Where?"

"Burma, then," he said.

"Oh," I said. "Rangoon."

"Hmm.' He tapped his bottom lip. "That's something. Tell me, Mr., uh, ... "

"Bledsoe," I said. "Scott Bledsoe."

"Mr. Bledsoe, I've been having trouble with the power steering on my 1980 Toyota Corolla."

"Like it doesn't have one?" I said. "That was just like George. Don't you two know anything about cars?"

"No," they said together.

"Then ask me a serious question."

"I thought you'd already decided to get a new lawyer," Leo said.

"And I thought you were sure I was a con artist."

Leo waved a dismissive hand. "I was just yanking George's chain."

George grunted. "I don't pay you to be my own personal second guesser!"

"Yeah," Leo said. "You do."

"And that was a bargain-basement quiz," I said. "Knowing capitals, even foreign ones, is just a memory trick. In no way does it verify our claim. He just wanted us to squirm, George."

Leo grinned and shook his head. "That little quip convinces me more than anything. But how do we plumb your depth of knowledge? Other than my favorites, I don't know anything about cars. Or about secretarial work. I know something about banking, but what would I ask you? How to convert simple interest to APR?"

I leaned in closer. "I'm sticking my neck out here and I need a lawyer. I couldn't care less if you believe who and what I am. Just do the job and keep your lips zipped."

"You say you were convinced early on in our conversation," George said, "but you were so unimpressed you continued to 'yank my chain.' What does it take to astonish you, Leo?"

Leo smiled at me and jerked a thumb at his client. "I would be astonished to make it through one of this guy's books."

II

Later, we sat around Sheila's kitchen table. Leo and George each had a hotel room, but I wasn't comfortable going where it was just the three of us. Who knows what kind of ideas people might get?

"Before I can do anything for you, Scott," Leo told me, "you have to tell me what you want."

I smiled. "Besides world peace and a long, healthy life?"

"I meant why do you need a lawyer?"

I rubbed my head. "I'm sorry I don't have a good answer prepared. It's not like I don't think about it."

Leo looked at George. "Aren't you helping him?"

George shrugged. "I know what I might want in his position, but Scott is his own man."

I blinked. "Thanks."

He gave me a smile. "I mean you're able to make mature decisions. Leo, I think that Scott is in need of options. I would bet he's reluctant to hope for anything at all, not knowing what's possible."

I sat up. "That's it to a tee."

"Okay," Leo said. He sighed so hard it pushed his eyebrows up. "How about we approach the question from another angle. What do you *not* want, Scott?"

I jumped on that one. "To be a guinea pig. I knew this would be big news in the scientific community, even before I spilled the beans to my mother. Everyone's going to want a piece."

"So, what?" Leo asked, "you want me to divvy you up? You need an accountant, too?"

"Maybe a butcher," I heard George mutter.

"How about a general business contract?" I said. "It can label what's up for grabs and perhaps, more importantly, what isn't. Services, compensation, et cetera."

"We'll have a little trouble with your minor status," Leo said. "It's a good idea to start with, though."

We were all quiet for a few minutes, letting our brains churn. The creator, the manipulator and the repository.

I sat up straight. "What if I were a celebrity? How did Macaulay Culkin's lawyers do it?"

Leo's grin looked devious behind his mustache. "Pretty well, is how. But his parents weren't anything like your mom, so you might end up in better shape, in the long run."

I hadn't been this excited since I met George. "Then that's the kind of contract we need. No matter what studio or production company wanted me."

"Studio?" George asked. "The celebrity thing was just an analogy, right?"

"It was at first, George," Leo said, "but we could be talking the real deal." Leo smiled with a squinty-eyed look meant to engender trust, but each of my four component wells of knowledge had its own reservations about lawyers.

"This isn't a profit scheme, Mr. Radcliffe," I said.

Leo looked to his other client. "Little help?"

"Come on, Scott," George said. "You do this, it's going to be big news."

"I already figured that out."

"But I don't think you've *thought* it out. This is a discovery that could potentially affect every single person in the world throughout the rest of history."

Leo stood and stretched his back. "You're getting carried away, George."

"No, I'm not. Remember what happened after the announcement that they mapped the human genome?"

I blinked. "They did that?"

"A few years ago." George looked at Leo. "The news was pandemic. One person in twenty could define the word 'genome,' but that week everybody and his brother was saying it.

"And Scott's not a bunch of numbers only scientists can decipher. He's a real live boy. Someone who can be seen, photographed, interviewed, quoted, misquoted ... "

"Annoyed," I said, smiling.

"Dissected," he finished, unsmiling.

Leo looked at me, then glowered at George. "It wouldn't come to that."

"No? I know you don't read much, Leo, but you watch movies."

"What movies?"

"Anything involving extraordinary human abilities and government intervention, usually to the detriment of the protagonist and human rights in general."

Leo looked gassy. "I'm not gonna get a call some night because you were arrested for setting lab animals loose, am I? You're sounding like an activist."

"I'm not. I'm just reminding you guys that Nobel Prize winners may have a small and exclusive fan club, but even they get on television."

"And," Leo said, now able to pick up the thread, "if it's bound to happen anyway, why not make the most of it?"

"Those sound like famous last words," I said. "I can say I won't let money change me, but just you watch. I'll wind up in a poolside chair somewhere screaming because someone used the wrong brand of vodka in my martini."

17

Discomfort

Sheila didn't really treat me like a child anymore, but she insisted I get eight to ten hours of sleep a night. I knew why, of course, but every moment I wasn't awake felt like a waste of time. My restless mind almost always woke me before the alarm clock. At least it gave me time to eat breakfast with Sheila.

One morning I awoke and Sheila wasn't preparing breakfast. She was sitting on the back patio in her robe, drinking coffee. Charlie was usually there by nine, so breakfast became the only time for just Sheila and me. The one semblance we had of a normal parent-child relationship involved oatmeal or Cheerios. We rarely skipped it.

"How long have you been up?" I asked.

"Too long." She peeked at her bare wrist. "I'm not running late, am I?"

"No. It's early yet." I sat on the opposite bench of the picnic table she'd built a few years before. A competent job, but it was from a cheap kit and very flimsy. I was careful not to bump it and launch her coffee cup into the bushes. "Here's an easy one: something on your mind?"

She smiled over her coffee. "Does 'everything' count as something?"

The previous evening, Leo had outlined the plan for my world debut. It represented hours of careful work and revision. To Sheila, though, he might have been reading my Selective Service draft notice. She didn't voice her reservations, but she had them.

I tried to be understanding. In a way, I did understand. After months of uncertain inaction — about seventy-five in my case — one decisive stunt would undo all my secrets. *Attention closet skeletons: Everybody out!*

"Anything I can help with?" I asked.

She shook her head. "Not without giving it all up, and you've already put too much into it." She reached across to pat my arm. "I'm just thinking how we're going to have to adjust things."

"Which things?"

She put down the coffee and tightened the belt on her robe. "Like what I'll say when someone at work tells me they saw you on the cover of *Time Magazine.*" She folded her arms, then folded even more, cocooning herself in terry cloth. "I don't know what I'll say."

"I wouldn't, either." I reached for her free hand but my arm was too short. She was staring into the future and didn't notice. "I didn't think about *Time.* Science journals, but nothing like that."

"Most science articles I ever read were in Time," she said.

"Or other news magazines. Remember that one about eels in USA Today?"

"They say there's no such thing as bad publicity." She still didn't see my hand, so I pulled it back. "As long as I don't show up in Weekly World News."

That got me a smile. "Oh yeah. That would go over well at work. Bonnie Lockhart will ask me if you've met the Bat Boy."

I rubbed my face. "I guess I didn't think how this would affect your job. But look at the bright side. Soon you won't have to work there anymore."

Sheila's eyes widened. "How so?"

I shrugged. "This deal will come with compensation. I mean, I'm not going to spill my guts for nothing."

She made a face at my choice of words but sat up straight. "What kind of compensation?"

"Leo brought it up after he talked to his friend Rob Mitchell," I said. "I was thinking show biz, but Mitchell compared it to a professional sports draft."

Sheila scowled at another word she didn't care for. "Sports draft," she said. She scratched one foot with the heel of the other. "Like you were going to play for the Orioles or something."

"Yeah."

"And how much does he think you'll get?" She stood up, grabbed her mug and headed for the kitchen. "Enough to live on?" I knew it wasn't greed talking.

"Rob Mitchell gave Leo the idea," I said, "though I'm sure Leo would have thought of it. My cooperation with the scientific and medical communities could be tantamount to sharing years of research. We might clean up."

"And that translates to ... ?" She stopped at the door.

She wasn't looking, but I smiled anyway. "Enough to live on."

She sighed. "I see." She went inside. I got up, too, but hung around a moment.

Our tiny backyard was more like an inside room. It was confining and not all that comfortable. Like extra closet space, but without a roof. Until that morning, on that porch, I didn't realize the most practical result of my exploits was — and should be — my mother's rescue from lower-middle class suburban purgatory. If nothing else came of my contacting George McCullough, getting Sheila out of that house would do.

When my father went from healthy to deathly ill to buried inside of five months, Sheila had to move somewhere cheaper. As her sister put it, the cancer ward was like an extravagantly expensive hotel where room service came only through a needle. James Stephen Bledsoe had small-cell lung cancer and a dozen stays at *Château Oncologie* before he checked out.

Sheila had moved here after he died, but other than leaving enough money for bottles and diapers, it hadn't helped like she hoped. I wondered if moving away would help her now. No matter how my brain worked, it wasn't something I could just come out and ask my mother.

"Are you going to want some of this?" she asked me through the window. "It's decaf."

I sighed and smiled. I wouldn't worry about her until she broke her maxim about children and caffeine.

"Sure," I said. "Now that I brought it up, how do you feel about me bringing home the bacon?"

She handed me a steaming cup. "I don't know." She leaned on the bar and cradled her chin in her hand. "I won't know until it happens. Easier to imagine than plan for." Then she grinned. "Like winning the lottery."

I carried my coffee to the table and sat. "That might not be far off the mark."

"In what way?"

"This could turn out to be a windfall. Our ship coming in, as it were."

She got out the Cheerios and plunked them on the table. "You think so?" She sent the milk sliding. She was being unusually free with Newton's laws, dropping the cereal box and sending me the milk as if it were a pint of beer. Of all times for her to have a poker face.

"Prospective research sponsors will probably vie for exclusivity." I dumped cereal in the bowl and poured milk, no stunt work involved. "Wealthy corporations pay top dollar for things like that."

Sheila bit her lip and stared into space. I ate Cheerios and waited for a response. When none came, I offered a penny for her thoughts.

She shrugged. "I don't know."

"What don't you know?"

She took a deep breath. "I don't know. I don't know what to think."

"Which part of it?".

"About any of it." She scooted her chair away. She went to the counter, then to the fridge, but didn't open it. Then back to the counter. She paced and paused, like a weak runner, tired after one lap.

"I know it's overwhelming." I put my spoon down, unable to eat while she fretted. "Maybe if you take it in steps. Figure out the things that bother y—"

"I can't fix this with a list of pros and cons, Scott." It was a mark of her mental strain that she interrupted me. I felt like a teenager after a night's carousing, greeted by the dawn's early light and a rocket-red glare from his mother.

Then, because she was a good, inoffensive soul, she sat next to me and smoothed my hair back. "*You* think that way, sweetie, but I can't. I can't be rational about why it makes me upset." She lowered her hand. "No, not upset. Just the feeling that something's a little off. It sits in your mind, but you can't figure it out." She gave me a tired smile. "And then you run for the bathroom and get a second look at your breakfast."

I looked at my half-finished bowl of cereal, then pushed it away.

She patted my hand. "Sorry, but do you get what I mean?"

"I think so." I covered her hand with mine. "You've got the early stages of queasiness?"

"See? You *can* think that way."

"No," I said. "I just condensed what you said."

She sighed. "In a weird way, that description is appropriate."

"How so?"

"It's the way I felt when I was first pregnant." She did not say "pregnant with you," but she had been about to. "I didn't know if I had flu or malaria, or if I was just tired and depressed. Jamie was working seventy-plus hours a week then. I got used to it. Then the feeling built up again and I almost recognized it.

"It dawned on me one Saturday ... about five seconds after I started scrambling eggs for your father. A baby was coming."

I learned more about my father in those three or four months than I had in all the years before. Sheila had pictures but no home videos of him. It would have been nice to see myself in him. Something of the man I might become instead of the man I already felt like.

"I'm beginning to have the same kind of almost queasy feeling, but I'm afraid it might mean the opposite this time." Without my noticing, she had begun to cry. I handed her a napkin.

"You think I'm going to leave?"

She sniffed. "I think you might end up having to."

I wanted to assure her it wouldn't happen. That I would be around until I was old enough to drive away to college. But I couldn't, so I kept quiet.

She held an envelope she had picked up from the counter. I thought she wanted me to ask about it, which I did. She bit her lip and handed me the envelope.

It was from the home school records office. Not a list of my most recent grades but a letter to Sheila. I skimmed it and grinned.

" ... and the high test scores compel me to suggest a more accelerated program. This will allow your child to complete rudimentary studies early and begin a regimen that will lead to *early graduation and ... ,"*

I started laughing and couldn't finish the letter. Sheila joined in only a moment later.

18

Feelers

I

When Leo first met with hospital and university representatives, I wanted to go. Leo said no. All the information and potential offers had to go through him. He knew what to look out for. I had a fair amount of knowledge in that area myself, but he still said no. He was my filter, he said. The meetings were lawyer-only events for a while.

Sheila went to work, though I suggested she call in sick. It wouldn't be a lie. She had eaten enough antacid tablets to leave chalky footprints. Charlie was at work or I would have asked him to come sit with Sheila while strangers planned my future in an office downtown. Then she'd have to stay home. If not for the company, then to make sure Charlie didn't dirty the kitchen.

She went to work anyway. I said I was glad she didn't work around dangerous machines with her attention so compromised.

"What do you mean, no dangerous machines?" she said.

"We still use Mimeographs. We're lucky someone hasn't lost fingers."

"I'll bet it keeps people from making copies of their rear ends."

She rolled her eyes. "You would think."

So she went, and I was left to my own devices.

II

MyAlterEgo: My day's shot. If anyone wants to get real deep, here's your chance

OneBrikShy: I just wanted to chat. why you gotta get all serious???

bArElYtHeRe: what's the matter hon? meds not come thru?

WottaNut: naw, hes just cranky coz of the dow plummet

OneBrikShy: bare's right. the MAN is getting me down

MyAlterEgo: what MAN is that?

OneBrikShy: my doctor. he won't hook me up with a real dose

MyAlterEgo: >< (blinks)

OneBrikShy: s'okay ego. I'm in a wheelchair. broke my back a few years ago

MyAlterEgo: sorry to hear that

OneBrikShy: don't be. I'm took care of. just a little edgy between hits

MyAlterEgo: and i thought *I* had problems

OneBrikShy: what kinda problems? might as well spit it out

bArElYtHeRe: don't spit i just windexed my monitor

MyAlterEgo: my lawyer's negotiating a deal for me

WottaNut: big mistake

MyAlterEgo: i thought so too. i wanted to go along

WottaNut: no i mean the lawyer. they is all minions of satan. didnt you hear?

MyAlterEgo: (smiles) you a lawyer, nut?

WottaNut: no way. official driver of the oscar meyer wienermobile

OneBrikShy: LOL fitting anyway

bArElYtHeRe: whats with the lawyer ego? divorce?

MyAlterEgo: i can't really say anything specific

WottaNut: for a group this intimate we do a lot of dissembling

OneBrikShy: look whos talking wienerman

bArElYtHeRe: that mean you guys'll never believe im a princess?

WottaNut: i think you're a queen bare

bArElYtHeRe: YOURE the queen

WottaNut: (fans his boa) oh hush you

OneBrikShy: so why are you here ego? march in on that meeting and lay down the law.

MyAlterEgo: I would but i can't drive

WottaNut: never learn?

MyAlterEgo: cars in the shop. the turbocharger is messing with my emissions permit

WottaNut: wotta pain

OneBrikShy: gonna tell us what your lawyer's doing or do you want sympathy because you have a lawyer?

MyAlterEgo: getting to that. i want to ask you guys a question first. how would you feel if your child wanted to leave home?

WottaNut: i have a catapult for that. they don't get far past the neighbor's yard but theyre getting the hint bArElYtHeRe: I don't have kids

OneBrikShy: mine are grown already. yours got his fill of life under your roof ego?

MyAlterEgo: it's a little more complicated than that. the child is younger. not even a teenager.

WottaNut: its a phase. they want to see how long it takes you to burst into flames.

MyAlterEgo: no behavior problems. well, not anymore. just ready to be out from under the protective wing.

bArElYtHeRe: ready? or says hes ready?

MyAlterEgo: therein lies the problem. he just might be

OneBrikShy: how does his mom feel about it?

MyAlterEgo: not thrilled but she's behind him.

bArElYtHeRe: how old is the kid?

MyAlterEgo: young

WottaNut: send a bunch of pampers with him. he'll learn to potty soon enough

MyAlterEgo: not THAT young

OneBrikShy: ego, if you're serious, you need to get the kid a therapist . You and his mom too.

MyAlterEgo: I have said this before. Our situation is unique. A therapist might help ... later.

WottaNut: I got it! you're a spy! can't go to anyone outside. car is an aston martin or something cool like that right?

bArElYtHeRe: cut it out, nut. we're trying to be serious

WottaNut: <---- look at the name bare. it doesn't say WottaSaneGuy. youre lucky I'm not in a don rickles or lenny bruce mood

MyAlterEgo: or Carrot Top

WottaNut: see? vindication muahahahaha
OneBrikShy: seriously, you'd send your child on his way?
    what, to make your life easier?
MyAlterEgo: no, to make HIS life easier. not away, though.
    maybe just to a boarding school. somewhere he can
    live his own life.
bArElYtHeRe: no discipline problems, so why boarding
    school? afraid he's gonna go nuts at home?
MyAlterEgo: could be getting there already
OneBrikShy: therapy, man. get some quick. for both of you.
bArElYtHeRe: brik is right, ego baby. no offense but you
    need it
MyAlterEgo: i thought this was a pretty good substitute :)
OneBrikShy: for you maybe, but not for your kid
MyAlterEgo: that's funny
bArElYtHeRe: what's funny?
MyAlterEgo: when we get into serious matters, everyone
    uses punctuation.

That was just great. I was okay with going to a therapist.
But was Sheila?

I bade farewell to the group and spent some time looking
up George's books and their reviews on Amazon. I got bored
and then frustrated when I realized I couldn't order any of
them. No credit card. Another disadvantage of being a kid.
Or poor.

Time to fix that.

19

Payoff

"How much?"

Leo blinked at Sheila. "How much what?"

Sheila wore no expression. "What did you get for him?" She tried and failed to snatch a paper from Leo's hand. Now I knew the specifics of her distress. Without me there to calm her, Sheila spent the whole day watering her guilt plant.

"What, you think he put me on Craigslist?" I felt unkind toward my mother for the first time.

"Might as well have." Seeing tears fall from dry eyes is disturbing, like watching a statue cry. "You get into a deal like this, it's like 'I used to be a person, but now I'm a publicly traded commodity.'" Her glare bored into Leo.

"It was *me.*" I spoke in a slow, forced groan to help stall my own tears. "I did this. I sent him on this job. Sure he's out there peddling my brain, but we've discussed this. A lot. If you don't want me to pursue it, why did you ever let me get this far?"

Sheila's eyes widened and she put her hand to her cheek, as if I had slapped her. I could almost see the tiny, glowing hand print.

Long moments passed.

After doing his best to be invisible, Leo opened his mouth without his lawyer smile. "Mrs. Bledsoe, I acted not only in Scott's interest, but on his specific instructions. He, not I, decided how to approach, how to present his 'credentials.' I had to go outside my office to get the right kind of contracts drawn up, but I am still Scott's attorney, not his publicity agent.

"That analogy — an actor seeking a role — was close but wrong, even if we do follow some of the same rules. This is more like a major league baseball draft. Scott shows his fastball and the teams make their bids."

Sheila's eyes stayed on me. Her face had softened. Her tears looked less creepy now, but I still didn't like them.

I went to her and took her hand, kissed and squeezed it, wondered how to allay her fears. "More has gone into this than who to talk to and how much to ask for. I didn't want to start this deal until I had fifteen anchors in place." Sheila sagged into her chair like a woman twice her age. I reached out to touch the imaginary handprint on her cheek and she cried into my hand. My actions and words were an odd match, but she needed both; why not at the same time? "Nothing is solid yet. Right, Leo?"

Leo nodded right away. "Right. So far the only people who have a clue are the lawyers." He mimed zipping his lips. "Confidential. Right now we have canary leverage."

I stopped comforting Sheila and we both waited for the

punch line.

Leo re-tightened his tie. "We'll know almost right away if someone sings."

"What if it's you?" Sheila asked. I couldn't tell if she was serious. Her face was puffy from crying.

I played along. "Yeah, Leo, what if it's you?"

Leo put a hand to his chest. "Do you already think so little of me?" We might have insulted his footwear rather than his integrity. "I never take the easy money. I always milk a client for all he's worth. I'm no scientist, Mrs. Bledsoe, but I think any company with a 'sciences' department is going to be interested in Scott. If the canary sings this early on, you'll know it isn't me. The first offers will be laughably small." He smiled, showing every one of his sharky teeth. "Wait until we get some big names interested."

Sheila definitely wasn't smiling now. "What names?"

"Pharmaceutical companies," Leo said. "They're some of the richest corporations in the world. As an industry, they pay hundreds of millions of dollars in tort settlements. They'll jump at the chance to do something proactive for the trade. It's good for both their wallets and their PR."

"Wait a minute." I dropped Sheila's hand. "I told you I'm not in this to get rich. I just think the only way I'm going to find the kind of help I want is through research." That wasn't entirely true, but I had to keep up some kind of charade. I didn't want Sheila to know I had decided money was a worthy goal, too.

Leo leaned back. "Scott, who do you think funds most of the medical research in the world?"

"People who profit most from it, and I don't mean the

patients." Knowing the answer made me feel dirty, especially after my little fib about money. Times like this, I didn't care much for my extended mental database, but it excited Leo like nobody's business. He grinned and shook his head.

"So how does Scott go up on the block?" Sheila asked. She wasn't angry anymore. Just weary.

"With discretion," Leo said. "On advice from Rob Mitchell, we're going to contact the heads of all the major medical research facilities and universities in the country. They, in turn, will seek funding from corporate sponsors." He turned a wry look on me. "I urged Scott to consider an international market, but he insisted on keeping it in the U.S."

"Don't ask me why," I said. "Might be chauvinism or something vague that's not quite a memory. I'm just more comfortable paying attention to the voices in my head."

"Just keep doing that," Leo said with a smile. "Those little voices are about to be your meal ticket."

It annoyed me that Leo thought he was tapping a bottomless source of wealth. It was attractive enough for me, too, but for Sheila's sake. Even with internet access and all my knowledge and ability, I had never thought to apply it to earning an income. Since I met George, then Leo, and found out what might come of just sitting back and being an object of scrutiny, working for a living was no longer an attractive option.

But for a six-year-old, is it ever?

20

Draft Day

If one more office decoration in short skirt, low-cut blouse, and brakelight-red lipstick tried to give me a Tootsie Pop, I was going to scream. We could have had this conference call in a closed room, but no, Leo had to show off. If not for his New York accent, I could imagine him as an auctioneer at a county fair.

Here the boy/fine boy/ who'll gimme four dollah? four dollah-four dollah/FOUR DOLLAH/ Alrighty, who'll gimme five? figh-dollah-figh dollah ...

Unseen, unknown people were literally bidding on *me*. I wanted Sheila elsewhere, but how would I suggest it? It was more pleasant than a prison sentencing, but the duty was the same. I was family.

I followed the legal talk pretty well. After all, part of me was a successful businessman. Details sailed right by me after a while, though. I attributed it to nervousness and I was glad Sheila was there. I wanted my mommy.

I felt lost when familiar words escaped me. I might have kept up if the men on the conference call had been lawyers or scientists. Instead, they were the scientists' lawyers. Scientists speak a language all their own, then hire lawyers to translate it into even more confusing mumbo jumbo. Everything was clear as mud.

The contenders were many. All had some ties to pharmaceutical manufacturers, just as Leo had said. Most of them insisted on conducting their research at a major facility, like Johns Hopkins in Baltimore or the Mayo Clinic. I liked that idea, but mostly because it was definitive. Some omitted research sites from their proposals, as if we might miss a clause requiring all research be conducted in Singapore.

Leo said a brief farewell and suddenly the call was ended.

I blinked. "What'd they say?"

"Weren't you listening?"

I frowned. "I kind of zoned out."

"Me too," Sheila said, "but I started that way."

"We're adjourning for party deliberations." Leo checked his watch. "We ought to go to lunch."

"But was anything decided?" Sheila wanted to know.

Leo shoved things in his briefcase. "Some of them decided they weren't big enough dogs to leave the porch. They won't be calling back." His grin had too much dental surface area. "Guess they'll be reading about you in the journals like everyone else. Come on. Let's eat!"

II

Charlie met us at the sandwich shop near the firm where

Leo had finagled office space. Leo hated to eat alone. Sheila and I were doing well to keep water down.

"Who's winning?" Charlie asked after ordering a chili-burger.

"Leo said it's still up in the air," I said.

Charlie whistled. "Wow. Who's in the running?"

The name of the bidding leader made Charlie's eyes pop. "Along with four others," Leo said.

Sheila shook her head. "I still can't believe what we're doing. Five major companies are fighting over Scott and we're just sitting back and watching? Like a girl watching boys fight over her and leaving with the least bloody one."

Leo nodded and winked at her. I didn't like his dismissive attitude.

"My mother was just voicing an opinion." I leaned in close. "Me, I'd like to know what to expect from the losers in today's bid."

Leo didn't even look at me. Just smiled and shook his head. That and his treatment of Sheila infuriated me. He seemed to get on well with Charlie, and that bothered me, too. I flicked a straw wrapper into Leo's beer glass.

"Don't patronize us, Mr. Radcliffe," I said. "Either of us. If you can't see our point of view, think about this: what kind of self-respecting big business corporation is satisfied to pick through a competitor's leavings? On a deal with this kind of potential?"

Leo looked stunned for a moment, then fished the paper out of his glass. Charlie snickered and stirred his Dr. Pepper. His snicker usually annoyed me, but this time it was his subtle way of cheering me on. The Boy and Daniel Webster.

"You think someone's going to be so jealous they'll come and, what, kidnap you?" His push-broom mustache pulled to one side, suggesting a grin. "Wanna hire a bodyguard? Bodyguards? Your ma might need protection, too."

"First," I said, "this isn't paranoia. Among my other charming qualities, I have scads of knowledge about the business world. When I thought of this, my mental switchboard lit up like Las Vegas." I slipped out of the booth, stood beside Leo and put my finger in his face. "Second," I whispered, "you and I don't have a contract. George McCullough paid your retainer, not me. You may have a future with him, but if you don't quit with the dismissive attitude, *I* will find another lawyer." I poked his shoulder. "Have I made myself clear?"

Leo didn't wilt or cringe. But he quit smirking. "I get you." He looked at his beer glass. "I apologize."

I glanced at Charlie. He was staring and I almost winked at him. I sat just as our waitress reappeared. No way to tell what she had seen or overheard, but I didn't fret about it.

"I changed my mind," I told her. "I'll have a Reuben with onion rings."

"Sure thing, doll." She shot a glance at Leo and winked at me. Awe from Charlie and now applause from onlookers. Maybe I should just go around and tell people off for a living. Imagine it: eloquent moral outrage from a six-year-old.

"What about Scott's question?" Sheila asked while patting my leg under the table.

Leo gripped his beer glass before he answered. "Most — if any — problems will arise from Scott's minor status. Once we cut a deal with a sponsor, one of the losers will try to nullify the contract by bringing to the court's attention that Scott is a young boy."

"Will that work?" Charlie asked.

"They can tangle things a little," Leo said. "Scott's income through this endeavor can be protected by the same kinds of laws that protect child performers. It will just take longer to finalize."

"How long?" Sheila asked.

"Years, I'll bet," I said. My appetite was ebbing, but to revive it I just thought about poking Leo and giving him what for. I wondered what it said about me that telling Leo off made my mouth water.

"Possibly," Leo said. "I'll draw up advance motions to contest anything our opponents might come up with." He sipped his beer and smiled at me. "They won't stop us."

"Another question," Charlie said. "Who is going to win this little game? You already know, don't you Mr. Radcliffe?"

Leo hadn't finished his tuna melt but he was on his third beer. When we first met, he hadn't seemed the type to drink his lunch. My eyes had been opened about a lot of things.

"The ones connected with Johns Hopkins," he said. He covered his empty glass with a coaster. "They're the top neurology center in the nation. Three of the five are in this together, whether they admit it or not."

"Would they really be so redundant?" Sheila asked. "After funding the original research, wouldn't they have dibs on Scott?"

"I love that about you," Charlie said. "You always believe that, deep down, people are fair. Fair-minded, anyway."

"Really," she said, ignoring Charlie. "Since it's up to us

anyway, why even consider the others? If Johns Hopkins runs the initial experiment, aren't they entitled to the data?"

I handled that one. I'd thought about it a lot. "Morally? Yes. Legally, probably not. To date, no one has proven George's experiment affected me at all. The technology to confirm it doesn't exist yet."

"But you know all those things!" Sheila said.

"Yeah," Charlie said, "but it's like trying to prove reincarnation. The evidence is intangible."

Leo enjoyed his suds, but he wasn't sloppy. "You're right, of course. For the same reason, you'd never win a case against the hospital where Scott was born. Faulty wiring might have caused their machine to blow, but so far, nothing about Scott has been 'diagnosed.'"

Sheila chewed her lip. She might have sued the hospital if one or both of us had been injured by The Surge. With no real injuries, she had no grounds.

"Something wrong?" Charlie asked her.

She wrapped herself in her arms. "Sorry, I've got the words 'kidnap' and 'bodyguard' going through my head." She looked at Leo. "I'm glad you're not a doctor. Your bedside manner sucks."

Charlie and I shared a surprised look. Sheila's epithets were usually more tame than other people's pleasantries. Maybe she was having a breakthrough. I hoped it wasn't a breakdown.

Leo's drop-it-forget-I-said-anything answer satisfied me, but Sheila couldn't let it go. Defending a young child from exploitation was important, but defending him from harm was a moral duty, especially her own son. Even a jest about bodyguards set alarms off in her head.

"How do you hire one?" she asked, as if considering a magician for a birthday party.

Leo made that scrunchy, dismissive face again. "You won't have to."

Sheila closed her mouth, but she wasn't mollified.

"Look," Leo said, "if there is a real problem, the principal investors would hire a 'security expert,' as they are now termed. Most are former police or military, but the best are former FBI or Secret Service. These sponsors can afford the best."

"I don't think it's the expense that bothers her, Mr. Radcliffe," Charlie said. "It's the potential necessity."

Leo took a deep breath and sighed it out. "Look, I'm sorry I gave you the idea. Believe me, I take Scott's safety very seriously."

"Of course you do," Sheila said. "The same way you put your money in a bank with a safe."

"No," he said. He sat back rubbed his eyes and pulled at his face. "I mean, yes, but ... " He looked at me. "I've sort of —"

I gave him a nasty smile. *"Don't ... you ... dare,"* I said. "Don't you dare spout something about how you 'feel close to me.' That might work for George McCullough, but you ain't him." I tried to keep my voice low, but Charlie's face told me I wasn't successful.

"No," said Leo. He sat back and held up his hands. "You're right. Of course not. But I've begun to take an interest in your future."

"And why is that?" Sheila asked.

"Because Scott may be my first client in a long time who really matters." He looked at Sheila. "I can't say I'm not in it for the money. I wouldn't be working for people like George McCullough if I wasn't.

"But I like my work. I might even love my work, because I get to see things *happen*. It's a kind of power."

I thought the Heineken had loosened Leo's tongue. But what came out wasn't a drunken confession. It was a speech. I wanted to get up and walk out, but I gave him another moment or two.

"In my eighteen years as a practicing attorney," Leo continued, "I never had a case I cared about after my part of the job was over. Divorces? They suck, even if they do make lawyers rich. Personal injury? They're almost as bad because huge settlements often *lead* to divorce."

"This is pretty eloquent for drunken rambling," Charlie mused.

Leo pshawed. "On three beers? No way. You ought to see me at home. And after this case, I might just give it up altogether."

"No, you won't," I said.

He shrugged. "I guess you're right." If he'd an ounce of comedic instinct, Leo would have flagged down the waitress for another bottle right away. He didn't. "What I mean is, I might have a financial interest in Scott, but I want to see him succeed, too."

"And therefore you will do your best to see that he's taken care of," Sheila finished for him. "That about it?"

"Yes, ma'am," he said. When we all just looked at him, he

pouted. "Oh come on! Can't I have some encouragement on my epiphany?"

Charlie golf-clapped.

Sheila's lip-chewing tension abated. "I can live with it, for now." She took Leo's hand and shook it. "Congratulations, Mr. Radcliffe. You have confirmed my faith in the human race. It is possible to be both a lawyer and a visionary."

We headed back to the office. Sheila, Charlie and Leo were excited. But I couldn't help feeling like a defendant hearing the jury was back.

21

And the Winner is . . .

I

Whether by merit or skullduggery, the expected contender won the bid. Oddly, a dollar amount was never mentioned. The others bowed out and left the game ball to the winner. Leo later told me the competing parties reached an agreement. Less fighting, more cooperation, *much* more contract legalese.

The next conversation — their three lawyers for our one — was on the issue of compensation.

To avoid some vague legal problems, I was to be paid as an employee of sorts. Rob Mitchell's influence came into play here. Our entertainment lawyer friend had drawn up a proposal. I heard it for the first time during the conference call.

"James Scott Bledsoe, six years old upon the drafting of this contract, shall be employed by Meritorious Studios according to the bylaws of the Screen Actors Guild for work in a documentary film series, title to be announced at a later date. Compensation shall be placed in blocked trust until the child shall reach the age of 18 years or is legally emancipated. He shall be educated in compliance with the compulsory education requirements of the Commonwealth of Virginia and/or any other state in which he resides. Pending satisfactory results on a high school equivalency test, he may pursue, at no cost to himself, a course of study of his own choosing at no charge at either Johns Hopkins University, Baltimore, MD, or Georgetown University, Washington, D.C."

There was a little more about money. Mostly that there would be a lot of it. Income would go into a trust, but bonuses would go into an account I could actually use ... which was kind of the point.

Leo smiled as he read. Charlie triumphantly pumped his fist and gave me a feral look. I assumed it was a male bonding thing. Only Sheila looked unsatisfied.

I think I wore a smile, but I still felt a pervasive risk. A less cynical person might ask, "What risk?" Right then, two came to mind.

My mother's happiness and my own freedom.

II

Leo smiled as he shoved papers into his briefcase. Charlie grinned as if he had just aced a test. Sheila looked as if she had swallowed the test paper and then chased it with the number two pencil.

"Some reason you couldn't share that proposal with me first?" I kept my tone calm and hoped the rest of me would follow suit.

"Nothing's final yet," Leo said. "That's why it's called a 'proposal,' Scott." He was so smug I thought again about canning him.

"Chill out, Scott," Charlie said. He looked at Sheila. Her mouth hung open, threatening drool. "Chill out, Scott's Mom."

"Chill out?" I wailed. "I went to a lawyer because I wanted some control over my life, not to have someone else run it for me!"

"Stop panicking," Leo said. He flipped open a copy of the brief and slid it to me. "Read the whole thing before you get too upset."

When Leo said that, I no longer remembered what had upset me.

So I read it. It was nine pages long, and in addition to outlining a very generous income, it addressed the issues Sheila worried about. More than one security company would be on hand to protect the parties' interests, especially the party who wore child's size-two sneakers.

But ... college?

I flipped the brief closed and tossed it on the table. "I don't remember anyone asking if *I* thought college was a good idea."

"Do you?" Charlie asked. "Think it's a good idea, I mean."

I blinked at him. "You did this?"

He shrugged. "I only helped."

Leo stowed the papers in his case. "That was Rob Mitchell's idea."

"Why?" My anger subsided and now I was just curious.

Leo gestured to Charlie and Sheila. "Your mother and Charlie told me, separately, that what your life lacked was newness. That with all that stuff from other minds, the only way you could have fresh experience is to actually do something outside your mind's ... what did you call it, Charlie?"

"Realm of focus," Charlie said. He looked guilty about his part in the chicanery, though he hadn't so much pulled a fast one as thrown a surprise party. "Something outside the scope of what he inherited from The Surge."

The Surge. George and Charlie used a proper noun to refer to the event that brung me. I remembered a short-lived lemon lime soft drink by that name. The catalyst of my existence could be nicknamed after a bottle of pop.

"I remember talking about that," I said, "but I was just letting off steam. It was nonsense."

Charlie shook his head. "Not nonsense, Scott. It came out because it was true. You can spout *facts* all day long, but when you're emotional, you tell the *truth.*" He smiled. "Not a good quality in a spy, maybe, but it helps us help you."

"What Charlie means," Sheila said, "is that someone decided for you, because you couldn't decide on your own. You couldn't do it because you couldn't diagnose it in yourself."

"What do you mean, 'diagnose?'" I asked. "I've known for a long time what irked me."

Charlie blinked. "Really? You've said it a hundred times. 'I've got so much knowledge. I'll never have any new experiences.'" To his credit, he did not mock my voice. "You've known it all this time, but what have you done

155

about it?"

"Hello?" I gestured at Charlie. "We came to *you*. I wanted a lawyer at first, but we didn't have the money. But when George said —"

"No, Scott," Charlie said. I glared but let him go on. "Not other people. Other than spilling it to Sheila and taking a few quizzes, you haven't really done anything. You're the focus of all this hoopla, but you're the most passive member of the team."

"Thanks," I said. "Remind me again how I'm a victim."

Charlie shrugged. "It's a life you chose for yourself."

"I think you've confused me with someone else." I stood up, pushed the chair away from the table. "How many newborns are embarrassed because they think it's obscene to suck milk from a woman's breast? You think babies enjoy the switch to formula? Believe me, the tastes don't compare. But I was *relieved*, Charlie. How old was I, three months?" Sheila didn't look at me but nodded. "Did I ever tell you I felt guilty being happy because this natural, beautiful thing was over?"

Charlie stood. "I didn't ask how you felt, Scott." He came closer and I backed up. "I asked what you've done. Before I came and George came and handed you a high-dollar lawyer on a silver platter." I looked straight up to see his face, but after a moment I scowled and looked away. "What did you do, Scott?"

"What *could* I do?" I barked. "Sheila's not rich. I spent all my time considering and rejecting ideas, and that was as fatiguing and disappointing as anything I've ever known." Sheila sank deeper into her seat, but her eyes were on me now. "Anything I thought of was too risky for Sheila or too deplorable to pursue. Don't make me go into it."

Charlie backed off a step, then straddled a chair and faced me. I kept my back against the wall. "If you'd been scared, it would've made more sense. Kids aren't able to make mature judgments for themselves.

"But you weren't really scared. Not for yourself, at least." He tilted his head at Sheila. "You were always worried about her, weren't you?" He reached to put a hand on my shoulder. "You've been under that restriction too long. You haven't given yourself a chance."

"The college idea actually came from Rob Mitchell," Leo said. "When I mentioned your need for new things, he said, 'Shoot, man, if I didn't have the wife and kids to worry about, I'd go back to college. There's always something new.'"

According to the brief, I would spend a total of between eight and ten hours a week in examinations with doctors — neurologists and psychiatrists — answering questions and submitting to non-invasive procedures. In return, I would get a full curriculum at one of two prestigious universities. Oh, and a largish bankroll.

Charlie grinned. "Isn't it great?"

Sheila smiled at me. "Looks like I don't have to come up with college tuition." Then she burst into tears and covered her face.

I looked at Charlie and Leo, not knowing what to do. My emotions had run rampant before everything was explained to me, but Sheila's had been ready to spill over since we sat down. Charlie and Leo bowed out right away, leaving me with Sheila. They knew something I didn't.

Her face was puffy and her nose red, not a good look for her. At the same time, she didn't look sad. I took her hand and ignored the wadded tissue in her fist.

"I should be the one crying," I said. "Charlie's right. Having someone else making decisions took a load off me I didn't even know was there." In truth, I was lightheaded and my knees were wobbly, not something that happened often. Then again, I could count on one hand the number of times I'd been this thrilled, ever. "Is there something you're not telling me?"

Sheila sniffled, squeezed my hand, then gave up and pulled me into a hug and wept into my ear. "I'm so happy for you, Scotty, but I've been dreading this day."

It was embarrassing how stupid I had been. I had thought about it for a long time, even discussed it on the sly with Brik, Bare and Nut. Sheila was experiencing Empty Nest Syndrome, for a six-year-old who hadn't even left home.

I hadn't been her baby since I had acquired the motor skills to dress and feed myself and the bowel control not to require diapers. I did housework without being told, including some things a child would not be trusted with. But I didn't think she was upset because I wouldn't be there to balance her checkbook anymore.

"I have an idea." I held her hands and gave her my best smile. "Besides the college tuition and an allowance for housing, initial bonuses amount to almost *ten thousand dollars a month.*"

"What are you getting at, Scott?"

I shrugged. "Let's get a new house. I don't think there's a

realtor around who would balk at that kind of credit."

"Scott, I don't think —"

"If anyone asks, I'll tell them it was my money, you didn't have anything to do with it."

"Sweetie, you're —"

"What is it, about two hundred miles from here to Washington? That's a long commute to see your kid."

"Two-forty," she said. "Or about two-eighty to Baltimore."

My mouth snapped shut and I sat down hard. I looked at her but couldn't say anything.

Sheila's face was dry and a little tougher. "I knew you'd need some prodding."

"That business with Charlie?" I asked. I felt my face grow hot.

"No, that was just to help you see what you've been avoiding."

"By getting me all upset?"

"Partly," she said. She scooched closer and put a hand on my knee. I would never be able to predict anyone's perception of me, responsible adult to innocent child in an eye blink. I wasn't even sure which this was. "You're always more honest when you're emotional." She covered my hand with hers. "You start to believe yourself, too."

I tried to grin. "Is this a motivational speech?"

"More like a commencement speech."

My grin turned into a frown. "From which school am I graduating?"

She smiled and the tears resurfaced. "The one at the kitchen table."

"What are you talking about?" I tried hard not to understand something very clear.

"Don't want you to take this the wrong way," she said, "like I want you out of the house. But Scott, dear," she patted my cheek, "I want you to move out of the house."

Part Two

Away

22

Emancipation

I

"Are you sure you understand the process here, young man?"

"Yes, ma'am, I do," I told the judge. "Possibly better than anyone else who has ever done this." This I said in an undertone. I doubted anyone but Leo heard me.

"Okay, then," the judge said. She shuffled papers and didn't look at me. Maybe she wondered what kind of parent would cut her kid loose at age seven. I could have told her, the kind with her unique child's best interests at heart and in mind. The kind who understood there wasn't much she could teach him.

Another thing Sheila and Charlie — and probably Leo — did behind my back was trickier than anything we had accomplished thus far. Charlie, with some small persuasion, would be coming with me.

The judge didn't take us seriously until Leo showed her

my test results. After that, the woman in the black robe looked at me in a different light, somewhere between suspicion and sympathy. Upon hearing me answer some basic questions, I'm sure she shifted the sympathy to Sheila.

By Labor Day, I was a legally emancipated minor. With polite suggestions from Leo, Sheila, and a helpful social worker, the court named Charlie my guardian *ad litem* for the duration of my college career, until I reached the age of eighteen. With some slick maneuvering, I might become a legal adult before then. I was told, however, that such a declaration, like same-sex marriage, would not be legal in all states.

When Leo told me my off-campus housing had been selected and furnished, I was ready to go right away and leave Sheila a note — *please FedEx my stuff* — but I didn't want to be unkind. Sheila had watched her son potty-train, by himself, at nine months, speak in complete sentences soon after and type when most kids his age were still learning their ABC's. Despite her heartfelt benediction, she wouldn't jump for joy that he was ready to fly the coop before his seventh birthday.

Again, I was mistaken. She didn't jump for joy, but neither did she show any sign of changing her mind.

"I know it will be better for you," she said. "In the long run."

With that and the admonition, "Take care of Charlie," she said goodbye.

II

I picked Georgetown University. As I have related *ad*

nauseam, I had scads of information but precious little of my own learning. If I could combine the info, skill in various fields, and youthful exuberance, I could learn scads of new stuff.

Charlie came along as my legal guardian, but mostly as a trusted friend. He was a watchdog, keeping an eye out in case some creative bureaucrat got any ideas. He was also there to remind the doctors that I was not a rhesus monkey.

It should have been an easy distinction. Lab animals live in cages. Courtesy of the project administrators, I lived in a comfortable, if very modest, apartment just off campus.

I wasn't completely alone, though. Charlie lived right next door. Twice in the first week I had to remind him to turn down his stereo. I never would have pegged him as a reggae fan.

23

Matriculation

The Georgetown campus was the most gorgeous place I had ever seen, though I had an inkling of something in Europe. But that didn't count. That had been seen with someone else's eyes.

It was freedom, though. For the first time in my life.

Until I got to the campus coffee bar.

"Young man, I'm not allowed to serve coffee to children."

"Excuse me?" I had asked for a latte, not a martini.

The cashier — not quite a barista — gave me a sympathetic look, but it was as fake as her hair color. People probably spoke to this woman all the time without ever learning her name. I wouldn't be one of *them.*

"Good morning ... " I checked her name tag, " ... Sally. I'm Scott Bledsoe and I'm a new student here."

Her eyebrows went up. I think they were eyebrows.

I smiled. "Yes, and I'm a child, not a dwarf. *And* a student, and since this is the *student center,* do you think the rule about not serving kids might be ... ?" I made a sweeping gesture, dispersing the rule like a bad smell.

Sally lowered her voice and looked down at me. "Young man, it is very rude to call an adult by their first name."

I was still standing speechless when another voice spoke up.

"That would be 'call an adult by *her* first name.'"

It was a young woman, fairly attractive, apart from looking like a walking culture medium for tetanus. Her body piercings were epic.

"It's on me, new guy." She smiled and I was relieved to see all her teeth were accounted for, none painted black. "There's no problem with that, is there, Sally? No contribution to delinquency?"

"No." Sally averted her eyes. Apparently my rudeness didn't hold a candle to the young woman's leather clothing, unnatural hair color and dermal accessories.

"You get a discount if you show your student ID when you pay," my rescuer continued. *"And let the Powers That Be monitor your caffeine intake,"* she added in an undertone.

While my new friend paid, I smiled and waited for my latte. I was glad Sally herself wasn't fixing the coffee. The foam on top might be soap flakes.

As she paid the tab, the decked-out damsel couldn't resist a final jab. "I'll bet you could avoid future problems if you'd have your last name affixed to your name tag, Mrs. *Oddchester.*"

I wanted to hide behind something but my benefactor — if that's what she was — led me to a booth.

She smiled as we sat. "Mister ... Bledsoe, is it?"

I grinned. "The same, dear lady. Thanks for the save. I didn't want to flash my note from Dean Barclay on my first day."

She dabbed milk foam from her nose ring. "That's a rare prize. I hear he hasn't signed his name in years. His personal staff has fifty rubber stamps of his autograph for emergencies."

"Mine's real," I said. "I watched him sign it."

She leaned closer. "Are you sure it was the real Barclay?"

I leaned closer, too. "My lawyer thought so."

She blinked, then smiled and reached to shake my hand. "Erin Bradley: English Lit."

I took her hand. "Scott Bledsoe: undeclared, but leaning toward foreign language."

"Which one?"

I took a deep breath. "All of them, I hope."

Erin's eyes widened behind the rings hanging over her eyes. "All of them? Aren't there like half a dozen?"

I sipped my latte. Oh, what Sheila had been keeping from me. "Fifteen in all," I said. "I won't do them all at once, though." I hoped for a laugh. Instead, Erin gulped and sat back. "So much for escaping notoriety," I said into my cup.

Her face changed and the sympathetic look was a hundred times better than Sally Oddchester's. "Sorry. I'm just used to being the center of attention."

I estimated how many ounces of metal were embedded in her skin and smiled.

"So, what ... is this like Make-A-Wish or something?" She gave me an appraising look. "No, I guess not. You don't look sick. I just meant ... I don't know."

"More like a one-man PBS series," I said, and framed the show's tag-line with my hands. "First grade to College Freshman in One Year."

"Gee," she said in a flat tone, "you-must-be-real-smart."

I grinned. "No more than any other freshman."

"Then why ... ?"

"A mishap on the day of my birth."

Erin smiled, but looked unsure. "Doctor with butterfingers?"

"No, but you might not believe the truth."

"I'm having coffee with a six-year-old college student," she said over the rim of her cup. "I'm still looking for the Candid Camera crew." She sipped through the foam. "Mishap," she mused. "Were you injured?"

"Not in the conventional sense. Just got a dose of something I wasn't supposed to get."

"Was your mom doing something weird?"

"Just the usual heavy breathing as far as I know." I couldn't believe my coffee cup was empty. Then I believed it. It was good but it had been little better than lukewarm. Erin didn't notice or didn't care. Maybe tepid java was the house specialty. "The weird part was a computer in the next room that couldn't cope with an electrical storm."

"Want some more?" she asked. A good hostess, she noticed my empty cup.

"No, thanks. My shoes probably won't touch the ground again today."

"So, there was a power surge," Erin continued. "What happened after that?"

I took a deep breath. "Ever see *Frankenstein?*"

"You mean ...?" She sat back. "No way!"

I nodded and smiled. "Yep. Totally way. The difference is that I didn't start off dead."

"And you didn't wind up with bolts in your neck."

"Or towel racks in my eyebrows."

She cackled.

"Anyway," I said, "we tracked down the guy responsible."

"The guy running the computer in the next room?"

"Yeah." I should have taken her up on the coffee. Maybe they'd microwave it or steam it or something. This little boy liked his coffee *hot*, for Pete's sake.

"I thought you were joking!" Her eyes darted around the room and her voice lowered to a near whisper. "Did that really happen? Like you said?"

I nodded. "Just like I said."

"Wow." Her buoyant manner disappeared. Even her pink hair seemed to dull. "That's like, I mean ... totally ... whoa."

"Let's hear it for the Georgetown English program." I raised my empty cup in a toast. "Too weird for you after all?"

"Hey, I don't give up on a guy because he's different. I don't want to go steady or anything, but ... "

"Oh, no," I said. "I couldn't think about a relationship right now. I've got my career to think of." We both chuckled.

We were interrupted by an earsplitting noise, a repeated, savage honking that sounded like Harpo Marx being beaten with his own horn.

The fire alarm. What a day.

With the alarm horn censoring Erin's yelps of profanity, we got up and aimed toward the exit. Customers were more annoyed than worried. I had thought the noise funny at first, but the flashing lights made it real.

"Attention, please. Calmly make your way to the nearest exit. The fire department is on the way."

Erin and I calmly threw our cups in the trash and joined the calm throng calmly making its way through the corridor to the cobbled sidewalks outside. The exasperated PA voice tried talking over the alarm twice more, then gave up. Students, employees and other, less identifiable people were moving, chatting and gossiping. Erin and I joined the swarm of chinos and corduroy like a couple of extras in a slow chase scene.

I halfway expected to be crushed in the exodus but managed to keep my head above the tide. I was surprised and a little disappointed when Erin didn't throw out a tattooed hand to rescue her new little buddy. Maybe her navel ring caught on someone's loose-knit sweater.

We poured out the doors into the student center's courtyard. I looked but couldn't see Erin, which was odd. She should have been visible through closed eyelids. I stuck around to see if she'd emerge.

She didn't emerge but the building manager did, half an hour later, to tell the few people who still gave a hoot that it was a false alarm. He disappeared back inside the building, muttering. I didn't feel like making friends with anyone else, so I headed back to my place.

Erin's disappearance didn't worry me as much as it would later. She was a grown woman with other things to do. Like analyzing something by Milton or Marlowe. Like working on a thesis.

Like telling the local grapevine that the new student who looks like a rugrat and talks like an adult isn't just smart, he's an experiment gone awry.

As I walked back to my apartment, I began to feel what Charlie called "hinky." Erin Bradley had appeared out of nowhere with an assist, bought me coffee and talked to me. Maybe it was a little too opportune.

Regardless, I welcomed the talk. So different from the chat room. Her voice was real and her facial expressions were not parenthetical. Over time, my little online cadre had adopted voices from inside my head. When Brik typed, I heard a public radio voice, like Robert Segal. Bare, for some undefinable reason, spoke to me in Janis Joplin's voice.

Nut, of course, sounded like Dwight Schultz as Murdock from *The A Team.*

Erin was none of the above. A real person. It was totally new, meeting and talking to someone who wasn't also meeting and talking to my mother and/or Charlie. My coffee morning with Erin Bradley had been my first ever conversation with an adult, outside of elementary school or business meeting, *sans* chaperon.

And I'd spilled my guts. Record time, too.

It would tear me up to think Erin was a shady character, maybe a brand new employee of the Association of the Defeated and Disgruntled from the Scott Bledsoe Auction.

Sheila's comment about *Newsweek* crossed my mind. Was Erin a journalist? Print journalist, of course. I didn't watch much TV, but I would have noticed pink hair on the evening news, especially on a reporter. Normal in L.A., but this was D.C. They weren't into that here. Yet.

In that guise Erin also claimed to be a fellow student, an English Lit major, to be exact. That would make her a sophomore or higher, unless she was lying. As I understood it, freshmen couldn't declare specific majors within a department. English, but not English Lit.

I opened my apartment door with my own key. On a key ring, not on a string around my neck. My new George McCullough autographed hardback — *Magellanic Cloud 9* — was on the coffee table. So far it wasn't totally unreadable.

Now, though, I wanted a different book: the student directory. I looked searched for a minute, then remembered Charlie borrowed it. At least I knew I wouldn't get it back with all the women's pictures rated on a one-to-ten system.

I knocked on his door. There was movement inside, but no answer. I rang the doorbell.

Charlie answered the door wearing his iPod earphones. Something loud, probably reggae, had covered up my knock. He wore the earphones out of courtesy to me. He was a true-blue fan of Bob Marley and his ilk, and they were okay in their own setting: out of my earshot. And he was forbidden to sing along. I told him if I heard one more *"Irie, mon!"* from his apartment, I was going to hire a Rastafarian witch doctor to make his tongue fall out.

"I wasn't singing." He yanked out the earphones. "Just reading."

"You still have my student directory?"

"Sure," he said, and replaced the earphones. "Come on in. Watch your step. I just did the floor."

I stepped inside and took off my shoes. The duplex was a nice place, complete with walnut flooring in the entrance halls. Charlie, who'd never had a hardwood floor, took serious care of his new one. He waxed the whole thing — all eighty some-odd square feet — twice before we'd lived there a week. I did well to vacuum my place once in that time. He might have been trying to attract a mate with his fine flat — "chick vortex" was a trendy term — and I knew Sheila would be impressed, but the chicks were more apt to think he suffered from OCD.

I scooped the directory from his kitchen table and flipped it open. Charlie was dishing up something from a tall soup pot on the stove.

"Want some gumbo?" he shouted. When he looked to me for an answer, I covered my ears and winced. "Sorry." He yanked out the earphones and draped them over his shoulder. "Want some gumbo?"

I was interested. "You made it?"

"Either that or Emeril found my extra key."

I wasn't tall enough to see into the pot. Charlie dipped me a bowlful. It did look good.

"You'll make someone a lovely wife one day," I said.

"Join me?" he said after swatting me with a dishtowel.

As we slurped gumbo, I flipped through the directory and looked at the tiny pictures of students. I was searching through the B's when Charlie spoke.

"You know, it's rude to read at the table."

Without looking up, I reached and flipped Charlie's own book closed. It was a heavy one, and that made me look up. I tried to look at the cover, but Charlie's hand came down over it. It looked like the one on my coffee table.

"Uh-uh," he said through chicken and okra. "Not until

you tell me what you're looking for." He aimed his spoon at the directory like a magic wand.

I wanted to laugh. I'd felt almost middle-aged most of my life. Since I moved to Maryland — or since I met Charlie — I felt younger, of an age with Charlie, who was almost twenty years older. Follow?

"I met a girl." I took a bite of gumbo. It was terrific, and I don't even like okra.

"You're having better luck than I am."

I didn't look up from my bowl. "That's because Sheila is still in Roanoke."

His spoon hovered. It dripped once before he spoke. "*Touché.*"

"Sorry," I said. I kept looking in my bowl, but I was hiding a blush. "I think I might have really screwed up today."

Charlie dropped his spoon. "You signed up for Columbia House Records."

"Please be serious."

"I am," he said. "I got in way over my head with those guys. What did you do?"

I flipped to the BRs. "I think I blabbed to the wrong person."

Charlie showed interest at last. "Was she pretty?"

"No," I said. "Yeah, I guess. Wait." I found the name, but the picture was different. Same face, minus hardware and war paint, plus a foot of dark brown hair. "Oh yeah," I said. "Very pretty."

Charlie took a peek. "I concur, Mr. Bledsoe. Bodacious, in fact. What gave you the hinky feeling?"

"I was at the coffee bar—"

"And signing my death warrant. I'm supposed to be watchdogging your java consumption."

"As I was saying," I sighed, "I was at the *juice bar*." I pointed at the directory. "That young lady, Erin Bradley, offered to buy my latte. Smoothie. Whatever. We talked for a little and the subject of majors came up."

"Of course."

"She's in English Lit. I told her I was in foreign languages and that started the whole mess."

Charlie grinned and sat back, gumbo forgotten. "And you just thought you would blend in with all the other collegians, did you?"

I shrugged. "I just didn't expect it to come up so soon. Maybe I'm spoiled, but I didn't think anyone would be so forward as to ask it."

He snickered. "Right on the heels of 'aww, are you lost?'"

"Yeah, go ahead and laugh. But while we were talking, someone pulled the fire alarm at the student center."

Charlie's eyebrows went up. "Really? A fire?"

"False alarm," I said. "Found out after. We left together, but I lost her, and the crowd wasn't all that big."

Charlie tapped the picture. "She looks like this? I'll help you look!"

I shook my head. "She's all punked out now. But you don't understand. It's not that she disappeared. It was the timing. Gone right after I spilled it."

"What, you think she had to tell someone else the amazing news right away?"

"Or write a blog," I said. "Or a news article. Or a report to the other side in the contract bid."

Charlie looked at the picture again and popped his lips a few times. That drove Sheila nuts, but it didn't bother me. I guess I understood it was the sound of a brain idling.

"I wouldn't worry about it," he said at last.

"You wouldn't?" I was dubious.

"Come on, man," he said, digging back into his gumbo. "You can't be afraid of everyone. Just don't tell everyone you meet." He took a bite and talked with his mouth full. "The way Leo tells it, you'll be all over the news by Thanksgiving, anyway."

There it was, again. One of those things so obvious it makes you feel impossibly stupid when you have to be reminded of it. Like looking for your glasses and finding them on your face. Or to stretch it even further, looking for your face and finding it right there on the front of your head.

All over the news by Thanksgiving. Joy. Well, I had asked for it, hadn't I?

"Charlie?"

"Mmm hmm?"

"You called me 'man,'" I said. "Thanks."

"Huh?"

"You said 'come on, man.' I think it was the first time. It was nice."

He grinned. "You're checking out *girls*. Welcome to the club."

24

Testing

I became acclimated to the Georgetown campus and my new residence in about three weeks. It took just about that long for my sense of obligation to kick in. I was ready to earn my keep, as it were.

Leo sure had earned *his* keep. After the initial few physical exams, I would be interviewed every weekday for an hour, undergo EEG and similar scans for another hour, then go to class the rest of the day. The project administrators — hereafter "The Doc Flock" — had arranged to leave my evenings free.

I thought it was gracious of them until Leo assured me it was a stipulation of the laws for employing a minor. X hours working meant Y amount in school and Z amount off duty. I said I meant I expected them to try squeezing more out of me than they were allowed. Leo said I was being cynical, but he said it with a hint of admiration.

II

Got up. Showered. Spent a few moments wondering where my razor was. Ate breakfast, just cereal and fruit in my own kitchen, but Charlie promised omelets later that week. Then off to class.

At nine a.m., Monday, Wednesday and Friday, I enjoyed a three-hour lecture in remedial geometry. I never suspected Georgetown had *any* remedial programs, but apparently everyone has his own strengths and weaknesses. Leo was a successful lawyer, but his paperwork contained boatloads of spelling errors. He said they were typos, but after the third "indefinate," I told him he wasn't fooling anyone.

After lunch, the real fun began. I treated it like a personally-tailored *Jeopardy!* but without the cuteness or pesky answer-to-question format.

Did I dream in black and white?

Did I have conflicting religious or philosophical beliefs?

Did any of my inherited knowledge come and go?

Did I notice traits I had thought were my own but then realized were inherited?

I answered the last one with a little joke.

"You mean like the fear of impending menopause?" If they hadn't laughed, I would have made plans to call the whole thing off. They chuckled, though. It was comforting to know that despite their stuffed shirts, they did have their ticklish spots.

After the first Q and A, I went to the University hospital for medical tests. Charlie took me. I told the Doc Flock I didn't get into cars with strangers. They laughed.

I was assured the first batch of tests would be the worst. I hoped they were right. I had skull x-rays, PET scans, MRI's and functional MRI's during which they asked me questions and watched my brain respond.

Worst of all was the lumbar puncture. I called time-out when they brought out the syringe tipped with a sharp flagpole. But someone had theorized some unique property in my cerebrospinal fluid might have facilitated the transference of data from EM radiation to brain memory. It was why I was there, so I bore it.

"This is scary," I said as they folded me in half. "Isn't there some other way of getting this stuff out?"

"Are you scared of needles?" the assisting medical student asked. Her name tag read "Gina Freytag."

"Just pain," I grunted. "I don't think this qualifies as 'non-invasive.'"

III

My medical duties were limited to two hours a day, but that did not include my visits to the shrink. I didn't see the need, but the Doc Flock insisted. Colleges accepted few very young students, they said, and with few exceptions, they suffered from depression. I didn't think I had anything to worry about. My future was so bright, as the song said, I had to wear shades.

My shrink had no bothersome stereotypical qualities, like an Austrian accent. She was girlish, in her mid-thirties, and I liked her right away. "Afternoon, Scott," she said. "I'm Cynthia Westbrook." She led me to a pair of chairs facing each other at angles, as if for a TV interview.

"Hello, Dr. Westbrook."

"You can call me Cynthia, if you like." She beckoned for me to sit.

I'd like to call you the future Mrs. Scott Bledsoe, I didn't say. There was no sexual attraction, of course. My body was far too young. But she was so attractive and welcoming, I couldn't help a little infatuation. Two visits later, if she had asked me to run away with her to Monte Carlo, saying no would have been difficult.

"Are you okay, Scott?"

I quit staring. "I've never been to a therapist before."

"And you already spend a lot of time answering personal questions."

I nodded.

She smiled. "We can talk about me, if you would prefer." Except for my school teachers, I hadn't been around many women, young or old. Sheila had her own charm and good looks, but Cynthia Westbrook was very different.

Take my mother, change the accent one hundred eighty degrees, give her a paler complexion, freckles, strawberry blond hair and a smile that spelunkers could use to light up a cave. That was my shrink. You're jealous, I can tell.

"Tell me about yourself," I invited.

She crossed her legs and held her knee. "I'm a fully qualified, accredited psychotherapist, but I think they chose me for my looks."

I wanted to say something witty, like *"how does that make you feel?"* Instead, I tried agreeing with her. "If you can trust the judgment of someone who has to look up to see your face, then you are quite a looker."

Cynthia turned pink. "Thank you, but I was referring to

my youthful appearance. I think their aim was to liken me to a teenage babysitter."

"For someone who lives in his own apartment?"

She pulled her feet up and sat nestled in her chair. "An age-old study shows young boys tend to get along best with teenage girls. The older the boys, the less compatibility, until the boys reach adolescence, and then the graph return to higher congeniality."

I smirked. "I've called my mother by her first name my whole life, at least in my head. From 'here comes Sheila to change my diaper,' to 'I better finish the laundry so Sheila can get some rest.' You make a good teeny-bopper, but I think it's the wrong medicine."

She looked at me for a long time.

"Do I need to be quiet?" I asked.

"No!" she laughed. "'You've come a long way, baby!' You know that one?"

"Yes," I said, "but 'L-S-M-F-T' is the one that pops out of my memory bank."

I had to explain the slogan to her.

"Okay," she said, "so what else pops out?"

I frowned. "About four hundred percent more than I would like."

"Yes, and you're here so we can establish the *you* inside the crowded loft upstairs." She smiled and swung her legs like a kid. Like me. I doubted she was even five feet tall.

"How?" I asked. "I even have trouble at breakfast because the integral parts of my brain want, in no particular order, doughnuts, cream of wheat, lumberjack rations, and Fruity Pebbles."

"For real?" Cute as that was, it wasn't encouraging to hear from the mouth of my therapist.

"Not always," I said. "If making decisions independent of the masses in my head constitutes having my own identity, then I am defined by Cheerios and peaches. Sometimes bananas."

She looked at me, a little longer than was necessary to read my expression. If she was gaping at my turn of phrase, she was being professional about it. Her next words were more what I expected from a shrink.

"Wonder what I'm thinking?" Her smile was probably supposed to be reassuring, but her tone was a little fake. She was the professional, though. I wasn't here to be entertained or even liked for who I was. I was being managed. Maintained, like an engine, so I didn't run out of oil and lock up.

I shrugged. "Probably the same thing everyone else thinks when I talk about metaphysics. But since you asked such an orchestrated question, I wonder."

"You wonder what?"

"If you want to know my answer or hear how I'll reach it."

She sighed and smiled. "I hate to admit it, but I was trying to figure out how to avoid staring at you in the future."

"Oh."

"It's unusual to hear a kid talk like that," she said.

"I thought everyone here knew what to expect."

"People know what to expect when they visit the Grand Canyon, too," she said, "but it still takes their breath away."

I grinned. "Comparing me to one of the Wonders of the

World?"

She tilted her head. "Answering the question you cleverly avoided."

"Sorry," I said with half a smirk.

"I've seen hyper-intelligent kids before." She raised her hand to stop me from correcting her. "I know your situation is unique. But even the smartest of those kids — some were so smart it was scary — couldn't really discuss the subject you just brought up."

"Metaphysics," I said. "Ontology, epistemology, et cetera." I cleared my throat and quoted, though I knew not from where. "'The fundament upon which all our knowledge and learning rests is the inexplicable.'"

Dr. Westbrook smiled. "Schopenhauer."

I blinked. "Really?"

"Yes, and you have a better grasp than you think. Most very young advanced program students could give precise definitions of those words, but you *understand* them. Plus, your overlapping, far-reaching knowledge gives you something they didn't have: subjective years of experience."

I frowned. "So, you're not amazed at my abilities. You just see me as a person with extra toppings."

She smiled and shrugged. "In a nutshell, yes. As normal medicine goes, I don't have anywhere to start."

"You mean as far as treating me?"

"Yes." I thought she'd break into some kind of jargon, but she was being honest. It caught me off guard. After so many hours with Leo Radcliffe, I looked for duplicity on all fronts. Was this a ploy or was she telling me, up front, that she was in over her pretty little head?

"So we have a problem." I said.

She nodded. "Of the kind Dr. Pott and his colleagues will view with suspicion."

"Suspicion?"

"Supposedly, I was handpicked for this job," she said. "First, for the reasons I mentioned before." Her frown made her look older.

"The babysitter persona?"

She nodded. "I also had the most experience and, forgive me, success with the super-intelligent young people that end up graduating high school before they're old enough to ride the big kid rides at Busch Gardens."

"So far, doesn't seem like a problem," I said.

She nodded again, in a scooping motion that took years off. "None of those kids — one thought I'd believe he had a four-figure I.Q. — was without problems. I shouldn't even mention these, but you won't tell, will you?"

I winked and she smiled.

"Most problems were anxieties, about what you'd expect. The need to impress, to outperform all their contemporaries. When those were conquered, they tried to outdo themselves. Raise the bar, set new records."

I sat forward. "Because if they stopped advancing ... "

She nodded. "They stopped being special. In their own minds, at least."

"I see."

"But with you," she said, "that approach doesn't work. If I were to ask you your biggest worry right now?"

"That after all the money is spent and the research is done, we won't have anything but expensive pictures of the inside of my head and a two hundred thousand-dollar education that'll get me far in the travel and tourism industry."

She smiled. "So, the world isn't crashing down on you, forcing you to impress everyone?"

"Doctor — Cynthia — at the moment, the mere fact of my existence impresses everyone who cares."

"Then let's take a look at something else that might be bothering you."

I winced. "My neighbor's — 'scuse me, *guardian's* — taste in music."

She touched the tip of her nose with a finger. "Bingo," she said. "Now we have something to talk about."

"Charlie?" I said, then gave her a dumb look. "Or his reggae?"

"You have a guardian, even though your mother is alive and well and you're on speaking terms."

"The emancipated minor thing." I smacked my forehead. I had hypnotized myself into thinking my therapy sessions were just timed conversations, enlightened or otherwise. Then I let slip that yes, I did in fact have fodder for therapy.

She didn't jump in and ask me how I felt about Sheila, but soon I was pretty sure The Doc Flock had found a way to get more time with their subject. The questions were familiar.

How old did I feel I was?

Thirty-five at least, but probably closer to forty.

Who did I feel like I was?

Trying to get a grip on being Scott, thanks.

Despite the sudden shift into professional gear, she was wonderful. After our third or fourth session, I easily could have asked her to marry me.

But she was my therapist. And she was married. And I was six. "It wasn't meant to be" didn't begin to cover it.

25

Partner

I

Doctor Willis, one of The Flock and a specialist in heuristic sciences, suggested I begin with the most difficult languages. Spanish, he said, would be a waste of my abilities. I disagreed. According to the news, the number of Mexican immigrants showed steady increase.

With the entire academic program open to me, one might wonder, why did I focus on foreign languages?

George McCullough theorized — and I agreed — that because I had a small child's brain, I would have a small child's powers of retention and absorption. If you think of everything a child learns between birth and first grade, it makes a four-year college degree look a little petty.

I was born already knowing those things, so my brain had been idling for most of my life. It only started revving when I began the self-investigation which ultimately led me to Georgetown University. I had been marking time, but now my brain was really being put to the test.

I had headaches almost at once. I spent a lot of time at lectures massaging my temples and popping children's dose ibuprofen tablets. I could concentrate on the lessons, but only just. After the first week of classes — and twenty hours' worth of headaches — I wondered if I had made a mistake. But give up after just a week? No way.

Of the languages Dr. Willis considered most difficult, Japanese looked the most attractive. The course instructor, Professor Margaret Ownbey, was a woman of some eighty years. Until the mid-nineties, she lived at the US Marine base on Okinawa, in Japan. She had taught Japanese to American servicemen, and she still expected her students to behave as though in uniform. All the students were somewhat diligent, but they weren't the crew-cut, straight-backed crowd Professor Ownbey had become accustomed to over the years. The venerable teacher had only to remark that slouching students would be ignored, not only during lectures but also during exams, and everyone's posture magically improved.

The course syllabus said students would be paired into study partners. I wondered who would fall all over himself to be my lab partner, but I was saved the trouble. Professor Ownbey made the class roll of thirty-six into eighteen pairs and projected the list onto the lecture hall screen.

"I assign the lab pairs in my classes," she announced my first Friday. "Only genuine schedule conflicts have the power to alter the list. If your assigned partner is a friend: congratulations, you are among the lucky few. If your partner is no longer a friend: too bad. This is a class, not couples therapy or Jerry Springer." There were a few chuckles. "Lastly, if your lab partner is a total stranger, take the opportunity and establish relations at once. Which category you fit into later is of no concern to your professor."

After class, during which I discovered my profound ignorance about Japan, I got up to find my lab partner. I thought it might take a while. It seemed a joke on the part of nature to surround me with nubile coeds and give me just the kind of body to make them say, "Awww, how cute!"

According to the list, my lab partner was Deborah Mulliniks. I hoped she didn't dress like Erin Bradley. Aesthetics aside, body piercing made me feel squeamish, like waking from a nightmare about fishhooks.

Young men and young ladies met with no apparent design. No thrown punches, no cries of outrage. Names and phone numbers were exchanged and some partners went forth together, if not arm in arm. The hall emptied so fast, I thought I heard the gurgle of a bathtub drain. Even Professor Ownbey had gone. I hoisted my book bag, prepared to spend the evening searching my directory for Deborah Mulliniks. I wished the professor had let us identify our partners before letting them escape.

Someone sighed behind me and I thought I might be spared that bit of clerical work. I turned to see an attractive young woman, tall with bright yellow hair. I smiled at her, but her mouth was the only part of her that didn't say "you gotta be kidding."

"Deborah Mulliniks?" I asked, just to be sure I was

ruining the right person's day.

She nodded, then shook her head, as though she believed she was being asked to babysit.

"Look at the bright side," I said. "At least I'm not an ex-boyfriend."

II

Fifteen minutes later, I was calling her Debbie, she was calling me Scott and we were on the walk betw. een the Language Arts department and the main hall of the university.

"I've wanted to be a linguist since the ninth grade and my Spanish teacher told me about Georgetown," she said.

"Excellent," I said and smiled. "You go, girl!" Making it to Georgetown was a testimony either to her ambition or to her parents' bankroll. To look at her, her ambition was full-body skin cancer by age twenty-five. Her blond hair had actual white streaks, but her skin was tanned nearly to the color of whole wheat bread crust. "I was told Spanish would be a waste of time for me."

"*Que lastima*," she said. "Spanish is loads of fun, and it's not all that hard."

"I'll get there, I guess."

"I'm a little behind," she said.

Due to Charlie's influence, I almost responded with a remark about her posterior. "How do you mean?"

"Well," she said and stopped walking, "I'm a freshman and I'm eighteen." With her hand, she measured my height against hers. I came up to the white belt on her skirt. "I don't think you're a dwarf."

"I think they prefer the term 'little people.'"

Debbie grinned. "But you're not one, right?"

"Right. I'm what you call a 'child.'" I made quote marks with my fingers and she laughed. If nothing else, I had Class Clown in the bag.

"So, you're on some kind of special exchange program or you've tested well."

"A little of both," I said, hesitant to say more. I remembered that the last person I gave the *Reader's Digest* version of my biography had disappeared. True, it was during the subdued pandemonium of a screaming fire alarm. And it had only been a few days. Since then, I was suspcious of everything. I had called Erin's number twice and left messages but received no reply. To avoid a comparable situation with Debbie, I contented myself with telling little and jesting much. "My elementary school was way advanced."

She giggled. "Now you're pulling my leg."

"Yep." I looked at the long, tan pins sticking out from under her miniskirt. "Let me put my books down and give the other one a good yank, too."

We walked and talked, but more about school than our personal histories. Debbie told me she was fending off advances from guys — and the occasional girl, which shocked her — right and left. She wasn't interested in serious relationships until she got through her first year and saw her GPA. "Then I might have time for a boyfriend," she said.

"Very wise," I said. "As I told someone not too long ago, my career is gonna have to come first. Sorry, ladies."

"You get all the study materials?" she asked.

I patted my pocket and nodded. The course materials included several CD's of vocabulary and phrases. I had transferred them to my new iPod, given to me by the The Doc Flock. It might have been a kind of bribe, but maybe it was just how affluent people treated little kids.

"Do you want to meet at your place?" she asked.

I winced at that. There would be no end of questions from Charlie if I showed up with a pretty girl before he even had a chance to show off his glossy floor. Debbie would be a little suspicious if I made her sneak in and out.

"Why my place?" I asked. That sounded rude and I winced. An impatient passenger in my conglomerate psyche had asserted himself over the polite guy who usually drove the bus. "Sorry," I said. "I have a neighbor I'd rather you didn't meet."

She smiled. "You're not ashamed of introducing me to your mother, are you?"

"No, no," I said. "I'm sure she'd be thrilled."

"So, my place it is," she said. "What's your cell number?"

I shrugged. So much for adult integration. "Sorry," I said. "I don't have one."

"Land line?"

I gave her my apartment phone number. It didn't have the three-digit prefix of a dorm phone line, but she didn't comment. She punched it into a tiny flip phone the exact shade of unchewed grape bubblegum. It looked like a little makeup compact.

"*Sayonara,*" she said and winked.

I grinned and waved. "Toyota Camry."

She laughed and walked away, and not to the tune of a fire alarm.

Someone in the back of my mind asked it because I was too chicken. *Would Debbie disappear, too?* I was paranoid. It was certainly too early to recognize a pattern.

I tried to forget it. Emotional stress affected the brain tests, I had been told. So far none of mine had affected the scans and I wasn't anxious to test the limits.

I avoided emotional issues and went over the material Professor Ownbey had covered in the lecture. I was happy to discover I could recite every phrase we had learned. It was no harder than any other subject. My headaches weren't brought on by a massive course load. It was just performance anxiety. With that worry gone, my headaches disappeared.

26

Absence Makes the Heart . . . etc.

I missed Sheila. At first I told myself it was just because she was part of my routine. I loved my mother, but natural mother/son closeness ended when I started on formula. I still called her every other day. Who knew I'd be homesick for the place I felt the most trapped?

Actually, the place I felt most trapped was first grade, and Sheila had rescued me from that.

I tried to return the favor. I knew her account numbers because I'd been keeping her checkbook for months. So I did a wire transfer from my new account and suggested she go house-shopping.

It didn't go over well. Sheila had resisted implications that she had sold me, but she also wasn't ready for me to support her. That was supposed to happen much later.

After three weeks, though, she relented, but only because she already planned to move closer. On a hunch, and long before my contract was secure, she had found a position with a junior college in Germantown, Maryland. Her life was no longer focused on me, and I believed it was better for both of us.

One Saturday, Charlie and I drove down to Roanoke to help Sheila pack. Correction, Charlie drove. I sat in the back, in a child safety seat.

Charlie had a '72 Camaro. I didn't really care for General Motors, but it was in good shape. I wished I could drive, but I could only sit in the back with reggae marching out of the speakers at me. Nine-plus more years until I could drive, unless the powers-that-be intervened.

Upon arrival, we learned Sheila had packed her own stuff. We were just there to help move. I couldn't lift much, but I had enough youthful coordination and energy for the hand truck.

During one trip to the van, I saw a little girl on the sidewalk. She looked familiar and after a moment I remembered her name.

She stopped a few yards away. "Hi, Scott."

I set the hand truck upright. "Hi, Barbara."

"You've been gone a long time."

It had been a while. I hadn't seen Barbara since just after New Year, when I decided to eject myself from school. If memory served, she was present the day Mrs. Miller tried to amputate her thumb with a desk drawer.

"Yeah," I said.

"Do you do home school now?"

She spoke so carefully, I thought. Sounded so grown-up. I remembered she was pretty bright and did good work at school. Her careful, well-bred speech was impressive.

"No," I said. "I'm going to a new school now."

She nodded and looked down at her feet. "School is a lot different without you."

I didn't know what to say. *Yeah, I bet* came to mind, but I kept quiet.

"Where is your new school?" Barbara asked. She looked at the sidewalk.

I smiled. "In Washington, D.C. Where the president lives."

Her eyes widened. "And you live here?" Then she looked at the boxes on the hand truck.

"I live there now," I said. "I'm just helping my mom move." She looked at me. "So she can be closer to me," I added and wished I had just kept quiet.

"Don't you live with your mom anymore?" She sounded sad.

Barbara was a nice little girl, but she asked too many questions. It was a little like a session with my therapist. I had to answer Barbara's questions carefully or there would be more questions.

Her gentle way was a little like Dr. West's. Quiet and calm. I must have been a brat to inspire such careful handling. Maybe she thought I was disturbed.

Kids don't say that, though. Maybe she thought I was *Looney Tunes. Cuckoo for Cocoa Puffs.*

"I live at the school," I said and cringed inside. So much for careful answers.

"Are there a lot of kids?"

I nodded and thought, college kids.

Barbara seemed at a loss for how to go on. "Well, bye-bye," she said, and left, just like that.

Kids are funny, I thought, and pulled the dolly up the ramp. I was just inside the van box when I heard a voice.

"Scott?"

I turned and saw Barbara standing on the ramp.

"Hi, Barbara." I almost told her not to play on the ramp. That wouldn't be a kid thing to do, but neither was stacking moving boxes in neat rows.

"I forgot to ask you a question," she said.

"What question?" I let the hand truck go. *Oh boy, I thought. What now?*

"When's your birthday?" she asked.

I blinked. "January 4th." Did she want to send me a card? How sweet.

"Where were you born?" she asked. With the grace and balance of a six-year-old, she walked up the ramp and stood in front of me.

"Here, in Roanoke," I said. "Roanoke" ended in a squeak when she grabbed the front of my shirt.

"Which *hospital?*"

"Memorial." I pried my shirt out of her grip. Under duress, I gave up some pretense of childhood. "What are you doing, kid?"

She grabbed my shirt again. "Does *MyAlterEgo* mean anything to you?"

At those words, some part of my mind expected immediate chest pains. I couldn't speak, but that was okay. Barbara wasn't finished yet.

She pulled me so close she could kiss me, or bite me. "Your birthday is the same as mine. We were born at the same hospital. We both had school issues. The timing is right." She stopped and took a deep breath. "I've been piecing it together for so long, this has to be right!" She shook me again. "Are you *MyAlterEgo?*"

I swallowed hard and nodded.

With a wordless sound of relief, she pulled me into a hug and squeezed all the air out of me. I had no idea a child could be that strong. She whispered all sorts of things I couldn't understand and kissed my face over and over. I thought she was drooling on me until she pulled back. Her cheeks shone with tears.

For all the piles of information in my head, I was slow on the uptake. A moment later, though, my own tears began. I returned her embrace and made my own sounds of relief.

We overcame our speechlessness and tried to speak at the same time. We clasped hands and looked into each other's eyes, each unwilling to let the other go. We were high on revelation, dreading the moment the drug would wear off.

Barbara released one of my hands to wipe her eyes. "I can't believe it."

"Me neither." An inherited habit made me stuff a hanky in my pocket every morning. I handed it to her and let my own face drip.

She dabbed at her eyes. "I waited so long to come and see you. To ask without your mom around. Does she know?"

"Yeah," I said. "She would have figured it out though. She's pretty bright." I smiled and squeezed Barbara's hands. "Did you?"

"Figure it out?"

"No, tell your parents."

She glanced up the road, toward her house. "I think it was

a relief to them, to understand why their little girl doesn't like playing with dolls but listens to the news every day without fail." She grinned. "It must be what coming out of the closet feels like."

I understood. "Sheila is very supportive, as much as a single mother could be in this situation."

Barbara smiled and it dawned on me why she reminded me of Sheila or Cynthia. Her smile was so ... grown-up. With a hint of something to indicate too much awareness in such a small person.

I suddenly understood why someone might find me disturbing, even if they didn't know the reason. I tried to act like a child, but at my most sullen moments, I was not cute.

"You know things?" I asked. "Things you shouldn't know? I mean, just to make sure we're on the same page."

"Remember that day in the chat room when you were ranting about 'unnecessary schooling' and I tried to get you to call me?"

I almost collapsed in a heap. "You're *BarelyThere*?"

She smiled and nodded. "Guilty."

I felt faint and put a hand to my head. "I didn't know what to think when *BarelyThere* started getting ... friendly. I had premonitions of fending off a stalker."

Her hands went to her mouth. "So that's why you went quiet on me!"

"Sorry about that," I said. "It was Sheila I was worried about. I was using her ISP."

"I understand," she said. And that was the best part. She really did.

We were silent for a few moments, letting everything sink

in. I looked at her and noticed things that had slipped by me before. For instance, she didn't wear jeans and a sweatshirt like a normal kid. She wore a mock turtleneck, cardigan, wool slacks and loafers. If she wore glasses, it wouldn't have surprised me to see them on a chain around her neck.

"What happened to us?" she asked. She put both hands to her forehead and sighed. "Please tell me you know something."

"A little bit," I said. The van was a bad place to have this meeting. Too easy for someone to listen in. I didn't want anyone to know about Barbara yet. If this was a dream, I wanted to enjoy it as long as possible. "Do you remember a Disney film with Kurt Russell, *The Computer Wore Tennis Shoes?*"

Barbara's eyes widened. She recalled, as I had, the early seventies film in which a high school student is mentally enhanced after being shocked by a big computer. Her hands covered her mouth and she spoke from behind them. "You can't be serious!"

"I am," I said.

"But computers don't know the things we know!" She whispered, but it wasn't quiet.

I pulled her hands from her mouth and held them. "It was the simplest analogy I could think of," I said. Briefly, I told her about my new friend, George McCullough.

"Are you telling me that our brains were juiced by a computer run by an eccentric science fiction author?"

"Given all you know," I said, "is this any harder to believe?"

Barbara put her head in her hands and closed her eyes. "I

kept thinking I had been reincarnated. That I was schizophrenic in a former life. Too many things didn't match up, like loving chocolate one day and hating it the next."

I had experienced that one myself. I even told Charlie about it. He told me I was Hershey Bipolar.

"I know what you mean," I said. "But it's all true. We've done tests to confirm our suspicions. They might not hold up in court, but I believe the answers."

"Are you really going to school?" she asked. "Or spilling your guts to the government?"

"School," I said. "Georgetown University, foreign languages major."

Her eyebrows shot up. "So living in Washington, D.C. doesn't have anything to do with Big Brother keeping an eye on you?"

One of my — our — "donors" harbored a special affinity for George Orwell. Barbara's thought was so close to mine it might as well have been the same thought. After all, it did come from the same source.

"Couldn't they keep an eye on me anywhere?" I asked. "I may be an emancipated minor, but I've got babysitters out the wazoo: all the guys from Johns Hopkins, Cynthia West, Charlie, the judge presiding over my emancipation ... and don't forget Sheila."

"The government hasn't put their fingers in the pie?" She looked skeptical.

"Someone from the National Institute of Health dropped by," I said, "to find out what's been accomplished. Some day, they might try to recreate what George McCullough did by accident. The military isn't interested in me."

Her gaze was very heavy. "You've given it some thought. I didn't even bring up the military." For all her momentary joy, Barbara looked troubled.

"I'm not sure I get you," I said. I was hip-deep in denial, though.

We both jumped when a voice called from behind Barbara.

"Who's your friend, Scott?" Charlie asked, his arms full with a stack of boxes. He must have tired of waiting for the hand truck.

Barbara didn't make a sound but pantomimed zipping her lips. I gave her a tiny smile and a nod.

"This is Barbara," I said. "She was in first grade with me at school." My tight face reminded me of the tears I had just shed. I hoped Charlie couldn't see. It would be easier for Barbara to get away "Scott-free," pardon the pun, if he failed to notice anything odd.

So I shot Charlie a look and rolled my eyes while gesturing to Barbara with a tilt of my head. He got the message I wanted him to get. *Kids!*

"Nice to meet you, Barbara," Charlie said, now more concerned with getting the boxes in a neat stack. For a moment his back was turned.

Seizing the opportunity, Barbara took a pen and pad from her pocket and jotted something down fast, talking as she did so.

"Here's my address, Scott." She pulled the sheet from the pad and handed it to me. She had indeed written her address on it, but before she had even approached me. She just added a few words.

Call me!
Ask for BarelyThere
Use a safe phone
Big Brother is watching!

And there was a number. After a glance, I shoved it in my pocket.

"I'm not allowed to use e-mail 'til I'm ten. My parents like me to write letters and mail them with stamps. If I write you will you write back?" She smiled and oscillated at the waist with her hands behind her back, playing 'little girl' very well. Her tone was so solemn I almost giggled. The effect was compounded when she stuck out her lower lip.

"It sounds like fun," I said, seeing Charlie's shoulders vibrate with silent laughter. I was glad he was amused.

"I hafta go now," Barbara said, watching Charlie as she sidled toward the back of the van and through the door. Though she still wore a troubled expression, she blew me a kiss.

And I think I fell in love.

With a six-year-old girl.

If not for my own age, I'm sure you might call me a sicko.

You might anyway, but then you haven't been there, okay?

27

Comparing Notes

I

After we got to Germantown and unloaded the van, Charlie treated us to supper at an Italian place.

More than once he expressed sorrow that I could not partake of *il vino*.

"I mean," he said *sotto voce*, in keeping with the theme, "we can't have you getting tanked and spilling the beans. *In vino veritas* and all that." If not for Charlie's silly streak, I might have thought him a little drunk, but he hadn't even finished his first glass of wine.

I didn't know what he was on about. My condition wasn't a state secret, nor had I been required to sign a non-disclosure agreement. I was preoccupied with a different secret, so I didn't respond to Charlie's banter.

"What," he said, "no pithy Latin phrases?"

I kept my eyes on my linguini. *"Requiescat in pace,"* I said. Give it a rest.

"Is something wrong, Scott?" Sheila asked.

I shook my head and laid my fork down. I didn't want anything in my mouth.

Charlie sobered right away. Almost. "Is it your girlfriend?" he asked. "I mean, 'your friend who is a girl?'"

I rolled my eyes, hoping the interrogation would stop.

But then Sheila picked up the thread. "What girl?" She was smiling.

"Barbara Davis," I said. I nudged my fork around the plate. "You know, from Lacrosse Drive? First grade?"

She nodded, smiled bigger.

"She cornered Scott in the U-Haul," said Charlie. "I think she wanted to cover him with kisses."

That's just what had happened. Sheila didn't see me blush, though, because she was making a face at Charlie.

"She just wondered where I'd been." I didn't like keeping my kinship with Barbara secret from Sheila, but the secret was only half mine. When and if Sheila found out, she and Barbara's folks might form a support group.

I could confide in her for one thing, though. When Charlie excused himself to the little boys' room, I spoke.

"Can you get me a cell phone?"

Sheila blinked. "A cell phone? Scott, what's —"

"Long story." I followed Charlie to the bathroom with my eyes. "I need a phone and it has to be secret. A prepaid cell phone will work."

She looked at me, watched my mouth.

"You're serious?" she said. "Of course you're serious, and I'm wasting the moment." She rattled her head and grasped my hand. "Of course I'll get it."

I breathed a sigh of relief. "Thanks." It was hard to keep a neutral face while squeezing her hand with wild gratitude. "Whatever you do, don't tell Charlie."

She leaned close. "So I gathered. But why not?"

"There's a ... " I fumbled for words. "There's been a development."

"I see."

"And I mean it," I said. I stared into my plate. "Don't tell Charlie."

"Scott, I —"

"Listen," I said behind my napkin. "You might think you're doing it for my own good, but it won't be. If I had a nickel for every book I've read or movie I've seen when someone reneged and caused a catastrophe ... " I paused to calm down and sip my soda. I gestured to the restaurant. "we could eat here every day for a week."

Sheila was silent.

"Please try not to decide I'm overreacting. I need to have someone I can trust absolutely." My fist clenched a handful of tablecloth. Objects on the table moved toward my hand as if by gravity. "I want that person to be you."

"I'll keep silent, Scott," she said. "Until you say otherwise."

I spotted Charlie talking to someone at the bar. Whoever it was had his full attention. I wondered, did he know anyone around here?

"You remember what I said that first day? About what worried me?" I gave Sheila a short, apologetic frown. "This whole deal is bigger than we imagined. I think I got us — you — into something." I squeezed her hand. "Until I find out, I have to keep tabs on everything." I glanced at Charlie again.

"So I can distinguish friends from enemies before anyone knows I'm getting bad vibes."

Sheila looked at our friend standing by the bar. "Charlie better be on the good half of that list, or I'm liable to kill him."

Her words sent a shiver through me. I turned to see her making a face, watching Charlie's approach. She looked to be in pain. "Quick," she whispered, "say something funny. I need a real smile. I can't fake one right now."

II

Later, Sheila had Charlie stop at a drugstore. She went in alone for a few last-minute household goods. I asked her to get me something for a tummy ache. When she returned, she handed me a small bag over her shoulder. I got out the bottle of children's antacid, but I left the tiny wireless phone in the bag.

III

The next day, I fled my math class at the moment of dismissal. There was time before my daily session with The Doc Flock, so I searched for a secluded spot and wound up on the top floor of a nearly deserted building. I ducked into the men's room, turned on my new phone and dialed Barbara's number. If not for the note paper with her handwriting, I might have dreamed our meeting.

At the first ring, I had second thoughts. Third and fourth

thoughts when a man's voice answered.

"Hello?" Deep, deep rumble, like James Earl Jones.

I cleared my throat and winced when it echoed. "I'm, uh, calling for ... BarelyThere."

A few seconds of silence on the other end.

"One moment, please," said the voice.

A moment later, Simon and Garfunkel sang into my ear. There I was, on the top floor of an empty building, hiding from pretty much everybody and listening to "Me and Julio." I almost tapped my foot to the music to ward off creepiness.

"Ego?" Barbara answered. *"Is that you?"*

I was so unused to hearing the moniker aloud I almost forgot it was me. "Uh, yeah."

"That was quick." She sounded impressed.

"I'm not getting any younger."

"Oh, funny," she said and chuckled. *"Before we go on, where are you calling from?"*

"A bathroom," I said.

"No, which phone?"

"Prepaid wireless, bought just for the occasion."

"Don't tell me you just went into Radio Shack and —

"No," I said. "Sh- ... my mom."

"Yes, best if we don't use names, just in case someone's listening." She was silent for a five count, then ... *"What did you tell her?"*

"That I needed a private number. I did not divulge that the little girl down the street is leading a secret life much like my own."

She laughed. *"That's what it amounts to, isn't it?"*

"Sorry if I worried you, but I had to pick someone to trust, her or Ch– ... this other guy."

"Who's the other guy?"

That question cued the abridged version of everything I've recounted thus far. When I talked about leaving home, she broke in.

"Remember when I asked if the government had a hand in your new lifestyle?"

"Yes, and I told you the military wouldn't be interested in me, meaning a six-year-old child. But you were about to say something else."

"Caught that, did you?"

"Thanks. Remember what you were going to say?"

"Look," she said, *"you're not going to stay six years old."*

"Thank God. I think I've outgrown it."

"I'm serious," she said. *"If they could begin training soldiers at age six, just think what they could accomplish."*

"That already happens," I said. "Middle Eastern warlords and Islamic radicals do it. Except what they get by sending six-year-olds to war is a bunch of tiny coffins. Or a bunch of shell-shocked, spoon-fed kids."

"Only at first," she said.

"But that doesn't make it less wrong," I said. "You have a different suspect than the military, though."

"You're a sharp kid."

"It pays the bills. Who'd you mean?"

"The alphabet groups. CIA, NSA, DOD, etc."

"DEA," I said. "FBI?"

"Sure," she said. *"Even them."*

"Why?" I asked. "Why would they be interested in a six-year-old?"

"*You can't guess?*"

"Humor me."

"*Same thing,*" she said. "*Early start on training. You're going to Georgetown, right?*"

"Yes."

"*Studying ... ?*"

"Languages." I began to feel sick.

"*You know the same things I do, so you should remember that Georgetown has cornered the market on State Department training.*"

"Yeah."

"*So if you took a certain six-year-old and taught him languages until his head bulged, because he had both an adult's world view and a prepubescent child's learning curve ...*"

I mulled it over. "You've given this some thought."

"*You bet.*"

"Who answered the phone?" I asked.

"*That was me,*" she said.

"I'm jealous. My voice won't be that deep for another ten or twelve years. Maybe never."

"*It's a synthesizer I use when I have to be an adult. It works better than when I pretend to be a grown woman.*"

"Nifty. Wish I had one."

"*I had help getting mine.*"

"Sounds way better than Radio Shack."

Several questions had occurred to me. I asked the most bothersome first.

"You haven't been approached by anyone, have you?

"*Like who?*" She sounded a little spooked.

"Like scientists." Barbara's birth was a matter of public record, and though her mother's stay at the hospital should have been protected under HIPAA laws, this *was* the twenty-first century.

"You're thinking they might check me out because I was in the same place at the same time?"

"Yeah," I said. "Charlie and I — mostly Charlie — guessed out how the transfer happened. I can't believe The Doc Flock —"

"The what?" Barbara asked.

"The doctors in charge," I said. "They wouldn't think of looking for other ..."

"Victims?"

"I was going to say 'recipients,'" I said, "but with the original occurrence being so unlikely, maybe they thought two would be inconceivable."

"I think it's probably because I played nice with other kids, didn't say derisive things to teachers, and didn't make one flatten her thumb."

"It got me out, didn't it?" I said, "which reminds me. Didn't you ... ?"

"What?"

I swallowed. I didn't taste any foot, and I didn't want to start. Not now, and not with her. "When you first came to me and ... dropped the bomb, you listed ways were were alike: born at the same hospital, born on the same day ... issues at school."

"You want to know how I missed out on a gold star."

"If you don't want to tell me ... "

"You don't have to walk on eggshells," she said. Her voice was

deep and soothing. *"I'm as anxious as you for answers. You won't offend me by asking personal questions."*

"So what happened?"

She sighed. *"I snapped."*

"Snapped?"

"Yeah," she said. *"Fortunately, six-year-old snaps are over faster than adult snaps. We just don't have the strength. Mostly I got a lot of broken nails and a skinned forehead."*

I was silent for a few moments. Barbara asked if I was still on the line.

"I'm here," I said. "How did you ... I mean, why—?"

"Why did I snap?"

"If your school career was anything like mine, I can guess. I just didn't figure you for the type."

"What's that supposed to mean?" Her tone was bitter. Or I might have been tasting foot after all.

"Sorry," I said. "That didn't come out right. I meant you seem so ... with it."

"Oh, okay."

"You must have done some good damage control if they let you back in."

"It wasn't really a choice. I would have gone the home school route, too, but I needed out of the house. Starbuck's was out of the question, so school it was."

"I'm sorry."

"Even if I — if we had found someone like your friend, I don't know how much I could have trusted them."

"I think I knew I'd have to trust somebody, someday. I went with the guy we approached rather than someone who approached us."

"But the more who know, the more there are who can talk," she said. *"One or two people can keep a secret. But five people? I don't know anything about sociology, but I know human nature. Someone will spill it, especially with gossip pits like internet chat rooms."*

"Look who's talking," I said, but my heart wasn't in it. A detail about my educational exploits occurred to me and I was loath to reveal it. Better to wait. We had enough problems.

"Hello? Still there?"

"Yeah," I said. "Just thinking."

"Well, don't think your airtime away."

"What I was thinking," I said, "is I'm already in the system, so there's no hope of keeping my own secret."

"If only we'd caught on sooner."

"You give me too much credit," I said. "I was almost too proud to ask my mommy for help. But now I'm in the system. You're not. Let's try to keep it that way."

"What do you mean?"

"Let's keep your options open. We both have extra people in our heads, but so far I'm the only one who has extra people on his tail."

"That's a relief," she said. *"I thought you were going to say we couldn't talk anymore."*

"Never," I told her. "I couldn't stand it. When you came to me ..." I couldn't finish.

She could.

"We only have each other. Of everyone in the world, you're my one and only peer."

We were silent for a moment.

"I should go," I said. "I spend too much time on bathroom trips and they'll stop examining my head and focus on my other end."

"Can't you just tell them you want to be by yourself?"

"Better to claim constipation for now. It's common enough in young boys. The university admin staff worries about depression in very young students. They might worry if I start demanding alone time." As if they could fault me for wanting everyone out of my hair.

It came time to say goodbye, which we did with minimum mush. I looked at the phone after we ended the call. Eighteen minutes. Nine hundred eighty-two left.

I could have talked to Barbara for hours. It was the first time I had been completely candid with anyone but Sheila and Charlie. I hated to end the call but was relieved all the same. I was so desperate for honesty my mouth might have kept running and blabbed my deepest, darkest secrets.

Like the thing I remembered near the end of the call.

I had taken a high school equivalence exam prior to beginning my "work" for The Project, so compulsory school attendance was moot. I went to Georgetown University as part of the compensation package agreed to by all the institutions involved ... but it hadn't been their idea. Nor had the foreign language program.

It had been Charlie's.

28

Paranoia

I faced a problem. The seed of doubt had been planted —
thanks a heap, Barbara — and it sprouted overnight. I had
become a conspiracy theorist. My eyes were on everybody.

For instance, Dr. Pott, the neurologist, asked a number of
questions I would have thought more appropriate for my
sessions with Dr. West, the psychologist.

Dr. Pott — I couldn't help giggling at the surname when I
learned his first name was "John" — never wore a lab coat.
Nor did he wear the overtly nondescript suit one associates
with government agents, whatever team they claim. Instead,
he wore a ca. 1970 three-piece charcoal pinstripe suit and
asked me about my knowledge and my ability to focus, while
taking whole minutes to spit out his questions.

"Do you ever experience, um," he searched for a word,
"anxiety — foreboding, perhaps — that is incongruous with
your ... situation?"

I wondered if Dr. Pott knew he was bowling in Dr. West's lane. "I got a little edgy around April 15," I said.

"Yes, income tax is and should be beyond the scope of a child." He made a note and smiled at me. He probably thought it a kind expression, but after talking to Barbara, I couldn't take anything at face value, pardon the pun. The smile creeped me out so I looked down at my lap.

"Anything else?" he continued.

I went with an old favorite. "I already mentioned fear of menopause. Maybe … regret over never having children?"

Dr. Pott and his constituents smiled. At my discomfort, I couldn't help thinking. "Have you had other feelings of a … cross-gender nature?"

I shrugged. "Odd feelings sometimes. I can't define them but I keep hoping they can be explained by hormones, or maybe the lack thereof." I shivered thinking about it.

Dr. Pott looked at the others and they reached a silent consensus. "I believe we will address those at another time," he said.

I hoped my sigh of relief would be taken for fatigue. Barbara had heightened my wariness, and while my comment about menopause and childlessness was true, I decided to ration the release of data. If I needed to keep silent about something, I feigned tiredness or emotional stress, the latter being the truest claim I made the whole session.

Running out of ammo scared me. As long as I had something to say or give, I was useful. What might happen if I suddenly dried up? *Sorry, ladies and gentlemen, the cupboard is bare.*

What would they do if I stopped volunteering information, try to take it from me? I had read enough books on the subject – well, not *read* precisely. When the government can't get what it wants by asking, it asserts the old "Eminent Domain" clause. The more squeamish bureaucrats might rationalize it by claiming they were drafting me.

I didn't want to be drafted. I was already in a situation I didn't volunteer for. Not the "research" gig, but the absence of a true identity.

Knowing myself included: what I knew, how I learned it, how I felt about it as I learned it, how I felt about it after mulling it over, etc. I knew loads of information, but in amongst the clerical skills and automotive minutiae, there was almost no feeling of Scott Bledsoe. Some people might see the data and skills as a gift, but I could take them for granted someday because like my hair, I didn't earn them. They just came with my head.

Something else bothered me. I enjoyed my phone conversation with Barbara, and it was extremely cathartic, but it scared me how reckless we'd been. We didn't use our real names, but we talked about home situations — mine, mostly — as if our call was not secret at all.

We had not spoken in code. We had not disguised our voices. If anyone listening didn't already know our on-line identities, they'd figure it out, given at least half a brain.

My friend and I had been unwise, and I didn't relish telling her.

29

Women

The phone became my security blanket. It rarely left my hand.

I struggled to keep from calling Barbara every time I had a new idea, as if she were an interactive diary. Sometimes I forgot she was doing her thing while I did mine. She never came out and told me to chill, but I'm sure she wanted to. She didn't tell me just what she was doing, either, but I was sure it involved her parents. I began to suspect they had more than just a conspiracy theorist's interest.

Instead of calling Barbara every five minutes with my idea *du jour*, I wrote notes to read her later. I almost wrote them in code but decided just to keep them vague. I was writing my vague notes Monday when a sharp voice nearly made me drop my pencil and notebook.

"There you are!"

I looked up and saw Debbie Mulliniks, hands on hips, making a face at me.

I managed not to drop everything I held. "What'd *I* do?"

"Didn't show up. Didn't answer the phone." Her nostrils flared. "You're supposed to be my *study partner.*"

I had forgotten our Sunday night study date. In my defense, I had a good excuse. Finding out I was not the only sufferer of my peculiar problem had driven mundane things right out my head.

I raised the notebook and covered my face. "Sorry." I peeked around the notebook. "I was called away."

"Uh-huh," she said, then looked at my hand. "And I thought you didn't have a cell phone."

"What?" I looked at my hand. "Oh, I just got it. Last night." When we should have been bouncing Japanese phrases off one another.

"I see," she said.

"Yeah, here." I'm sure I looked disheveled and a little evasive but I pulled up the number and read it off to her. She took it down and I was glad. "I'm really sorry about last night. I spent the weekend helping my mom move."

"Doesn't she live in Roanoke?" Debbie asked.

"Not anymore." I peeled the phone from my hand and pocketed it. "She moved closer. I had no idea she would. At least not this soon."

Like in the Eagles song, I had seven women on my mind. Barbara — who definitely counted as a woman — Prof. Ownbey, Sheila, Dr. Westbrook, Sally Oddchester — who still wouldn't sell me coffee, even decaf. I wanted to go to the coffee bar wearing a scarlet "C" on my navy blazer, but I wasn't sure she'd get the reference — Debbie Mulliniks, and Erin Bradley.

I meant to discuss Erin with Barbara. Erin's disappearance looked more and more suspect. No doubt Barbara would speculate that the fire alarm had been sounded to disrupt our introduction.

But Debbie was right there and deserved my undivided attention.

"Are you happy she's closer?" she asked. Her hostility was gone. "I don't know how I'd feel if my dad moved up from Savannah."

"I'm about as happy as I can be for someone who is still sore from carrying boxes." We started walking.

"You didn't have to move anything heavy, did you?"

"I left that to my pal, Charlie. He'd try to carry a piano if she asked him." Charlie had insisted Sheila let the menfolk move the boxes, which left him doing most of the moving. Sheila ended up doing little actual work but worrying herself into exhaustion over her breakables.

"Where did she move to?" she asked. "You said she was closer."

"Just outside of town," I said. I almost said more but held my tongue.

I thought I saw Erin Bradley walking toward the coffee bar, though I had to look twice to be sure. The sunlight glinting off her every surface should have been a dead giveaway, but after three weeks of staring at overhead projections, PowerPoint presentations and good old chalkboards, I began to suspect I needed glasses. Funny. If I'd still been at elementary school, someone else might have noticed before I did.

"Excuse me," I told Debbie, "but I have to go talk to

someone while I've got the chance." I glanced at Debbie, but only out of courtesy. I wanted to hurry and catch the elusive Ms. Bradley in the open, where there was no fire alarm to separate us.

"Well, okay," Debbie sighed. "Don't you be late or Ownbey's gonna go all *banzai* on you."

"Don't worry." I took off at a jog. "I'll be there."

Erin had reached the door when I stepped up beside her.

"Allow me," I said, and pulled the door open. She stopped and looked at me for a moment, as if trying to place me. Then her face hardened.

"What are you doing?" she asked, her voice low. She checked around us for eyes. *Like anyone thinks we're dating,* I thought. Or maybe she worried someone might think I was *her* kid.

"Where'd you go the other day?" I ushered her through the door and then followed. "At least let me return the favor about the coffee."

Erin did not look tough as she had at our first meeting, despite all her flair and the flesh accessories she wore. She shrank into the alcove but her eyes stayed in the corridor. For someone who dressed to attract attention, she was being awfully shy.

"What's the matter?" I whispered and followed her to the alcove, where we hid. "You don't look happy to see me."

"Good guess," she said. She looked at me once or twice but kept her eyes moving. "I can't be seen with you."

"Did I scare off all the guys?"

She stepped closer. "No, but you might scare off my scholarship!" She didn't yell, but in the enclosed space I almost felt my hair blown back. "I need you to stay away from me!"

"I'm beginning to see that," I said. "Can you at least tell me why?"

She still didn't look right at me, but her face softened. "Somebody slipped me a note during the fire alarm the other day." She looked at me again. "It said I wasn't to 'fraternize' with you or my financial aid would be discontinued."

I frowned. "We weren't exactly fraternizing. We had just met."

She huffed a hot breath. "Yes, and normally I would think this was just a dirty prank. But the note included a detailed list of all my financial assistance sources. Somebody seriously wants me to steer clear of you."

I pushed at her elbow. "Then for heaven's sake, go! Don't get yourself in more trouble."

She looked at me for a moment, undecided. "Okay," she said. "Sorry, but I can't let anything happen to my funds."

I nodded. "Supposedly, I've got connections. I'll see if they can do anything about it." I made a shooing gesture. "Go on. Get."

She turned to enter the coffee bar, but she turned back. "Mr. Bledsoe?"

"Yeah?"

"Thanks for understanding."

I shrugged. "I'm getting a lot of practice."

30

Alarm

Erin's plight was upsetting, but it reminded me of Barbara's admonition to keep my head down. If I was being watched more during my off-time than during my interviews, and acted as though I knew it, someone might consider damage control. Probably the kind of thing that was harder to ignore than to discover.

When the office door opened, I looked up from my magazine. The woman looking at me was not Cynthia Westbrook. "Hello, Scott," she said. "I'm Dr. Oesche. Please come in."

Damage control? I thought. I stood and tossed a Newsweek half my age onto the coffee table. "Forgive me, but should I know you? My sessions with Dr. West are a closed affair." Of course, all sessions were supposed to be, but this was *me.*

"Dr. West had a family emergency and had to go out of town for a bit. I'll be taking over your sessions for a while."

"Is she okay?" I got conspiracy vibes, but the story could

be true. Cynthia had become a friend, but I didn't know anything about her family.

"The note just said she would be on leave for several days." Dr. Oesche wore a tight, clinical smile, as if she had only a passing acquaintance with bedside manner.

She held the door and I stepped into the office through a cloud of perfumes and feminine scents women apply to smell fresh. From the amount used, she might have been trying to conceal a dead animal in her pocket.

Dr. West held sessions in two sling-seat directors' chairs, like old Barbara Walters interviews. I sat in my usual spot. Dr. Oesche took the chair opposite me, but I could tell it was not her first choice. She was the new factor in the equation, and I almost felt sorry for her. Paranoia and her assault on my nose helped me get over it.

Seated, she seemed warmer but still unsure of me. People meeting me for the first time usually wore big, fake smiles. Cynthia West was an exception. And Charlie, of course. When he wasn't teasing me about my height or lack of body hair, Charlie treated me like one of his intellectual college buddies. Cynthia treated me like any of her adult patients, with the solidarity of someone who has graduated from childhood.

And then there was Sheila.

Sheila treated me the way a mother treats her child, even one who's well into adulthood.

From the start, Dr. Oesche seemed to humor me, as if I were putting on an act and it would be politic for her to play along. Maybe I was paranoid. Maybe it was just professional behavior.

"According to Dr. West's notes, you have feelings of confused identity." She wore that odd smile that made me uneasy. "What is it you feel like?"

I borrowed a page from her book and played along. If she paid no real attention to my problems, I could always complain to The Doc Flock.

"I think I can cover only so much ground by contemplation," I said. I rambled on a few more moments and then stopped. Dr. Oesche still smiled at me, but she had softened somehow. I no longer felt queasy. Perhaps her scent had skewed my perceptions. Behavior modification through aromatherapy.

Then I relented. "I'm sorry. You asked what I felt." I looked at my hands, then held them up. "I feel like these aren't mine. When I have a thought, I can't decide whether it's really mine or I pulled it out of my ... supplemental files."

Dr. Oesche still wore a smile. Now it belonged there, as if her face had been built for it. She was a completely different person than when I stepped in, and I didn't think the change lay with her.

Vulnerable and a little ashamed, I let loose.

"I don't know who's in charge inside my head."

II

Less than an hour later, I bade Dr. Oesche farewell and left the building. I felt like skipping. The only thing stopping me was a feeling of lightheadedness. And a twinge of guilt.

Lightheadedness because in one fifty-minute session, I made more progress than in any one — shoot, any three — before. Amazing insights about my judgment, emotions, adjustment ... all of it. Guilt because I betrayed my other therapist. I felt bad that another shrink helped me so much more than the one Doc in the Flock I actually liked. I enjoyed Cynthia's company, but I felt like I'd been seeing a compassionate but unskilled psychology student.

Oh, and here was a lovely thought: is that what was holding me back before? An unhealthy attachment to my therapist? Did I pay more attention to her as a person than as a professional? Another thought occurred to me, but I couldn't articulate it. Something about a "master plan."

Perhaps it was for the best, though. No previous discovery, epiphany or divine revelation had thrilled me like my hour with Dr. Oesche. I hoped she didn't have a full calendar or a booming social life. I intended to visit the lady three or four times a week. Every day, maybe.

I smiled at everyone, bebopped along and acted my age. What I had been given amounted to a second childhood — never mind that I couldn't remember the first — and I wanted to enjoy the full use of those young limbs. Unlike other kids, I understood the regret of not being able to skip anymore.

So I skipped, and skipped, and skipped. My youthful lungs had not begun to tire when I reached the sidewalk to the building where I met with The Doc Flock. Right there, in mid-turn, I realized I had blown it.

I wanted to kick myself. All the information I had sworn to ration, just a few days before, was now so many pencil scratchings in Dr. Oesche's notebook. If I really was dealing with professional conspirators, they had just racked up a thousand-point lead.

I stood still and watched the building, forbidding now for an entirely different reason. I felt like a small-time mafioso who had to give *da boss* some bad news. I doubted cement overshoes would enter into it, but sweat still seemed to squirt out of me. I didn't often get ominous feelings like this, but to date they were more or less one hundred percent accurate, in fact if not in detail.

Erin said someone didn't want her fraternizing with me. Anyone, I wondered, or just her? Getting close enough to be a friend and therefore learn a few secrets. Or notice something I hadn't. Call into question my future autonomy ... or even safety.

I started moving again, but didn't skip. Past the research building, through the alley beside it, and arriving at a hidden alcove, I pulled out my phone and entered Barbara's number. I had promised not to call her every time I had a new thought, but this was a potential nightmare. My heart pounded so hard I could see pulses in my peripheral vision, as if my eyeballs were throbbing.

I heard two rings and then the most annoying three note chime in the known universe. It must have been chosen because it sounded like the total opposite of music.

"The number you have reached has been disconnected or is no longer in service."

I checked the phone to make sure I had entered the number correctly. I tried it again, hoping perhaps that my call had been misdirected by a computer glitch. The chime came again, sounding resentful that I hadn't understood the first time. Barbara's number was disconnected.

I was on my own.

When I saw the research building, where all the tall people in suits and lab coats waited, my foreboding grew into something else. A feeling I recognized but hadn't experienced. Not in this life, at least.

Panic.

31

The Show Must Go On

I found courage, turned off my cell phone, and marched into the building to face the music.

Despite the oddity of my meeting with Dr. Oesche, if indeed that was her real name, I had a normal session with The Flock. Not *really* normal since I was on pins and needles the whole time, but at least no one jumped up and said, "We have you now!"

One guy on the new rotation told me I seemed in a terrific mood.

"Made a breakthrough in therapy today," I said, which was true, though the real one came after. "Don't worry, though. I'm not cured yet." I gave them a politician's smile and they chuckled.

With *Project Me* good and underway, the sessions moved from a conference room to a lecture hall, just to accommodate all the white coats. I was in the lecturer's spot but I felt as if I were a courtroom witness, or auditioning for a play, over and over.

Today in particular, I awaited the sound of a gong. Someone just visible over the footlights to say, "Sorry, not what we're looking for." Or they would stick me in a straitjacket and tell me to keep at it until I sang the right song.

Dr. Pott finally adjourned the session. After making my way through half a dozen *good evenings,* I split. The first lavatory on the floor above was vacant, so I sat in a stall and tried to use all the oxygen in the room. I didn't wheeze, but I sounded about as manly as a Lamaze practitioner. My vocal chords were pulled taut like the neck of a balloon. I looked in the mirror and tried to tell myself it was okay, but I could only squeak reassurances at my reflection.

I exited the bathroom nearly twenty minutes later. The entrance hall was deserted. There should have been a guard on duty, but he was probably on rounds. The setting sun shone through the space between the glass doors. I could see the lock wasn't engaged.

I couldn't have left faster if I'd been fired from a canon.

A few minutes later, though, I wished I had a bike. Mental stress had burned through my youthful reserves and my apartment was so far away. *Forget a bike,* I thought. *Gimme one of those Segway electric scooters.*

The door clapped shut behind me. I flopped on the couch and kicked off my shoes. One landed on the coffee table. After the harrowing fight with my own imagination, I just wanted to relax. But my conscience wouldn't let me.

I turned my phone back on, re-tried Barbara's number and got the same cruel message.

Her e-mails were often nothing more than cute pictures of cats in cute poses tagged with cute captions. Other times she sent inspirational messages, compatibility quizzes and personality questionnaires. She did not stoop to chain letters, and for that I thanked her.

But the messages were inconsequential. What mattered was the message time stamp. A message — feline photo or otherwise — in my inbox posted at 17:45 on Thursday afternoon meant to call Barbara at 17:55 on Friday, twenty-four hours and ten minutes later. We'd done it half a dozen times and it had worked perfectly. We synchronized our watches by the e-mail server and we were golden.

It was just one possible layer of protection. We harbored no illusions that we were clever. We just didn't have the resources to cover our tracks any better.

And it didn't help now. Even if I'd spent normal sessions with Cynthia and the Docs' Q&A, I still would have been unable to call Barbara.

I still would have no e-mails from her in my inbox.

But there was one from George McCullough. I felt a pang of guilt, even through my near-panic. I hadn't called the guy since I'd gotten to Georgetown. I needed to thank him for all he had done — not counting the initial achievement.

Though I wasn't sure how thankful I was right then.

Hey Scott

Much as I'd like to be there to cheer you on, this trip is just what I needed. Relaxing as a tranquilizer dart.

I'm lying, of course. I told the publisher I needed to get back to you, but he insisted I stay for the whole thing. Yeah, I know

Brain Child

someone else paid the bill, but if I were getting married, these guys would fly the bride out to me.

Hope everything is going well. Charlie wrote the other day and said your mother moved to a town nearby so she could be close. I feel kind of responsible for her empty nest. She hasn't answered any of my e-mails. Can't really blame her. I hope she's okay.

BTW, I thought you might find this interesting.

George had included a link to an international news service article. When I clicked it, a picture of a man in a suit popped up. I recognized him, but I couldn't remember from where. Maybe from television, I thought. I had been watching TV a little more. In my defense, there were some really good shows on. Even SpongeBob got my attention every now and then.

I read the caption.

Seen here with New York Mayor Bloomberg, Mark Norton is advancing his ideas for tax reform.

Mark Norton. I read the name four or five times before I identified it.

He was one of the four people in my head.

I read the article and found that Mr. Norton had made a fortune investing, made another fortune with a book on investing, was running for the US Senate as an Independent from Connecticut and ... at that moment, I could not have cared less.

I needed something, but I didn't know what. My feet carried me around the apartment. My brain tried to roll uphill to an answer.

I thought about reheating some of Charlie's gumbo — he

had made about twelve gallons — but settled for water. I didn't even crack open a bottle. I climbed a chair at the sink and splashed water in my face, not caring how much I swallowed. When something in my belly loosened, I realized I'd been lucky not to vomit.

A short while later, I noticed my wet shirt stuck to my chest. My queasiness gone, I just looked like I hadn't graduated from the Sippy-Cup. I opened the dishwasher and wrung my sodden polo shirt into the door. I didn't want to drip on the floor.

I peeled off the wet shirt, tossed it into the hamper, and went to my room for another. I wasn't going into the cool autumn night wearing a wet shirt, but I didn't think I needed a sweater. I was an emancipated minor, after all. I could make dumb choices like that all on my own.

A couple of minutes later, I knocked on Charlie's door. With my luck, he would have managed to talk some woman into sampling his mysteriously good cooking. I had suggested he advertise on one of the dating websites, but he chose to rely on serendipity, awaiting that special someone who would follow the smell of cooking chicken to his apartment. Fate hadn't told him if it would be Marsala or Kiev.

To my relief, Charlie answered after the first knock. He said nothing but pointed to the button on the door just below the peephole. Then he closed the door in my face. Any other time, I would have laughed.

I sighed and pressed the button.

"Just a minute!" he called. He soon opened the door and smiled at me. "Sorry, I was in the other room."

I gave him a half smile and wedged my way into his pad. Rude, I know, but I didn't want to use a lot of words. I just stood in the entrance hall and admired my reflection in his floor.

"What's up?" He caught my mood right away. "I was just about to get something to eat. Wanna join me?"

I shook my head and laid fingertips on my belly. "Not hungry. Just need a friendly face, I guess."

"Sure," he said. "Come on into the living room. The couch needs breaking in."

"My couch is okay," I said.

"You *sit* on yours." He plopped down and tested the springs with a few bounces. "I'm weird that way. I don't sit on a seat for two unless there are two people. I have a set of dishes and glasses and I only ever wash one plate at a time."

"You'll have a mismatched set if you don't cycle through them, you know."

"I know," he said. "I don't do it with clothes, you'll notice. I don't have one threadbare bath towel and three pristine."

"Good to know." I wanted to keep up the small talk, to keep my mouth running, talking about nothing important. It was all I could do not to tell him I couldn't reach Barbara.

From Charlie, the correct response would be, "Barbara who?" If he knew right away whom I meant, I would run for the door. I might kick him in the shins first.

Charlie tried to jolly me out of my bad mood, but he got nowhere. I responded to his voice and avoided his eyes. He tried to keep the flow going, but I was not helpful.

"Obviously, something's bothering you," he said. "But if you're still looking for missing girls, you're in the wrong place."

I looked at the office space in the living room corner. His computer showed the white on black text of a word processor. "What are you working on?" I asked,

"Oh, nothing," he said. An instant later he was across the room. He nearly left his kneecap on the corner of the coffee table but didn't fall down. At the desk, he flipped shut manila folders, closed out the word processor window and stood there a few moments, trying to slow his breathing.

"Gee," I said. "I wonder if he's hiding something."

Charlie's face was blank. Then it grew a feeble smile. His glasses were askew but he made no move to fix them.

"I caught you," I said. "Though at what, I couldn't say." I climbed onto the coffee table and faced him down from across the room. "What's going on?" I asked. "I have enough going on right now without your keeping secrets. Whatever it is, please don't make me torture it out of you."

He looked me over, as if trying to decide if I were serious. Then he took a deep breath and opened a text document. The title read, *"Brain Child."* Not *brainchild.* As written ... well, it wasn't hard to figure out.

I looked at Charlie. He was chewing his lip hard enough to draw blood. I looked back at the screen and took in the document. The first few lines were just vital statistics: DOB, weight, length ... vital statistics at birth. Nothing exciting, but when coupled with the familiar manila folders, it made me suspicious.

"I didn't want you to be upset," he mumbled.

"Why would I be upset?" I must have sounded sarcastic because Charlie cringed.

"I talked to Sheila," he said. "I asked her how you would — how *she* thought you would react if I asked your blessing on my biography of you."

I didn't answer. I was doing some mental and emotional housekeeping. Charlie's guilty conscience made him defensive. I waited to see if there was more.

"I've been writing a little here and there," he said. "I went back and looked at my original notes and listened to the tapes we—"

"You didn't want George McCullough to get first crack," I cut in.

Charlie frowned. "No, it's more than that. I want to see it done *right*. I was there, Scott. Not from the very beginning, but at least since you decided to make contact with the 'outside.'" He scratched his head and yanked off the crooked glasses. "Being involved meant — *means* a lot to me."

We were silent for a moment.

"You're not gonna write it like Truman Capote, are you?" I asked. "The nonfiction novel?" Charlie was no gold digger. If he really had as corny a reason as "because I was there," I would believe him.

He shrugged. "Would you rather George did it?"

"I think he's written enough books," I said. "And he got me into this mess. He might want to write it, but I'll tell him the only one that's gonna get authorized is yours."

Charlie smiled, but his eyes went misty. "That means a lot, man," he said and lightly punched my shoulder. Then he grabbed a tissue from a box on the desk and faked a sneeze.

I had come over because I was emotional and now I'd brought Charlie to tears. Since he was already in a warm and fuzzy mood, I almost told him about Barbara. Emotional outbursts — even other people's — had a way of loosening me up, and it was all I could do not to tell him another great story he was in the middle of.

I patted Charlie on the shoulder. "My work here is done. Think I'll go call Sheila."

"Sure you don't want some supper?" he asked.

"No, thanks," I said. Rediscovering Charlie's integrity had distracted me from my own woes, but I still planned to fret over Barbara all night. Unless she got in touch somehow. "I've got some studying to do."

"I saw your lab partner, by the way," Charlie said. "Does she know she's robbing the cradle?"

I chuckled on the way out the door.

At my place, I noticed three new messages. From the time stamps, though, they must have been there before. George's note hadn't thrown me into fits of distracted despair. It just … wasn't from Barbara.

One was from Dr. Oesche. Cynthia Westbrook would be out for another week, she said. Her brother-in-law had been in a bad car accident. As family shrink, Cynthia was probably getting an earful and unable to bill a soul. I guessed at that last part. The consummate professional, Dr. Oesche would not have said such things. Not in writing, anyway.

One was from Debbie. It was a reminder of our Saturday morning cartoon-fest and study date. She was a great study partner: fun, diligent and with an impressive intellect.

An impressive tan, too. She smelled of coconut, even at the onset of autumn. "I got three letters for you," I told her one day. "S-P-F!" She giggled and kept on smelling like a

Polynesian appetizer.

The third was from OneBrikShy, which was a little weird. As long as I had been chatting with Bare and Nut and the rest, I had never received an e-mail from any of them. Barbara e-mailed me as part of a huge group of recipients, to throw off suspicion.

hey ego,
bare dropped me a little message earlier. said she might not be on for a couple of days and that I might want to tell you and nut too. not sure but it sounds like she might be having a family problem or something.
later,
brik

God bless you, Barbara, I thought. Whatever was going on, she had gotten through. By including Nut, it didn't sound as if BarelyThere and MyAlterEgo had a relationship outside the chatroom. As far as Brik knew, the one female group member would be absent for awhile.

A little while later, my mind finally at ease, I discovered it was possible to fall asleep sitting up in a computer chair.

32

Spilling the Beans

The following Saturday morning, I did something I knew I might regret. Hopefully I would just feel foolish. After an early Japanese session with Debbie Mulliniks, I went to the Georgetown University bookstore and gift shop where I bought an entire new outfit. T-shirt, hooded sweatshirt, sweat pants, a pair of Nike basketball shoes and matching socks, and to top it off, an embroidered ball cap. Even GU boxer shorts. And a tote bag. All in school colors, blue and gray. I looked like a Virginia State Trooper on his day off.

It was a good thing I had a weekly grocery allowance and that I hadn't spent much money thus far. With almost three hundred dollars' worth of new apparel, I could have been reduced to eating with Charlie every day. Not that I would mind.

In the restroom, I changed clothes and stuffed my old ones into the tote bag, along with my wallet and key chain. I left the bathroom and went to the bank of lockers near the cafeteria, chose one at random and fed it enough coins for a week's rent. The full tote bag went inside, and I closed it and pulled the key. The key didn't matter much. I wasn't sure if I would even be back for my clothes.

A spy movie aficionado would recognize what I was doing. All my own clothes, anything that might contain a tracking or listening device, was now in a bag, in a locker, miles from the place I was about to be. Even my cash on hand came from the ATM outside the bookstore.

If my paranoia paid off and someone was tracking me electronically, I had done all I could to thwart him. If I wore glasses, I would have spent the afternoon with fuzzy vision.

I went for a walk and called Sheila. "Want to have lunch? My treat."

"*It's always your treat,*" she said.

"That's because you have to drive. Charlie caught me eyeing his Camaro and now he hides the keys."

"*With all that automotive knowledge in your head, you ought to be able to hot-wire it.*"

I smiled. "Piece of cake," I said. "But don't tell Charlie."

She picked me up a little while later. "Where to?" she asked.

"The Farmers' Market," I said. "It's only a few blocks away."

"Farmers' Market?" she asked. "For lunch?"

"It's the USDA Farmers' Market, the best there is. They have an outdoor café. Great salads, I hear."

"You're my kid, all right."

Sheila parked and we got out. As we walked through the crowd toward the café, my hand found hers. She gave mine

a squeeze and smiled down at me. I felt safer with Sheila, but
I still wondered if someone was homing in on a locker full of
electronic tracking devices. And if someone had managed to
insert one into my body ... oh well. It was Washington, D.C.
What were you gonna do?

"First off," I said, standing close enough that I didn't have
to shout, "you can cross Charlie off the suspect list."

She blinked, then breathed a sigh and smiled. "Good to
know," she said. "He tell you about the book yet?"

"Yeah." But I didn't want to get into that. "Let's not go to
the café just yet."

"No?"

"Let's check out the cucumbers." I angled us that way,
leaned closer and spoke in an undertone. *"It's harder to listen
in if we're on the move and mixed in with people."*

Sheila stiffened, eyes on rows of veggies. She swallowed
hard and then nodded once.

"Just keep walking," I said, and flinched. It was something
people with guns in movies said. "Squeeze my hand
occasionally to let me know you hear me. I don't want to be
loud."

We paused beside a huge table mounded with all varieties
of cauliflower and broccoli, like white and green brains.
Sheila squeezed my hand.

"Remember when Charlie mentioned Barbara Davis at the
restaurant?"

She squeezed my hand.

I took a deep breath. "She's like me. Born at the same
hospital, in the room next door."

Her head jerked and she looked at me. Her face was part

worry, part something else. I tried smiling at her, but she turned her head away and led me through the vegan horde.

"She approached me at the moving van," I said. "I was just trying to be nice, but she asked me questions about where I was born. Then she mentioned something ... about me."

Sheila squeezed my hand, but slowly. As if she were saying "yes," but dragging it out. *Yesssssssss.*

We continued in that vein for several more minutes, moving among the health nut shoppers and fragrant produce. I said a little something. Sheila squeezed my hand, like signaling with a single telegraph click.

Me: *Barbara was the person I had in mind when I asked you for the phone. OVER*
Sheila: *Acknowledged*

Me: *We've had a few conversations, but mostly about who might actually be behind this enterprise. Not the medical community, but the government. OVER*
Sheila: *10-4*

She might as well have *been* a telegraph for all the feeling in her responses. Either she played her part well or she was so stunned it was all she could do to answer. When I caught a glimpse of her face, she looked confused, as if searching for something without the vaguest idea what it was. I knew how she felt, but I'd had time to get used to it.

To keep the blanks filled, I had to mention Erin Bradley and, thus, the coffee bar. Sheila didn't flinch at my admission, which made me glad I understated Erin's affinity for ink and ironmongery.

"When I finally saw her again," I said, "she told me someone threatened to cut off her financial aid if she batted an eye at me. Ready to eat?"

"What?" she said, thrown by my odd segue. "I don't know. My appetite kinda went away." Her usually warm hand was clammy and slick.

We stepped into the café. Even under cover, I could still feel eyes on me. The whole blue and gray ensemble could have been for nothing. It didn't take electronic devices to watch me. Just eyes.

I watched Sheila pick over her baby arugula salad while I worked on how to tell her the rest of my worries. The Dr. West/Dr. Oesche thing was worth mentioning, along with the e-mail from George. He was safe to mention. Anyone who didn't know he was involved wasn't much of a threat.

"I got an e-mail from George," I said. "He says New Zealand's the pits."

"I got one too." She stabbed at a mound of greens, then put the fork down. "He doesn't seem to be able to take a hint."

I looked at her mangled salad. "How so?"

"I think he's hitting on me." She gathered the remains of our salads into a container and closed the lid. "It's the apologies. All the offers for help, but not directed at you." Her mouth formed a grin I didn't see often. The one reserved for when Charlie had it coming to him.

"Maybe if you told him you were seeing someone," I said. The words had just come to me. Someone in my head had a secret yen to be an advice columnist.

She gave me a blank look. "Like whom?"

I shrugged. "You don't have to. Just tell him you are."

She shook her head. "That's too complex for me." She picked up the salad in its polystyrene box and we left the table.

"I need to visit the restroom," I said. She turned to me and I made meaningful eyebrow gestures. "You ought to go after I get back." She got the message and nodded.

In the bathroom, I grabbed a few brown paper towels and locked myself in a stall. Unwilling to say more out loud — I'd begun to wonder if Sheila's car might be bugged — I wrote about the mysterious Dr. Oesche, Cynthia's replacement, and my foreboding about what all I had revealed to her.

I wrote that I couldn't reach Barbara and that I was worried for her.

Finally, I wrote about how sorry I was to get her mixed up in all this. I tried not to be overly contrite. I didn't want this to require a second paper towel. Plus, George had already made her suspicious of apologies.

When I came out, I passed a tiny folded square to Sheila before she disappeared into the ladies' room. Then I tried hard to watch everyone in the café. For the moment, we were almost alone. A balding older man in the corner held open a newspaper, and when he looked over the top of it, our eyes met. I felt the blood leave my face and was glad I'd just been to the toilet.

The man put down his paper, got up, and walked right toward me. I froze, held my breath. Any clever ideas I'd been saving vanished. I glanced toward the ladies' room. Did I dare barge in to seek help from Sheila?

The man, tall and threatening in his black mock-turtleneck, kept coming. I turned my head aside and held the salad box against my chest, as if I could hide behind it. My eyelids pulled back and I prepared to scream something they tell kids to scream when accosted by strangers.

He stepped past me, laid his hands on the counter and called to the people fixing food. "Excuse me! Hello? I'm still waiting for my salad."

I sighed, and tried not to let it turn into hysterical giggles. For such a scary-looking guy, he had a prissy voice.

"You okay?" Sheila stood very close and I could see a fading redness in her cheeks and nose.

I nodded and took her hand. "Yeah, let's go. Did you ... ?"

She nodded. "I flushed it." She looked back over her shoulder. "Who was that guy?"

"Nobody." I urged her out the door. "I'm ready to go home."

Sheila amazed me sometimes. Once again, I delivered amazing, life-altering news and she had put that on hold long enough to sneak and pay the check. Lunch wasn't my treat after all.

And now it looked like nothing would be.

33

Confirmation

Sheila didn't stick around, though I'd bought decaf just for her visits. I thought she was avoiding Charlie, but I hated to bring it up. No matter how special our relationship, I just couldn't ask my mother about her social life. I thought Sheila and Charlie would be good for each other. They both had my best interests at heart, and that was a great way to begin.

With no guest to entertain, I walked to the student center to retrieve my belongings. No sense in leaving them there forever. I might never find out if my trick had actually worked. I still had a nice new blue and gray ensemble.

About halfway to the student center, I noticed a noisy crowd. I thought someone might be staging a protest. I didn't see any picket signs, but this was Georgetown. They probably used embossed business cards.

But this was a different type of crowd. People clumped together on the sidewalk as though poured out of the building. Evacuees. The fire truck and the throaty *brank, brank, brank* through the building's closed doors confirmed it. No smoke, so there must have been another false alarm.

It had apparently interrupted a late lunch crowd. Now rain threatened and the coffee bar and grill patrons wanted back inside. They didn't mind microwaved food as long as they didn't have to get wet. I didn't blame them, but I had already eaten. I just wanted to get to my locker.

A tall young man sat by himself, eyeing the goings-on. His cigarette produced the only smoke around. "How long have you been waiting?" I asked him.

"About half an hour," he said. "Fire department just got here a few minutes ago."

I frowned. "Half an hour? They're only a few blocks away! I walked here faster than that."

The guy looked at me through his smoke and eyed me up and down. He smiled. "Yeah, they've had like four false alarms already this year. Somebody been cryin' 'wolf.' You know that story, kid?"

"They're getting apathetic."

He grinned. "Yeah. That. Better than last year, though."

"Why's that?" I asked.

"Somebody had fun pulling fire alarms in the dorms." He took a long drag on his cigarette and blew it away from me. "Last January, he waited until about four a.m., right around the time when everyone was getting in real deep, snoring away. Then ... " He made a pulling-down gesture. "Had to stand outside like forty-five minutes, in my jockeys and bathrobe. And socks, I think. Of course you don't think about dressing warm with that noise going on." I let him ramble.

He must have been bored, and it sounded like one of his favorite stories.

The alarm went silent and a fireman came a moment later. A collective sigh of relief rose up from the crowd.

Then there was a commotion, indignant outcries from those closest to the doors.

"But I've got stuff in there!"

"Hey man, I gotta get back to work!"

The fireman held up his hand. "Not yet, people. We've got a problem."

I moved closer, weaving in and out of the clots of people on the sidewalks. When I got close enough, I heard the fireman talking to the building manager, whom I had seen at the last false alarm. There was another man, too. A police officer.

"Looks like you got some vandalism in there," the fireman told the manager. "A whole bank of lockers busted open. With a crowbar, looks like."

"Lockers?" the supervisor asked. "Not the cash drawers? We lock them down when there's a fire alarm." He looked at the police officer. "We've been getting a lot of practice, mind you. But lockers? It doesn't make sense."

Unless they were looking for something specific, I thought. A certain tracking device, say. Only then did it occur to me that the lockers were also large enough to conceal a small boy.

Trying to be even smaller than I was, I detached from the discontented group and headed back toward my apartment. Then the guy with the smoke and the story called to me, durn him.

"Hey, little man," he said. "What you doing here? Are you gifted or something?"

"Something like that," I said, not turning to look at him. "I gotta go."

If someone were looking for me, I had just given him a peek. He and whatever outfit he worked for had another free shot at me. Of course they could sneak into my apartment, grab me and make off with almost no fuss; what kind of fight could I put up?

If it were just a matter of finding me, I was in the directory. But tracking? I had apparent confirmation of that, but I had also let them know I was wise to them. Even more, that I knew how to foil them. I was no poker player, but I knew you weren't supposed to let the other guy find out you knew his tell. Shame on me.

My only comfort came from being right, and small comfort it was. Someone was keeping tabs on me, and I was sure it wasn't done legally — witness the destruction of all the lockers to cover a search. Maybe they thought I had ticked off somebody who then decided to teach me a lesson by cramming me into a locker. Whatever they had thought, they now knew the truth.

The destruction of all those lockers meant someone was serious about finding out how I had given them the slip.

I had one more comforting thought: if they had been watching Sheila already, they wouldn't have bothered to trash the lockers. But if they happened to see Sheila at my apartment, I had given them another target to watch ... if they hadn't been already. It was a matter of intelligence, in more than one sense.

While I walked, my brain churned, putting faces on imagined conspirators. A rail-thin man with with a freaky facial scar transecting his eye, wearing a black trench coat. His boss, a wheelchair-bound, bald man in an old fashioned three-piece suit, bejeweled fingers stroking a Himalayan cat. Cheesy, but very creepy, nonetheless.

The wheelchair idea brought Brik to mind. His message said Barbara/Bare indicated she was experiencing technical difficulties. But what if it was worse? What if she had been forced to abandon her online persona, like a spy torching a forged passport?

I had either too much spy movie information or not enough. Too much, meaning I had an overwhelming number of ideas about what could go wrong, and not enough, meaning I didn't have a clue how to escape any of my growing number of dilemmas, imagined or real.

I was almost relieved to see a familiar face when I arrived at the apartment. Debbie was sitting on the small stoop, smiling at me.

"There you are," she said. "I hoped you weren't gone for the weekend."

"Didn't you get enough of me this morning?"

She held up a book. "You might need this," she said. "I don't think the school bookstore has any more." It was my Japanese 101 textbook.

"Thanks," I said and took it from her, "but you didn't have to bring it all the way here."

She shrugged. "I wasn't busy. The library is really tedious after five hours or more."

"Speak for yourself."

She grinned. "I forgot who I was talking to. Anyway, no boyfriend, so no date tonight. I haven't made many friends yet, so I haven't been invited to any parties. I've just been walking to and fro across the campus."

Since going public, I took most unsolicited attention with a grain of salt. Her visit was a comfort, though. I'd been wondering if I'd find my apartment ransacked: couch cushions butchered, drawers upended, toothpaste ejected from the tube — I think I saw that last in a movie. But the only thing I had hidden was tracked down elsewhere.

"Back and forth, carrying a Japanese 101 textbook," I said. "Wouldn't little pink dumbbells would be more your style?"

She wrinkled her nose in amusement. "Where are you getting back from?" she asked and took in my attire. "The football team is at an away game. Did you miss the bus?"

I chuckled. "As a matter of fact, I'm just returning from lunch."

She looked at her watch. "It's nearly four-thirty."

"I eat slowly." *Why the sudden interest?* I thought.

"Eat at the grill?"

"Nope. Went out." My little amateur detective ploy. Remain laconic, let her keep talking. Right then, of course, my only suspicions were based on her being pretty as a James Bond film *femme fatale*. That, and how she showed up right after I learned I couldn't trust my own clothing.

The apprehension from the student center was still with me, but it was oddly relaxed. I was adapting to the stress of multiple layers of subterfuge. Or maybe I was just tired.

She nodded. "Campus meals get really old. My mom told me to get an apartment off campus so I could have a kitchen." She shrugged. "She forgot I can't cook. I settle for a microwave, a hot plate and ramen noodles."

"At least you can't burn them."

"Sure I can," she said. "I may be responsible for the campus's only legitimate fire alarm this quarter." She laughed at my look of surprise. "Don't worry. No real danger. Just the super-nasty smell."

"I've got it good," I said. "Charlie cooks pretty often. For a straight, single guy, he does a great job. Lots of cooking show stuff. Most of it's pretty palatable."

She looked at me for a moment longer before laughing. Like she was waiting for my words to register.

"Something wrong?" I sounded calm, but my paranoia came to periscope depth. Her pause made me think of someone receiving orders via radio earpiece. I knew it was unfair, but by this time I had reason to suspect just about everyone, short of Sheila.

Nixing Charlie from that list might have been premature. This was his second chance, even if he didn't know it. He would be offended had he known, but the reason I trusted Charlie in the first place was that, despite his intelligence and manner, he was guileless as a toddler. And if he wasn't, I would suggest he give Hollywood a try. He'd win an Oscar in no time.

Debbie was still looking at me. I reminded myself I had seen precious little of her day-to-day behavior. No patterns on which to base an informed opinion.

"Hello?" I said. I waved my hand in front of her face.

She closed her eyes and shook her head. "Do you think you might ... I don't know, grow a goatee or something?"

I blinked and frowned. "Excuse me?"

Debbie shook her head and got to her feet. "I'm sorry. Please forget I said anything."

"No," I said. "It's all right. What is it?"

She stopped before she was fully upright, as if "old lady hunch" hit her decades early. She bit her lip. "I don't want you to think I'm being mean."

I smiled. "Come on. Now I'm curious."

She ran a hand through her five-pound blond coif. Consternation made her even prettier. "I was thinking, if you looked ... I don't know ... older, maybe, it wouldn't be so weird to hear you talk like ... like — "

"Like an adult?" I suggested, smiling.

She let her hand fall. "Yeah. I'm sorry, Scott. It's just freaky sometimes."

I nodded. "Believe me. I see the freak in the mirror every day."

Her hand went to her mouth. "Now I *really* feel like a real b—"

I cut in. "Don't worry about it. It's still weird to me, too. I can't expect others to be more comfortable with it than I am."

She looked at me for a moment before speaking again. "You told me once that you weren't really a child prodigy or anything like that. Do you feel like elaborating?"

I thought about it for a moment. "One day," I said. "I'm still dealing with it, so I don't know how much I want getting out."

Then she looked hurt. "Geez, I'm not going to tell everybody."

I sighed. "My life is tied in about five kinds of knots right now. I'm trying to figure out if it's the kind of thing I want to tell people. Would you ask someone in a wheelchair why he wasn't walking?"

"You're not in a wheelchair, Scott," she said. "It might be more appropriate to ask you where you keep your flying saucer." She winced. "Sorry. I'm not being mean, really."

I wanted to say, *if that helps you sleep at night.* But I didn't. "It's okay."

"Please," she said. "I don't want you to be angry at me." She folded her hands in front of her and shook them at me. "I don't want you to think I'm prying. I think a lot of you, Scott, and as I said, I don't have many friends."

I wanted to say something snide about her hair, her beautiful, tanned skin, her expensive clothes. How she shouldn't lack for friends when she looked like a third generation country club member. I bit my tongue and decided to give her a chance.

"It's okay," I said. "Truly. I don't mind being friends. I *like* the idea of being friends. Every time I make a new one, it's a big percentage increase."

"I just keep thinking of you as a really short adult," she said, and winced again. "I hope you don't take it the wrong way."

It was way better than the norm. Most of the adults I knew either thought of me as an opportunity or an obstacle. "It's fine. Sounds good, in fact. Maybe you could convince the courts to let me get my driver's license."

She smiled. It was nice. Making up was less painful when it didn't involve taking back unkind words.

"You just got back from lunch," she said, "but it's time for me to have supper. Are you too full to join me?"

If I had been ten years older — and a normal kid — I would have been thrilled to do anything with a knockout like Debbie. But I had to say no. "Sorry. Lots to do tonight."

"Like?"

I smiled. "I have to start growing a goatee."

She laughed.

"And you might want to go off campus for supper," I said. "The student center is probably still locked down." I slid from friendliness to intrigue. It was easy, completely involuntary, and I hated it.

I mentioned the student center to provoke some kind of reaction. With luck, she wouldn't react at all, possibly exculpating her from the plot.

She looked in that direction and my heart sank a little. "Yeah, another fire alarm." She shook her head. "Shame they don't have security cameras to watch for that sort of thing."

"Yeah," I said, both relieved and confused. My little experiment had yielded nothing. Maybe if I had worded it differently.

"Okay, then," she said. "You have your book and I am walking upright again. I will now return to my dorm and decide whether to stay in and eat noodles or go out and eat noodles."

"I'd go out," I said. "Keep the fire alarms to a minimum today."

She chuckled about two syllables worth and gave me a *you silly boy* pat on the cheek. "See you tomorrow night? Try not to forget, will you?"

"I'll be there," I said. "I'd say 'with bells on' but the library staff would gripe." I was fishing for class clown votes, but it was fun, and I knew I'd never get BMOC.

We said goodbye and I watched her walk across the road and down the sidewalk, arms swinging. Maybe she was celebrating not having to carry all those books. It was hard not to run after her and share in the mood. I could have used a bit of cheer and forgetfulness right then.

I stood and watched until she rounded the corner. Then I sighed and turned to go in, but was stopped at the door. My conversation with Debbie had helped me forget the clothes I'd ditched at the student center ... and the keys in my jeans pocket.

I started to walk around and knock on Charlie's door, but before I went a single step, I saw something on the concrete stoop at my feet. Had I been an adult, I would have missed it. Being short wasn't always a disability.

In the flowerbed, hiding behind the stoop's brick column, there was a styrofoam coffee cup from the student center coffee bar. I picked it up and detected a foul odor. A dozen or more cigarette butts had soaked up the remaining coffee.

Someone had been watching my apartment.

34

Coming Clean

Charlie took me out to eat at a west D.C. area mall Sunday night. It was the second time that weekend I'd eaten on someone else's dime. I either felt clever or guilty.

If there was guilt, it was over fat grams in the sub Charlie had bought me. Uncountable kinds of meat, a couple of cheeses, olive paste ... I could hardly concentrate enough to tell him what I was on about. I was telling myself lettuce, tomato, olive oil and vinegar put the sandwich in the "salad" category when Charlie raised the question.

"Why are we here, Scott?"

"You picked the place." Which was true. With the number of good restaurants near our place, it wasn't practical to bring me all the way across town for a sandwich. But that was Charlie. If visiting New Orleans, he would forego the famous five-star restaurants in favor of Mama Boudreaux's, specializing in animal parts that don't feature in *The Joy of Cooking.*

Charlie wiped his lips. "I meant, what's on your mind?"

My eyes went around the food court, by no means a lonely place. My five-way mind had argued with itself over where and how to disclose my theory, but it came down to avoiding eavesdroppers. That meant a crowd. Or a quiet rendezvous. The board meeting in my head hadn't reached a consensus.

If anything would make my watchers nervous, it was exposure. The threat only worked on me because, through a serious lapse in judgment, I hadn't told anyone yet. I just didn't want anyone assuming the stress was getting to me.

But I had ignored the real problem, or put it on the back burner. Discounted worries that turned out to be legitimate. Avoided dealing with the problem, hoping it would turn out to be imaginary.

"I'm pondering a problem," I began. "I'm still trying to decide what I ought to tell you."

"About what?" Charlie dabbed his face again. The sandwich oil made everything south of his nose shiny.

Though Charlie's glistening face amused me, I almost broke down and boo-hooed all over the place, freeing the child within. I took a few deep breaths before I spilled it all.

Charlie reached across the table to pat my hand. I looked up, saw real concern in his face and wondered how I ever doubted him. He was like a big brother who had adopted me, or vice versa.

"Someone's ... doing something." It was all I could think of to say.

Charlie's eyes widened. "What kind of something?"

"Keeping an eye on me, for one thing." That said, I let my

own eyes wander around the food court. I didn't worry about being conspicuous. The clothes-in-the-locker experiment had alerted whoever it was that I was onto them.

"You *are* cute," he said through a mouthful of pickle. "Maybe someone's keeping an eye on his investment."

I fixed him with a stare. "With electronic tracking?"

"Like ... homing devices?" he asked, his voice raspy. He took a long swig of soda. Before, Charlie's attention had been token. Now he lit up as if I'd dripped hot wax on him.

I nodded. "In some of my clothes. Or all of them." I tugged my hoody's drawstring. "Thus the wardrobe alteration."

"Seriously?"

I detailed the events of the day, starting with my shopping spree and lunch with Sheila, continuing to my discovery of the locker break-in, and ending with Debbie's visit and my finding the hidden coffee cup full of butts.

"The coffee cup doesn't necessarily point to Debbie," he said.

"No," I said, "that cup belonged to a dedicated smoker."

Charlie patted his shirt pockets rhythmically and grinned. "I guess you'd know."

I put my hands on my head and grunted. "It's like a mystery movie. I found a vital clue, but it feels like it's from another movie." I shook my head to settle the debris. "That's why I need you. I can't make a decision based on my own judgment."

"What's wrong with your judgment?"

I shrugged, but it felt like a nervous tic. "It's like I don't have my own best interest in mind. Part of me wants to ignore the problem. See if it disappears. Another part wants me to jump up on the table and yell 'incoming!'" Panic was setting in, so I shut up and slowed my breathing. The calm had boiled away fast and I didn't know why. Charlie was there, and I should have felt safer.

"Do the ideas have equal value in your mind?" Charlie asked. "Like two generals with equal power issuing conflicting orders?"

"Maybe more than two," I said. "Anyway, it's the irresistible force and immovable object problem. I need a tiebreaker."

Charlie sighed and gave me a smile he hadn't shown before. The kind you see at funerals. The I'm-here-for-you-in-your-time-of-need smile, which was kind of bleak. I wasn't sad, I was *scared*.

"What's that look all about?" I asked.

"I'm glad you told me," he said. "I was beginning to think you didn't trust me anymore."

"What gave you that idea?"

He smiled. "You haven't introduced me to Debbie."

"Didn't I just explain that she might be part of the problem? Playing on the opposing team?"

"Yeah," he said. "But she's an attractive co-ed who likes brainy guys."

"You might be meeting her soon," I said. "I'd like to be able to eliminate her as a suspect." In truth, I suspected that if Debbie was a really bad guy, her true assignment would be seducing Charlie.

Could Charlie be taken in by a pair of pretty eyes? Well, add her long legs, payload of wavy blond hair, and winning personality, and he just might ... if he wasn't already seriously crushing on my mom.

Charlie watched me as I thought. "You through here?" He spoke out of the side of his mouth.

"Yeah," I said. Though I believed Charlie was devoted to the Scott Bledsoe Cause, he was acting odd. He collected his trash in quick, jerky movements. Without looking up, he stuffed his refuse into the overfull waste can and fidgeted while I did likewise.

As we left the food court, Charlie guided me along but stopped short of taking my hand. He kept pushing me forward, his hand on my elbow. Before long, he moved too fast for my short legs and my pace began to flag. When he pushed again, it was easy to imagine he was abducting me. That was absurd, though. Why grab me here if he knew where I slept at night?

As Charlie pushed me along the mall floor like a piece of flimsy furniture, I considered his behavior at supper. Little things, like not speaking unless his mouth was covered. Or full. It was the very limit of good manners to cover one's full mouth while speaking. But every single time Charlie spoke, he covered his mouth ... or stuck something in it. Or mumbled, like a ventriloquist.

I took back everything I thought about his lack of guile. He must have decided we needed to make a quick departure. With no time to explain, he just prodded me along.

Charlie's strides were so long I soon had to jog, and I wasn't used to it. I never played tag, or kickball or any of the things that made kids get up and run. My legs and lungs tired very quickly and every other floor tile threatened to trip me up.

I kept moving, despite the growing burn. No one stared so I must have looked like a normal hyperactive child, unable to behave and walk at sub-light speeds. I got tired very quickly but wove back and forth, stopping short of putting out my arms and pretending I had wings.

My foot hit something, maybe a loose tile. I pitched forward and smacked the floor as if trying to belly-flop in a hot-asphalt mirage. If the wind hadn't been knocked out of me, I would have screamed in pain. I couldn't even gasp. I just flopped around, trying to find my breath, like I had just dropped it on the floor.

I knew what was going on — my diaphragm was temporarily numb after hitting the floor — but I felt like I was dying. When breath still didn't come on the third try, I began to wonder if, instead of tripping, I had actually been brought down by a bullet.

There was no huge pool of blood, though. The floor where I lay was pretty clean. Recently mopped, by the scent. Smelling the floor seemed a waste of my rebooted lungs, but I was happy to be breathing again.

Where was Charlie? I thought I had been only an arm's length ahead. Now I was so obviously alone that a clerk came to check on me. She looked relieved that I was getting to my feet. Charlie was nowhere to be seen.

"That must have hurt! Can I help you find your mom or dad?" the lady asked. That was nice, I thought. She didn't scold me.

"Thanks. I'm on my way to meet them." Before she could say any more, I took off again. In the same direction, but at a slower pace.

I couldn't see Charlie anywhere. I felt as if I had ditched a tail without even trying. From behind a huge potted plant, I looked back the way I had come. I saw nothing encouraging.

The mall's businesses were suffering because of newer retailers nearby. The remaining shops' few faithful patrons strolled here and there. The other storefronts were boarded up. There were few places Charlie could hide.

Keeping an eye out for helpful adults, I made my way back down the long corridor and tried to remember where I last felt Charlie's hand on my arm. It was a long way back to our dining table and I kept my eyes peeled, trying to identify every person I saw.

Thirty paces into my third trip along that leg, I saw where Charlie might have gone. There was a vestibule leading to a back corridor that ran the length of the mall. Behind the stores instead of in front. The employee entrance.

Just inside the door, I found Charlie ... and a whole lot of Charlie's blood.

35

In the Line of Duty

I

I cried out and ran to Charlie's side, almost losing my footing in the slick pool.

"Hallelujah, you found me." His voice was tense and his face pale as could be, but he was conscious and lucid.

"What happened?" I asked, looking for the hole where Charlie was leaking. "Why'd you run off? I was almost out of the mall." I wanted to complain that he hadn't been around to pick me up after my spill, but that was unkind. "Are you shot? Stabbed?"

"Gimme a minute." Charlie had his hands pressed to his upper thigh, near his groin. "He got my cell phone!" he groaned up at me. "Find someone to call 911!" Then he grunted something about "overseas calls" and "a six-figure phone bill."

Instead of running down the corridor to call 911, I pulled my own cell from my pocket. If I had been thinking — and if

Charlie weren't catching his own blood by the handful — I would have kept the phone a secret. But if I couldn't trust Charlie with everything by this point, I might as well give up.

"911 Operator. What is your emergency?"

"There's an injured man in the south employee entrance corridor at the Cherry Acres mall." I looked at Charlie. "Shot or stabbed?"

"I don't know," he grunted. His eyes were closed.

"Just a moment," I covered the receiver and hissed at Charlie. "You don't know?!"

"It happened fast." His head lolled back. "I don't remember a gunshot."

"Some kind of stab wound," I said into the phone. Extreme upper right thigh. Looks like an arterial bleed. Not bad enough to be the femoral." *Thank God,* I added silently.

"Did the wound penetrate the ... uh, pari-tonium?"

"You mean the *peritoneum?*" I asked.

"If that's how you say it."

I repeated the question to Charlie.

"Do I even *have* one of those?"

"Yes. Think 'hernia.'"

Charlie considered. "No."

Back to the phone. "No peritoneal penetration," I said. "You heard me say 'arterial bleeding,' right?"

"Yes, ma'am, I did. Ambulance is on the way. Can you get someone to lead the way when the EMT's get there?"

Ma'am? Sheesh. "Someone will meet them."

I ended the call and turned to Charlie. He lay against the cinder block wall like a crumpled food wrapper leaking ketchup. My eyes blurred. Nerve tears. "What do you have to say for yourself?" I asked.

Charlie had both hands on his wound now. "Ouch."

"A comment on your injury or on my question?"

He grinned. "Where'd you get the phone?"

It was a fair question. "Sheila got it for me when I discovered I had reasons to be suspicious."

"You mean when you met Leo?" He chuffed once, like a dog laughing, made a nasty grimace. *"Please,* don't make me laugh."

"Here's something to sap all your funny," I said. "Do you think your attacker's still around?"

Somehow, Charlie's face grew paler and darker at the same time. "I hope not. It's why I didn't holler for help in the first place."

"Who was it?"

Charlie grunted. "Didn't know him. Small, wiry guy in a hooded sweatshirt. Some kind of team logo." He closed his eyes and added more pressure to his wound, as if massaging his brain. "Patriots, maybe?"

Even with my large scope of knowledge, I had no in-depth knowledge of sports or sports teams. If I had inherited such, though, all the statistics would have predated my birth. "New England Patriots?" I asked. "Where are they from, Boston?"

"Yeah, but that —" He stopped and gasped. "It doesn't mean he's from Boston. I wear a Forty-Niners shirt all the time, and I've never been to California." He was already light-headed from blood loss and shock. In his growing stupor, he repeated that last word over and over, with the

Teutonic resonance of Governor Schwarzenegger: *Kahl-ee-fohr-nya.*

Charlie needed help *now.*

"Okay," I said. "Ready?"

He frowned, his eyes closed. "For what?"

I covered Charlie's ears and opened my mouth. I had never done this in living memory, so I was afraid of what might happen. Closing my eyes, I took a deep breath and screamed until I saw hot toaster wires in my eyelids.

It must have been something. Every able-bodied person in the whole mall arrived in a matter of moments. An aged security guard wielded his radio and took control of the situation like a SWAT captain. Charlie tried to tell him we called an ambulance, but the uniformed senior citizen just put a hand on his shoulder. "You'll be just fine, son," he said, and waited for someone to okay a call to the National Guard.

Thought I hadn't seen many people in the mall, they filled the corridor now. It was the perfect time for Charlie's assailant to show up and, in the confusion, stick Charlie again ... or me. Now fearing for both of us, I hunkered at his side, not even avoiding the blood. I put my hands on his shoulders and stayed with him until the paramedics arrived.

In the ambulance — another first for me — the paramedics asked about the "doctor" who had made the 911 call. Charlie wasn't too out of it to brag on me, though I wish he hadn't. He must have been bursting at the seams for months. I just hoped he would regain control along with consciousness.

II

In a much shorter time than I would have thought possible, Charlie was in a semi-private room. He was under light sedation and trying to say something about Sheila. But the attending nurse kept cutting him off, saying he needed to rest.

"Hey!" I told the nurse. "Shut up and let him talk!"

I might have levitated and shot sparks out of every orifice for the look she gave me. She took a deep breath and backed off.

"What is it, Charlie?" I asked.

"Call your mom," he said. His voice rose and fell like an ocean wave. "Call ... right now. Tell her to ... careful. Come to the hospital."

"Gotcha." I patted his arm. "*Now* rest."

I watched as the nurse resumed her duties, occasionally looking over her shoulder. Maybe she thought *I* had stabbed Charlie and was just waiting around for another worthy target. I escaped into the corridor and pulled out my phone to call Sheila.

"Young man," said a voice. "I'm sure you're proud of your little phone, but it's against the rules to use it inside this hospital." I turned to see a man in hospital garb smiling at me. Charlie's nurse was only the beginning, I saw.

"I need to call someone," I said. "Is there a nearby phone I can use?"

"Would you like me to call them for you?"

I huffed. "I *know* how to use a phone."

"You ought to watch your tone, young man," he said. "Let's just go find your parents, shall we?"

"Leave me alone," I said. I felt like a cat, back arched and hissing. "I've had a rough night and I don't have time for this."

"Is your mother on this floor?" he asked, oblivious to the pile he was stepping in.

"If you don't get out of my face and tell me where a phone is, I'm going to make you *very sorry*." I glared at him. "All it will take is a police line-up."

He squinted against my words, but he could have been shielding his eyes from spittle. Then he straightened and I heard someone enter the corridor behind me. "There's a phone in the visitors' lounge," he said. "End of the hall. Dial nine for an outside line."

"Thank you," I said. I wanted to say *"See how easy that was?"* but with a witness, too much could go wrong.

"Are you Scott Bledsoe?" asked a deep voice from behind me. I didn't want to turn around, but pretending to be deaf is rude. There was a big man with a round face and an ill-fitting tan sport coat. Something about him said "cop," but I pretended ignorance. I wasn't sure I liked cops, but like with chocolate, that was changeable.

"Yes." I stood still and tried to palm my cell phone. It was tiny, but so was my hand.

"I'm Detective Tim Rogers." He didn't shout, but no one had ever taught him when to use his inside voice. He probably wasn't popular at hospitals. "Mr. Bailey is sleeping right now but he said you might be able to fill me in on a couple of things. Is that right?"

Almost everyone looks down to talk to me, but Detective Rogers remained where he was and it wasn't necessary. I was happy to avoid that tableau: cop bent at the waist, hands on his knees. Norman Rockwell came to mind.

"What did Charlie tell you?" I asked.

"That you could fill me in on a couple of things." He smiled, and I knew he was hip. It hadn't taken him long.

"What can I tell you?" I didn't want to be a pain, but I didn't want to talk without my responsible party, and he was in drug-induced dreamland. "I didn't see anything. I wasn't there for the attack." I also wasn't sure Charlie had been coherent enough to vouch for me.

"Why don't we get out of the corridor?" He turned to one side and gestured down the hall. "I'll bet you aren't the public sort."

"Okay." I walked past him toward the lounge the disorderly told me about. I passed Charlie's room and saw a blond woman of about forty standing by the door with her arms folded. With her blue blazer and white blouse, she looked like my elementary school principal, Mrs. Bowman. Unlike Rogers, this woman displayed a badge, worn on a lanyard around her neck.

"That's my partner," Rogers said. "Detective Sandy Allen."

"You must be Scott Bledsoe," she said and held out her hand.

I smiled but my handshake was a little limp. "What department are you with?"

Detective Allen smiled, and it looked sincere. "Before you asked, I might have sidestepped the question, even said I was a social worker. Mr. Bailey advised against treating you like a normal kid, though."

I persisted. "And the answer is?"

"Narcotics," she said. "At least I am. Tim is in violent crimes."

"Why narcotics?" I asked.

"We ought to talk in the lounge, Scott," Rogers said. "Detective Allen will stay here and make sure no one bothers your friend."

I looked past Detective Allen at the door that hid Charlie from view. Then I sighed and led Detective Rogers to the lounge. It was big and almost empty. The emergency room had been pretty slow, too. It was probably a rare night when only one violent attack victim was hospitalized. Maybe Charlie was the only one to survive the emergency room.

Rogers filled one of the umpteen identical chairs with his large body. I had not met a man this big in all my six point seven years. I sat on the coffee table a discreet distance away — or, as I thought of it, out of reach.

"I'd like to get some background on you, Scott," he said. He opened a marbled cloth-bound notebook. "Are you related to Charles Bailey?"

"No."

Rogers waited. Waited longer. "Where're your parents?"

"My mother lives in Germantown," I said. "My father died before I was born."

"Do you have her phone number?" he asked. "I should call her to come get you right away."

"She's on her way," I lied. I didn't have a chance to call her yet.

Rogers scratched his head. "I don't really need her for background, but she ought to be present before I start in with questions."

"I'm an emancipated minor," I said. "She's not actually in charge of me anymore. Charlie is my guardian."

Rogers looked at me as if I had been the one to flash a badge. "Emancipated minor. Pretty rare thing, that, though you sound like someone who might get it."

"Does that mean I'm special or incurable?"

"Why don't you tell me?" he said. "Mr. Bailey said you would shed some light on this mess, as long as I didn't patronize you."

"I don't think I can tell you any more than he did."

"Should be easy," he said. "Mr. Bailey passed out about ten seconds after I showed up." He smiled. "The timing was so good, I would have thought he was faking, if not for the blood loss."

I shook my head. "It didn't seem like that much at the time." *Liar,* I thought. It had looked like gallons.

"Believe me, with the right kind of jeans, like Bugle Boys, you can sop up a couple of quarts, easy. Never spill a drop until you wring 'em out."

"I'll have to buy a pair," I said. "All I know is that I found Charlie in the back corridor after he had been stabbed. I can tell you what he said about the attacker, but you'd better let Charlie tell you."

"You can go ahead and tell me, too."

"Small, wiry," I said, remembering. "Wearing a Patriots sweatshirt. The kind with a hood."

"Patriots, eh? Not Redskins." He wrote in a full-size notebook, like a journal. I was curious to look at his notes, because he didn't scribble. With that kind of care, he could have been drawing a sketch. Maybe little football players.

"Anything else?"

"Charlie said the guy took his phone," I said, just remembering. "It might have a GPS locator, but I don't know." I gave him the number and he called it in to dispatch with instructions to check the GPS status. Apparently cops were allowed to use cell phones in the hospital.

"So, any idea why this guy would stab your friend?"

"As I said, I never saw the guy. Charlie's about the most inoffensive person in the world, unless he's ever played reggae at you." I looked in the direction of his room. "That can change your mind."

Rogers smiled. "So, you found him in the back corridor, bleeding from a stab wound, but you never saw the knife man?"

"Right," I said.

He looked at his notes. "Does Mr. Bailey work at the mall?"

I shook my head. "No."

"So what was he doing in the back corridor?"

"I don't know. We were on our way out."

"But Mr. Bailey went off on his own?"

Rogers was as polite as could be, but his voice literally hurt my ears, so much that I had trouble paying attention to his words. It almost made me forget he was pumping me for information. But the man that stabbed Charlie was still on the loose, and I wanted him caught.

"We were leaving, but we got separated." I retraced the route in my head. "When I discovered Charlie wasn't with me, I doubled back to find him."

"And how did you know to look in the back corridor?"

Rogers asked, still reading from his notebook.

I waited until he stopped and looked up at me. "I'm a perceptive guy."

He smiled at me and wrote something else in his book. "A witness at the mall says you were running full tilt on your way out of there, with Mr. Bailey nowhere in sight."

"Your witness is mistaken." I folded my arms, losing the desire to be helpful. "I never got above a medium jog. And Mr. Bailey was *too* there. He bought my supper."

"So, you were ahead." Rogers checked his notebook. "At a 'medium jog.' When you found you had been separated, you doubled back to find him."

"Do I need to write this down?" I asked.

"I've just about got it," he said. "Again, why did you check the back corridor?"

I sighed. "It was just one more place to look. Like when you check pants pockets you haven't worn in forever to find something you just lost."

Detective Rogers wrote fast, as if trying to empty the ink from his pen. He finished and looked at the page. He looked up a moment later, as if just remembering I was there. "You found Mr. Bailey in the back corridor because you just happened to think of looking there."

"Are we having a breakdown in communication here?" I asked. "I said as much already. My story won't ch — "

"Was Mr. Bailey looking for someone?"

I wasn't sure which member of the committee upstairs didn't trust cops, but I was weary of evasion. "I think," I said, "that Charlie was following someone who had been spying on us."

"Why would someone spy on you?" Rogers asked.

Weary, I slipped off the edge of the coffee table and onto a chair. "That's a long story. To begin, would it surprise you to learn I'm a freshman at Georgetown?"

He smiled. "Not now, it wouldn't."

"Sorry for the prevarication," I said. "And the rudeness. That's really unlike me."

"I doubt it," he chuckled, "but apology accepted. Now, from the beginning ... ?"

"Okay," I said. "I started —"

"*Stop!*"

The voice from behind me nearly loosened my bowels. I spun around and saw Dr. Pott standing in the doorway. I recognized the man behind him, but I couldn't remember his name.

"Don't say another word, Scott," Dr. Pott said. "Our attorney is on his way."

36

Keeping Lids on

Detective Rogers got to his feet. "Gentlemen, can I ask what you're doing before I confuse it with 'obstructing a police officer?'"

Dr. Pott was at my side in half a second and took hold of my arm. He looked different, but I couldn't think why right then. The way he handled me, I thought I was in for a beating. He pulled me away from Detective Rogers and swung me around behind him. I felt like a jacket being discarded before a fist fight.

"Scott has nothing to say to you, officer," Dr. Pott said, more animated than I had ever seen. From behind, I realized why he looked different: he was dressed head to foot in black leather. The other man — Dr. Hanson, I remembered, one of those people with very vague titles— wore matching attire. I almost laughed out loud. We had interrupted a weekend bikers' outing.

"Neither of you gentlemen is Scott's parent or guardian.

Therefore your interference is ... inadvisable." Rogers rattled a pair of handcuffs in his palm. "Please don't make me ask your intentions again."

"Our intentions," Dr. Hanson said, "are to protect this young man from his so-called guardian's egregious flouting of responsibility." He looked at me again. Though he was an official with The Project, it was only our second or third meeting. Maybe he was making sure he had the right kid.

Detective Rogers flipped his notebook shut and put his hands on his hips. "As I have said, gentlemen, Scott is not a suspect but a witness. Since he enjoys emancipated minor status, only his guardian or a judge can direct him not to talk to me."

I was about to say I wasn't exactly *enjoying* my emancipated minor status when the voice I had been waiting for spoke from the doorway.

"His own lawyer can do that, too."

I pulled away from the Drs. Fonzarelli to see Sheila standing in the door. Right behind her, Leo smiled and winked at me. I had no idea how Sheila had learned of my troubles, but I doubted she'd had to do much wrangling to get Leo to come along.

Leo rounded Sheila and stepped forward. "Detective, I'm Leo Radcliffe, Scott Bledsoe's attorney. Should I worry about this line of questioning?"

Rogers looked at me and smiled. "Not unless Scott slips up and tells me *he* stabbed Mr. Bailey."

"Go ahead, Scott," Leo told me. "Then come talk to me."

That shook me. "Don't you need to sit in on this?"

He shook his head. "Of all people, I know best how laconic

you can be, Scott. Just tell the truth."

As the interview was about to restart, Detective Sandy Allen stepped into the lounge and did a double-take, with special attention to the two awesomely-attired academics. "Did I miss something?"

Detective Rogers sniffed. "Dispatch let a name or two slip and someone obviously picked it up on a police scanner."

Detective Allen smirked. "Jolly." Then she turned to Sheila. "Hello, I'm Sandy Allen. With the police."

"Weren't you watching Charlie?" I asked, a little nervous that she was here instead of there.

"They're draining the wound and changing his dressing." She closed her eyes and gave a delicate shiver.

Sheila's hand went to her mouth. Her face paled behind her fingers.

Detective Allen put a hand on Sheila's shoulder. "I'm sorry. I shouldn't say things like that out loud."

"It's not that." Sheila covered her mouth again and sat, breathing into her closed fist. "I've just been running on adrenaline since I got the news." She looked at me. "Is he okay?"

I shrugged. "So far, so good."

She stood. "I'm going to go see him." I think she wiped away a couple of tears.

"I'll go with you." Detective Allen threw a sisterly arm over Sheila's shoulder. "You know how doctors are."

I agreed with that sentiment and gave Dr. Pott the thousand-yard stare. Rogers saw me do it.

"I take it he's not your gramps?"

"More like my employer. Dr. John Pott."

Rogers nodded. "And the other guy?"

"Dr. Hanson," I said. "Don't remember his first name. He's an administrator for the project I'm involved in."

Rogers whistled and gave the two leather-bound, bookish men another once over. "Did you know they were bikers?"

I chuckled. "They seemed more like amateur Piper pilots to me."

"Let's go somewhere else," he said. "All that leather is making me sweaty."

We ended up outside Charlie's room again and the conversation was less formal. I gave Rogers my practiced, abbreviated autobiography, finishing with admission to Georgetown. I mentioned the perks that entailed, including being watched by persons known, Drs. Pott and Hanson, and unknown, the guy that skewered Charlie's leg. I almost told him about my clothing and the trashed lockers, but decided to wait for the recap.

I peeked in and saw Sheila at Charlie's bedside, speaking to Detective Allen. I couldn't hear her, but she didn't look sick anymore. I couldn't see Charlie but I saw his watch, a burnished stainless steel diver's watch that must have weighed half a pound, resting on his bedside table.

Beside me, Detective Rogers chuckled. "That Nine-One-One operator just about had a fit when she learned there *was* no doctor on the scene and that the call had been made by a six-year-old kid."

I smiled, but I wanted to gag.

"Do you know why Charlie was back there?" Rogers asked. He didn't have his notebook out. He was done recording facts.

"I want to kick him for it," I said, "but I think he was following a guy that was watching us eat."

"You don't like people watching you eat?"

"The timing was kind of spooky." The next words were out of my mouth before I could recall them. "We were discussing my apartment and clothing being bugged."

Rogers looked at me for a moment. Then he opened his notebook and wrote something. "That sounds pretty serious," he said. "But it has nothing to do with drugs."

"Right," I said, still nervous about my slip. "Charlie isn't a health nut, but he doesn't do drugs. Do them, sell them." I remembered Charlie's refusal to buy me cigarettes I hadn't asked for. "Advocate them," I added to the list.

"Mmm hmm," Detective Rogers said. He looked at me, put a finger to his lips and handed me a sheet of note paper.

Bugging your apartment and clothing?

Is this true? Nod twice

I folded the paper, handed it back to him, and nodded twice as if watching a bouncing ball. I wanted to hug him for taking me seriously. I also wanted to kick myself talking about the bugs out loud.

Rogers stuck the paper in his pocket and whistled through his teeth. Right then, he seemed more like a regular person than a cop. He was still the archetypal paunchy detective with the smart mouth and repetitive questions but I now saw him in a new light. A file labeled 'Detective Rogers' moved to a different drawer in my brain.

Like with Dr. Oesche, I didn't know if the change was in my perception or the other person's behavior. Right now, it was just another datum to save for The Project.

"I'd like to call you," Detective Rogers said, "if I have any more questions."

"Sure," I said and gave him both my phone numbers. "Anything I can do to help." I looked in the room. Sheila and Detective Allen stood at Charlie's bedside, whispering. "I feel more than a little responsible."

"And why's that?" Intentional or not, Detective Rogers reverted to cop mode. I exercised the right to keep my big mouth shut.

"Never mind," I said. "I've just got a lot on my mind these days."

He patted my shoulder. "I don't doubt it, son. By the way, we've got the security videos from the mall. I'll bring them here to the hospital, see if Mr. Bailey recognizes his attacker in any of the shots. You'll want to have a look, too."

I almost reminded him I hadn't seen the attacker, but Rogers was twirling his finger and cuing me to answer in the affirmative. With his other hand, he showed me the note he had written moments before. I almost hadn't expected him to remember. If he showed interest, though, I had an obligation to see it through.

"Yeaahhhh," I said, watching his face for another signal. "Sure. Any reason I can't do it tonight, though?"

"Yeah," he said, "'cause you look like you've been up since Labor Day." He pointed into Charlie's room. "And your mom might need some hand-holding."

"Yeah, okay," I said, thinking I might need some, too.

Detective Rogers leaned in and gave a discreet whistle. Detective Allen patted Sheila on the back before coming to the door, shaking my hand and wishing me a good night. I almost expected a pat on the head or a peck on the cheek. I couldn't believe she was a narcotics detective. She was more like the kind of teacher kids actually liked.

I heard a sniff from Charlie's room and decided I had avoided Sheila long enough.

I went in and my first look at Charlie stunned me. His true condition hadn't registered before, apparently. As if ignoring his fragile state made it less true.

It was, though. All too true.

The bed was inclined a little, maybe the only thing that made him look alive. It must be some kind of psychological trick. Elevated torsos and hospital gowns make patients look less like they're on the slab. No matter how discolored, bruised or lacerated, if we make him look like he just dozed off while watching *Seinfeld,* he'll be fine.

I was glad he was propped up. I couldn't have seen his face if he were lying flat.

"How did you know to come?" I asked Sheila, taking her hand.

Sheila nodded toward the bed. "Charlie called from the hospital phone. Said there was trouble, to bring Leo. Something about you being detained by the cops." She sniffed. She wasn't really crying, but she wore depression like a mat of sodden cobwebs.

It was just like Charlie to watch out for me, even half-drained of blood and doped up. Perhaps he just didn't want Sheila to have police call and ask, "Are you the mother of Scott Bledsoe?" He did both of us a favor on that count.

Charlie's glasses lay on the over-the-bed table, a little smudged. Perhaps a drop of blood from the faucet in his leg.

His glasses were always so clean you'd think he wore empty frames. That smudge must have hit me pretty hard, because before I knew it, I was wiping my eyes and burying my face in Sheila's side, trying not to sob. Sheila ran her hand through my hair and held me.

"I can't believe this happened," I whispered.

"I still can't even imagine it," Sheila whispered back. "I told that lady detective — Sandy — I can't imagine why anyone would want to hurt Charlie."

"Yeah," I said. I didn't want to say anything when there were possibly microphones in my clothing. I couldn't really concentrate with Charlie lying there, so naked and fragile without his glasses. He wasn't pale, but without glasses, his face looked different. His eyes looked small and feeble.

I reached out and touched his cheek. It was stubbly and warm and that made me feel a little better. If he had been clammy I might have gotten weak in the knees.

After we spent a few more minutes watching Charlie not move or talk, a nurse told us that we ought to go home and go to bed.

Sheila took me to her house and, for the first time in years, tucked me in.

37

TV Time

Charlie looked miles better the next morning but he hated not to be up and cooking breakfast. As he ate his fruit cup, I reminded him that even heroes wind up in nursing homes. He threw something at me that might once have been a grape.

Sheila stood at his bedside, pushing his hair back off his forehead. Was this a spark between them? I had never even seen them shake hands. But no. She was so hard up for someone to look after that Charlie's boo-boo brought out her maternal instincts.

"How are you feeling?" she asked him.

He was throwing fruit, I thought. How hurt could he be?

Charlie grinned at Sheila. "About a quart low."

Sheila's next question was less solicitous. "What on earth possessed you to follow that guy?" She swatted his arm. "All by yourself! Were you trying to get hurt?"

"I never thought I'd get stabbed." He winced and lightly

touched his bandage. "I won't make that mistake again. This is not a comfortable place to have stitches."

"Why didn't you stay with me?" I asked Charlie. "When I looked around and you weren't there, for a minute I thought ... "

"What?" Charlie asked.

I sighed. "That you might have been in cahoots with ... them."

Charlie laced his hands behind his head. "I hope this clears me."

I nodded. "Your blood gets spilled, you're acquitted."

Charlie grinned. "I could have died, then you could have felt *really* guilty."

Sheila sniffed at that, but I returned Charlie's grin.

"How's everyone this morning?" Detective Rogers said as he and Detective Allen stepped through the door. Another man followed, trying to hide in Rogers's shadow.

"Hungry," Charlie said. "Otherwise, much better than last night."

Detective Rogers shook Charlie's hand, then mine. He nodded to Sheila. He noticed us watching the young man who had entered with them. "This here is Troy Baldwin, our favorite tech guy."

Troy put a laptop computer with a huge monitor — probably twenty inches across — on Charlie's over-the-bed table. He tapped a few keys and brought up a window. It was security camera footage from the mall where two of us had eaten and one of us had been stabbed.

"The extra large monitor is to help ensure accurate visual IDs of suspects," Troy said. "People make mistakes or worse, guesses, when they can't see things clearly."

"Watch a little while and see if you recognize anyone," Detective Allen said. "This one starts about fifteen minutes before your sandwich shop receipt says you got your food."

"That wasn't when we got our food," Charlie said with a sneer. "It's when they got their money."

Charlie and I watched the show, noting our own entrance and the time we spent in line getting subs. Sheila hadn't been there, but Detective Allen invited her to watch, too, saying she might recognize someone that we didn't. No one mentioned it, but I realized what it might mean: if Sheila recognized Charlie's assailant, it suggested a conspiracy dating back months.

All the way back to Roanoke.

"Can we fast-forward it a little?" Charlie asked. "I didn't even see the guy until we finished eating."

"All the more reason to watch the whole thing," Detective Allen said. "You might see something you missed the first time."

The picture was amazingly clear, scrolling through four views of the food court, shot from near the atrium's high ceiling. Two seconds at a time, each camera gave us a look at ourselves from a new perspective. No wonder I'd felt watched, and long before Charlie noticed the unwelcome eyes.

"There he is," Charlie murmured. He used his fruit cup spoon to indicate a hooded figure gliding across the field of view. Then the view changed and we saw him from the front. Charlie swore under his breath and ran his fingers over the computer. "Where's the pause button?"

Troy Baldwin stepped forward to push a key. The picture paused, then backed up one frame at a time until the hooded figure's face was in the center of the screen. "Well, that doesn't help much," he said.

"Why not?" Sheila asked.

Baldwin used the touch pad device to enlarge the shot from the center, giving us a close-up.

"He looks familiar, all right," I said. "He looks like the police sketch of Ted Kaczynski."

Troy looked up from the keyboard. "Who?"

"The Unabomber," I said.

Troy still gave me a blank look. "Kid, I know who the Unabomber is," he said. "How do *you* know?"

I ignored Troy and looked at Detective Rogers. "He's right. This doesn't help much. We have a lookalike for the most famous suspect composite sketch ever."

"Keep watching," Detective Allen said. "You don't want to give up on the plot after only half the movie."

We paused the recording from time to time, watching the people. But my eyes kept going to the table where Charlie and I sat, stuffing our faces. To all outward appearances, we seemed to be having a father/son, big brother/little brother moment. I had never seen myself on camera before, only in the mirror. The difference was profound.

I really did look like a kid, six going on seven. Until I moved. The way I held my sandwich, sipped from my soda cup. On an adult, it would have looked normal. On me, it looked fastidious and prissy. The sub and soda could have been a cucumber sandwich and a cup of Earl Grey.

"There," Sheila said, pointing. Troy paused the shot and

we all looked. The hooded figure was walking by a custodian with a broom and dustpan. "That's definitely the walk of a man."

"Or a teenage boy," Detective Allen agreed. "The guy sweeping up looks to be a little over six feet, but our guy is a tad shorter."

"Height isn't everything," I said.

"It is when you're trying to make a visual ID."

I shrugged. "Yeah, he's pretty short. I might have noticed were he next to me."

"He was," Charlie said. "He walked past you three or four times."

I blinked. "I was so fixed on identifying him, I didn't watch where he went." The frame changed and we saw the suspect from the front. "You were right, Charlie. Patriots."

"What?" Sheila asked.

"The guy's wearing a Patriots sweatshirt," Charlie said. "Great picture quality."

"Got to have it these days," Troy said. "Too many people watch *CSI*. Keeps us on our toes, though."

"He *does* look familiar," I said. "I can't place him, but I know the walk. The way he holds his spine absolutely straight, like he's got a flagpole up his ... back."

"It's a trick short people sometimes use to look taller," Detective Allen said. "Makes him stick out, doesn't it?"

"He make any calls from my phone?" Charlie asked.

Detective Rogers shook his head. "That would be nice, wouldn't it? Too bad he's not dumb enough to try it."

"He was smart enough to take the phone away and leave me bleeding to death in a remote spot," Charlie said. "It didn't seem like a spur of the moment decision."

"You never know what you'll do when the moment arrives," Detective Allen said.

"Yeah," Charlie said. "I thought I'd scream bloody murder if stabbed anywhere, but four inches from my groin and all I do is gasp and wheeze."

"How could you not know whether you'd been shot or stabbed?" I said.

"Probably shock. I remember it now, though." Charlie elevated his bed even more and looked at the figure on the screen, almost a caricature of criminal notoriety. "I noticed him watching us, walking past every now and then. I thought he was working up the courage to ask for a handout. Then what Scott was saying hit home, and I knew we were being watched."

"Was that when you told me to skedaddle?" I asked.

"Yeah." He tore his eyes away from the screen and shifted on the bed. "I had this feeling things were about to go down. Like maybe a shootout. I wanted you out of there ASAP."

"But why did you go after that guy yourself?" Sheila asked.

Another time, Charlie might have blushed. Once you're in a hospital gown, though, you save the blushes for when you're up and about. "It was a combination of things, I guess. Scott telling me about stuff going on, then seeing that guy ... ." He paused, took a deep breath and shifted again. "I just lost my temper."

"What, you hit him?" Detective Rogers asked.

Charlie shook his head. "I just walked after him. The guy came so close, I thought, he obviously wanted to be seen.

Maybe I was just trying to show him I wasn't intimidated.

"Catching up to him was easy, but when I put my hand on his shoulder, he popped like a mousetrap. Next thing I knew, I was on the floor, trying to hold my blood in." Then Charlie tilted his head, resembling a TV news reporter hearing updates through an earpiece. He looked up at Detective Rogers. "Another thing," Charlie said. "The guy had braces."

"Seriously?" Detective Allen said. Detective Rogers was scribbling in his notebook.

Charlie took off his glasses. "Would I make up something like that?" He picked up the nurses' call button and pressed it hard.

"Can I help you?" the wall said.

"Ow!" Charlie said. "Very ow!"

"Room a little crowded?"

"Yeah," he told the wall, "but they kinda need to be here."

"I'll send someone right away," the nurse promised.

"Braces?" I asked. "Like on your teeth, braces?"

"Right," Charlie said. "Not British suspenders."

"Two decent clues," Detective Rogers said. "Height and dental appliances."

"He looked kind of young, too," Charlie said. "High-school-young not college-young," Charlie said. "Of course, maybe he's like Scott. Early admittance."

"What," I said, "you think he's from Georgetown?"

"Easiest way in the world to keep tabs on you."

Charlie's idea sounded clever, but I was sure I'd notice someone that young at Georgetown. Of course, most very young students were more reclusive than I. They probably lived on campus, too.

Detective Rogers mumbled to himself as he scribbled. "Check ... all ... underage ... students."

"Hold that thought, Tim," Detective Allen said. "I want to check something before we start harassing every kid with braces."

"Okay, okay," Rogers said. I couldn't help seeing him as a henpecked husband. Neither he nor Detective Allen wore a wedding band, but not every married person did. "One more thing, though, and we'll let Mr. Bailey here get some rest." Rogers gave Troy Baldwin a significant nod and stepped aside to let him approach.

Then Detectives Rogers and Allen took turns rattling off best and worst case scenarios for the outcome of the search for the Dentally-Enhanced Unabomber Lookalike.

Without a word, Troy Baldwin handed me an index card before unplugging every electrical device in the room. While he opened his second attaché case, I read the card.

Remain still and quiet while I scan you for listening and tracking devices. It will take a few moments. Tim and Sandy are talking to distract whoever may be monitoring. If you have a cell phone, hand it to me.

I handed Troy my phone and he scowled as if it were a used Kleenex. Not to his taste, I guessed. Too bad. My mother bought it for me.

Detectives Rogers and Allen read Charlie the *Magna Carta* and the first six Articles of the Constitution, or so it seemed, before Troy clicked his tongue and stowed his high tech equipment.

"Tim," he said over the detectives' recitation, "it's over. You can stop."

"What?" I said. "What did you find?"

"Four devices," he said. "Jacket collar, jeans waistband — rivets, maybe — shoes, and watch."

I blinked. "And you're saying this out loud because ... what, you've disabled them?"

"They disabled themselves," Troy said. "I can't tell if it was automatic or manual, but right when I got an accurate count, they all shut down. It might not be significant, but it took the same amount of time as someone flipping four separate switches."

"So, they're onto us?" Detective Rogers asked.

Troy stared at my jacket collar. "Maybe."

Detective Rogers responded with a word that would make Sheila's blood pressure spike. His partner chided him for it, but he didn't seem to notice. He looked at me and he looked worried. "Troy, can you find out who's running them?"

Troy shrugged. "If we can catch them transmitting, we might get a signal to trace. We could open up the devices and tinker with them, but that would raise red flags on their switchboard and —"

Detective Rogers *ahem*-ed and made a get-on-with-it gesture.

"As they are right now?" Troy shook his head and clicked his tongue.

"Scott, I'd like to — " Rogers began, but Allen put a hand on his arm. Something unspoken passed between them. After a few moments, he seemed to agree to do something —

or maybe not to do something — and nodded his head.

"Troy," he said. "Go to wherever it is you do your thing and find out what you can about the stuff in the clothes." He gestured to me. "You're sure they're off right now?"

Troy checked the device in his hand again and nodded. "Still off."

"Any reason to believe they might not know we're onto them?"

Troy shrugged and clicked his tongue. "Maybe when I scanned, they thought the kid was getting feedback from a nearby machine and they shut down because they only heard noise."

Detective Rogers nodded. "Good enough. We're going to pretend that's what happened. Scott," he turned to me, "don't let on again about the bugs. We ought to assume they're scattered all through your everyday clothes." He looked a question at Troy, who shrugged and nodded. "Keep wearing your old clothes," Rogers told me, "but shut up about them. Same for everyone else." He zipped his lips like a veteran school teacher.

Something about that nagged at the back of my mind. It only took a second to figure out why. "I already did that thing with the locker."

"I know," Rogers said. "But as long as we're pretending one thing, we'll just stretch it to include that. Make believe you did that in all innocence. Fewer ulcers that way."

"I don't get why they put them on him in the first place," Troy said.

"Troy!" Detective Allen said, her voice rising in pitch and volume.

"They're off right now, Sandy," he said. "Remember? Anyway, the range on gadgets of this sort is notoriously short — at least the listening devices. You have to have a relay station if you want to receive more than, say, half a mile away if you're in a building."

"So?" Detective Rogers asked.

Troy raised one finger, about to make a point. "So, most likely they would only be used in certain situations."

"Such as?" I asked.

"When you're in or near buildings on campus," he said. "If they could put those things in your clothes, they probably did it at your house. If they got in there, they can wire the whole place."

I gulped, not liking the sound of that. "That makes sense, but I'm not there all the time."

"Hence, the tracking device," Charlie said. He almost punched the nurse button again, but by the same law that brings dinner to the table while you're in the restaurant lavatory, the nurse showed up at that moment with a covered tray.

"You can put it down, Mr. Bailey," she said. "It's not a remote control. You can't fast-forward me."

Charlie shook his head. "I'm keeping it, in case you're a mirage." He looked at the tray. "I wanted pain relief, not food."

The nurse whisked away the tray's cover to reveal four large hypodermic syringes. "Don't worry. We'll fix you up."

"Thank God for IVs," Charlie said, relaxing back on his pillow. "When you need a shot, it just goes through the express tunnel."

The first syringe the nurse selected appeared to be loaded with mayonnaise and looked like something you'd use to sedate a buffalo — or bring one down at a hundred yards. "Not this one."

"What?" Charlie groaned.

"This is your post-op antibiotic shot," she said, cradling the syringe in her hands like a rifle. "I need you all to leave the room while I make Mr. Bailey cry."

We left him to his doom.

38

Tech Support

I knew it would help catch the culprits, but the idea of leaving the bugs in my clothing gave me the willies.

And it seemed like an awful lot of trouble to bug all my clothing, then only listen to the conversations I had at home. Chats with Charlie, mushy phone calls to Sheila, speaking Japanese along with my iPod for an hour each evening, and G-rated potty mouth when I forgot to start the dishwasher. Why would someone go through so much trouble to listen to that?

I stopped him. "Is it possible that the bugs—"

Troy shook his head and clicked his tongue. "'Listening devices,' kid. Bugs are a thing of the past. Like, twenty, thirty years ago."

I rolled my eyes. "Whatever. Is it possible they have a greater range than you thought?"

"It *is* possible," he said, "but not likely. Anything with

high enough wattage to transmit long distance without a relay station would require bigger batteries. Harder to hide."

I sighed. "So, to get their money's worth — and I'm sure they spent a bundle — they probably would use relay stations, and put them in strategic spots."

Detective Allen looked at me and then at Troy. "Such as?"

"If they can get into my apartment and handle my clothes, it isn't a stretch for them to get a copy of my class schedule."

"And put relay stations in the buildings where you have classes?" Detective Rogers asked. He looked impressed.

"Only if Troy thinks it's possible," I said. "I don't guess these things are cheap."

"Cheap?" Troy said. "Most aren't even legal, strictly speaking, for the same reason you resent having them in your clothes." He got out his electronic wand again and waved it over my torso and extremities again. When it didn't make a peep, he wiped his brow.

"Maybe we ought to just shut up about this, right?" Detective Allen said. "Or maybe speak in code?"

"Another minute, please?" I asked. "I'm on a roll here."

"Okay, Scott," Detective Rogers said, checking his watch. "For another minute, anyway."

I turned to Troy. "If the relay stations are tracking me at school, would it matter where they were in the building?"

"So much for 'speaking in code.'" Allen said.

Troy winked at her before answering. "It could go anywhere, except near load centers or big wiring clusters."

Detective Rogers seemed to catch my idea. "How big

would it have to be?"

Troy clicked his tongue and shook his head. "Not very."

"Think you could find them?" Detective Rogers asked.

"Get with the University people and clear it," he said. "I don't want to get booted out by some prof who thinks I'm trespassing."

"Wait a second," I said. "I'm still cogitating."

They all looked at me the way Charlie used to before he became accustomed to my vocabulary. Detective Rogers stuck his hands in his pockets, maybe to keep from checking his watch again. "Okay," he said. "Shoot."

"If they did place the relay stations," I said, "they're probably at the Research Resource Facility, where I have my 'interviews.' They might be near the classrooms, but all they'd get there are geometry proofs or people asking 'Where is the hospital?' in Japanese."

Troy didn't seem to be listening to my last thoughts. "So we find that one and ... what, turn it off?" The question was not directed at me.

Detective Rogers turned to me. "Scott?"

"Instead of that," I suggested, "can you just mess with it a little?"

"How do you mean?" he asked.

"You know how a short in the co-ax messes up the TV picture?"

"Sure." He folded his arms and looked at me. I couldn't believe he hadn't understood yet.

"What do you do when the picture is messed up, Troy?" Detective Allen asked, so I didn't have to.

"First," Troy said, "don't use co-ax. Use an HDMI cable.

Much better quality."

Detective Roger grunted. "Okay, Troy, what does Joe Sixpack do when the picture is messed up?"

Troy smirked. "Just kidding, folks. I know what you're getting at." He looked at me. "That's a pretty good plan. Fiddle with it and provoke a field response."

I nodded. "And if you can, make it look like an accident. Rats chewing the wires, maybe."

He winked and clicked his tongue. "I'll think of something." He picked up his little duffel bag and walked out of the room.

"I'm going to Georgetown's admissions office to check the student ID photos," Detective Allen said. "I should be able to get copies and bring them in for Mr. Bailey to look at. How are you for classes today, Scott?"

"At the moment, I'm not all that interested in going to class." Someone cleared her throat from the doorway and I remembered who else was listening.

"I know you don't feel like it, Scott," Sheila said, "but you'd probably better go. 'Life as normal' to help avoid suspicion."

"'Life as normal,'" I said. "Right. I'll just have my mommy drive me back to my apartment, leaving my friend-*slash*-guardian in the hospital while I go study Japanese and tenth-grade geometry and wait for a growth spurt so I can reach the soup cabinet without a step stool."

Sheila took a deep breath and sighed it out. "Yes."

Everyone was silent for a moment, especially the detectives.

"Okay," I said.

Detective Allen looked at Sheila with pity and awe. Detective Rogers looked at me. No pity there. I didn't need it anyway. Self-pity was enough for me.

"I'll call you later," Rogers told me. "Let you know when Troy has done his thing. Let's keep the number of people in the know to a minimum. Don't tell anyone else, got it?"

"Fine," I said. Sheila looked at me but I couldn't read her.

Rogers left the room first, followed by Sheila. Detective Allen remained a moment longer, as if deciding to say something.

"I'll be apologizing to Sheila for the rest of the day," I told her. "If it makes you feel better."

"You don't call her 'mom?'" she asked. Instead of a Sunday School teacher, Detective Allen now reminded me of Cynthia Westbrook. Boy, I was starting to miss *her*.

I shrugged. "When I'm talking to her, sure. Not *about* her, though. It's the whole ... brain anomaly ... thing." For the first time in a long while, I had trouble talking about it. For just a moment, I remembered my speculations about the well of knowledge drying up.

But it was mostly embarrassment from being caught at my worst and knowing I wasn't Mr. Popular.

"I see," she said. "It's not any of my business, but do you talk to her like that all the time?"

I snorted. "That's right, it *isn't* your business." Then I sighed. "But I only talk to her like that when I'm under a lot of stress." I stuck my hands in my pockets and wondered if the listening devices had been reactivated yet. If so, they were getting the real dirt now.

"Do you miss her, or are you glad to be out of her house?"

"I miss her plenty," I said, "but she kind of insisted that I leave." I was uncomfortable having this conversation, Sheila possibly within earshot. I didn't want her to overhear something worse than I had said to her face.

"She sent you away?" Detective Allen asked.

"I'm not a pyromaniac or anything," I said. "She just thought I'd be better off on my own. I wasn't all that keen on it then, but that's changed."

"Sounds like she knew you pretty well."

"She still does," I said. "Her advice is good, even if her timing stinks." My memory resonated with the detective's last statement. "You seem to know Detective Rogers pretty well."

She blinked. "We've known each other for several years."

"Not married, are you?" Right away, I wanted to bite back the words, afraid I'd royally stepped in it.

But Detective Allen laughed. "No!" she said. "We've just worked together forever. Twenty years or so. Why do you ask?"

"You stopped him from asking me something," I said. "He seemed to read your mind."

"Stopped him from ... oh!" she said. "When we were in Mr. Bailey's room." She looked at her hands and rubbed them together. "He was going to ask if you knew who might ... " she laid a finger on my shirt collar, " ... want to cause you grief."

"Who might have planted the bugs," she didn't say. She was taking no more chances.

"Why'd you stop him?"

She sighed and looked down at me. "Because regardless of

his demeanor or intelligence level, we can't just ask a young boy to offer up a list of suspects."

I scowled. "Why? Because my list might include the boogeyman?"

She grimaced and shrugged. "Solicited or not, we'd have a hard time getting a D.A. to act based solely on your say-so."

I threw one hand up in disgust. "That makes no sense at all!"

"I know," she said, "but for now, just count yourself lucky Troy was able to, uh, get a good picture of Charlie's assailant ... *among other things.* That's real evidence that can be acted upon."

"Fine," I said. I didn't count myself lucky, though. Troy's finding them meant there was something to find. Add that to the attack on Charlie, and it meant I *wasn't* paranoid.

I almost wished I were.

39

Keeping in Touch

I

I did *not* want to go to my session with The Doc Flock that afternoon. Call me irresponsible, call me unreliable, but all I wanted to do was sleep. I put on my new Georgetown sweats in preparation for a nice, mind-wiping snooze.

Almost all the participants were out-of-towners, though, so it would be very bad form to play hooky. These guys weren't likely to say "oh, well" and just drive back home, especially with the astronomical price of gas — or the astronomical price of *me*. Even if I bought a round of pizza, they'd have good reason to gripe.

I wanted advice, but I didn't have many options. Charlie was laid up, Sheila wasn't feeling maternal and I didn't know Detectives Rogers and Allen well enough to ask. I could always wait until my therapy hour, but I had reason to distrust Dr. Oesche, no matter how effective she was.

I convinced myself that only Barbara could provide the advice I needed. It was a cheap way to get past my conscience, but I couldn't give all my decisions equal rumination. I didn't relish a five-way migraine.

On a whim, I took a short walk — on the theory that my walls had ears — and called Barbara's number, ready to hang up when I heard what I thought of as the "denial tone." I nearly dropped the phone when Barbara picked up.

"Did I forget what day it is?"

"I can't believe I got you!"

"Maybe you didn't. Check and see what number you dialed."

"What happened to your phone?"

"Couldn't pay the bill. Finances aren't great right now."

"Now I feel like a snob."

"It's okay, but what possessed you to call today?"

"Can't I just call to say hi?"

"You're the one who made the rules."

"That one was dumb," I said. "I don't know what I was thinking."

"Do you want to discuss how dumb it was or did you have something on your mind?"

"You might have heard something about it," I said. "I know it made the local news."

"Only thing I saw in the news from your area was about a stabbing at some mall drug deal."

"Wow," I said. "I'm impressed. They got it half right."

"You have my complete attention," she said. *"Whom did you stab?"*

For a moment, I thought the same thing everyone else did when they heard *me* speak: *When was the last time you heard a six-year-old say "whom?"* "I just made the 911 call," I said. "The victim was my guardian."

There was silence.

"Are you there?"

"I was going to say 'you really know how to pick'em,' but I didn't want to be mean."

"Thanks," I said dryly. "It wasn't a drug deal. It was a stalker, but he wasn't very subtle about it. He could have been wearing a sandwich board reading 'I'm stalking you' and been less obvious." I was exaggerating, of course. It was embarrassing not to notice the guy.

"And you got into a knife fight with him?" She sounded more impressed than upset.

"Charlie did," I said, "but he forgot his knife."

"From the lightness of your tone, I take it he's doing okay."

I took a deep breath, remembering how he looked before I left the hospital. "He's got a nasty three-inch-deep stab wound, made with a serrated knife. Extreme upper thigh."

"Peritoneal penetration?"

"No," I said. "One of the first things we checked for." I paused. "How is it that we know that kind of medical terminology?"

"I don't know about you, but I watch E.R. from time to time."

"Yeah," I said, "but I didn't speculate. I actually gave the inbound EMT's fair warning about what they would find." I smiled. "They kept looking for the 'woman doctor' who had called in the emergency."

"That's funny," she said. *"Without my voice synthesizer, I still sound like a little girl over the phone."*

"No, *I* sound like a little girl. *You* sound like Lauren Bacall. Do you have an answer to my question?"

"You could ask the project people," she said. *"Like it or not,*

they've got the most info about the original project. Maybe one of the donors was an army medic or something."

"Maybe," I said, unconvinced, "but that brings me to why I called. I kinda, sorta ... went to the police."

"Excuse me?" She didn't sound upset, but maybe it just hadn't sunk in yet.

"I was telling one of the case detectives about my recent mental state," I said, "and I happened to mention the likelihood that my clothing was bugged."

"You said it ... out loud?"

Cold sweat formed along my spine for a moment before I realized I was in my one sure set of safe clothes.

"Stupid, I know. But I didn't say anything else. This morning, Detective Rogers, the guy in charge, brought in a tech guy with a sweeper for bugs. The moment he found them, they all shut off."

"I don't like this." Now she sounded worried. *"Someone could be onto you."*

"The cops don't think so," I said. "Or at least the tech guy doesn't. He thinks the shutdown might be an automated response to excess feedback. He guesses interference from all the hospital machines might have masked our talking."

"He guesses?" she asked. *"I'm no expert on those devices, but that's pretty lax. What did you say when they asked whom you suspected?"*

"Not a thing," I said. "No matter the weird stuff I'm involved in, it all comes down to my being too young for my word to be trusted."

"If you'd accused them of ... other inappropriate behavior, they wouldn't hesitate to act."

"I already thought of that," I said, though I hadn't. "But why ruin someone's life with a random accusation? It could be *anybody*. But I've got another plan."

"Do tell." She didn't sound excited.

I explained my idea about jimmying with the supposed relay stations in order to flush out the bad guys.

"Forgive me for doubting you," she said. *"Excellent. When will you do it?"*

"Soon," I said. "As soon as Troy, the tech guy, gives the go ahead."

"Then ... I wish you luck," she said.

"So ... you think I should?"

"I'm not sure, but you may not get another chance like this."

I took a few breaths before uttering the next sentence. "I wish I could see you again."

"Me too, but you better go to your therapy session."

We said bye-bye and broke the connection. The phone call might turn out to be more therapeutic than my session with Dr. Oesche. I was accomplishing more on my own than the Project was on my behalf.

II

I had my first pleasant surprise in days when I showed up for my evening therapy session and Cynthia Westbrook greeted me.

"Welcome back! " I said. "I got a little worried when you were gone two whole weeks."

She smiled. "I appreciate that. A number of people resent

a substitute therapist. I trust Dr. Oesche didn't do you irreparable harm?"

I bit my tongue and let her draw her own conclusions.

Before long, we were off and running. I would have said "just like normal," but we'd only met twice before Dr. Oesche's turn. We just got on well, I guessed. Just like before.

"Since you've got proof someone's spying on you," she said halfway through our session, "I obviously can't label you 'paranoid.'"

I had wrestled with the idea of telling Dr. Westbrook about the bugs — forget what Troy said; they were still bugs to me — and decided to go ahead, just because I was still in my Georgetown sweats. I wore the tainted garments at other times, but I didn't want *anyone* listening in on my therapy sessions.

"I keep thinking how easy it was," I said. "People believed me, right away. I was afraid they'd think I was nuts, like in the movies." I smiled at her. "Sorry. 'Paranoid.'"

She wrote in her notebook and shook her head, smiling. "No paranoid delusions. How about other feelings? Stress?"

I almost laughed. "This doesn't qualify as stress?"

She shook her head. "I mean your day-to-day life. Anything freaking you out?" She tucked her feet under her. "If you were a little older, I might ask you if you were having romantic or sexual problems."

My eyes widened. "No, none of that."

"I didn't think so," she said. "What about Charlie?"

"I think he's too busy healing for that right now."

She chuckled. "I meant your relationship with him."

"What about it?"

"You don't talk about him much," she said. "How do you feel about him being your guardian?"

I scratched my head. "Well, I talked a little about Charlie with Dr. Oesche. 'Guardian' is just his official title. He treats me like an adult. He's here mostly because my mother trusts him. To make sure I'm not overburdened with protective adults."

She wrote in her notebook again, though I didn't think I had said anything earth-shattering. "Other protective adults being most everyone else. Am I right?"

"Oh, yeah," I said. "Sally Oddchester at the Student Center coffee bar, who won't even give me decaf. Drs. Pott and Hanson, showing up at the hospital when Charlie was stabbed." I sneered. "Like I was some mafioso's kid in trouble and the *consigliere* was there to box my ears and make sure I kept my yap shut."

Dr. Westbrook's eyes widened. "Pardon?"

During the couple of minutes I spent explaining the family hierarchy in *The Godfather,* I reached the unsettling conclusion that, no matter how much I liked Cynthia's company, I preferred Dr. Oesche's treatment. I didn't have to explain every analogy to her, and she didn't make me feel like a subject for a dissertation.

I could learn to cope with Dr. Oesche's perfume ... if I knew I could trust her.

III

The last thing on my schedule that day was a Q and A

with the Docs. I was on time, as was most everyone, but Dr. Pott was late. I pictured him in his old three-piece suit, checking his watch as he rode his Harley down the campus's cobbled lanes, edging past pedestrians. When he showed up ten minutes late, he didn't carry a helmet. He was a little disheveled, but looked more sleep-deprived than windblown.

There was a new schedule rotation that day, but few changes. Just new people asking the questions. One young English doctor even made the session entertaining, with the most eclectic word association game I've ever played.

He said, "skateboard."

I said, "helmet."

Leprechaun.

Breakfast cereal.

Napkin.

Lap.

Darwin.

Award.

Dr. Pott, the usual master of ceremonies, was oddly silent, lips pressed together as if he were chewing something with his front teeth. Questions dwindled to a trickle, the interviewers' lists having been depleted for the moment. Dr. Pott ostentatiously pulled a pocket watch from his vest, checked it against the wall clock, stage left. I thought he would conclude the session and thank everyone for his or her participation, but he didn't. He clicked his watch shut, then looked at me.

"*Mister* Bledsoe ... " he began, and I suddenly felt as if I were before a congressional subcommittee.

"Yes?" I hoped no one heard me gulp.

"Do you ever have ...," he paused, maybe for effect, "that is ... do you suffer from paranoia?"

I blinked. That was a remarkable coincidence, paranoia being the subject of the greater part of my hour with Dr. Westbrook. It was also not the kind of question I would have expected of Dr. Pott. He was more subtle, like a timid chess player who bites all his nails before collapsing your ironclad strategic position like a house of cards.

"No." The best kind of answer. No ambiguity.

"No?" Dr. Pott seemed surprised.

"That's right," I said. "I do not suffer from paranoia. Paranoid schizophrenia or even the non-psychotic, 'poor me,' blues."

Dr. Pott watched me and I watched him. The rest of the Flock watched both of us. I began to expect some sort of reprisal for the hospital scene. Despite his words — and his impressive costume — Drs. Pott and Hanson had seemed more like ambulance chasers than concerned patrons.

I sat a few moments longer while the Docs gathered their belongings. Those who didn't already know each other exchanged pleasantries and business cards. Dr. Pott handled questions from two or three younger participants and did his level best not to look at me, even when I was in his line of sight.

I was glad I hadn't mentioned the bugged clothing to him or Dr. Hanson. Maybe I had just identified a suspect.

I left the room and almost ran over Troy Baldwin. I nearly spoke to him, but shut up immediately when I realized why he was there. When I kept my mouth shut, he breathed a sigh of relief.

Instead of his nerd outfit he wore twill khaki work pants and shirt. He carried a toolbox and wore a visitor badge on his breast pocket. He had no ladder and wasn't dirty, so he'd probably just arrived. He stood just outside the lecture hall and acted as if he were waiting for someone. He was in the right place. After all, who better to have such a thing installed than the man in charge of the project?

I gave Troy a discreet wink and left him to his work. I wondered what he would think if he knew I had already figured out who the culprit was.

Later, a voice mail from Detective Rogers confirmed I was right. Just not the way I thought.

40

Roundup

"Please run that by me again." I reached Detective Rogers in his car on the way to the police station. He had an interesting collection of arrestees.

"Well, first we found the knife man," he said. *"Wasn't too hard. Showed his picture around the mall, then the campus."*

"Who was it?" It made me a little ill to think I might have known him.

"A young fella by the name of Whitney Horton," he said. Then, maybe because good cops are mind readers, he asked, *"Know him?"*

"I don't think so," I said. "Who is he?"

"One of your crowd."

"You'll have to elaborate."

He chuckled. *"Underage college student. He ain't seventeen yet, but he's four years in. Imagine that."*

"Just think what I'll be like after four years. Any leads on why he did it?"

314

"The young Mr. Horton fingered Dr. Levon Hanson as his puppeteer."

"Hanson?"

"You sound surprised."

"No too much," I said, "considering the company he keeps."

"The kid's kind of in a bad way right now, though."

"In what way?" I asked.

"He's schizophrenic, but there's evidence that he's not been medicated in weeks. Put up a heck of a fight when we went to pick him up. He had to be sedated and now he's at the University Hospital on suicide watch."

I was glad I was sitting. "Did he say how Hanson got him to do it, or why?"

"Haven't gotten that far yet. Clinically paranoid he might be, but there were enough details in his story that I'm compelled to believe him. As it was, his insistence that Hanson had a hand in things was enough to get the D.A. interested. When I told the D.A. about the all the unwanted doodads in your clothes, he got a judge to issue a warrant and we went to pick up Hanson at his office."

"I sense a long story coming on," I said. "You didn't have to shoot it out with him, did you?"

"Nope, he came quietly as you please. He smiled the whole time and chuckled to himself. Actually said, 'Okay, okay, you got me.'"

"So you've got the culprit and the conspirator," I said. "Assuming Charlie can make the positive I.D. and the D.A.'s convinced Hanson was the string puller, will they be arraigned soon?"

"I'm not finished!" Rogers wasn't giggly by nature, but he was excited. *"When Hanson saw the precinct, he must have felt a*

little less confident about his chances. Before he even called his lawyer, he tried to cut a deal by offering up another conspirator."

I waited for it.

"We're on our way to pick up Dr. Pott right now," he said. *"You ever hear something so convoluted?"*

"When this is over, I'll give you the details regarding my matriculation at a prestigious private college at age six-point-something." I smiled to myself. "You might as well tell Troy he can leave off crawling around in attics. We won't need our better mousetraps anymore."

"Shoot, no!" he said. *"The more evidence, the better. Let him find what he can. He might end up getting to keep the hardware when the trial's over."*

"By that time it'll be obsolete."

"You're kinda pessimistic," he said.

"Just a little."

"Go ahead and tell Mr. Bailey the good news while we go flush out Dr. Pott."

I groaned but offered a warning. "Be careful. You've got Hanson, but he might have the rest of his biker gang with him."

He laughed and said goodbye.

II

"I knew there was something I didn't like about that man." Charlie sounded a lot like Sheila over the phone. *"Did they have reasons for doing what they did, or are they just plain evil?"*

"Detective Rogers didn't say, but I can guess. I'm just worried they'll let Whitney Hopkins take the fall, claiming that he was delusional. Even after Hanson offered them

Pott."

Charlie chuckled. *"It sounds like he tried to bribe them with marijuana."*

I grinned into the phone. "Well, where there's smoke ... ."

Charlie guffawed and repeated my words before continuing. *"I still don't get why Hanson ratted Pott out."*

"Even smart people do dumb things sometimes," I said. "Like not making sure the hospital electrical system is up to code before conducting an experiment involving brain waves."

Charlie repeated what I said, but a background chuckle told me he wasn't the only one enjoying my wit. *"By the way,"* he said, *"your mother would like to know if you'd like to join us for dinner."*

I wasn't sure what to say. Sheila was there again? Or there still?

"I don't know," I said. "Are we dining *à l'hôpital?"*

"I was thinking steak house," he said. *"I might be wearing your mother down. She said she's willing to try red meat."*

"When are they letting you out?"

"Sometime this evening, supposedly. My wound hasn't had to be drained for twelve hours so they figure infection's being kept at bay."

"Yuck, but good news," I said. "Someone gonna come by and pick me up or do I need to walk?"

"Scott, you couldn't run fast enough. We'll pick you up."

"Are you okay to drive?" I asked. "Friends don't let friends, et cetera, et cetera."

"Don't worry, your mom's driving. With these stitches, I can't even push the gas pedal."

I wondered where in Sheila's Honda he was going to put his crutches when I overheard him say, *"Sure you can handle the Four-in-the-Floor?"* He was gonna let Sheila drive the Camaro while I sat in my little booster chair? Just for that, I was going to order lobster.

"See you soon," I said. "Please don't honk from the driveway."

"You got it. I'll bring a bullhorn."

"As long as you don't honk."

As I hung up, I was almost certain I heard Sheila giggle, which was almost as odd as hearing her swear. I hadn't exactly pushed Charlie at her, or her at Charlie, for that matter, but I had hopes ... and a few reservations, too. Now that she wasn't looking after me all the time, she might be able to try living a life of her own.

But Charlie was the proverbial first-guy-to-come-along. That character who led to so many unhappy endings. It would be unbearably awkward for all of us if things didn't work out.

I was going to take a shower and change clothes before Charlie arrived but I don't remember what happened in the few minutes after I spoke to Charlie.

I didn't make the dinner date.

41

Change in Scenery and Wardrobe

I opened my eyes, but that doesn't really count as waking up. I saw darkness and things moving in it. I heard music, like from a stereo with one blown speaker, but I couldn't tell if it was vocal or instrumental. I could discern nothing else.

I closed my eyes again.

I opened my eyes again. It felt like the hundredth time. I didn't even know if I opened both at once or alternated. I imagined red flashing things and a *ding-ding-ding* sound warning of something big and metal on the way.

I opened both of my eyes and saw words. Well, letters. I couldn't make out the words. J-E-S-S-U-P. And numerals. Four and one together. I wondered, did that mean five? No. Duh. Forty-one. Then another sign. A red and blue shield with the number ninety-five on it.

I saw something else. A sign of some kind with lights underneath. Cooke Tire Inc.

Cooking tires in ink, I thought. *Or would that be braise?* Either way, it sure would turn out *black*.

Charlie's Camaro sure had grown, I thought. A moment later, I realized I was in a van. I couldn't move and thought I was still too groggy, but it was only a double shoulder harness, like a race driver. Or a straitjacket.

My clothing felt odd, too. Itchy, but not as uncomfortable as looking into the front seats and seeing no one I recognized. Even in the dark, I knew neither Sheila nor Charlie rode up front. A stinking miasma of old tobacco smoke confirmed it: these were strangers.

The driver's head turned, so I closed my eyes and let my mouth hang open. I didn't squeeze my eyelids too tightly. If they fluttered a little, it might look like REM sleep, and I could peek from time to time.

The driver was a man. I smelled perfume, too. The other person was a woman, but probably not Dr. Oesche. It didn't necessarily prove her innocence, but at least she wasn't a kidnapper.

In less time than it takes to tell it, I put some things together. I was traveling north on Interstate 95 with people I didn't know, in a van I didn't remember getting into, wearing a dress I didn't remember putting on.

This last didn't really shock me until I thought about it. The sleeves felt scratchy on my arms, just like taffeta worn under a coat. I let my head loll forward, strained to see what I was wearing, and then noticed the wheelchair.

I was in a wheelchair, in a van equipped with a wheelchair lift. Too weird for words.

The folks up front were very quiet now. No radio played now, music or talk. On any other car trip, I'd have gone right back to sleep.

Obviously, I'd been abducted from my apartment. The idea was still a little sluggish, working through my mind like a drunken caterpillar. When my brain was firing on all cylinders again, I decided the dress was a disguise. My neck itched, too, as if the barber forgot to brush little bits of hair away.

But it wasn't hair clippings. I wore a shoulder-length wig. In my puzzlement, my forehead wrinkled and I felt where it had been glued to my skin near the hairline.

Whoever they were, they had laid it on thick. I had gone from average-sized boy with short hair to wheelchair-bound girl with long hair. It was good thing I didn't wear glasses or they might have taken them away, leaving me even worse off.

They had kidnapped me, disguised me and transported me across a state line — Washington, D.C. to Maryland, anyway — so I expected cold, calculating professionals. But from the way the driver kept checking the watch on his right wrist, despite the clock on the dashboard, it wouldn't be long before someone's nerves frayed.

Soon my patience was rewarded.

"The search is on." A woman whose voice I didn't recognize spoke quietly from the passenger seat. "State Police are on alert." She popped out an earphone. Green LED's flickered like tiny airport runway lights on a hand-held device. A police scanner.

"Don't tell me you're worried now," the driver said. *He* sounded worried.

"I'm not," the woman said, stowing the scanner and its

earphone. "Do you need to stop and pee?"

"I'm too uptight to let go."

"Chill," the woman said. "Now would be a good time."

"To chill or to pee?"

"Both," the woman said. "Pull off at the next exit."

"Is that smart?" the man asked. "Why don't we keep going?"

"Because I need to pee."

"You just said they're on alert!" he whispered at the top of his voice. I heard rustling fabric and knew he had turned to look at me. Luckily, my eyes were already closed. "How long will the kid be out?"

I heard another rustle and a squeak from the passenger side. "I'm not an anesthesiologist."

"You know more than me," the man said.

"I used enough to put him out!" she snapped. "You want his heart to stop?"

Perhaps they had consciences after all, I thought.

But then the driver said something that made me wonder.

"We should have put him in a steel drum," he said. "Punch a few holes in it, stick it on the back of a truck—"

"And what if there's a wreck?" the woman asked. "Or an inspection at one of those weigh stations? And what would our clients think if we got there and said 'Here's the kid. Hope you got a can opener?'"

I had relaxed too much. The little jest made me exhale a short, sharp laugh, like a polite sneeze. The driver started so violently that the van swerved. He and the woman both said a few things I won't repeat, while he got it back under control. A moment later, he seemed to be pulling off on the shoulder, but then I saw the freeway exit sign. Exit 41, toward Jessup and Columbia.

The woman turned to look at me. "I hoped you'd sleep until we got there. Now we have to come to an understanding."

"Understanding's good," I said. "I'd like to understand who you are and why you've taken me from my home." I tugged at my sleeves. "And then you can tell me why you put me in such an itchy dress."

The woman sighed and shook her head. Then it hit me. I couldn't see her face, but I knew that dismissive head shake.

Are you scared of needles?

No, just pain.

What was her name? Gina? Gina ... Freytag. The intern at GU Hospital.

"I know you," I said. "Do I know him, too?"

She grinned. It looked nasty in the dark van. "Who and what you know doesn't matter to me, so long as we meet our sponsor's minimum requirement: you, alive, with your brain intact." There was a click and a flash of metal. She turned the blade of a knife, flashing light in my eyes. "Your brain. Not your fingers."

I swallowed hard. "I'll be good."

"That's what I wanted to hear." She quit with the flashing blade.

"But if it doesn't matter what I know, why not tell me?"

"Don't tell him anything," the driver said.

Gina and the knife turned to him. "When I want your opinion, I'll ask for it. Your fingers aren't worth much to me, either." He didn't reply, but I could see his throat convulse in a hard swallow. He removed his right hand from the steering wheel and kept it in his lap.

"You're a lucky boy, Scott," Gina told me. "Not only did someone foot the bill for a very expensive college education, they put you up in nice digs and they're filling up a bank account for you on the side."

"And what, you're jealous?"

"No." She clicked the knife closed and put it away. "Someone else would like to have given you the same treatment, but they weren't given the chance." We entered a parking lot and slipped into a parking space far from the fuel pump islands.

"I didn't have anything to do with that. You wanna be mad at someone, call my lawyer."

Again with that patronizing, dismissive head shake. By the parking lot lights, I could see her smiling. She knew I wasn't a normal child, but I'd bet she treated most people this way.

"The group I represent has a more practical use for studying your condition." She smirked. "And *they* don't claim it's all to further the realms of neuroscience."

"What are you talking about?" I knew, but I didn't really want to hear. George McCullough's imagination was good for more than writing novels, like polluting my world view.

"You haven't guessed it already?" she asked. "The most practical purpose for studying your condition is to advance the production of true clones."

I waited for more, but nothing came. Something else was coming, though. I wasn't actually sick, but I felt my gorge rise. What came out was a fit of the giggles.

Gina looked annoyed. "Think about your fingers and how many times you think you can afford to anger me." The knife clicked open and flashed at me again. "I grew up on a hog farm. Blood and squeals are nothing new to me."

Despite the threat — did she really think it would take more than one? — my giggling didn't peter out right away. "Sorry," I said. "A friend of mine mentioned that idea not too long ago, but he thought the government might be the guilty party." I frowned at her. "You don't work for the government, do you?"

She didn't answer, but faced the front again.

"So," I thought out loud, "a country where cloning projects are still legal? Or somewhere they don't care about little things like laws?"

Gina shrugged. "Where is really not important. He could do it at *Disney World* for all I care. From you, though, he can get data that will make cloning a whole human being — body *and* mind — a possibility."

"Sounds like you're a believer," I said.

"I am," she replied. "They might advance the science of human replication by comparative decades with the data your brain will yield. The important thing is that you exist at all. Enough to get the scientific community's ball rolling."

I snorted. "Nice to know I'm dying for a cause."

"Who said anything about killing you?"

"How long do you think I'll survive under those conditions?"

"They'll keep you healthy," she said. "Unique as you are, your survival is paramount."

"That's nice to know," I said. "And as such a visionary,

playing a part in the advancement of People-Xeroxing ... you're working for free?"

"We're being paid well," she said. "Our survival is important."

"To you, anyway."

She didn't smile. "Our disappearance will be connected to yours. With the money we'll collect, we can start new lives."

"Just thinking out loud here," I said, "but if I weren't above the international crime of human trafficking, I could think of cheaper ways to tie up loose ends than setting them up with lots of money."

Gina looked at me and bit her lip. No dismissive head shake this time. To my relief, there was also no flash of knife blade.

"I'll be back in a couple of minutes," she told the driver. "If anything happens — anything at all — call me immediately."

"Bring me a pack of cigarettes?"

Oh, no, I thought. With smoke in the van, I'd probably get nauseated. Even worse, because I'd inherited more than auto mechanics from Jarvis Tracy. I'd probably get an intense craving.

"Not a chance," she said. "Smoking in a van with a handicapped child? First activist that comes along will be all over you."

"Anyone gonna call the Health Department if I smoke outside?" He was itchy for a smoke and I was appalled to find the itch contagious. If I weren't bound to the seat, we might be doing the Pall Mall Shuffle together.

"As long as you keep both eyes on the van."

I thought she might glance at me before getting out. She didn't trust her jittery partner and I didn't blame her. He'd probably bolt at the first hint of trouble. To make myself look harmless, I leaned back and acted stoned on knock-out drugs. I don't know if it was my act or her bladder, but she got out and headed for the building.

After she left, I said, "You know, it won't be long until they find me."

"Shut your mouth."

"And if it isn't my friends or the police, there's another party that will object to your absconding with me."

"I don't think I mumbled," he said. "Shut up." He wrung the steering wheel as if revving a motorcycle throttle. The rubbing sound got on my nerves, but it was an apparent comfort to him. Maybe even more than a cigarette. He still hadn't gotten out to smoke.

"I'm being monitored by some pretty sophisticated surveillance equipment. If they show up and see you holding my leash ... " I *tsked*. "I don't know what they'd do."

He turned and looked at me. He had calmed down, but he didn't speak.

"I mean," I continued, "I know where we are, and I was out cold. It's a pretty sure bet they do, too, and they're pretty rough people. Did some major damage to school property last time I gave them the slip."

That provoked a reaction I didn't expect. He laughed so hard he started coughing. *"I'm the 'other interested party,'* kid. Those bugs were *mine.* Besides being a tech nut, I'm pretty good with a sewing needle. Every shirt collar, every jeans waistband, every pair of shoes. Even your cute little

L.L. Bean knapsack."

"Oh," I said. All those resources and no smart comeback. Then I made a connection. "My locker. That was you outside the student center after the fire alarm." It must have been his makeshift ashtray outside my apartment, too.

"You sure tipped your hand on that one. Helped me retrieve some of that state-of-the-art spy gear our client supplied. It's part of my payoff for this little job. European stuff that won't be on the U.S. market for years yet. I can crack a couple of them open, reconfigure the layout, reverse-engineer my way into the patent office, and bank *way* more than these guys are paying me."

"I didn't think you two were doing this in the name of science," I said.

"Gina is," he said. "She's a medical student, after all. I'm no scientist, though. I'm just into expensive gadgets."

"But Gina's not doing it just for the life experience?"

He shook his head and stared into the parking lot. "Like she said, we're both gonna have to move, change identities, stuff like that. That takes money."

"And someday, you'll flood the patent office with your 'inventions.'"

"Yep," he said. He laced his fingers together, cracked his knuckles and smiled.

I shook my head. "Too bad."

"Too bad, what?"

"About the Patriot Act."

He angled the rearview mirror to look at me. "What about it?"

I shrugged as much as the taffeta and my bindings would

let me. "Since 2001, all patent candidates of a scientific nature are given a thorough background check."

His eyes grew wide in the mirror. "Huh?"

"It's true," I said, though I was probably making it up on the spot. "After the terrorists infiltrated America so deeply, Homeland Security started scrutinizing patent applications, to see if any of them had potential terrorist applications."

When he responded, it was with foulmouthed disbelief.

"Don't you remember what this project's about? I've got *libraries* in my head, from four different sources: some technical, some to do with government and a lot having to do with the stock market. Ergo, I know this stuff like the back of my hand."

"Shut up," he said. "You don't know anything."

"I know that after 1994 and the Oklahoma City bombing, it became a lot harder to buy large amounts of fertilizer."

"Shut up!" He looked out the window.

"I know Gina's been gone a lot longer than she ought to." Despite my anger, I was surprised I could keep digging at this guy. He hadn't been the one to flash a knife, but neither was he just the chauffeur.

Had Mr. Jarvis been a POW, jabbing at his jailers? Maybe Mark Norton's business savvy included skill at hectoring. It could even be Kevin Adams, the *über*-nerd whose picture had amused Charlie. Of course, it might have been all me.

My sole remaining captor looked out the windshield toward the well-lit building. Neither of us saw Gina. I had just been mouthing off about her lengthy absence, but now her partner must be wondering.

Perhaps my captors planned on my sleeping the whole

trip: they had not tied me up. Only the safety harness held me. While spinning my patent office fairy tale, I'd worked my hands under the edges of the harness straps. When Gina's partner turned to look for her, I thrust my hands through the straps. With the heavy coat, they might not notice, and now my arms were free.

Poop, I thought. I forgot the buckle on my chest.

I needed him speaking again, to cover the noise of my escape, so I tried another jab.

"I don't think you could have picked a worse time to nab me."

He turned from his vigil and glared at me. I don't think he disagreed so much as he couldn't believe I was still talking.

"You had me bugged," I said, "but did you even listen to my phone calls?" He turned away and I covered the harness buckle with my hand. "My mother was on her way and I'll bet she arrived twenty minutes after we spoke. She would have been tipped off right away." The last word of that sentence covered a muffled *click.* My arms were more or less free.

"You should have done it during the day." I patted around in the dark to make sure I was free of hindrances. "On schooldays, there are times when I wouldn't be missed for a couple of hours." I slid forward the tiniest bit. "Or in the middle of the night. I never have visitors after ten. You wouldn't have needed this awful dress. Just pluck me out of bed in the dark and make it all the way to Philly before anyone's the wiser."

He was biting his lip now. Gina was still nowhere to be seen.

"If you want that smoke you'd better take it now," I said. "She won't want to stick around for anything when she gets back."

We hadn't exactly established a rapport, but I expected a murmur of agreement at least. Instead, he popped the door and jumped out as if he had spilled coffee in his lap. I felt a rush of brisk air and noticed for the first time that it was a chilly night.

In the glow of the parking lot lights, I could finally see and recognize the driver. He was a technician in the Research Resource Facility, near the University Hospital, where I had my initial CAT scans and MRI's. He wasn't a student, just a hospital employee. Kevin. Kevin Ward.

Kevin smoked like a man whose wife was giving birth to a baseball team. I scanned the parking lot and tried to edge out of the wheelchair without being obvious. As I scooted, my glance shifted between Kevin and the building. I didn't see Gina, but I thought I saw a police car. I got excited until I saw it was a civilian Chevy Caprice. Easy mistake to make.

I was a hair away from scrambling for an exit when Gina burst out of the store. Kevin saw, pitched his cigarette and got back into the driver's seat. Even if Gina wasn't heading for her own door, my chance was gone. I'd never get Gina's door open and get away. Either of them could grab my stupid dress with no trouble.

Unable or unwilling to control his language around children, Kevin asked what had taken her so blankety-blank long. Gina said the blankety-blank bathroom didn't have any blankety-blank toilet paper. Kevin said he was tired of sitting at this blankety-blank gas station and it was time for them to get the blank out of Dodge.

I almost asked them to watch the swearing, but if either of them looked at me closely, I'd lose my only advantage.

I wasn't practiced at things like this, but I knew timing was important. Luck and not a little bit of Divine Providence wouldn't hurt, either. I waited, for the van to be in the right position and for a moment when both Gina and Kevin were turned away.

Kevin backed out of the parking space, sped to the road, jerked to a stop, and waited for a gap in the traffic.

I freed my arms from the bulky coat while Kevin played Steve McQueen with the steering wheel. Just before he gunned the engine, ready to shoot into the street, I shot out of the wheelchair. Gina noticed right away and I had to dodge as she clutched at me. Her arms flailed over the seat back but the seatbelt held her tight. The wheelchair's lift door would be too slow, so I leapt for the back of the van.

It would have been just my luck for the back to be full of cargo I hadn't been able to see, but there wasn't a thing in my way. I reached the door just as Kevin hit the gas and zoomed out of the parking lot. Whether he was jumpy or thought I'd be less likely to jump from a moving vehicle, he eliminated my alternatives. Before we had moved twenty yards, I banged on the door handle, let it swing open and launched myself into the night, praying that I wouldn't land in the path of a speeding truck.

42

On Foot

Depleting my miracle allowance in one stroke, I landed on my feet. Now I just had to stay on them. They had taken my shoes but left my socks. Loose gravel bored into my feet as I ran.

Behind me, Kevin braked hard and shifted into reverse. Then the brakes squealed again, and as I hied for well-lit freedom, I heard Gina scream at Kevin for almost running me over. That particular danger had never occurred to me. Next time I exited a moving vehicle, I'd make sure to bail out from a side door.

It didn't take Kevin long to back the van alongside where I ran. He shoved his door open and tried to jump out, but he had forgotten to remove his seatbelt. *Must be amateur night,* I thought.

Kevin swore a blue streak, managed to extricate himself, and got out. The van, still in reverse, idled backward, and the open door almost knocked him off his feet before he could climb inside and move the gearshift. Suddenly in "Park," the van barked to a halt with Kevin's bracing hand on the doorframe. Like a crocodile, the Ford Econoline's sturdy door clamped on his hand and held it, firm as concrete.

His cry of pain and shock must have been all breath. I heard nothing, even with the van's back doors open. He continued the silent-movie screams and tried with all his might to pull free from the evil van's jaws, as if he couldn't remember how to open the door,

Whatever else Gina did, she kept her priorities straight. She left Kevin, wounded and blocking traffic, to chase me, the dummy who stopped to watch the show. Only when she rounded the van and came at me did I remember I was supposed to be escaping.

But Gina was halted by oncoming cars. Impatient motorists honked and veered past Kevin on the shoulder. Had Gina been a movie villainess, she could have hurdled the line of cars. Given chase, regardless of the danger. But she only stood and fumed, as if at a scaled-down railroad crossing. I took advantage and limped away to safety.

If I had been watching where I was going instead of watching Kevin's performance, I might have made for the right door. Instead, like a cockroach, I veered past the gas station to hide in the dark near the truck gate. I risked a glance back and saw Gina looking around, not seeing me. I couldn't have been in shadow for more than a second, but the path along the fence was darker than dark. My abductors had even given me nighttime camouflage — a dark blue dress. It was definitely easier to hide in the dark after Labor day.

Moving in the dark was more difficult. The wind made the chain-link fence jingle, or else I would have run headlong into it. With my hand, I followed it along the edge of the parking lot and stepped in things I didn't want to think about. Some was grass, some was mud. Fortunately, none was broken glass. Unfortunately, most of it was wet and icy cold.

I dropped to the ground fifty yards from the opening to the parking lot. Headlights were sweeping my way. While I hid behind a mound of unkempt grass, the van crawled in exaggerated slalom patterns, strafing the fence line with its headlights. I couldn't see who was driving, but Kevin was probably in no shape for it. It was possible one or more of his fingers had just popped off. Investigators would find a couple of digits in a puddle outside a truck stop in Jessup, Maryland. Forget dusting for prints.

Did you misplace something, Mr. Ward?

The van moved past. They hadn't seen me. Hiding in the dark, though, I had made an important discovery: the dress had been put on over my clothes. I'd left the bulky jacket behind and I was already getting chilled, but the dress helped. Not even Halloween yet and here I was, dressed up. No candy, though.

I discovered something else, too. I didn't feel the lump in my pocket until I lay there for a few minutes. While the van went to the truck entrance and got turned away for not being a truck, I rolled onto my side, hoping and praying I hadn't crushed it, wondering why in the world they didn't take it, and pulled out my little cell phone.

The van returned, rolling even more slowly, passenger side toward me. I went prone, ducking so low I couldn't see over the scrub. From very close by, I heard feet hit gravel as someone got out on the driver's side.

"Shut up!" Gina hissed into the van. *"You'll get some ice when we find the kid!"*

I heard a weepy moan of protest before the door slammed. Then shoes on gravel. A pause. Steps in tall grass.

"Might as well come out!" Gina told the darkness. "We can track your clothes!"

Says the criminal mastermind stymied by a mere parking lot attendant, I thought.

Her footsteps almost reached me, but then she turned and walked away along the fence. My night vision had returned, and as she walked away, I got into a crouch and watched her go. Something shiny and metallic — a hair clip, maybe — made spotting her easy.

Quiet as I could, I crab-walked to the fence and pulled at the galvanized wire, testing its elasticity. I had to be careful. That same fence ran alongside Gina's path. If I moved it too much, she had only to follow the wobble and I'd be a prisoner again.

My arm went right under with no trouble. I had worried the bottom would be lined with clipped wire ends like those on top, which deterred climbers. But the bottom edge consisted of looped chain-link wire. Slipping under it was as easy as a few scoots in that direction. My gaudy blue dress didn't even catch on anything.

The first truck was a Peterbilt with a single forty thousand-pound coil of sheet steel, like a huge roll of toilet paper, chained to its flatbed trailer. I crawled underneath to hide behind one of the big tires and gagged from the stench of the ancient pavement beneath me. It reeked of automotive fluids, garbage and worst of all, urine. Over the years, constant additions and summer heat had impacted the smell. In daylight, wavy lines might have risen from it, like in a comic strip. I was surprised it didn't glow in the dark.

Trying for a less fragrant spot, I moved on and found a car hauler. It wouldn't hide the stench, but by clambering onto the low trailer, I got my sock feet off the toxic tarmac. The trailer held used cars, most of them wrecked. I tried to find a way in, but if any had unlocked doors, they were on the top level. I'd never make it up there in the dark, wearing a dress.

I was already hidden from view on all sides, so I sat on one of the cars' hoods. The recent cool weather made air-conditioning unnecessary, so the parking lot wasn't too noisy. I wouldn't have a better chance and hated to waste it. I dug into the taffeta dress's skirt, dug out the cell phone, found the battery almost full, and called 911.

Or tried to. I pushed buttons but got no numbers. I pressed and held the "end" button, turning it off. I pressed it again, doing internal commentary about the absurdity of pressing "end" to turn *on* the phone. Like clicking "start" to turn off your computer. Like graduation being called "commencement."

I tried 911 again. The number buttons still didn't work, so I tried others. Volume worked. The menu activated, but with the directional keys, I could only select things that required use of the number pad, which didn't work.

The "send" button worked, but it would only redial the last number I had called.

Barbara.

She might have been a child, but she wasn't helpless.

She answered after half a ring. *"Scott, is that you?"*

I sighed with relief. "Who else?"

"What happened?" she asked. *"Where are you?"*

"From what I hear, I'm officially a missing child." I checked to make sure no one was sneaking up on me. "They drugged me, grabbed me, and took off with me. I just escaped."

"Who was it?" she asked. *"Can we get the police after them?"* She paused. *"Wait, why didn't you call the police?"*

"The number pad on my phone's broken. Nothing but redial. It's just a Barbara Hotline, now."

"But you know who took you? You could identify them?"

"A couple of flunkies from the project," I said. "Gina Freytag, a neurology intern with a thing for needles, and Kevin Ward, a radiology tech at the University Hospital."

"Did they hurt you?" She sounded worried.

"I"m okay," I said. "Embarrassed, though. They must have chloroformed me or something. I don't feel sore, like from an injection."

"You didn't tell me where you are," she said. *"Do you know?"*

"Jessup, Maryland," I said. "Miss Freytag had to tinkle. They didn't tie me up. Just knocked me out and put me in the van, like a sleepy kid on a long trip."

"Jessup?" she asked. Then she spoke to someone else for a moment. *"Did you say Jessup?"*

"Yeah. Why?"

"I'm only ten miles from you."

"What do you mean?" I asked. "How?"

She was silent for a moment. "I've talked to Sheila."

My heart missed a beat. "How'd you manage that?"

"Not now. Listen, I'll call the police, but I'm coming to get you. We'll probably make it there first, anyway."

"How are you so close?" I asked. I jerked around, feeling like someone was close enough to lay hands on me, and not the way they do at prayer meetings.

"I called Sheila, just to talk, and she said you were missing. I didn't know what I could do, but I offered help."

"You didn't make it here from Roanoke that fast, did you?"

"I was in Chevy Chase, visiting friends."

"You can drive?" I asked. "I'm jealous."

"No, silly," she said, sighing into the phone. "I've got a 'Charlie' of my own."

"Handy."

"Just stay put," she said. "You couldn't have picked a better place to hide."

"Maybe," I said, "but these are the guys that bugged my clothes, and I'm still wearing them."

She groaned. "Don't you ... I mean, can't you take them off?" She took a deep breath. "Wait. You better not, or you'll freeze." She paused again. I heard her muffled voice and figured she was talking to her chauffeur. Then she was back. "Where are you, exactly?"

I gave her the name of the truck stop and the exit number.

"Man, we're good."

"Since you're on speaking terms with Sheila, you could have visited me in Washington and they wouldn't have grabbed me."

"Or they could have grabbed both of us."

"You always notice more than I do." I smiled, and though I'd spent only minutes with her in person, I missed seeing *her* smile. "You would have seen them coming."

She would have seen Kevin coming. There I sat, on the hood of a car, in a blue taffeta dress, like a jilted prom date, when he came down the aisle and spotted me. He stopped and looked and I just sat there, clueless. If I hadn't been so caught up in the phone call, I might have found a better hiding place. Now I just sat on my perch like a little kid fresh out of ideas.

He glared at me, just out of his reach, and foamed at the mouth.

"Gotta go," I said into the phone. "I've just been found."

"Try to make it outside the gate!" she said. *"We just turned off the exit ramp!"*

"Bye," I said. I turned off the phone and faced Kevin. "Hi," I said. "Manage to keep any fingers?"

His hand was wrapped in a yellow cloth — maybe a T-shirt — and looked hugely swollen. He must have packed the bandage with ice. I know I would have.

"Get down!" Kevin hissed.

"With my bad self?" I asked, thinking this was an odd way for Tourette's to manifest.

"Get ... down." His voice carried, but his intentions came harder. I offered no more flippant answers.

I climbed off the car and stood on the narrow platform.

With his mangled paw, he couldn't come after me, so he stood and urged me down with vicious grunts. I wasn't high up, but I was small and climbing in a dress was hard. Enraged at my slow descent, Kevin said one of the stupidest things I ever heard.

"Hurry it up, you cross-dressing little freak!"

I'd had enough of his mouth and I lost my temper.

"Maybe *you'd* like to try it!" I yanked the wig from my head and pitched it at his face. When he put up his good right hand to catch it, I jumped down, grabbed his injured left hand and wrenched. There was a sound like bubble wrap in a laundry mangle. Kevin howled and tugged his hand from my grasp. He doubled over, protecting his wound, while I scooted under the trailer to my left and retraced my steps to the fence.

I had forgotten how cold the asphalt was, but not how nasty. My feet would need a soak in disinfectant. With Kevin spouting curses behind me, I ducked under the trailers, some lower than adult waist level, until I got to the fence.

The return trip under the fence was faster and easier, with no worries about the wig snagging on the fence. I got to my feet and immediately tripped on the hem of my dress. I rolled over the clump of tall grass, once my little duck blind, and almost into the street.

Brakes screeched.

A man's voice called from the small car that had stopped. ""Scott? You okay, buddy?"

I got up and looked in the car's passenger window. The car was small and boxy — a Scion, I thought — and the driver was roly-poly. He looked like the last melon in a crate, crammed into the corner.

"Uh, fine," I said.

He waved me in. "Come on!"

I was about to relax my rule about getting in cars with strangers when Barbara leaned over the front seat and gave me that smile I'd been missing.

The back door popped open, I jumped in and the roly-poly driver floored the gas pedal. There was no sign of Gina. She might still be stomping through the weeds. I pictured Kevin driving off without her and smiled.

"Scott?" Barbara asked. "Are you okay?"

"I think so," I said, "but my feet may need decontamination." I held my nose. "Ten thousand times worse than a movie theater floor." I glanced at the front seat. "Who's your friend?"

Without taking his eyes off the road, the driver offered his right hand. "Larry Myers. Nice to finally meet you." He glanced back at me. "Nice dress."

Barbara giggled nervously.

I let out a long breath and closed my eyes.

43

Face to Face

"What's the matter, Scott?"

I opened my eyes. I told myself I hadn't passed out. I had just dozed off within a minute of escaping abduction and getting in the car with Barbara and her friend, Larry.

"Everything hurts," I said. "I haven't been this active since ... well, ever. I never get any exercise."

"Don't feel bad," Larry said over his shoulder. "This drive is more exercise than I've had since before you was born."

I eased sideways to lie down. "Add whatever they knocked me out with, and I'm not feeling top shelf just yet."

Barbara put a hand to my forehead before smiling down at me. "You're not overheated." Then her nose wrinkled and tried to withdraw into her face. She checked my feet and let out a cry of disgust. Using a handful of tissues to protect her hand, she yanked my socks off and tossed them out the window onto the freeway.

"Litterbug," I said. My feet could breathe now, but the

stench lingered.

"I think they allow for apple cores and other biodegradables," she said. "Those socks won't last the night."

I heard an aerosol can spraying in the front seat and a voice saying, "Shoulda tied him to the luggage rack."

With baby wipes, Barbara gave me the barefoot version of a shoeshine. Had I been less exhausted, I would have giggled when she flossed between my toes. The swabbing didn't eliminate the odor, but it helped.

"Did you call Sheila and Charlie?" I was slipping away again. "Tell them I'm okay?"

She squeezed my hand and watched Larry's driving. "We're going to meet them. University Hospital," she said. "To check you out and everything."

The getaway car was nice, but I hadn't really relaxed until I was in Barbara's care. She cleaned my hands, face and then my feet again. The baby wipes were warm from the car's floorboard. It was hard resisting the urge to doze. I thought, why bother?

A short, blank period later, I opened my eyes and saw bright street lamps overhead. Not the hospital, though. I was still in the car, moving in fits and starts. Another moment and my tired brain figured it out. We were at a toll station.

I leaned back and looked up at Barbara. She watched the road, though the car was crawling. "Who's Larry?" I asked.

Barbara glanced at me before looking forward again. "OneBrikShy," she murmured.

"Does he know?" I asked, looking up at her. "About me, I mean?"

"He does now," she sighed. "It's okay, though."

"Okay." It was too taxing to think about, anyway. My fuzzing was thinky, but I didn't think it was the knockout drug. Some idea hadn't settled. Something almost ... contradictory.

I gazed at the intermittent scenery as we drove through the toll plaza. There wasn't much. Just the tops of semi trailers as they inched by. Because of the bright overhead lights, I couldn't even see if any stars were out.

I moved before I could think. Sat up, bending at the waist, and yanked the door handle. It fell open like a trapdoor and I tumbled onto the concrete amid slow-moving cars. Larry's arm slapped at the back of the car seat as he reached for me and grabbed only air. Barbara yelled something as I kicked the door closed in her face.

She didn't call my name or cry out in fear for my safety.

The car door slammed on a shrill *"Damn it!"*

As I got to my feet, the car screeched to a halt. Larry — was he really Brik? — was a little better than Kevin at this part, but I was already three lanes away by the time he got out. Barbara, I noticed, had not deigned to follow.

It had happened fast, and I wanted to stop and think. No time for that while being pursued. I only knew my actions were instinctive, based on something inherited in the surge. It had just now surfaced in my conscious thought: there was no toll plaza between Jessup, Maryland and Georgetown University. Larry had driven north, the wrong way. I noticed at just the right time and escaped a second abduction attempt just outside the Fort McHenry Tunnel, on the southern end of Baltimore.

"Hey, kid!" Someone called from a nearby car, like I was going to stop and chat. Others honked their horns, probably to shoo me off the road. It was cool out. No sense letting the heat out to yell at pedestrians.

My bare feet felt like hamburger. My damp, shoeless trip through God-knew-what had further tenderized my already tender soles. Any other time, I would have worried about infection from running through broken glass and runoff debris. But I didn't have a destination. I was just fleeing pursuit.

My feet hurt so bad I almost stopped to beg assistance from the nearest motorist. That inclination disappeared when I saw an off-white Ford Econoline with a wheelchair lift door, little blood streaks on the driver's-side door frame. Gina was at the wheel, and if I hadn't stopped to gape, she might have missed me. She braked, slammed the van into park and popped the door. No seatbelt stopped her this time.

I ran by the van's hood, crossing two more lanes of traffic, heading for the shoulder and possible safety in the darkness beyond. Gina didn't call out, but I heard boot soles hammering the concrete, getting closer and closer. I knew I shouldn't risk it, but I caught myself peeking over my shoulder.

"Run for it, *muchacha!*" someone cheered from a nearby Jeep. Four people sat inside, bundled against the night chills and riding with the canvas top down. I don't know why I didn't ask them for help, tell them I was the kid advertised on all the freeway marquee signs lining I-95 from Florida to Maine. I guess I just didn't feel like trusting anyone just then.

I reached the curb faster than I expected and hit it at a full run. I screamed as I tripped — my foot felt as if I'd broken all the toes — and kept on screaming, rolling over and over until I hit the guard rail. Like sports fans witnessing a vicious quarterback sack, the folks in the Jeep let out a collective "oooooooh!"

The fall knocked the wind out of me, but somehow I ignored that — and my throbbing, growling toes — to check on my pursuer.

Make that pursuers. Gina was only a lane and a half away, and a stout Larry Myers brought up the rear. He hadn't fibbed about his lack of exercise. His face was so red he looked sunburned. I'm ashamed I hoped for it, but maybe he was only a few labored steps away from a massive coronary.

Still gasping, I rolled under the guard rail into darkness, off a ledge, fell several feet and hit hard-packed dirt. If I hadn't already been struggling for breath, that would have done it. I couldn't think, just kept rolling and rolling until I hit a brush patch.

I stopped moving and breathed the night air in shaky gasps, forced to relearn respiration. From the bottom of the steep berm, I saw Gina leaning on the guardrail and peering down into the darkness, like a sailor looking for a man overboard. Larry staggered up with his hand on his chest, puffing hard. She turned to him and said something I couldn't hear. He said something back. Both his tone and his expression told me Gina was not the boss of this shooting match.

There was a short argument with violent hand gestures.

The only word I understood was "flashlight." They both threw up their hands. It looked like neither had planned for this contingency. Amateur night, indeed.

Larry pointed a meaty finger at Gina and spoke so softly I couldn't hear at all. Gina heard, though, and it made her wilt. He turned his back and disappeared from sight. Taking his cue, she climbed over the rail and followed me into the darkness.

I walked and tried to keep an eye on Gina while biting back screams with every other step. I wanted to reach the toll plaza, but I didn't know exactly where it was. We were near the tunnel, which almost bisected the city, so I was just happy to find unpaved ground. The cold dirt and occasional grass were a lot better than pavement for my poor foot.

I had never been a soldier, of course, but some kind of training asserted itself. I noted the wind, moving only when the breeze pulled at the grass around me. The dead stalks crunched loud enough to hear when stepped on, so I tried hard to keep to the dirt.

Gina, without benefit of light, headed in the wrong direction. This was good, because my regained breath generated heavy plumes, like big gray flags. *Just keep on walking,* I told her silently. *Nothing to see over here.*

A cruelly placed bit of rock or concrete caught my bad foot and I crammed my wrist in my mouth to catch the scream. My little toe, already loose from its framework, felt as if it had been crammed all the way into my foot. My vision blurred and I thought I would pass out. My eyes filled with tears, but they gushed so fast they were like water dashed in my face.

I unclenched my jaws and released my arm so I could wipe my eyes. I would have been happy to bite a chunk out of my arm if it would quell the pain in my foot. It pulsed so hard I was surprised Gina couldn't hear it.

She had moved out of sight, going in the wrong direction, I hoped. If she was closing in on me, I was sunk. I couldn't run anymore. If only I could sneak my way to the toll plaza. There were always police around toll plazas, where arguments often occurred. But if there were cops, why didn't they come running when they saw a couple of adults chasing a kid across five lanes of traffic, at night, with an interstate Amber alert in progress?

A shout came from the guardrail above. I turned, hunching low, and saw Larry waving and calling for Gina. In his other hand, he held what looked like an old army field phone. A moment later, I caught on.

He was shouting for Gina ... and pointing in my direction.

44

It Just Ain't Fair

I almost screamed in frustration, but it would just make me easier to find. It wasn't as if they needed more help. No less than twice, Kevin and Gina had reminded me about the devices in my clothes. I couldn't do much about that, though. I couldn't very well pull out the seams on a pair of Levi's with my fingers.

I looked up the berm and noticed, without surprise, that Larry was closer. I wasn't moving fast, but my injuries weren't the only thing slowing me down. I had relied on my pursuers' ineptitude. I never thought about my own.

I neither saw nor heard Gina, but I had to assume she was now moving in the right direction. I avoided looking toward the freeway street lamps. The ground was treacherous enough without having spotty vision. I slid downhill on my rear in the grass whenever I could, but even with the aid of gravity, I was too slow. I didn't want to think about what my captors — both sets — were going to do to me after this.

Especially Barbara.

I could stay on the run forever, maybe justify avoiding the thought for the rest of my life. Tired as I was, I found the idea attractive. But even thinking about *not* thinking about it was thinking about it, so I hid the thought away, sealed it in a mental paint can. I'd have to think of something else to ease my heart.

A few more controlled slides and I reached a ledge. There was a knee-high concrete barrier and a deep drainage culvert a long way down. I backed away from the edge, hid among tall, brittle weeds, and tried to gather my wits. I couldn't hear Gina behind me, but my own hammering heart and throbbing foot had most of my attention. I just sat, weighed my options, and found them slim.

The cold grass was actually good for my hurt foot, but the tacky dress itched like nobody's business. I yanked at the collar and decided the few female traits I inherited from Marie Huntsacker weren't enough for me to tolerate wearing a dress. I wanted to take it off and throw it down in the culvert. Watch it float away. Maybe get eaten by a big fish.

I didn't even know if there was water down there. It was too dark to see the bottom.

Like my leap from the car, I acted again without understanding why. After a quick look to see if Gina was close, I began to pull off the dress. I couldn't reach the zipper, but as stuffed full as my head was, it went through the hole with no problem. In a few seconds, the dress was off. Much as I wanted to, I didn't throw it into the culvert.

Gingerly, as not to jostle my foot, I took off my own clothes. Jeans, shirt, and after a brief debate, underwear, too. I rolled them into a bundle, looking up to gauge Gina's intercept distance, and tossed the clothes over the side into the darkness.

Then I didn't mind the dress so much. Shivering like mad, I put it back on, and moved back to my hiding spot. I wanted to huddle against the cold, but I needed to be ready to move.

I was losing hope — along with feeling in my fingers — when Gina came sliding down the hill, muttering about the cold, my escape, and the ugly things she would do to me. At the bottom, she stood and brushed herself off. She held a device like Larry's, maybe the same one. I hunched in my cold hiding spot and gritted my teeth to stop their chattering while she checked the device, her face glowing green.

After a moment, she looked over the edge into the darkness. Then she stood back up and rechecked the device. "No way," she groaned. "You gotta be *kidding* me!" She lowered the device, braced herself with both hands, and leaned over the barrier.

She made a perfect target, like a tackling dummy. With a horrid pang from my foot, but absolutely none from my conscience, I launched myself from the weeds and rammed into Gina. She went headfirst over the edge, never crying out, not even when she hit the bottom.

Though I could ill afford the time, I looked for Gina in the shadowed culvert. The bottom was still dark, but now there was a tiny green light — the display from the tracking device, no doubt. There was no movement. At the time, I had no qualms about pushing her. Later, though, I wondered what it said about me that I turned my back and walked away.

I didn't worry about Larry. Not about him chasing me, anyway. The footwork was all Gina's and I was pretty sure Kevin was sitting in the van, wondering if he'd ever count to ten again. Larry was probably still on the shoulder above, or in the car.

With Barbara.

Tears ran down my face, but only partly from the pain in my foot. Only fifty more yards, up the hill to safety, but it was far enough for me to distill my earlier thoughts. To realize that my entire relationship with Barbara had been a lie.

She never called the police, anyway. I'd probably realized that as soon as I saw we were going the wrong way. Realization, or maybe instinct. Whichever, it was enough to make me jump from a moving car.

I had to stop, just ten yards away from the light. Had to stop. Had to sit. Had to understand.

Larry hadn't been driving fast enough. Once we were underway, he gave no sense of hurry. He might have been a cab driver.

And Barbara's farewell words. Her curse confirmed fears that, unknown to me, had quietly churned in my brain for less than ten minutes.

"*Damn it,*" she had said. I thought I could still only say one of those words by quoting scripture.

But that difference between us paled beside her betrayal. We were the only two people like us in the world. Did she think that was one too many?

I sat crying, shivering and holding my injured foot. I was grief-stricken and outraged, but I couldn't match reactions to emotions. The only person who could really understand me was someone I never, ever wanted to see again.

45

Hospital Blues

Both my feet were treated and bandaged. A tox screen showed traces of chloroform and a standard tranquilizer whose name I didn't bother to remember. My hospital bed was too big, too hard, too well lit. I just wanted to go home and sleep until I felt like facing the world again.

But no one would let me.

The woman who sat in the room with me should have been a nurse, but she wasn't. Underneath the sympathetic smile and minimal makeup was an FBI agent. I closed my eyes and tried to ignore her along with everything else.

"Your mother and your friend Charlie are on their way," she said. Her name was Coreen, but she had asked me to call her Reenie. The nickname sounded like an outdated term for a kidney ailment.

They should have just let me have a regular nurse. Or maybe Detective Allen if they thought I needed an authoritative female presence. Better yet, a pain pill and some let's-just-leave-the-kid-alone.

"Did you hear me?" Reenie asked.

"Yeah," I said, not looking at her.

"I'm sorry you don't want me here," she said, "but my boss wants to keep you isolated. Except your mom, of course."

I closed my eyes. "It'd be easier to ignore you if you quit talking."

She sniffed but went silent. Just as well. It wouldn't do to escape kidnapping only to antagonize my bodyguard into throttling me.

There was a knock at the door and I opened my eyes. I tried to smile as Sheila walked in, followed by Charlie in a wheelchair. The door was held by a tall, slim man dressed like Reenie.

"Oh, honey!" Sheila cried, rushing to my bedside. She fiddled with the bed rail for a moment, trying to get to me. Then Reenie helped out, lowering the rail — or opening my cell door, as I saw it. Sheila was on me a microsecond later, wrapping me in a hug that did more for me than all the drugs I'd been given.

She held me a few moments and wept in relief. Then she took me by the shoulders and looked at my face. I smiled but it was an effort, just for her benefit and Charlie's. I had to maintain it consciously. Fatigue and emotional debris kept weighing it down.

"How are you doing?" She brushed hair back from my forehead.

I reinforced my smile, but tears came to my eyes and she held me again. Charlie rolled forward and reached for me. I took his hand and squeezed.

"What's with the wheelchair?" I asked, wiping my eyes. "You were ready for crutches a couple of days ago."

Charlie looked down and scratched his head.

Sheila spoke up. "When we got to your apartment, I let myself in, but you didn't answer when I called. With no response and no sound from the shower, I got worried.

"I went to your bedroom, thinking you might be lying down or something and just didn't hear me." She swallowed. "You've always been so fastidious about putting up your clothes, ever since you were first able to walk and open drawers. So when I saw clothes strewn all over the place, I got really worried."

"She's being modest," Charlie said. "She screamed."

"Charlie tried to run to the rescue," Sheila continued, "and tore out his stitches!"

I looked at Charlie, who winced as he smiled.

"Damn," I said.

That drew stares from everyone and surprised even me. Sheila actually felt my forehead, perhaps thinking me delirious. It felt so much like Barbara's touch that I shied away before I knew it.

"Scott?" She lowered her hand and rested it on my hand. "Are you okay?"

I had wanted to growl my answer, so it wouldn't be a sob. It didn't entirely work. "No."

The man who had entered with Sheila and Charlie cleared his throat and Sheila scooted to the foot of my bed, staying close but careful not to nudge my foot. My feet were still full of Lidocaine. A resident in the E.R. had stabilized my toes and stitched up the cuts that, due to the cold, I hadn't been able to feel. At least I didn't have to worry about frostbite.

"Hello, Scott," the man said. "I'm Special Agent Darrell Moore. I'm with the D.C. area FBI." He scratched his chin and squinted. "Now, normally kidnapping falls under the jurisdiction of the FBI anyway, but from what you told State Trooper Woods, I'm inclined to think potential foreign involvement."

Obviously Agent Moore had been briefed and knew I'd understand grown-up talk. He didn't look surprised at all when I responded.

"By implication only," I said. "I was trying to keep them talking, to get info out of them or maybe just to distract them. Gina said— Wait, what happened? Did you find her?"

"We did, but one thing at a time. Okay, guy?" He smiled, but it wasn't patronizing. A man's smile. He was much better at this than Reenie. Probably why he was the boss.

I nodded and leaned back. "Gina never said that her sponsor was foreign, but everything she said pointed that way. Her and Kevin's compensation package, new lives, new identities." Despite my weariness, I gave him a nasty grin. "Kind of like what you guys do, right?"

He grinned right back. "Not my department. Anything else you can remember?"

I shook my head. "No more names, other than Larry Myers." I frowned and looked at my hands. "And Barbara Davis."

"Right," he said, weighing my tone. "Here." He handed me a newspaper I hadn't seen him holding. It was a well-known tabloid.

I groaned. On a front page photo, a small figure in a dress ran across several lanes of traffic. There was a blurry figure in pursuit.

FOREIGN SPY CHILD DEFECTS!!!
PINT-SIZED MATA HARI SEEKS ASYLUM IN THE U.S. SAYS GOVT. SOURCE

Sheila and Charlie were both angling for a peek so I held it up for them to read. I felt a little like Truman with the erroneous Dewey headline.

Charlie stifled a giggle. Sheila looked stunned, but then smiled. "At least it's not Bat Boy." Normally, I would have expected that comment from Charlie. I could tell they'd spent a lot of time together.

"That picture was from a Maryland Department of Transportation traffic control camera." Agent Moore's smile was a little on the stuffy side. "Yes, they are for exactly that. Not Big Brother or anything."

I was reminded, uncomfortably, of Barbara, but said nothing.

"Anyway," he continued, "right now, a traffic camera monitor is probably holding a check from the tabloid in one hand and a pink slip in the other. Something similar awaits one or more members of the Baltimore P.D., EMTs … whoever else heard your debriefing then blabbed. We can thank our lucky stars the tabloid reporter didn't believe the real leak and wrote his own version."

"Sorry," I said. "Next time I get kidnapped I'll keep my mouth shut."

He shook his head. "I don't blame you at all, Scott. You did everything you could to help us catch the bad guys. I appreciate that, considering how traumatized you were." He handed me another newspaper, *The Baltimore Sun.* I didn't make the front page on that one, but I wasn't offended. You didn't have to be famous for your abduction to make the papers. It worked the other way around.

A page-three headline read, "RUNAWAY CAUSES TRAFFIC TIE-UP AT FT. MCHENRY TUNNEL."

"This one's only half right," I said. "The traffic was already crawling when we got there. It's why I didn't die when I jumped out of the car."

"Geez, Scott," Charlie said, whistling in awe. "That move took some really big—" Sheila cut him off with a stare. "Guts," he finished. "Big guts." When Sheila looked away from him, he gave me a big wink.

"In effect," Agent Moore continued, "that's what the public knows. No actual names — you, Gina Freytag, Kevin Ward, anybody — were known at press time."

"And the spy thing?" I asked, thinking about the absurd tabloid headline.

"We'll ignore it," Moore said. "Forceful denial makes people think 'cover-up.'"

"What about Gina?" I asked. "Once she went over, I didn't wait around to see if she ..." I swallowed, "died."

"She didn't die," he said. "No lasting damage, either, I don't guess. Scratches, concussion, broken femur. They found her trying to tie a splint on her leg with your jeans."

Charlie shook his head. "That was pretty sharp, man. Ditching the bugged clothes, I mean. How'd you think of something like that while you were on the run?"

"It must run in the family," Agent Moore said. "If not for your mother's contribution, Scott, finding Mr. Ward would have been much more difficult."

I blinked and looked at Sheila. She blushed and looked away, but she was smiling.

"Yeah," Charlie said, "the van was too nondescript to track down by camera — mud on the tag and all that. So Sheila called Troy Baldwin because he knew about the transmitters. They tracked him down by following the signal from your shoes."

I shook my head. "I can't believe they left them in the van."

"And if you hadn't already told us about Ms. Freytag's swan dive," Agent Moore added, "we could have tracked her down the same way she was tracking you."

"Is that poetic justice or irony?" Charlie asked.

"Both," I said. "So they're in custody now?"

Agent Moore nodded. "Oh, yeah. They're in custody. In this hospital, in fact. They're patching up Ms. Freytag's leg and head and trying to save Mr. Ward's fingers."

I sighed and looked away. "I get the feeling that if they hadn't been such ... "

"Dweebs?" Charlie suggested.

"Amateurs, anyway," I said. "If they hadn't been so inept, I might not have gotten away."

"Well, you did a great job," Agent Moore said. "And think about what you learned during this little caper."

"Oh, yes," I said. "I learned that persons unknown spent serious money to get their hands on me."

"I don't think he meant that, Scott," Sheila said.

"I know." I scooted down and pulled up the blanket. "Unfortunately, that and one other thing are taking up most of my attention right now." I looked at Sheila. She seemed far way, though she was right next to my feet. "I really don't want to think or talk about either of those things. I just want to work on fixing my mistakes."

Sheila laid a hand on my knee through the covers. "You didn't make any mistakes, honey."

"Nobody's pointing fingers at you, Scott," Charlie said. "Don't you do it either."

"Hiring a lawyer as my P.R. agent and pimping myself out to the scientific community?" I scooted farther under the covers. "Doesn't that count? I could have been discreet, written letters to doctors ... "

"What were you going to do, Scott, live in a box?" Sheila scooted closer. "You were never going to get results and keep the secret at the same time. Besides, Barbara was already onto you. Something would have happened eventually."

I shook my head. "According to Gina, my fate was sealed the moment the bidding was over."

"Forgive me for intruding on a family discussion," Agent Moore said. "I'm sorry you feel bad about your decisions, Scott. You can 'what if' and 'I wish' all day and all you'll get is an ulcer. I'd like to talk about the two other people involved, if you don't mind."

I sighed and shrugged.

He read from small notebook. "Mr. Larry Myers — his real name, by the way — was pretty easy to catch. He drives

a popular car, but his was the only Scion to exit the
Tunnel in the hour following your report to Trooper
Woods.

"I thought you'd like to know," he added. "Larry Myers is
not, in fact, *OneBrikShy.*"

"Are you sure?" Charlie asked. "After giving his real name
and all?"

I shook my head at Charlie. "That's not what he means."
To Agent Moore I said, "I thought not, but it's nice to have
confirmation." I squinted at him. "Morbid curiosity: how
long have you been watching me?"

"We haven't been."

I snorted.

He held up his hands. "Really. Our computer guys just
checked out all your recent e-mail contacts. At your
suggestion, really, since you said *OneBrikShy* might be an
alias for Myers. But that online identity has been continually
active since we've had him in custody."

I swallowed before asking the next one.

"What happened to Barbara?" She *was* my chat room
acquaintance. I didn't like her much anymore, but I couldn't
stand to think of her in police custody.

Agent Moore showed me empty hands. "We don't know.
She wasn't with Myers when we picked him up, and he isn't
talking."

I didn't know what to say. After running from Barbara
and never wanting to see her again ... I was suddenly
terrified I'd *never* see her again.

Then I had a shrewd thought. "You could have just *said*
you didn't find her. Maybe you have her locked up

somewhere, not an adult so maybe exempt from full constitutional rights. With the 'potential foreign involvement' angle, you could hold her indefinitely. A witness no one can touch."

Agent Moore was stony-faced for a few moments. "There may be some government employees that engage in that kind of — "

"Spare me!" I said, scowling at him. "This isn't conjecture or cynicism. Deep down, I know about this stuff." Sheila took my hand, but I pulled away.

Agent Moore stuck his hands in his pockets. "Regardless, we do not have her. If we did, we couldn't deny her representation. Children actually have more rights, not fewer."

"I'm sure you could come up with justification for holding either of us as long as you deem necessary."

He sighed. "Is that what you think we're doing here, Scott? Trying to stake our claim on you?"

"Maybe not you," I said, "but I'll bet you have people figuring out just how to do just that."

He turned to Sheila. "Has he always been this paranoid?"

"Did you actually say that?" I asked before Sheila could answer. "I was just kidnapped. Right before that, I discovered someone keeping tabs on me with high-dollar electronic equipment. My friend was stabbed for no reason other than associating with me." I shook my head. "Federal Bureau of *what*?"

Sheila tried to comfort me or shush me or something. Charlie looked proud of me, but worried that I might practice my newfound ability to swear. Despite my insult of his entire organization, Agent Moore looked sympathetic. He went on as if I hadn't said a thing.

"We don't know where Barbara is. We may never find out."

"Sounds like you're not even looking for her."

"Oh, the word is out," he said. "But it's not an Amber alert."

"Why not?" I asked. "Who's looking for her?"

"We're circulating her picture, but I don't think we're going to find her."

I blinked. "Why not?"

Moore crossed his arms over his chest. "We think the clients Mr. Ward and Ms. Freytag spoke of probably picked her up from Myers, to cut their losses. After all, she's like you."

I had trouble breathing normally. I hated what she had done, but I wasn't vengeful. At least not enough to wish on her what they had planned for me. It couldn't have been as good as, say, freedom.

"If she was abducted," I said after a few moments, "and taken overseas.— to Belgium, maybe — and considering she's a wanted person, how much effort is anyone going to put into getting her back?"

"Why Belgium?" Sheila asked.

"Among other things," Charlie said, "it's one of the few countries that still allow human clone research."

I looked at him in surprise before realizing that he must have heard something of my debriefing. Sheila must have told him about Barbara. He didn't make a single comment about her, and for that I was thankful.

"Belgium makes sense, then," I said. "But my question still stands. Would anyone try rescuing her from a foreign country?"

Agent Moore scowled and shifted on his feet. "Scott, she's not a garbage bag that fell off the truck. She's an American, whether she's an innocent child or a criminal."

"What a nicely oblique answer," I said.

"We'll keep an eye out for her, okay?" He looked at Reenie for assistance. She didn't return his look. Maybe revenge for the time she had to spend with me. "Sorry if passive investigation is too laid back for you. Without clues, though, that's how things work."

"What about her parents?" I asked. "Surely they know something."

He gave me a half-sympathetic look. "I thought you knew: Barbara has been in foster care since she was a year old."

I pounded my leg with a fist. *"Do the foster parents know anything?"*

Agent Moore finally sat down. "The foster mother, Suzie Myers, says she only knows Barbara went visiting with her foster father somewhere out of state."

I couldn't believe it. "So, Larry Myers ... "

Moore nodded. "Larry Myers is her foster father."

46

Instant Replay

I didn't think I'd ever sleep, but I did.

I awoke in the wee hours, thought I was still at the hospital and almost pushed the nurse call button. They weren't stingy with pain meds, but if I made a pest of myself, they might opt for a full knockout. Maybe it would keep me from dreaming.

This was Germantown, though. Sheila's new house. No nurse. Sheila would come if I called, and I would welcome her efforts, but what I really wanted was drugs.

After staring at the dark ceiling for half an hour, I got edgy. That was normal. What wasn't normal was trying to remember if my room had a mini-bar.

Barbara's image kept showing on the inside of my eyelids. The way she looked just before I kicked the car door shut in her face. Had I given her a nosebleed? Would Agent Moore mention finding blood in the car? He could have dismissed it as mine, but I didn't start bleeding until later.

I didn't want to see her image, but you know how that goes. "Don't think of aardvarks," someone says, but then they root right into your mind. I didn't want to think about Barbara, or the car, or my leap from it, or my kicking the door shut in her face.

But I closed my eyes and there she was.

I knew I was done sleeping, so I got up and limped to the living room where Charlie was asleep on the couch. Sheila's new house had four bedrooms, but Charlie had crossed his arms, leaned to one side, propped his feet in the wheelchair, and zonked out sitting up — aided by a pain pill, no doubt. Sheila had draped an afghan over him. I wondered if she'd kissed his forehead like she used to kiss mine.

I turned on the television, careful to mute it right away. The click and hiss made Charlie stir a little. He snored for a five count and then faded to silence again.

TV didn't help. I didn't want to sleep, didn't want to be awake. Wanted to be alone, but fought an urge to wake Charlie and talk his ear off.

Barbara's face, just before I kicked the door shut ...

Now I didn't even have to close my eyes. I tried to watch TV, a grainy nineteen-eighties comedy I'd never seen yet could almost quote. But another recording, much less grainy, was on a playback loop in my head.

Why do we insist on revisiting painful and traumatic moments? Why do we stare at a car wreck, knowing we might see something horrible? Why do we repeatedly relive moments in our lives that we'd rather forget?

While I watched the broadcast of a videotape on what could have been its six-hundredth playback, I came up with an answer to one of those questions.

We relive unpleasant moments for the same reason we watch and re-watch the saddest moments in movies: because we believe, deep inside, that this time Old Yeller won't go mad. That this time, the Titanic won't go down with more than a thousand people still on board. That this time, Joan of Arc won't be roasted alive.

That this time, Barbara won't give me that pained look through the car window, as if I had abandoned her.

Wait, I thought. For the first time, I forced myself to recall the entire incident.

I moved before I could think. Sat up, bending at the waist, and yanked the door handle. It fell open like a trapdoor and I tumbled onto the concrete amid slow-moving cars. Larry's arm slapped at the back of the car seat as he reached for me and grabbed only air. Barbara yelled something as I kicked the door closed in her face.

She hadn't said, *"damn you,"* in anger. She had cried it. *"Damn it!"* Frustration.

Frustration and grief. Grief that I had escaped. But not *from* her.

Without her.

I wanted to give myself a swift kick. I didn't know what I was talking about. I just couldn't let go of loyalty and face facts.

But if there was the slightest chance I was wrong ...

"Charlie!" I stood up and hobbled to him on my stitched-up feet. "Charlie, wake up!"

His right eye opened like an observatory dome with a slow motor. "Am I bleeding on the couch?" He sounded more alert than he looked.

"No," I said. "Listen, I need you to wake up."

He had both eyes open now, but they were a bit dull. I got his glasses from the coffee table and slipped them onto his face.

"Are you awake or do I need to bang some pots together?" I asked, holding him by the shoulders.

"Don't you dare." He yawned like a lion. "I'm awake. What time is it?"

"I don't know," I said. "Late. Early. Whatever. I have to call Agent Moore."

"Why?" His eyes finally focused on me. "What's wrong?"

"The movie!" I said, hobbling toward Sheila's room.

"Scott, are you awake?" Charlie asked. He threw off the afghan and moved as though his leg were held on by thread.

Sheila came out of her room, tying her robe's belt. "What is it, honey?"

"Barbara! She's not one of them!" I raked my fingers through my hair. "We have to call Agent Moore!"

Sheila frowned. "What happened, Scott? Did you have a dream or something?"

"Not a dream," I said, "a movie." They both gave me blank looks so I tried again. "I replayed it in my mind over and over. I don't think Barbara's with them."

"Of course not, dear," Sheila said. "They didn't find her."

"I think Scott's trying to say Barbara wasn't in on it," Charlie said, a yawn nearly obliterating his words.

I snapped my fingers. "You got it!"

"But why do you think that now?" Sheila asked. "And why do you have to call Moore at this hour?"

I hitched my way to the desk where the phone sat. "I

think I was wrong about Barbara. I might have misunderstood her motives."

"Scott," Sheila said, "wait just a second before you go waking people up at three in the morning."

"Yes?" I leaned on the desk and tried tapping my foot, but it was still too stiff from all the stitches.

"What are you going to tell him?" she asked. "That she's now guilty for an entirely different reason?"

"No!" I said, picking up the phone. "Charlie's right. I don't think she was really in on it."

"Based on what?" Charlie asked. "Scott, I know you don't want to see your friend on a wanted poster, but think about what she did, man! What's changed?"

"Everything!" I said. "I had to replay it in my mind, over and over, but I finally saw it. Not proof, but enough to give her the benefit of the doubt."

"What is it, Scott?" Sheila asked. "I'd like to think my little boy knows how to share."

So I told them. I was so antsy, it took several tries to make it cogent.

Charlie grimaced. "It's a nice theory, Scott, but there's a hole in it. Barbara could have jumped out of the car with you."

"And I'm betting she wasn't barefoot," Sheila added.

"But she couldn't!" I said. "Myers had grabbed her! I thought he was grabbing at me, but now that I can think clearly, I *see* it. I was already out the door, but he was grabbing at her because she was about to follow." I looked at the floor. "And I slammed the door in her face."

They looked at each other before looking at me again.

"I'm sure about this," I said. "Please don't try to talk me out of it."

Sheila and Charlie frowned while I rubbed my feet against each other. They itched and I couldn't pace. Then Sheila went to her bedroom, returned with her cell phone and handed it to me. "I hope you're right about this," she said. "I already put the number in. Just hit 'send.'"

I did.

47

Sorry, My Bad

"I know everyone has asked you this already," Agent Moore said, "but are you sure, Scott? The other night, you were ready to walk her to the cell block yourself, just to make sure the door shut tight."

My eyes were on his desk blotter. "I was still reeling from all the action." I looked up at him. "I made a big mistake leaving her in that car."

Agent Moore didn't look at me for a long moment. "One more time, Scott. We need to make absolutely—"

"I already told you!" I tried hard not to shout. "I was calm. It was analysis, not wishful thinking."

Agent Moore looked at the ceiling and tapped a pencil on his knobby knuckles. It sounded like a metronome set on *prestissimo.* I hoped it reflected his mental processes. It was all I could do not to knock it out of his hand.

He began to nod his head. Just a little at first, then more. He smiled at me and slapped his desk. "Okay," he said.

"You've convinced me."

The tension went out of my spine and I nearly poured onto the floor. "What do we do now?"

Agent Moore picked up a pen and clicked it. "We change her official status with the Big List. Or, more accurately, we remove her from the list."

"What's the Big List?" Sheila asked.

Moore smiled at her like someone who enjoys shocking people. "FBI's Ten Most Wanted. For a very short time, she was a rare number eleven and one of two not specifically charged with some kind of homicide. 'Suspected of conspiring with foreign nationals to abduct American citizens and remove them from U.S. soil,' or something like that. We should try acronyms for those long charge lists."

I frowned. "How did you stick all that on someone you never laid eyes on?"

Agent Moore stood up. "It's what we're charging Larry Myers with, but within the hour, Barbara's status will change from 'fugitive' to 'abductee.'"

"And what else?" I asked.

Moore clicked his pen closed. "What do you mean?"

Charlie wheeled himself a little closer to the desk. "I think Scott would like to know how this changes the search for Barbara."

Moore pinched the Windsor knot in his tie. "At first, it just means checking and double-checking a lot of airline manifests. But they probably didn't fly commercial, that being the most closely scrutinized form of travel in the world."

"So we just have to wait," I said, almost to myself.

"Unless you know something we don't," he said. Then he smiled. "Or something *else* we don't know. But you're right. Mostly, it's a matter of waiting."

I nodded and looked at the floor. The change in Barbara's status only meant they wouldn't go after her with guns drawn. I doubted the degree of the search would be increased, even a little. The way they saw it, I figured, the moment she left U.S. soil, she was someone else's problem.

Sheila drove us back to Georgetown. We should have been a little less somber. Sheila was shifting the Camaro like a pro and bulleting down I-95. We had already been in a blue funk, but the tune had changed. I could no longer tell if it was blues or funk.

I didn't bear guilt as easily as I had borne betrayal. Intellectually, I knew she might forgive me for mistakenly running off without her. She must have been waiting for just the right moment, and I jumped the gun.

I thought about that beefy arm flailing over the back of the seat. *"Damn it,"* she had shouted, maybe right when he grabbed her. She watched me bail out of the car and leave it all behind.

I wished I could tell her how I felt. That if I could do it over, I would have stayed.

So why did I still feel like a sucker?

Charlie invited me over for some reheated homemade chicken and broccoli soup, but I begged off. Sheila stayed to play "mommy" for a while ... and to help with my recuperation. Also, she and Charlie were becoming closer. It was only fitting. He was already almost family. If not for present circumstances, I might have been happier for them.

I went into my apartment, alone. My computer desk showed signs of recent use. The FBI Agents liked coffee in Styrofoam cups but didn't like to empty them. After throwing several cups away, I checked my e-mail inbox.

Only two new messages. Did the FBI read everything?

The first new message was from Brik.

not sure what this means, but bare wanted me to ask if you got home okay. I know you two are prolly sweet on each other, but how about springing for a phone? feels like the third grade, passing notes and stuff

ttyl

The second was an E-card notification.

YOU ARE THE RECIPIENT OF AN

E-CARD

COURTESY OF

Bqrbqrq Dqvis

Before I knew it, I had clicked the indicated link.

"HAVING A WONDERFUL TIME IN

europe ,qybe; not sure zhere

WISH YOU COULD BE HERE!"

I'm so sorry. Pleqse help.

Unable to access her normal e-mail account, Barbara had sent an E-card, maybe a free one from a website that ran on advertisements alone. But on which computer? With current technology, she even could have sent it from a cell phone.

Surely Moore's people could find out. If it came from a phone, there were tricks with triangulation and GPS tracking and ...

I held a breath and let it out. I had just seen the message and was already planning raids on a warehouse in Downtown Benelux, with or without the FBI. I was adding two and two and getting hot lottery numbers. All my assumptions were based on Barbara's being an innocent pawn in all this. And to my shame, even though I still wasn't totally convinced, I had propounded the idea. As Charlie liked to say, "when you assume, it makes donkeys of us both."

But an FBI Special Agent in Charge had greased the wheels of his bureaucracy on the word of a small child. It didn't matter what I believed, only what I claimed. I could claim Barbara was an alien and he'd be on the phone to NASA. Maybe even Spielberg.

What could I do? Why, I could get him to let me in on the investigation. The same ruse I used in The Project: disseminating all the pertinent info as it "came to me." Sheila and Charlie might suspect, but if they trusted me, it would be okay.

And if they didn't? I would do it without them.

I called the number I had memorized.

"Agent Moore, are you ready to put your money where your mouth is?"

To Be Continued

Alan K. Garrett

Thanks to my Beta Testers

Angie, Chad, and Joyce

www.ingramcontent.com/pod-product-compliance
Lightning Source LLC
Chambersburg PA
CBHW032131190626
46814CB00005BA/1642